# In Safe ARMS

## ANN GRECH

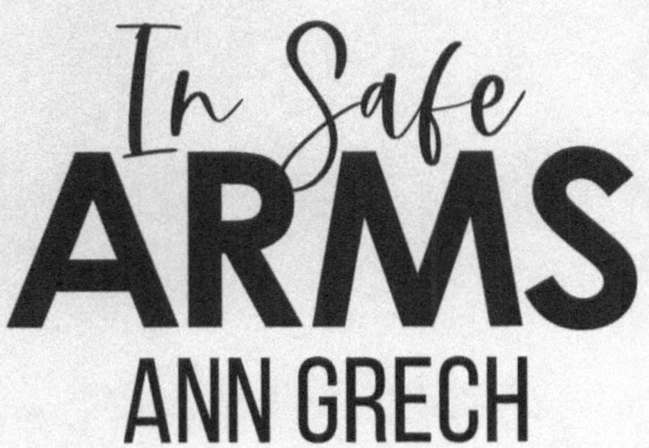

HOT TREE PUBLISHING

# IN SAFE ARMS

## MY TRUTH
### BOOK 2

## ANN GRECH

HOT TREE PUBLISHING

*I had the privilege of teaching you a few years ago. You shared your story. This isn't a retelling, but know that your strength inspired Trent's story. Thank you, BB. This one's for you.*

For information, contact the publisher, Hot Tree Publishing.

WWW.HOTTREEPUBLISHING.COM

EDITING: HOT TREE EDITING

COVER DESIGNER: BOOKSMITH DESIGN

E-BOOK ISBN: 978-1-925853-71-1

PAPERBACK: 978-1-925853-72-8

# ALSO BY ANN GRECH

All He Needs

In Safe Arms

# CHAPTER 1
## KEIR / TRENT

"Yes, yes! He's over the line! Parata scores his second try of the night," the excited commentator called through the television. Its volume was set to blaring but it couldn't compete with the cheering my godfather and I were letting loose. On my feet, fisted hands up in the air, I celebrated our side scoring. Elation filled me and I whooped excitedly. *We can do it. We can win.* Parata's six points left me riding a high. It'd been a nail biter of a game, the score going down to the wire. Five more minutes left before the final buzzer. It was enough time for the other side to score if they got a move on, but we were going to win. I could feel it. Nothing could go wrong.

Our goal kicker lined up, and I held my breath. He was standing dead center. All he had to do was kick straight and another two points would be added to our team's score. Could we extend our lead to four points? I knew we could. We had this. *Come on.* His powerful legs worked in a practiced motion, and I watched enraptured as every muscle flexed and contracted. Our kicker's legs were F. I.

N. E. But I couldn't be distracted by that; it was the match-winning point. His boot connected with a thwap and the ball sailed into the air. As if it were in slow motion, I watched the ball travel on a high arc toward its destination. With every millisecond that passed, it neared the posts. It was straight. It was true. It was perfect.

"Conversion," yelled the commentator as my breath came out in a jubilant shout.

Punching the air, I yelled, "Heck, yeah." I was careful with the language I used around my parents and godfather. They'd clipped me across the back of the head enough times that I naturally curbed my swearing around them. My godfather, Ryan, and I high-fived each other, and we each took a swig from our bottles of beer. It was the first one he'd ever given me, but I'd drunk it before at parties and with mates. I cringed as the yeasty flavor hit my tongue and knew I wouldn't be able to stomach the rest unless I chugged it. I may not have liked the taste, but I wasn't going to say no to beer. What sixteen—nearly seventeen—year-old would? Friday night football was our thing. Our tradition had always been popcorn and soda, so his offering me beer was like saying "welcome to manhood."

The cheerleaders came out onto the field and shook their booties, kicking their legs up high and waving their pom-poms around to celebrate the score. "Now that's a sight to see, isn't it?" Ryan leered as he watched the girls like a dog eyeing a bone. It was so typically him—always blunt and mostly inappropriate—but he was a good guy. He was my father's best friend and a second dad to me. He'd helped raise me. He was the guy I could always count on to fix things when shit was going wrong. He'd help take me to practice or to games and come collect me when Mom or Dad were late. He fed me when money was tight at home and stopped the bullies at school in their tracks—walking through the schoolyard with a giant truck wrench would do that.

I followed Ryan into the kitchen to dump our empty bottles in the bin, the glass clinking against the others Ryan had drunk as I let it go, while Ryan grabbed another for him and a soda for me. I was relieved, but he must have mistaken my look as disappointment when he passed me the bottle. "One's enough, bro. You've already got a buzz going."

"Yeah, I do." I gave him a small smile and turned to glance at the television again. More cheerleaders—they were most teenaged boys' dream, but not me. I was keeping a secret. I looked away and cracked open my can of soda, slipping it into a neoprene cooler. It was a nice design—Chris Hemsworth dressed as Thor.

"What's goin' on, Keir? You not interested in them?" Ryan pointed his bottle to the television, and I knew I'd been busted. I was usually better at hiding my disinterest. I would stare mindlessly at the beautiful women so my mates and my bro'd up dad and godfather wouldn't figure out my secret.

The high I was riding from my team scoring jarred to a screeching halt. My pulse leaped, and my heart beat hard against my rib cage. *Thud. Thud.* I should tell him. I wanted to. I hated keeping a secret, but I was scared. How would he react? How would Dad? I'd heard them insult people like me before, but it was just because they didn't know. I was sure they'd change, that they'd realize how wrong they were to judge. After all, that's what we learned in church every weekend, wasn't it? Don't judge? Our church was pretty progressive—at least it wasn't one of those fire and brimstone places were the priest shouted about how evil "the gays" were—so I knew it'd all be okay. I just needed to figure out how to break the news to my dad, to ease him into the idea that his boy was gay.

"Keir?" he prompted again, this time using his "dad" voice. Tonight was the night. I steeled my nerves and took a deep breath. I was going to tell him. Squaring my shoulders and looking across to him, I shrugged.

"The cheerleaders, ah… they, ah…." Shit, this was harder than I expected. My palms sweated and my knees went weak. I leaned against the linoleum counter and wiped my hands down my sweats. The too-warm room had me fanning my flushed skin with my football jersey.

"Yeah, man, I feel you." Ryan grinned at me like we had a private joke going on and happily turned back to the television. "One night alone with two or three of those beauties and I could die a happy man."

"I'm gay," I blurted out and sucked in a breath as Ryan stilled, not looking at me. Nerves clawed through me and the verbal diarrhea kept coming, my mouth ignoring my brain's attempt at giving my godfather a second to absorb the news. "I… I don't like the cheerleaders. I like boys. Men." I was on a roll and I couldn't stop. Now that I'd said the words, the rest of them just kept flowing, as if a dam had been breached. First a trickle, then a tsunami. "There's this one boy at school, he's cute. I don't think he's like me, but when I imagine kissing someone, I think about him. Men, not women…." I turned to the television and trailed off.

The fist grasping my jersey in a vise grip startled me,

the pull to turn me toward Ryan had me off-balance. There was something in his eyes I hadn't seen before. He looked calm, but the apparent façade couldn't hide the boiling rage behind it. Nerves spiked in me, crawling up my throat until I couldn't swallow. Furiously, I blinked back the tears that I was powerless to stop. All the while he held me there, staring at me. Not saying a word, not moving a muscle.

I sucked in a breath, my movement seeming to unlock something in him. His eyes flashed and the rage in them had me recoiling, but it was his words and the ice-cold tone behind them that put the fear of God in me. "What did you just say, Keir?"

"Nothing," I backtracked. "Nothing. It doesn't matter. I was wrong."

"No, you were pretty adamant a minute ago. Repeat it. Tell me what you just said to my face. Now." His hard, angry tone and his clipped voice had me swallowing hard, trying to beat back my anxiety. I was tall, already six foot. My years of rugby training had sculpted my body so my shoulders were broad and my legs thick. But I was still a kid in front of this man. Totally outmatched by him. He was a truck mechanic, his grip stronger than anyone's I'd ever met. As he held me there, I saw the façade of calm he'd shown me a moment ago crumbling. His nostrils flared as he breathed, daring me to disobey him.

"I'm gay," I whispered, this time my voice timid.

His hands shook, but they sometimes did that when he'd only had a few. It was as if his body was desperate for that fix of liquor. His grip hardened. I was afraid. Of him. Of what he'd do. Of what I'd just told him. I tried to pull away but he wouldn't let me. Holding me there, he loomed over me, his stale breath making me want to gag. "You're not a faggot," he seethed.

I saw his hand coming, it was like watching a car accident in slow motion—I couldn't turn away. Couldn't move. I stood there frozen as his clenched fist connected with my face and pain exploded in my head. Everything went hazy; my mind swimming through soup. My body sagged against the countertop and I struggled to stay upright. I knew I needed to, but the darkness beckoned. I wish it had captured me, drowned me to never wake again. The last thing I wanted to remember was the blind rage that Ryan spat at me when he shouted, "No boy of mine is a good for nothin' faggot." The truth was, I remembered everything. Every painful detail of him pulling down my sweats and pushing me down over the counter. Every nanosecond of my world being torn apart and my body being violated by a man I thought I could trust while he spewed his venom at me.

***

I STUMBLED THROUGH THE DOOR AND CLOSED IT AS QUIETLY AS I could. I had no idea what time it was, but it was late. There were no lights on in any of the houses I'd passed, and even the barking dogs were fast asleep. I wasn't sure if I'd blacked out or not, but I didn't remember getting tossed down the front steps of Ryan's house. When I'd woken up, my head throbbed like a bitch and every muscle in my body ached. I was cold, my shivering so bad that my teeth were chattering. I couldn't feel my fingers or toes. I was sticky, from what I wasn't sure but at least some of it was my own blood—my nose? My eyebrow? There were other places I couldn't think about that were sticky too. My skin crawled. I wanted nothing more than to scrub myself down with a steel brush, to remove every particle, every cell of his off me. I shuddered.

I was dirty. Exposed. Weak.

After I'd woken, I had to get out of there. I had to leave before I vomited all over his front lawn, and there was no way I'd let him see how much he'd destroyed by doing that. So I'd crawled along the path to the brick letterbox and used it to pull myself upright. The world spun around me and I'd breathed through my swollen nose, groaning from the pain. Stepping away tentatively, I'd stumbled down the street. I fell, grazing my hands and knees on the pebbled drives and the tarmac roads. It was hard to keep upright but the fences helped. The streetlights had hurt my eyes. I'd shied away from them.

I was numb. Distant. Far away.

The walls supported my weight as I stumbled through the house to the bathroom. Leaving the light off, I closed and locked the door, propping the washing basket behind it—as if that would stop anyone getting in there. I looked in the mirror, but it was dark enough that I couldn't see myself. Thank God. I reached behind the curtain and turned the hot water on, not even bothering with the cold. My socks were wet. Did they get wet when I toed my shoes off outside? I didn't know why, but it seemed important in that moment. I needed to figure it out, to know exactly what had happened to get them that way. I dropped one in my fumbling and reached down to pick it up. A piercing pain sliced through my head, fireworks lighting up behind my eyelids. The throb behind my eyes pounded. My head swam, the pain so visceral that my stomach heaved. My knees hit the floor, and I reached for the lid on the toilet. I retched into the bowl, over and over until I was spent, purging myself of everything I'd eaten. If only I could do the same to my memories. To my body.

Steam filled the room and its warmth cocooned me. I peeled my clothes off, leaving them wherever they fell before crawling in under the spray. I sat there, curled on the floor as the scalding hot jets flowed over me. But I was still cold. Still shivering. The tears came then. I couldn't help them. I didn't want to cry. I hated myself for doing it. It was weak. *I* was weak. Why didn't I fight him off? Why didn't I yell and scream and kick? Why didn't I use the knife we'd used to cut the popcorn bag open—the same one that sat on the counter—to cut off his dick? Why did I let him do it? I just stood there. I froze. Panicked. He was right, I'd hated those moments he was inside me. *I'm not gay.* I couldn't be. I hated the thought that anyone would ever be inside me again. I'd never let anyone do that to me. Never. I hated myself. I hated him. I hated what I had been. But I wasn't gay, not really. I'd just thought I was. But I wasn't. I was delusional thinking that. Clueless. *I hate myself.* But I'd been wrong. I was straight. Anger bubbled up inside me, overflowing and drowning out the sorrow. Covering the pain like lava flowing over the ground, hardening to solid rock.

Like a phoenix rising from the ashes, I scrubbed my bruised body, washing away the old me. Washing away the gay me. Washing away the stupid teenager that I had been. I held my head up and let the hot water cascade down over my hair. Still it didn't warm me. The water tasted of copper—my blood. I washed my hair, furiously scrubbing at it like I'd done to the rest of me.

The water cooled, its tepid drops making the chill set in deeper. I turned the faucet off and pulled back the curtain, stepping out and drying myself. The sun had started to rise, its rays piercing the black night to light up the room. I saw myself then. The drop of blood trickling down my forehead with the rivulets of water in my hair. My swollen eye. My split lip. I could see fingerprints too, from where that bastard had gripped my neck as he came at me from behind. Choked me while he held me in place.

Rifling through the cupboard, I found some Band-Aids and stuck them on my forehead before scrubbing dry my hair. Why was every strand on my head hurting? Had he pulled them? I didn't remember. I didn't want to remember, either.

Wrapping the towel around my waist, I looked at my clothes spread around me. Mom would kick my ass if I left them on the floor, but I didn't have the energy to find a bag and bin them. Hell would freeze over before I stepped into any of those clothes again. I'd burn them, together with anything else he touched. Maybe I should throw myself into a pit of fire too. Would it cleanse me if I did? Would I always feel dirty? Would I be me again if I didn't have this body anymore?

I took a breath, steeling myself for the world outside my little locked room. The house was quiet. Mom and Dad's door was still closed. The peace surrounding me was superficial. Any ripple on the surface would reveal the rip that would drag me under and drown me.

I went to my own room and slipped inside, pushing the door shut after me and shifting my desk partly against it. I wasn't scared. I wasn't a pussy, but in truth I was. I was tired. Weary. I wanted to close my eyes and never,

ever open them again. I wanted to sink into a black abyss and never come up again. I wanted to be safe again. Secure again. But how?

My room didn't look like my space anymore. It was a child's room, a delusional little teenager's who had no idea what the world was like. I'd changed. I was no longer that kid anymore. Maybe now I knew what people were really like. They told me I'd remember my first time. Fuck, I hoped not. I hoped that when I woke up, I'd be clueless again, that I'd be that dumb teenager who thought the worst thing that could happen on a Friday night was his team losing.

My folded washing sat in the same place I'd left it—on my bed. It seemed inconsequential, but I was grateful for the sweats and hoodie I donned. I hoped that the thick fleece might somehow make a difference to the cold that had settled within me. My bed and its heavy covers beckoned me, and I crawled in, curling into a ball and waiting for sleep to take me. The blackness swallowed me fast, its turbulent waters pulling me under and holding me there, drowning me. And I was relieved. Maybe I wouldn't wake up. Maybe this was all a nightmare.

***

I WAS BEING PINNED DOWN, HELD THERE. I THRASHED, desperate to pull free. Something dark loomed over me, evil in its nature. I gasped, opening my eyes to a light-filled room and shouting, fists pounding on my door.

"Keir Trenton, get your ass up. Now. What the hell do you think I am? Your personal maid?" More banging, loud enough to wake the dead.

I groaned. My head throbbed. Every inch of me hurt. I now knew how the losing boxer felt after a fight. I pulled the covers higher and desperately tried to drown out the noise. Each thud on the door made me want to puke. The banging, the yelling, it was all too much. "I'll get it in a minute," I whispered, but even that was too loud. My stomach turned and I puked all down the side of my bed, my throat now on fire with the rest of me. I couldn't stop. Once I'd started, I heaved again, but there was nothing left inside me.

"Did you hear that?" I heard Mom ask before she rattled the door handle, trying to push the door open. "Keir, you better not be spewing on the carpet."

"Go away," I groaned between heaves, but it was clear she wasn't going anywhere. Dad must have been there too now because the knocking on the door and the jiggling of the handle stopped. Instead the whole door shuddered. Dad was using his weight to bust it open. He was an ex-rugby player, still bigger than me even though he hadn't played in well over a decade. My puny student desk and bedroom door stood no chance against him. The furniture skidded across the room and the door slammed against it, splintering on impact.

"What the hell?" Dad roared as he saw the mess we'd both made. "This is how you repay being treated like an adult? You're given one drink and you finish the rest of the beer in the fridge as soon as Ryan turns his back? You go five rounds with the pavement after disappearing without a trace from his house? You think that's what a man does? I'm disgusted with you." He was shouting, and the words jarred my skull like physical hits. It took me a moment but then his words sunk in. Getting drunk and disappearing?

Is that what happened last night? Confused, I dragged myself out of bed and swayed on the spot, trying to piece back together the night before. A beer, the game, the kitchen. The words. The hit. The pain. *Oh God, no.*

"I…" I breathed through my nose trying to stop myself from spewing again. "I didn't. I…."

"You didn't get drunk? You didn't fall over and give yourself a black eye? You didn't leave your clothes everywhere? You didn't just spew all over your bedroom?" Mom asked in rapid fire, her words like slaps to my face.

"After you clean up this mess, you're going to Ryan's house to apologize. Then you're going to do whatever he wants for as long as it takes to pay him back for the beer you drank and the damage you caused to his garden." Dad was in my face, pointing his thick finger at me, poking me in the chest as I swayed. All I could do was stare at him like a deer in headlights.

"No," I breathed, shaking my head. It hurt. I was going to vomit again, but they couldn't make me go there. I wouldn't. I couldn't. Not again. *Please, no.* "No," I said louder when Dad paused and stared at me. I saw the disbelief that I answered back to him and the moment it turned to anger. But fear propelled me. Ryan had clearly gotten to them. He'd told them some bullshit story; they wouldn't believe me. Dad would never accept that his best friend would hurt his kid, especially if I couldn't tell him why it happened. And there was no way I'd give him the full story anyway. What? I thought I was gay so I told Ryan but then I realized I was wrong? What sort of rubbish was that? It didn't even sound believable to my own ears, never mind Dad's.

"You answering back to me, boy?" Dad snarled.

"I'm not going there. You can't make me." I was screaming, terrified of the monster lurking a few streets away and angry all at once. My heart pounded in my ears, thudding so hard it was all I could hear. My breathing shallowed out. The walls began closing in on me, crushing me. I needed to get out. I needed to lock myself in. I had to protect myself. He wasn't going to hurt me again. Not ever. I lashed out like a cornered animal using attack as its first line of defense. "I won't go. Never again."

Dad stepped forward, bringing himself chest to chest with me. He was only a few inches taller, but so much heavier. I was intimidated. He'd only ever done that once before. Last time, I'd respected him and apologized, immediately doing what he'd asked. But this time I reacted on instinct. I lashed out at him, kicking and punching, trying to hurt him the same way I wished I'd hurt Ryan. I was crying and screaming incoherently, shaking with anger. Ryan had hurt me. He'd broken my trust. And my parents let him. They let me spend time with him, they sent me there so they could get a night alone. I hated them all. I hated myself. My fist connected with Dad's face, splitting his lip. But it wasn't until Dad wiped the drop of blood away with his thumb and looked at it, that my brain registered I wasn't hurting Ryan but my dad. I stopped short and Dad took his opportunity to grab me by my sweater and drag me. I couldn't get purchase on the carpeted floor sliding under my feet as Dad pulled me to the door. Flailing around, I tried to grab onto something, anything, but all I did was knock a picture off the wall. I watched as it fell to the floor, the glass shattering as it landed on its corner. The photo was one of the four of us—we were all in our jerseys cheering on our team. I didn't remember the day. I was only a toddler, but it must have been one of the first football matches they'd taken me to. That image, the one I'd grown up seeing, was a fraud, just like my life. The shattering glass matched the splintering of my soul. I'd never be the same again. But that was okay. Now I knew what bastards human beings were. Now I knew I needed to protect myself.

"You think you can disrespect me like that in my own house? You think you're a big man now, drinking and playing up? We'll see how you like being a big man. Get outside and stay the hell out. You sit out there in the cold until your attitude gets readjusted. Then when you're done thinking about it, clean up. You *will* be going to Ryan's no matter how long you try to put it off. So stay out for an hour or a whole bloody day, I don't care." He pushed me out the front door and pointed to the chair on the front porch. It was the same chair he'd punished me in since I was a kid. He made me sit outside in a time-out until I was ready to come in and apologize. They'd chosen the front yard because of the neighbor's kids, my best friends growing up—they loved riding their bikes and skateboards up and down the street. Seeing them but not being able to join them was the purest form of torture. Now it seemed insignificant. Pathetic.

As soon as the door slammed, I looked down and saw my sneakers at my feet. I kicked them over to the chair and inched down, propping myself on one ass cheek. I was too sore to sit down any other way, and the last thing I wanted was to start bleeding again.

Lacing up my shoes, I didn't conscientiously decide to leave. But once I stood up, I knew I'd never see them again. I gazed at the house, trying to remember happy times. But every one of them were so intimately tied with the monster I called my godfather that I couldn't. I lifted my hood up over my head, shoved my hands deep in the pockets, and trudged down the front path away from them. I had nothing, not even money for a bus fare, but in that moment, it didn't matter. I needed to get away, and it needed to happen right then.

# CHAPTER 2
## KEIR / TRENT

I WALKED WITHOUT A DESTINATION IN MIND, BUT I SOON found myself in front of my best friend's house. We'd started as freshmen in school together and had been in all the same classes for that first term. By the end of the first week, we were inseparable. Mom and Dad would know that's where I went, but I needed something warmer than what I was wearing. I hoped Jake could help me.

When I knocked on the door, he opened it and took one look at me before stepping aside and motioning for me to go in. I went for the stairs, but he stopped me, pointing to the kitchen. "Go in there. Mom and Dad are upstairs putting their laundry away."

I did and found myself being watched like a hawk. "What the hell happened? Who did this to you?"

I shook my head. I couldn't tell him, couldn't tell anyone. They wouldn't believe me. Or maybe they would and that's what I was scared of. I was ashamed of how badly I'd screwed up. If I hadn't been dumb enough to think that I was gay, none of this would have happened. It was my fault. I'd made him so angry that he punished me in a way I'd never forget.

He must have seen something in my eyes, or maybe my best friend knew me well enough to know what I had planned. He blinked back tears and shook his head. "No, Keir. Don't leave. Stay here. Mom won't mind."

"I can't stay," I whispered. "They'll find me here."

"Your dad did this?" he asked, horrified. When I shook my head, he breathed out in relief, closing his eyes momentarily. "Then stay. Dad can call your dad, talk to him for you. Tell him that you're staying here for a while. Weeks, months, they won't care. Please. Don't leave. Just… stay." He was begging, but it was futile.

"I can't. I can't tell you why, but trust me. Please. I can't stay." My voice broke on the last words, wobbling as I fought back tears again.

"Where will you go?"

"My cousin's in Hamilton. I'm going there." I didn't have a cousin in Hamilton—they all lived close to us in Auckland's suburbs—but the city was an hour away from my house. It was far enough away that I could get lost between the two. Disappear. Jake looked at me and shook his head. He knew I was bullshitting but didn't call me out on it. "I can't stay."

From his turned-down mouth and the unshed tears glistening in his eyes, the sadness etched in his features was obvious. We both knew this was goodbye, and it killed me knowing I'd never see him again. But I had to get away. I had to run. I couldn't keep a secret like this staying in Jake's parents' house. They'd ask me why I ran, and avoiding a punishment wasn't a good enough reason. They'd walk me straight back home themselves. No, leaving was the only option. I'd hit the road, get a job and a place of my own. I didn't need school anyway. I was just filling in time until Dad would let me leave, and I could start my apprenticeship with him at the body shop.

"It's too cold out for you to wear just a hoodie. Lemmie get you some stuff." He placed his finger over his closed lips to shush me and motioned to the stairs. I followed him up, skipping the creaky third step by second nature. We entered his bedroom and he closed the door quietly behind us. Not talking, he opened his closet and started with his heavy coat, passing it to me. It was expensive, the best quality ski jacket. He pulled down a backpack and stuffed socks and underwear in it, together with tees and more hoodies, a beanie and gloves.

"Jake, I can't—" His hand on my shoulder stopped me.

"No, Keir. You can. You need this stuff way more than I do. If you're leaving, at least let me give you the best shot." He reached into the drawer of his desk and fished out his wallet before passing me his ATM card. "You know the PIN. There's only a few hundred dollars in there, but it's everything I have. I'll keep putting money in there as long as I can."

"Thank you," I whispered. "I'll try to keep in contact but…."

"Get yourself set up with your cousin, and I'll come visit next weekend. Text me the address." I nodded, but I didn't have my cell. I doubted I'd have one again anytime soon. "Come on, we'll go raid the kitchen too." I nodded again and followed him back down. He went straight for the dry storage pantry, plucking cans of fruit and tuna off the shelves and a bag of candy before stuffing them into the already full bag.

"I don't know what else you'll need, bro." He turned to me and looked helpless, his brow creasing and his lips turning down.

"You've done more than you could ever know, Jake. Thank you." I hugged him close, holding him tight as the telephone on the wall started ringing. I stepped away from him and eyed the device before turning back to him. "I'll see ya round, okay?" My voice broke and I blinked back tears. I wasn't going to cry again. I didn't have time.

"I'll walk you out."

I stepped away from the front door, carrying the bag and wearing the warm coat just as Jake's mom called out to him. "Jake, have you heard from Keir?"

"Go," he mouthed before he spoke to his mom. "No, not today." I nodded my thanks and sprinted down the street before realizing I had no idea where to go. Dad hadn't let me get a job yet, wanting me to concentrate on my studies and rugby training until I had finished the school year and started my apprenticeship, so I supposed the first step was to get some work. I figured I'd have a better chance closer to Auckland than in the burbs where we were, so I headed for the train station.

---

I'D HAD NO LUCK JOB HUNTING DURING THE DAY. MOST turned me away as soon as I asked. Some were polite. Most weren't. They dismissed me before I'd even finished the sentence. Those who told me they'd keep my enquiry on file wanted a copy of my CV and my ID, but I didn't have either. I could do up a new resume, but I needed my birth certificate, which I didn't have. Maybe someone would pay me cash under the table—a restaurant or maybe a tradie. Either way, getting a job was going to be harder than I thought.

Now, as night fell, I knew I needed to find somewhere to sleep. I'd seen a motel near the train station that looked as rough as they came. Hopefully it'd be cheap enough. I didn't have much, and I had to make it last.

I trudged down the streets to the hotel, relieved to see the neon Vacancy sign out the front lit. I pushed through the door to reception and smiled at the lady behind the counter. She looked up, gave me a once-over, and went back to her book. "You lost, kid?" she asked when I still stood there a moment later.

"Ah, no? I want a room?" I hesitated.

"You sure about that?" She put down her book and stared at me. "You need to be eighteen to rent a room. You eighteen?"

"Ah, yeah. Absolutely." I nodded, replying quickly, "Turned eighteen a few weeks ago."

"Are you in some kinda trouble?"

"No. No trouble." I shook my head, hoping that I didn't have that deer in headlights thing going on again. "I just wanted a place to stay while I was passing through."

She sighed. "It's sixty bucks a night, payable upfront." I pulled out Jake's ATM card from my bag and handed it over. I finally got a smile from her. "Okay, Jake, let's get you set up."

Less than five minutes later, I had the key to the room and I'd been lectured on the check-out time and how I wasn't to do drugs or kill myself on their property. It'd apparently give them a bad rep. Like they needed help with it. Room 103 was on the first floor of the motel, up a set of rickety stairs and along an open passageway. The spackle on the walls had fallen off in places to expose the gray cinder blocks underneath. Paint peeled off the doors, and they'd swelled from the moisture. It looked straight out of the seventies and clearly hadn't been remodeled since. The door to my room needed a good shove with my shoulder before it would open and again close. Still, it was home for the night, and I was grateful for having even that.

The bed sagged in the middle and the pillows were flat and lifeless. The carpet and drapes were definitely original too, the orange and mission brown on them contrasting wildly with the faded green carpet. The room resembled what you'd see in bad seventies porn. Even though the bathroom was just as outdated, it was clean and warm. More than I could ask for with sixty dollars. I dropped my backpack on the floor and slumped onto the bed, immediately regretting it. Pain shot up my spine, taking my breath away. The predicament I found myself in hit me like a freight train. Everything was foreign, my whole life entirely different now to what it was twenty-four hours ago. I wanted to go home. I wanted to see my mom and dad and eat dinner with them. I wanted to pile up on our old sofa and watch trashy game shows on television together. I wanted to go to sleep in my own bed and have my stuff back. I wanted to finish school—something I'd always just assumed I'd do, but that I now wanted desperately. I wanted to be *me* again. But it'd never be. That innocent part of me died a painful death the night before, when he had violated so much more than my body.

I lay down and clutched the stale-smelling pillow and cried into it. What the hell was I going to do? Jake had given me everything he could, but it'd barely last me the weekend at this rate. I had hardly eaten all day, trying to ration out my supplies, but I needed food. There was so much I took for granted before. And now everything was uncertain. Would I even have a place to stay after tomorrow? I cried until no more tears would come. I was utterly spent. Exhausted. But it wasn't an exhaustion that could be solved by a good night's sleep. I felt old. Worn out. Like I had nothing left to give. What would I be feeling in a week or a month? What about a year? Would I even make it that long?

The cold was back again, chilling me to my bones, but at the same time my skin crawled. I wanted to pull it off in layers, to scrub myself raw. To be clean again. The urge to disinfect everywhere he touched hit me. I crawled into the bathroom and sat on the floor, rocking myself gently. What I wouldn't do to feel my mom's arms around me again like when I was little and she'd hold me after a "bad imagination." My childhood nightmares had nothing on this hell.

I flicked on the faucet and as the water warmed I slowly pulled off my clothes. I had to figure out how I could wash them. It wasn't like I could stand in a laundromat in underwear while my only pants were in the washer. Maybe I'd be able to afford another pair of sweats when I found work. Just that thought had tears brimming again. I curled up on the floor of the shower, letting the hot water envelop me while I closed my eyes and imagined my dream life again—being back at home. When I opened them, I looked up to see small bottles of shampoo and conditioner and a tiny soap sitting in the dish above my head. I reached up for them and washed myself. I scrubbed away at my skin. Even though I wanted to do the same to my ass, I couldn't. Even touching my hole had me wincing. I was swollen and torn somewhere. Inside or out, I wasn't sure, but the dried blood that I'd seen on my legs the night before made it obvious.

The water cooled quickly, the heat nowhere near as good as home, and I found myself shivering in the tepid water. Turning it off and drying myself, I looked in the mirror for the first time that day. No wonder no one was willing to give me a chance at a job. My swollen eye had angry black and purple bruising all around it and my lip was split and inflamed too. I looked like I'd been beaten to a pulp. And I had. I'd managed to walk for most of the day, but I ached. My head throbbed worse than it ever had, and my muscles protested my every move. Another thing to wish I could change.

I slipped into the sheets wearing a pair of Jake's underwear. It was a foreign feeling. He always wore briefs, but I'd only ever had boxer shorts. He was also a size smaller than me. But I wasn't complaining. I was grateful, so very grateful that my friend had given me everything he could without question. One day I'd pay him back. One day I'd say thank you to him for helping me when I needed him most. I loved that boy like a brother. He was my best friend in the whole world, and I had no idea when, or if, I'd ever see him again. That cut me to the quick. And I only had myself to blame. I'd screwed up my life so badly. And for what? To realize I was wrong? Shitty way to learn a lesson.

ANOTHER DAY, MORE JOB SEARCHING. MORE REJECTIONS. Three days I'd been at it and I still had no luck. Not even a spark of interest. Nothing. I'd given up just after noon and ended up going to the library. At least I had a printout of my CV, as short as it was. I'd updated it with my middle name. I wasn't Keir anymore. I was Trenton, or Trent. I didn't have any work experience on there that would need to be checked, so I figured it'd buy me some time before people started reporting me to the police. My teachers were always telling us that the more extracurricular stuff we did, the better it would look when we applied for a job. I'd always figured that focusing on sport would be enough, but it wasn't much help when you were desperate to eat. Right on cue, my stomach growled, an inhumane sound, and I clutched it, hoping it didn't cramp this time. It didn't, but I couldn't take much more of not eating either. Three full days of little to no food was making me light-headed and weak.

I walked around, wandering aimlessly until I ended up back at the motel where I'd been staying. I didn't have enough money to pay for another night there, but it didn't matter anyway. I wasn't going inside. A police car sat in the small parking lot. No doubt Mom and Dad had called the police in the hope I'd be found. It was awful knowing they were probably out of their minds with worry. But I couldn't contact them. Not yet anyway. I knew it was self-ish, but if I spoke to them I'd cave and go back. And I couldn't do that. No matter what happened, I couldn't be anywhere near my godfather. I sat on the sidewalk, in the gutter between a couple of parked cars, and scrubbed my hands over my face. What the heck was I going to do? If the police saw me, I'd be going home in the back of the cruiser. *Can I go back but just not see him?* I dismissed that thought immediately. It was impossible. He and my father were such close friends. I could never ask Dad to give that up. But God, even if I did see Ryan, anything would be better than this constant fear, the constant worry hovering over me. Wouldn't it?

The all-too-vivid memories of that night sprang forth, and I clenched my jaw tight. I'd have somewhere warm to sleep—if I was ever comfortable enough to close my eyes —and food to eat, but I'd never be safe. I'd never relax enough to let my guard down. I couldn't do it. I couldn't live like that. I couldn't repeat the hell that Friday night was, what I'd caused by being so damn stupid. No, I wasn't going home.

I pulled the ATM card from the pocket in my jacket and sighed. That was how they'd found me. It had to be. I hadn't called anyone, hadn't let anyone know where I was. Jake would never have told them he gave it to me. But they probably didn't even need him to. It wasn't like we were adults. All Mom had to do was call his mom and she'd check the bank records herself. As soon as anyone saw the motel charges, it'd be obvious who was using it. I needed to toss the card if I was ever going to free myself from the risk of getting dragged back to my godfather.

But all of it would have to wait. I needed to eat more than I needed my anonymity at that point. So with my mind made up, I picked my butt up off the ground and walked away, hitching my backpack on my shoulder as I went. I'd buy some food and take out whatever cash I could. After it ran out, I was officially on my own.

I WALKED OUT OF THE GROCERY STORE WITH MY FEW MEAGER supplies in hand and went straight past a restaurant. A staff member hanging a Help Wanted sign in the window lifted my spirits. My heart beat hard. Hope. Finally, some hope.

I ran my fingers through my hair, checked my reflection in the window to make sure my face was clean, and pushed through the door.

"Hello, can I help you?" the middle-aged lady behind the maître d's table asked, not so subtly looking me up and down. The fancy restaurant had dark timber walls, white tablecloths, and lots of sparkling glasses on each table. The chairs were luxurious too. A deep red, they looked like you could sink into them and never leave.

"Ah, yes. My name is Trent. I saw that you've got a job available. I'm looking for work, and I can start immediately. I'm happy to do anything."

"It's a cleaning job in the kitchen—dishes, pots and pans, emptying rubbish, that sort of thing. Evening work mostly." She was saying it like I'd be turned off by it, but the position was perfect for me—I didn't need any particular skills to do it.

"That sounds great. I can do a trial run if you need, and like I said, I can start tonight." I sounded overeager even to my own ears, but at this point I was desperate, not just keen. She paused and tapped a glossy red-tipped finger to her ruby lips. Her stare unnerved me but I'd been in intimidating situations before, and it wasn't the first time I'd erected a façade to hide those nerves. Seemingly satisfied, she nodded.

"I'll need a CV. Do you have one?" I fished the creased paper out of my backpack before handing it to her. It'd have to do even in its less than perfect state. I didn't have a choice at that point. She read it over and raised an eyebrow. "Do you not have a cell?"

"No. It got stolen and I haven't been able to get another one yet," I bluffed, hoping that it wasn't going to ruin my chances.

"ID?"

"Same as the cell." I pressed my lips together, feigning frustration. "Gone."

She seemed to think something over for a moment. "Okay, well once you have a new set bring them to me. We can get you started straight away, but I'll need both from you." The lady held her hand out to me. "I'm Renee, Trent. I own the restaurant with my husband, Mal. Come out back and I'll show you around." She spun, and I followed close at her heels. I didn't care who I had to impress, didn't care what I had to do, I would make this job work. Relief coursed through me and hope shined bright. I could do this.

I was introduced to the waitress, Katrina, who was setting the few remaining tables in the back corner of the restaurant before we went through to the kitchen. The head chef was an older man, portly and severe. Scary as he barked out instructions to the other chef madly chopping and cooking at the massive stoves. I learned that he was Mal, Renee's husband.

"You can put your bag down here." She pointed to the corner of a storage cupboard filled with cleaning supplies. I set it down hesitantly and immediately wanted to reach for it again. I hadn't let that thing go in days; it'd become my security, my safety net. It held everything I owned; it was the only thing I owned. If I lost it, I'd be lost.

"You wash whatever the chefs give you. Plates, cutlery, and glassware all go in the dishwashers. They're full, so when you're unloading, you can see how it's stacked. Scrape off all the food first, rinse, and then pack it. Wash the pots and pans by hand. Make sure everything is pristine. If we get meals or drinks sent back because of dirty dishes, the cost will come out of your wages."

"Yes, ma'am," I murmured.

"Don't touch the chefs' knives. They wash them themselves; they're very particular about them. You do whatever the head chef tells you, when he tells you, and don't let the washing stack up."

"Got it." I nodded, confident that I could manage. Hoping I could anyway.

"I'll write up the times of your shifts, and you're required to be here fifteen minutes before you start. You don't leave until the head chef clears you to go." She ran through the other things that were expected of me and left me to it. Finding myself in front of the industrial dishwashers, I opened them up and looked carefully over how the dishes, cutlery, and glassware was stacked. It was pretty straight forward. It wouldn't be hard to replicate. Maybe Mom insisting that I learn to stack the dishwasher properly was a good thing after all.

Once I'd emptied and reloaded the dishwashers, I got started on the pots and pans that the two chefs were using for their prep. Scrubbing away elbow-deep in water kept me busy for hours. It was a fast-moving kitchen, and I enjoyed the renewed purpose I had. I hadn't realized how utterly rudderless I'd been until then. My life before was gone. My new life was starting. I'd been in limbo until then. But now, I had purpose.

It was late when Mal, the head chef, ordered me to have a break. "Spaghetti or penne for dinner, Trent?" he asked.

"Um, no thanks." I shook my head. There was no way I could afford the dinners here in the restaurant. "I'm good."

He looked at me with the same look my father would give me—with patience—and my knees almost buckled. God, I missed them so much. "We feed all our staff during the dinner shift, so pick—either spaghetti bolognaise or penne alfredo."

My throat closed up and tears sprung to my eyes. How did I tell him that he'd saved my life? That without them generously giving me this job, I'd be homeless and broke? They were paying me for my time and feeding me. That meant more than they could ever know. "Bolognaise would be great. Thank you."

He smiled a small smile and dished me up a huge serving. "You've done well tonight, Trent. Now, go and eat this. There's a small table outside that the staff use. I think Katrina's on break too. She'll be out there."

I pushed through the door to the alley and, sure enough, Katrina was sitting out there with an empty bowl of pasta and a smoke in her hand. She smiled and gestured to the spare chair. I took it, groaning as I relaxed into the seat. My sore feet and aching legs attested to how long I'd been standing before the sink. And my back was killing me. But I was so grateful too. I'd stumbled onto an opportunity that made everything possible again. This was it, the job that I'd be able to make my own, and who knew, maybe I'd even be able to work my way up into a cooking position in the kitchen.

Katrina started speaking, telling me about herself. A few years older than me, she was trying to break into the theater scene and working at the restaurant to pay rent. She seemed like good people, easy to talk to and funny.

"So, new guy, tell me about yourself."

"I'd better get back to it," I deflected, looking at my nonexistent watch. When she asked me whether I lived close by, I couldn't be rude and walk away. Turned out that she hated walking to the station by herself after closing and wanted some company. The thought of her doing that, then making her way home alone late at night didn't sit well. I'd happily walk her to the station. It wasn't like I had anywhere in particular to be.

"Come on." I motioned to the door and collected our bowls, taking them straight into the kitchen with me as Katrina headed to the handwashing basin.

My shift ended in a blur, more dishes, more pots, more hot soapy water. I scrubbed and dried and stacked all with a smile on my face. I loved every minute of being in there, with Mal barking out his orders and the other cook working frantically, Katrina and the other waiter coming in and out to collect plated-up dinners, and Renee looking in once or twice to watch me. I washed the suds from the sink and wiped down the stainless steel counters with the cleaner. "Can I help with anything else, chef?" I asked, not sure what I was supposed to do.

"No, Trent, you've done everything I needed you to do. Go and see Renee, and she'll give you your hours for the rest of this week."

I grinned. "Awesome." I grabbed my backpack from

the storage closet and walked through the swing door into the restaurant, spotting Renee immediately. Standing at the till, she was counting receipts, tallying up the day's takings by the looks of it. "Renee, Chef asked me to speak with you—" She held her hand up, silencing me midsentence, and I stood there awkwardly, stuffing my hands in my pockets as her fingers flew over the calculator. Katrina bumped me with her shoulder, smirking as she walked past. I narrowed my eyes at her but couldn't stifle the grin when she gave me a thumbs-up behind Renee's back.

A moment later, Renee looked at me with raised eyebrows. "Yes, Trent?"

"Oh, ah, Chef wanted me to speak with you about my hours. He wants me to come back to work here."

"Good, good." She nodded and handed me a slip of paper. I looked at it and my eyes nearly popped out of my head. I was rostered on every night. Long shifts. I'd totally make enough money to rent a room somewhere, and if I ate dinner at the restaurant every night, I'd be set. Relief swept through me.

I stuffed the slip in my pocket and looked at her. "Thank you, Renee. I... you have no idea how much this means."

"See you tomorrow, Trent."

I smiled and nodded before walking out the front doors to find Katrina waiting for me.

"So, new guy, when are you coming back?" she asked as I stepped up beside her, pulling on my coat.

"Tomorrow, and every night this week. I'm doing every dinner shift." I couldn't hide the incredulousness in my tone.

"Fantastic." She motioned to the street, and I pulled

out the gloves and beanie I had stuffed in the front of my pack as we began walking.

"I'll walk you to the station if you like," I offered, not wanting her to do it alone. I didn't want to waste the little cash I had on train fares, so I'd leave her to make it the rest of the way home, but it was the least I could do for her if she was uncomfortable.

"You didn't answer me earlier, where do you live?"

"Oh, around the corner from the station," I improvised.

"With your parents?"

The pain in my heart was like a knife slicing deep. God, I missed them so much, but there was no way I could go back. "Hey, what time does the train come?" I asked, an obvious attempt at a shift in the subject. I didn't want to lie but I couldn't tell her the truth either.

She stopped walking, and I turned to see why she'd fallen behind. "Okay, I get it, you don't want to talk about your private life. I'm just trying to be friendly. I don't know all that many people here."

I sighed. "No, I get it. It's been a rough week for me. I'm just a little guarded, you know?"

"I feel you." She linked arms with me, and we walked the few blocks to the station, the cold wind howling through the buildings. I shivered, tugging my coat tighter around my middle. It was futile. My sweats weren't warm enough for the weather. My breath fogged the air in front of me with each exhale, making me dread the next few hours.

After I'd said goodbye to Katrina, I looked up and down the street, trying to figure out where to go. There weren't any buildings open at that time of night. Even the grocery stores were closed. I was absolutely clueless on what to do next. Longingly I thought about the motel I'd stayed in. I never thought I'd take a bed, four walls, and a roof for granted like I had in the past. If only I'd realized how lucky I was and how stupid I'd been to risk throwing it all away. I should have kept my mouth shut. I should never have told Ryan. If I hadn't, he wouldn't have gotten so angry at me. He wouldn't have had to teach me the lesson he did. He'd always done that, always tried to show me the right way to do things. This time he'd hurt me though. He'd broken a piece of me that I wasn't sure I'd ever get back. But I couldn't get past it being my fault. If only.... It was a hard lesson to learn, but he was right. I learned, and I'd never make the mistake of thinking I liked men again.

The eerie quiet of the late-night streets unsettled me. Every shadow made me jump, every passing car had me tensing. If I got caught out here, I'd be in the back of a police car fast, but I was more worried about what'd happen if the wrong sort of crowd found me instead. The type Mom always warned me about—the drug dealers and the violent ones. I'd always laughed her off, thinking I was invincible, but I had no idea how scary it was to be walking the streets that late at night, alone and with nowhere to go. It was like I was a little boy again, wanting to hide behind my dad's strong legs whenever something freaked me out. But I didn't have that luxury anymore. Now I had to stand on my own two feet.

I turned a corner and saw them—three men walking toward me. I looked for a way out. Anything. But there was nothing, nowhere I could go. There were barricades along the other side of the road blocking the sidewalk, protecting pedestrians from the construction site there.

Next to me were shopfronts lining the street, old buildings with straight facades and small insets where the doors were. I was trapped and standing there wide-eyed, waiting with trepidation to see what fate would befall me. My heart rate picked up, my pulse thrumming in my veins. Fear spiked, sending adrenaline crashing around my body. I breathed fast, my shallow gasps betraying the terror of being confronted by them. I wasn't even sure whether I had a reason to be scared by them, but my flight instinct was firmly locked on.

I desperately wanted to hide, but unless there was a laneway coming up in the next few yards, I'd have to walk straight past them. Even if there was a laneway, the last thing I wanted was to get caught in it alone, potentially three-on-one. There was nothing I could do but face them head-on.

I walked past them, and their conversation continued uninterrupted. They barely looked at me as I shifted to the edge of the sidewalk to let them pass. The breath I'd unknowingly been holding whooshed out of my lungs, and I held my hand up to my chest, my heart racing. Being alone at night had never bothered me before, but now was different. I was out of my element, away from the safe streets of my neighborhood. Away from everyone I loved and everything that had been a comfort to me. I staggered over to the doorway of a bookstore and sank to the cold ground, thankfully out of the wind. My head swam and I breathed out again, trying to stop myself from vomiting up my dinner.

I clutched my backpack close and held tight to the knowledge that this would only be until I got paid. I hadn't even asked when it would be; I'd been so excited to get the job that I didn't even know when or how much I'd be getting. It didn't matter; anything was better than nothing. As long as I had enough for a room to stay in, I didn't care what the pay was.

I didn't know what was more unnerving—the darkness or the quiet. The streets were a very different place than during the day, and I'd never been so scared to close my eyes in my life. My mind ran wild, vividly playing through every worst-case scenario possible and in graphic detail. What if someone tried to hurt me? Could I defend myself? What if I got picked up by the police? What if someone stole my bag? It wasn't worth anything, yet it meant everything to me. What if my job fell through? What if this wasn't temporary? What if I got sick or went nuts? What if this was my life?

But I couldn't think like that. They always said in church that as long as we had faith, we had a chance. I'd misplaced my faith somewhere along the way, but I had hope. That would have to do. I was one of the lucky ones. This was only temporary. I'd make sure it was. As soon as I got on my feet again, I wouldn't be sleeping out in the cold, and the night's work I'd just finished would make sure of that.

I rubbed my eyes, trying to keep awake long into the night. It wasn't just the cold that had shivers running up and down my spine. Fear clawed at me, keeping my eyes open. But I was fighting a losing battle. I tried to keep vigilant, tried to listen out for risks but my eyelids were getting heavier, my blinks slower.

# CHAPTER 3
## TRENT

I MUST HAVE FALLEN ASLEEP SOMETIME BECAUSE WHEN I opened my eyes, the inky black of the sky was turning a dull gray, a chilly morning setting in. The pinch in my neck from sleeping curled up in the corner had me groaning. If I thought I was sore from standing all night washing dishes, sleeping on the ground was worse. So much worse. I stretched and immediately regretted it, the cold air assaulting my extremities. Traffic had already picked up in the streets, and workers passed me at a steadier pace. Across the road at the building site, tradesmen were arriving in their vans and trucks, coffee in hand as their breaths fogged up the air in front of them.

My body screamed in protest as I unfolded myself and managed to stand up. I would have done almost anything for a hot drink right then, but I had a bit of a walk to get one. I strode up the street as fast as I could toward the gas station I'd seen a few days earlier. The coffee there would probably taste like dishwater, but I knew it'd be cheap.

Stepping into the little shop at the gas station was

heavenly, the heated air melting the cold from me. I stood there a moment just enjoying the change, hoping that spring would finally make an appearance. I filled the cup and immediately sipped the steaming brew, which had me sighing in absolute pleasure. It tasted like watered-down tar, but as the warmth spread through my veins and I defrosted from the inside out, I knew I could face the day. A smile tilted my lips. My task for the day was pretty simple—find somewhere to have a shower. Maybe even wash the clothes I'd worn.

Fishing a dollar out of my bag, I handed it to the attendant and said thank you. Standing by the door, right under the main heater, I slowly finished the cup. "Refills are half price if you use the same cup," the attendant called out to me. "It's shitty coffee, but it's warm."

I nodded my thanks and headed straight back over to the machine. Who knew something so bad could bring such simple joy? I fished out some change and handed it to him, asking on a spur of the moment, "Are there any public restrooms around here? One with a shower? I'm going for a run but won't have time to go home and get changed before work." I hoped my white lie was convincing, but the attendant looked like he saw straight through me.

"There are toilets out back that you can use to relieve yourself. You'll need this." He handed me a key with a hunk of wood attached to it. "But if you want to wash, the best place is the shopping mall. The one with the library. They have clean toilets and showers there but be careful of security. If they see you hanging around there for too long, they'll ask you to leave. The public library is fine though. It's only small, but they don't mind if you pull out a book and stay all day. I used to study there all the time."

"Thanks, bro," I replied, touched that he'd given me such valuable information.

"Anytime." He nodded as I finished my coffee and made a move outside to the toilets. I was learning just what I'd taken for granted. Toilet paper was precious. Having a place to go more so.

I handed the key back and found myself needing to fill the time again. It was too early for both the mall and the library. Opening would be at least a few hours away, so I figured I'd look for a place I could stay that night.

The hours of wandering around, aimlessly moving killed me. I couldn't help but think of the people curled up in their beds or taking a shower, the ones reading a newspaper over breakfast, watching cartoons or yelling at kids to get dressed. I thought about my parents and what they'd be eating and Jake sleeping in until his mom ripped the blankets off his bed to get him up for school. I even thought about Ryan and what he was doing. If I sat still too long, my thoughts wandered. At least walking the streets gave me something to look for—a place to keep warm that night.

I got to the mall where the library was an hour before opening. Figuring I'd just hang around like I'd been doing all morning already, I wandered through the parking lot toward the entrance. I hoped no one would think I was acting suspicious. Movement behind the loading dock had me pausing as I passed it. I looked again and saw a lady there. She rolled up a sleeping bag and put it in the shopping cart to the side, filled to the brim with stuff.

"Hey, hi," I called out, moving over to her.

She eyed me suspiciously. "Whaddya want?"

"I, ah…. Never mind." I shook my head and looked back at the cardboard boxes lying on the ground where her sleeping bag had been. I was about to walk away when something stopped me. Even if it was only one more night out here, I needed to learn the basics. Where was safe? Where was warm and dry? "Is it a good spot here? Safe, I mean?"

"Listen, kid, don't go bringing any trouble my way," she warned, stepping closer to me. She was tiny, but she carried this don't-screw-with-me attitude that I liked.

"No, I wasn't trying to cause trouble," I explained, stuffing my hands in my pockets and looking down at the ground. I toed the tarmac with my sneaker. "I slept in a doorway last night. It was freezing. I was just wondering if it was warmer here. And safer."

Her whole demeanor softened, understanding filling her eyes. I hated that. I hated how young and stupid and vulnerable I felt. I'd learned since Friday night that it didn't matter how big and macho I thought I was. I was just a scared freaking kid. It was a hard pill to swallow. "It is warmer. The cardboard helps. It's good insulation and there's always a supply here from the shops. As long as I clean it up before I leave, I've never been moved on. I think security like having someone here to keep the criminals away." I helped her pick up the boxes and throw them in the compactor before wiping my dusty hands on my sweats.

"Where do you go during the day?" I asked. "I'm not sure where I should stay." She pushed the cart around the corner out of the way and plucked a messenger bag from it.

"I work full-time, so I'm at the office all day. I go to the soup kitchen sometimes to help out after work, then come back here at night. It's quiet, so...." She shrugged.

"You work full-time but still sleep here? Why?" I didn't understand. Surely she'd be able to afford something.

Her laugh held no humor. "Because my credit rating is shot, and I can't get a lease. I got sucked in by a con artist a few years ago—he stole my identity and took everything, racked up a bunch of debts that I'll never be able to repay. Now I'm living here, but it's not so bad. I earn enough that I can eat, and I know where to go for showers and bathrooms. You'll get used to it."

"Yeah, I hope not," I murmured, horrified that someone like this, someone who had a job and looked normal would sleep on the streets at night.

"I need to go get cleaned up for work." She motioned to the library. "The soup kitchen is on Main Street, near the church. I'll be there tonight volunteering for the dinner service. Swing by."

"I'll be at work. I've just started, but maybe I could hang here tonight with you?" She eyed me over for a long time before nodding.

"What's your name?" she asked.

"Trent." I stuck out my hand to shake hers, and she grasped mine with a firm grip.

"Edith." I smiled at her and shoved my hands back in my pockets. "Well, Trent, I need to go. See you tonight." She turned and began walking away before stopping and turning back to me. "Don't bring trouble with you, Trent. I don't need it." I told her I wouldn't, and seemingly satisfied, she left. I wandered off, walking around to the front entrance of the library. It hadn't opened yet, but the gated-off bathrooms had been unlocked.

---

THE SECOND NIGHT'S WORK WAS MUCH THE SAME AS MY FIRST —hot soapy water, scrubbing pots and pans, a dinner of pasta primavera, and a walk to the train station after my shift was over to drop off Katrina. I liked her. She was cute and fun, someone who I might even consider asking out on a date if my life wasn't so upside down and I wasn't so utterly broke. At least I had somewhere to go. The walk to Edith's spot didn't bother me. It was secluded enough that we wouldn't get hassled by police or passersby and sheltered from the weather too. The well-lit area made me more comfortable. I felt safer there, undoubtedly helped by security patrolling the area. Hopefully, once I got paid, I'd be out of there. I contemplated my conversation with my boss about my wages as I walked.

*"I'm running a business, Trent. I can't make exceptions and pay you before I pay everyone else." Renee turned away from me and started sorting cutlery into the buffet along the back wall. She looked engrossed in the task, but I needed to talk to her so I interrupted again.*

*"I understand. I don't have access to my bank account at the moment though—remember my cards being stolen? Well, the bank has frozen the account and I need ID to get a new card or open another account. But I can't pay for the ID because I don't have access to any money. I was hoping I could get paid in cash so I can sort this mess out?"*

*"Sure, that's fine." She nodded, not once stopping her task.*

*She was good at dismissing people, and her withering stare when I hovered there had me backing away.*

*"Okay, great. Thanks," I muttered, trying not to sound scared.*

I frowned. I'd approached her with two questions and she'd barely even answered one. I'd have to ask Katrina when she got paid. At least she'd give me an idea.

When I arrived at Edith's spot, she was already asleep. My footsteps roused her and she pulled her sleeping bag up higher around her beanie-clad head and rolled over when she saw it was me. I pulled a couple of cardboard boxes out of the cage and laid them out before finding a larger one that I could curl up in. I didn't have any blankets or a sleeping bag, so sleeping in the box was about as good as it was going to get for me. Anything had to be warmer than the night before.

Using my backpack as a pillow, I lay down and closed my eyes, trying to relax and fall asleep. Rustling nearby had me cringing. Mice, or worse, rats would be around the mall, the rubbish from the fast-food joints and cafes drawing them in. Oh God, if one ended up in there with me…. I shuddered, my skin crawling. But maybe it was birds or hell, a mountain lion—not that we had them in New Zealand, but still. Anything would be better than mice or rats.

Exhaustion slowly overtook me, and sleep dragged me under, my makeshift bed no more comfortable, but so much warmer than the cold pavement the night before.

# CHAPTER 4
## ANGELO

**TEN YEARS LATER**

*"Mamma mia,"* I breathed, taking in the view of the bridge before me as I flew over the curves in the road in my new-to-me baby, a Mini Cooper S. The turnoff was just after the wooden structure, but even though I knew it was coming I still nearly missed it. The sight of the narrow road passing over the roughhewn log bridge that straddled two cliffs had me captivated. A sheer drop was between them, with the clearest aqua-colored water I'd ever seen at its base. I'd photographed it on my first visit here, and now I was being hired to do it as a professional. It wasn't the first job I'd ever completed, but it was my first in the country I'd now called home for three weeks.

I passed over the bridge, my car bumping on the uneven surface as the flash of a lone figure standing against the pillar whipped by my peripheral vision. I'd already been warned that the bridge wasn't for the faint of heart—it was barely wide enough for two lanes of traffic, never mind pedestrians. The safety railing was nonexistent too. But it did have the best views of the bungee jump platform, and I was getting paid to photograph it and the crazy-assed jumpers hurling themselves off a perfectly good walkway with nothing but a glorified elastic band wrapped around their ankles. *No thanks!*

I closed the driver door with my ass, juggling my camera bag and tripod. I waited for the truck to pass before jogging out onto the bridge, then stopped short when I got a better look at the man standing there. Head held low, his dark hair was spiked messily like he'd repeatedly run his fingers through it. Even though he wore a heavy, leather jacket and was hunched over, his broad shoulders were unmistakable. His faded blue jeans were wrapped like a second skin over thick thighs, the muscle flexing as he shifted his weight and peered over the edge. I was captivated by him, drawn in like a fish hooked on a line. He was beautiful. A photographer's dream. Without even realizing what I was doing, I had my camera out, zooming in on his profile and snapping photograph after photograph. *What's his story? Where is he from? Why is he here?* He was a perfect blend of strong and vulnerable; beautiful in his flaws. The bump on his nose hinted that he was a scrapper. *Has he broken it before?* His pouty lips softened his features, even though they were turned down in a harsh frown. He tilted his head slightly, a drop of water on his eyelash shining like a diamond in the soft light of the winter's day. *He's crying.* My heart ached for him, wanting to fix whatever it was that'd brought him out there. I sucked in a breath and found myself stepping forward—

Tires squealed and a horn blared, making me jump out

of my skin. Looking around, I realized I was in the middle of the bridge, right in the line of oncoming traffic.

I waved in apology to the driver impatiently waiting for me to get out of the way and jogged over to the support columns the man leaned against. He looked me over but said nothing, turning back to the view before us. I clicked a few photos, landscapes including the buildings and a few close-ups of jumpers about to leap off the podium. I tried to line up an action shot to get a reel of the tandem jump about to occur, but my bags were in the way.

I'd never once asked for another person to help me out while I photographed my subjects, but instinct screamed at me to trust him. I assessed him again, trying to drop my photographer's eye. Despite my near proximity he paid no attention to me, keeping his head low and gaze glued to the sheer drop below. The tight set of his shoulders and stony facial expression certainly weren't an invitation to speak to him, and I wondered why he appeared so closed off. I couldn't resist looking at him though. What had he witnessed, experienced, to make him like this? I went with my gut and reached out to him, hoping I'd be able to get through the scowl he looked to carry around as a shield. "Hey, hi," I called. "Think you could help me for a minute?" I smiled at him, trying to get his frown to disappear. Silently, he nodded and reached out, taking my bags from me. "*Grazie*," I added while I adjusted the settings on my camera and snapped the first of many photos of the bungee jumpers.

"You know who's jumping?" he asked in a smooth voice after I lowered my camera. Hearing it sent a shiver through me. Quiet but strong, I wanted to hear him speak again.

"No. I'm a photographer." I paused, grinning to myself. "It's my first job here. I'm Angelo by the way."

"Trent."

I reached out and took his hand, my gaze snagging on his eyes. I sank into their fathomless depths. They say the eyes are the windows to a person's soul, and his were no exception. The darkest brown I'd ever seen, his eyes were filled with a grief that both transfixed and saddened me. What pain had he been through? Instantly I knew I'd been wrong in my original assumption. He didn't have a bad attitude. Something or someone had hurt him, and it made me want to reach out and heal him. I didn't warm up to people easily. I didn't like making new friends. Ironic really, when you consider I'd left my best friend—my sister, Gabriella—in Italy to join my brother in New Zealand. He was the only person I really knew, even though I'd met a couple of his other friends too. But looking at Trent, I was certain I'd met someone who would become important to me. It was crazy, but I just knew we'd become friends.

When he withdrew his hand, I jerked back in surprise, embarrassed that I was still staring at him. I expected him to be creeped out and leave quick smart. If it were me on the receiving end, I totally would have dropped the bags he was holding and walked back to my ride. But Trent didn't move. Instead, he stayed beside me and, in another first for me, helped swap out my lenses so I could keep photographing the scenes playing out in my viewfinder. When the sun reached just the right height in the sky, he held up a light reflector. For that split second, the lighting was perfect. I scrambled to adjust the exposure rate and held my finger down on the shutter. I hoped it'd give the shots a natural glow, softening them at the same time as adding the perception of speed. I easily had a hundred shots by the time I wrapped up a couple of hours later, my arms aching from keeping the camera steady.

"I could eat a horse," I announced, taking the last of my bags from Trent and sliding them in the trunk of my car. "Want to join me?"

"Nah, I shouldn't," he replied. He may have said no, but I wasn't convinced he really wanted to. Hands jammed in his pockets and his head low again, he looked like he carried the weight of the world on his shoulders.

"Let me say thank you for helping me. It would have taken me much longer to get the shots if I didn't have your help, and I wouldn't have been able to take some of them at all," I persisted. Seeing a small smile tilt his lips, I added, "Your choice of place." That seemed to push him over and he gave me a small nod. "Great. Where are you parked?"

"Oh, I ah, caught the bus out."

"Great, hop in and you can give me directions." I slid into the driver side and waited for Trent to follow me. I couldn't say that I'd ever picked up a man on the side of a highway either, but I was apparently in for a day of new experiences.

"You're Italian, right?" he asked, not waiting for me to answer before he continued. "Don't they drive on the other side of the road over there?"

"*Sì*," I responded, smiling. "I'm getting used to driving on the wrong side."

We ended up at a sports bar I'd never have guessed was there. Nestled away down an alley, it was up a rickety set of stairs and behind an unmarked door. I had no idea whether only locals were welcome, and I didn't care either. The atmosphere immediately drew me in. Mood lighting set over the booths gave the place a sense of intimacy, but the match playing on giant wrap-around screens that lined the walls of the bar added enough light that the room wasn't filled with shadows. International beers on tap and mouthwatering-smelling burgers and hot dogs on a constant stream from the swinging doors of the kitchen had my stomach grumbling.

I'd heard of rugby being referred to as football before, but I'd never seen a game. After five minutes of watching I had yet to see the players kick the ball, and it was lost on me why it could be called footy. I was familiar with the real football, the world game, soccer, whatever you wanted to call it, but I gathered Trent knew quite a bit about rugby. He caught my confused look when the ball was simply handed over to the other side after what looked like an all-in brawl.

"That was a penalty, so the team lost possession of the ball. Those guys tossing it now are your forwards. They carry the ball toward their try line and through the back rowers—the defensive players. See how they're passing it back? No one can throw the ball forward; the players catching it have to be behind the person throwing the ball. The other team can tackle players to get the footy, but there are rules on how you can do it. Too high or too low and you'll get a penalty. The aim is to touch the ball on the ground past the try line within five tackles. If they don't, they lose possession of the ball."

"Okay." I nodded. *Makes sense. Kind of. Not really.* "So what's the try line?"

He attempted to stifle his grin but failed. "The line at

the end of the field where the goal posts are. Cross that and you'll score six points. Then, if the team can convert it, they'll get an extra two." Before I could ask how to convert it, Trent continued explaining, "The team's kicker will kick the ball and try to get it through the posts. That's a conversion."

"Which team do you support?" I asked around a sip of my beer.

"Neither of these two." He pointed to the screen with his glass. "They're Aussie teams. I used to go for the Hamilton team, but I'm not much of a follower anymore." He quietened and seemed to lose himself in his drink, staring at the ice cubes floating in the amber liquid. The pain I'd seen etched into his expression flashed over his features but was gone a second later when he shook his head and looked up at me. I would have missed the somber moment if I'd blinked, but it was definitely there.

I wanted to return to the easy banter we'd had a moment ago, but I fumbled for a question, not knowing much about him. Then I realized it was the perfect opportunity to learn more. I asked him about his work and his expression cleared. He sat straighter and a smile broke out over those model-worthy lips.

"I'm a paramedic." His job was obviously something that made him proud, as he should have been. "During winter, I work on the slopes at the Remarkables, and the rest of the year round I'm in a bus answering emergency calls."

"Yeah? You might know my brother's friend. Ford, I think his name is. I met him the other night. I think he works at the Remarkables too."

Trent laughed. "Small world. Ford's my boss. Who's your brother?"

"Riccardo. Well, Ricky. He's a pilot."

"I know Ricky. He's good people. Tell him I said hi."

When my brother had first moved out here with his freshly minted helicopter pilot's license, I'd thought he was crazy. He'd moved literally across the other side of the world from everything we'd known, spurred only by the job offer in his hand. But when I visited, I understood why he loved flying here. I'd seen it the moment the plane started to descend toward the runway nestled between the mountain range capped in white. It had taken me two days into my first visit to decide I wanted to move to Queenstown too and another year to make it happen. Now, sitting in that bar watching a game I still didn't understand with a person I wanted to become a friend and a budding photography business, I was hopeful and happy.

"To new friends," I toasted, holding my nearly empty glass up to Trent's, who mirrored my move. I smiled and knew I'd made the right decision.

The next time I looked down at my watch it was after six. Trent and I had spent the whole afternoon talking and laughing. We both loved skiing, but he'd only ever experienced it in Queenstown. My hometown in Italy, Santa Caterina di Valfurva, was on the slopes, and I'd travelled through Europe. We both liked to keep fit, but where I enjoyed swimming and hiking, Trent ran and often lifted weights. We both had a sweet tooth; desserts were our weakness, but cannoli—those perfect pastry cylinders filled with vanilla and chocolate custard and coated in icing sugar—were our Achilles' heel. I also wasn't alone in my weird obsession for the reality TV documentaries *Alaska: The Last Frontier* and *Deadliest Catch*.

We both needed to get home, but saying goodbye was kind of a downer. I'd had fun, and I didn't want it to end. I wanted to ask for his number so we could catch up again but felt ridiculous asking for it. How does a grown man ask another dude to be his friend? Figuring that I'd see him again through my brother and our mutual friends, I let him go, watching as Trent weaved through the crowds on the sidewalk.

---

It was Saturday morning when the knock on my door sounded. The sun hadn't even risen when my brother called me urgently. "Angelo, get up. You have a call you want to take." I rubbed my eyes groggily, wanting to ignore him and sleep in. It was cold out and I was warm under the down covers. But then his words sunk in and I was instantly awake.

"What call? Who?" I asked around a yawn, stumbling from my bed and tripping over myself to get to the door. When I opened it, Riccardo was wearing sweats—much like me—and a grin that lit up his face.

"It's Ford. He said you met Trent?" Ricky held out his cell to me as I nodded and took it from him.

"Hello," I spoke into the device, "Angelo speaking."

"Angelo, hey. I'm so glad I caught you. I've just been on the phone with Trent. He's got a friend who's getting married today and their photographer called in sick. She's got gastro or something." He sounded annoyed and frazzled as he spoke a mile a minute. My brain struggled to wrap itself around his pace this early in the morning. "Anyway, Trent said that the couple are in a panic but thought you could help them. He didn't have your number, so he called me. Can you call him? They'll pay you." I stood there stunned for a moment after Ford finished speaking; it took a second for his words to sink in. As they did, I grinned, and the soft spot I'd developed for my new friend grew. *Hell yes!* I had my second job because of Trent. I was likely the only photographer in Queenstown who wasn't booked months in advance, so they didn't really have much of a choice, but I still took it as a win. And the fact that Trent had referred me made me smile even wider.

"What's Trent's number?" I asked, knowing I'd do whatever I could to help his friends.

Ford rattled off Trent's details, and I called him. In an hour I'd managed to pack my gear, shower, eat, and get dressed, but I was flustered. I hated not doing things precisely and this felt very half-assed. I had no idea of what the couple wanted and I hadn't even thought to ask what the dress code was. For all I knew, it was a lumberjack-themed wedding and I was wearing a bow tie.

"You look good, Angelo," Ricky said encouragingly from the doorway to his bedroom. He was getting ready for work too, his sweats having been replaced by an olive-green flight suit.

"Thanks." I nodded and threw him a smile as I adjusted the clip on my suspenders. "Guess I'll see you sometime tonight." I dashed down the stairs and out the front door, clutching my camera bag like a lifeline and counting my equipment out in my head. I hoped I hadn't forgotten anything. It was only ten minutes later that I was standing at the hotel's reception asking for them to call up to the bride's room.

The man who met me at the elevator took one look at me and engulfed me in a hug. "Thank you. I don't know what we would have done if you hadn't come through." I patted his back uncomfortably, and he pulled back, laughing at himself. "Look at me, I'm all emotional. My baby girl is getting married and I'm gushing. Come on up…." He hesitated, and I took my cue.

"Angelo di Pasqua. Congratulations on the wedding. And really, it's no problem. I'm new to Queenstown and still building my client base here, so you're doing me a favor too."

Photographing the bride getting ready had me loving every moment of this job. Jenna had had a shit of a morning but was still beaming. One of those rare super-chilled brides, she was fun to be around. Her brides-maids, on the other hand, were both tipsy and handsy. As pretty as those ladies were, they were like ravenous wolves too. By the third time they referred to me as a "sexy slab of man meat" I was grateful that it was time for me to head over to the groom's house where he was dressing.

I didn't expect to find what I did at the groom's house. The men in every wedding party I'd ever photographed had always left getting dressed until the last minute, but they were usually drinking and watching sport. This groom and his friends were up ladders building a gazebo in the yard of a house that was mid-renovation. "G'day, mate," he said by way of greeting, a giant power drill in hand. "Gimme ten and I'll be down."

"You've only got twenty minutes before you need to

leave for the church," I sputtered. "You're wearing work clothes!"

"I'll be down in a sec to grab a quick shower and get dressed. She'll be right."

"I'm not worried about *her*," I muttered under my breath. "*She'll* be at the ceremony on time."

Clearly that wasn't the right thing to say because the groom's friend boomed out a laugh and clapped me on the back, his meaty paw nearly sending me sprawling. "She'll be right's' a saying, bro." I shook my head and snapped some photos of the groom walking along beams and screwing down sheets of roofing to the frame. The friend continued talking to me, "That's his missus's wedding present. She's wanted one for years, but you know how chippies are—they build everyone else's shit and leave their own place half finished."

"Like you can talk, Jay," the groom called out. "Now shut the fuck up and catch this, will ya?" He lowered the drill by its cord, and Jay reached up for it, unplugging it and putting it in a hard case.

As he finished tidying up and locking tool chests he added, "He's been working on it for half the night. Wasn't there yesterday. I'll come in and stain it, and the decorator will furnish it so it's finished while they're away."

"Impressive." I nodded at Brad, the groom, as he hopped off the ladder and headed inside. Less than ten minutes later he emerged dressed in a navy three-piece suit, his tie hanging open along his collar. Jay and another man followed a few minutes later, and within fifteen they were ready to get in the cars. I'd been snapping candid photos the whole time, but it was standing at the front door while the trio were about to exit that sent pangs of longing through me.

Jay reached out for Brad's tie, adjusting it so it was centered. "This is it, bro. You're marrying my little sis. Nervous?"

"Nah, mate. I've waited my whole life for this moment."

My heart thudded in my chest, hearing the love in his voice. I wanted that, I really did. The thought of coming home to my partner, of holding them at night, taking care of them, of loving them was like a pipe dream. But it was one that'd probably never happen. People tended not to stick around when they found out I just wasn't interested in sex. I barely even thought about it nowadays. It wasn't like I hadn't tried. When I was in my senior year and in college, I'd had more than one attempt, but it was "meh" at best. I'd watched porn, I'd tried hooking up with a few girls in my senior year and others during college, but there was nothing there. No spark, no energy, no desire. Nothing. Doctors had told me there was nothing wrong and I could take drugs to increase my sex drive if that was what I wanted. I'd held off, trying to look for another option and spent countless hours trawling through the web trying to figure out alternatives. Then I came across a forum for aces, or people identifying as asexual. I knew I'd found my tribe. My worrying over my lack of sex drive was because I was so focused on what everyone else deemed "normal." Once I realized that I was my own "normal," I stopped being concerned that there was something wrong with me. As much as I hated putting myself in a box, because I was more than my sexuality, once I knew the right label to apply, I was comfortable in my skin. I wanted romance, I felt attraction, but it just wasn't sexual. I wanted the feel of arms around me, of a kiss, but I didn't have a thing for sex.

Problem was that most people still had no idea what that meant. They assumed the same thing as me initially—I was impotent—or worse, that I'd been abused as a kid and sex scared me. For the record, I could get it up without a problem—I jacked off occasionally when I needed the endorphin rush—and no, I hadn't been abused. I was one of those lucky kids who grew up in a stable house with parents who loved them and were understanding and accepting of me. But I was a complete failure at dating. Most didn't get past the first date if they started to get physical and I didn't move things along. But the kind of love I could hear in Brad's voice? I wanted that.

I shook off my musings and followed them out the door, snapping photos of the gorgeous red Chevy Bel Air parked in the drive and of the groom and his friends getting into it.

I saw Trent at the ceremony handing out booklets and ushering people to their seats, and later getting up to read out a poem. His voice was hypnotic. It wasn't overly deep, but his measured pace had the room riveted, and as he spoke about everlasting love and honor just about every tragic romantic in the room, me included, sighed. I'd loved getting close enough to take photos of him as he spoke, his dark eyes haunting in my lens.

It wasn't until the reception that I could say thank you to him. With the bride and groom speaking to their friends and family and taking endless selfies, I stayed out of the way, leaning against the mahogany bar. I toyed with the ice cubes in my empty glass as I watched Trent with his date. It didn't look like they were having a good time.

Trent shook his head, and his date went from looking like she was giving him puppy-dog eyes to then hardening her gaze. He didn't hang around, picking up his glass and turning his back on her. When he made his way in my direction, I moved to meet him in the middle of the bar. "Hey," I greeted, smiling at him. "Thanks for thinking of me today. I appreciate it."

He reached out for my hand, shaking it. His grip was firm, his hand warm. He had strong hands, and I knew they were talented—anyone who could make it as a paramedic had to be. "Anytime, bro. You're good at what you do, so I knew Brad and Jenna would be looked after."

"You never saw my photos though," I replied, my brows furrowed in confusion.

"So show me them then." He laughed and shook his head like it was the most obvious answer ever. I supposed it was. "I had a gut feeling about you. The way you analyzed every shot and adjusted your camera until you were happy? It's obvious you're good."

"Or maybe I'm just faking it." I grinned at him.

"Maybe. Sucks for the happy couple, doesn't it?" He smirked in my direction and held up his empty glass. "Want one?"

"I'm on soda water tonight, but yeah, sure." Trent didn't hesitate, ordering the same drink that I'd had at the pub when we were together and getting a whiskey for himself. "You need to get back to your date?" I asked, tipping my chin in the lady's direction. She was watching us with a sour expression, her red lips thinly pursed.

"She can wait a minute." He continued when I looked at him incredulously. *You don't just ditch your date.* "She's pissed at me. We've gone out a few times, nothing serious, and I made the mistake of asking her to come along tonight. She took it as me wanting to go steady or whatever, 'cause now she's telling me she's gonna catch the bouquet." At my hum and slow nod in understanding, he continued. "Wasn't too pleased when I said it wouldn't be me giving her the ring."

"Harsh let down."

"Needed to be said, but yeah, I probably should have been nicer about it." Trent took another swallow of his whiskey, and I watched the bob of his Adam's apple. He was strong all over, not just his hands. Even his neck was thick, muscular, and, in a suit, he looked damn sexy. His broad shoulders had filled out the jacket nicely when he was in church, and now with the sleeves of his shirt rolled up and his beefy forearms on display, I could understand why his date had wanted him to herself.

"You ever done modelling before?" I blurted out, my brain-to-mouth filter apparently on the fritz. He looked at me, startled, and shook his head. "Sorry, was thinking out loud," I apologized. "You could easily be a model. Photographers would love you."

"Yeah, no." He scoffed. "I'll stick with what I'm good at." He swallowed the last of his drink and turned back to the bartender. "Can I grab another two soda waters with lime, bro?" He passed me one of the drinks and sipped his own. "So, I start work late tomorrow. Want me to bring over some breakfast and you can show me those photos?"

I smiled. "As long as you don't mind Riccardo in pajamas shouting at the TV. There's a football match on. Our team is playing, and he got it on pay per view."

"Sweet."

# CHAPTER 5
## ANGELO

Trent and I had managed to spend some time together nearly every day after he'd come over to check out the photos I'd taken with him at the bridge. For nearly three weeks, we'd gone hiking in the hills or jogging along the lake, we'd checked out a few pub bands, watched football —both rugby and the real kind—and ate countless meals together. It was easy being with him, and we had a good time no matter what we were doing. I'd laughed a lot with him, but the last couple of days were different. There'd been radio silence since Thursday when he'd called to cancel our plans. I'd messaged him and had no response for two days. It was unlike him, but he was probably just busy.

Today though, I had news and I couldn't wait to tell him. Usually I told my sister everything—Gabriella was my confidante—but she wasn't the person I wanted to talk to now. Bursting with excitement, I'd dialed him, but his reaction wasn't what I expected. He was preoccupied. Quiet and withdrawn. Maybe I'd caught him at a bad moment. Perhaps he was in the middle of something, but his tone left me with that niggling feeling in my chest. Something was off and that worried me. I loved seeing him smile. When he did, the world around him lit up. His grin, his personality drew people in. I'd been scooped up and was in his gravitational pull from the moment we'd met. But in talking to him I knew there wouldn't be any smiles that day.

I'd headed straight to his townhouse, the niggling worry turning into a hole in my chest. I wasn't sure why, but I knew I had to get to him as quickly as I could. When I arrived, I thought I'd missed him. All the blinds were closed, and the silence surrounding the house had my nerves prickling. He hated silence. He was always playing music or had the TV going.

There was still no answer after I'd knocked twice. I turned on my heels and stepped away from the door, my mind preoccupied with where he could have gone. Then I heard it. Glass shattering, splintering against a hard surface. My gut dropped. Fear pulsed through me. Trent was inside and something was very wrong. I'd never moved so fast. Spinning around I jammed my hand down on the handle and yanked the screen open, almost falling through the door in surprise. *It's open.* I yelled out his name, the panic in my voice clear as I found my footing and ran through the small lounge room to the kitchen. I saw him standing there. Glass was smashed on the floor and amber liquid splashed on the white cupboards. He held an open bottle of Jack in his hand, barely gripping it. His shoulders were slumped. Even with his head held low, I could see the pain etched on his face. I wanted to take his sorrow away. Dressed only in basketball shorts, he must have been freezing. I shivered in the icy breeze coming in from the still-open front door behind me.

I reached out, and he flinched; my heart broke at the move. I took the bottle from him and hesitated to touch him again. I didn't want to make things worse, but I had no idea what the issue was. I wanted to help him. More than anything.

I murmured his name, and all hesitation fled when he swayed on his feet toward me. I slipped my hand around his waist and pulled him to me, holding him tight. It was as if he melted into my touch, letting me support him just for a moment. I wanted that—to be his friend. His skin was chilled to the touch and he was bleeding. Nicks along his legs left droplets of blood trickling down his shins. It had to have been from all the broken glass. The smell of liquor wasn't just from the mess on the floor. Trent was drunk. *What's going on?* His bloodshot eyes connected with mine, and in them I saw pleading. Raw pain. He swayed again, and I held him tighter.

"Come on, let's get you cleaned up," I spoke quietly, trying to soothe him as I led him to his sofa. Kneeling at his feet, I checked his legs and realized a few Band-Aids would be enough to cover the small cuts. Resting my hands on his knees, I looked up at him. "You want to talk about it?" When he shook his head, I nodded and squeezed his leg. "I'm here if you change your mind."

I went into the bathroom and searched through his cupboards until I found his first aid supplies. Neatly boxed up, just like Trent. Everything in the one-bedroom townhouse was always clean and ordered. Everything had its place. You'd never know below the surface were turbulent waters. I'd seen glimpses of pain, of how he closed himself off, but now I had no doubt there was something more there.

I grabbed what I needed and saw his robe hanging over the edge of his laundry basket. I snagged it and went back to him so I could tend to the nicks on his legs. The bleeding had already stopped, but I still needed to look after him. I needed to show him how much he'd come to mean to me in such a short time. I wrapped the robe around his shoulders and kneeled to clean the cuts, wiping away the blood and sticking the plasters over his hairy shins.

I smoothed the strips down and looked up into his eyes. I'd never seen so much sadness and agony in them before. I couldn't help but reach out and take him into my arms. He didn't hug me back, but he leaned into my touch. I gave a piece of myself to him in that moment. This man before me was already the best friend I had, even though we still had so much to share. He was so vulnerable, so incredibly sad, and I wanted to help him, to give him back his happy. But how?

He pulled away after a while and turned away from me, wiping his face. He'd cried silent tears on my shoulder, and despite every instinct in me, I backed off, not wanting to crowd him. Standing, I went into the kitchen and put a pod in his coffee machine. I couldn't help but worry about him. At only ten in the morning he'd been drinking. *Why? What happened?*

He was quiet but more settled after he'd downed a cup of the strong brew. I left him to get dressed while I cleaned up the kitchen. Lost in thought, I didn't hear him walk back into the kitchen until he was standing before me, freshly showered and dressed in jeans, a polo shirt, and his leather jacket. "You don't have to stay," he said quietly. "I'm okay."

"I know." I tried to sound convincing, but it was strained even to my own ears. "I figured we could get some food and chill for a few hours until you had to work."

"I'm not going in today," he mumbled. "Ford changed my roster. Said he didn't need me."

"What? Why wouldn't he need you?" I asked, and Trent looked like he had a bad taste in his mouth. Almost as if he were ashamed. But why? When he didn't answer I continued, trying to fill the silence with babble. "Maybe we can go out then. There's a gallery that I was going to visit this afternoon to drop off a card to. We could walk there if you wanted. It's not far."

"Sure." He nodded and shook out his shoulders, smiling at me. But it didn't reach his eyes. I let him maintain the façade for the moment. I wouldn't push him for answers. He had to want to tell me. Hopefully one day he'd trust me enough with whatever was bothering him. Until then, I had to be patient. "I could eat too," he added.

"Come on then."

We walked next to each other, our pace relaxed, neither of us in a hurry to get anywhere. I enjoyed the chill of the winter day. My favorite time of year was spent bundled up in warm clothes, drinking hot chocolates by the fire or skiing on the slopes surrounding my new home. I loved it. My breath fogged up in front of me with each exhale. The weak winter rays did barely anything more than light the sky. There was no warmth in it, leaving my nose and cheeks chilled.

We passed through the park, the blossom trees in full

bloom. The light pink flowers weighed down the broad branches of the old trees and littered the grass below them. This little park was one of my favorite things about Queenstown. The babbling brook, the old foot bridge crossing it, and the sandstone buildings surrounding it made it quaint. Trent stopped at the top of the bridge and rested his elbows on the heavy wrought iron and railway sleeper railing. "I fucked up at work," he admitted after a moment of silence.

"How?" I asked, leaning my butt against the handrail, one foot propped up against the balusters. My arms were crossed lightly over my chest and I turned, waiting for him to respond.

"Had a few drinks night before last, then went to work the next day. Ford said I stunk like a brewery and wouldn't let me clock in. Told me that I needed to get my priorities straight before I came back in. He gave me a few extra days off to remind me not to go to work still lit." Trent shook his head and blew out a breath. His lips were pursed, and he closed his eyes, his disgust in himself evident.

*Oh, Trent.* "You had a date that night, didn't you?" I knew the answer to that question. When he'd cancelled the plans that we'd almost naturally fallen into, I was far too disappointed. It'd soon turned to annoyance, but I wasn't sure whether I was annoyed with him or me. Thursday night football had become our thing, but I was hardly dependent on Trent to do something. My brother had gone out with Ford, inviting me along too. I could have hung with them, but I didn't want to. I'd wanted to spend time with my friend. It wasn't like I had any claim over him, and his date had been a reminder of that, which rubbed me the wrong way.

He huffed out a laugh that held no humor. "I did, but it was a no go. She wasn't looking for someone like me, and I definitely wasn't looking for someone as uptight and damn critical as her. I left before we'd even ordered dessert, and I'd been looking for an excuse for an hour before that. In the end, I told her I needed to get cat food for Dodge before the grocery store closed. It was like eight o'clock when I left."

"The cat you're minding?"

"Yep." He nodded. I bit my lip trying not to laugh. It wasn't funny. He was telling me about some shit that'd gone down that had upset him, but come on. How was I supposed to react? He'd used needing food for the cat he was sitting as an excuse to get out of a date. And the cat's name was Dodge? You couldn't make that shit up. I snorted, unsuccessfully trying to stifle my laugh, and wiped my eyes, tears welling from the effort. Trent paused and looked at me, confused, and I couldn't hold it in any longer. I laughed and shook my head, holding my hand up to him.

"I'm sorry, I don't mean to laugh at you, but seriously?" I sucked in a breath, my side hurting because I was laughing so hard. "Cat food? For Dodge?" Trent's lips twitched, and I could see him fighting the smile. I looked at him again and laughed once more, nudging him with my shoulder. "You didn't even realize how it sounded until now, did you?" When he shook his head and finally let that smile loose, I sucked in a breath, happy for a whole other reason. It was his story and he'd told it, but he was smiling and I couldn't help but take a little pride in that.

"Fuck me. She looked so damn horrified when I said that, but all I could think about was getting out of there." He chuckled and ran his fingers through his hair. "I'm such a dumb ass."

"Nah, you just didn't think." I nudged his shoulder playfully, letting him know that it wasn't all bad. "At least tell me you got the food."

He nodded and sobered up. "I couldn't wait to get out of there, but I didn't want to go home either. Figured you would have been busy, so I stopped by the sports bar. Watched a footy match. Haven't done that by myself in years, and I hated every minute of it. Suppose I had too many drinks."

My heart clenched, and I wanted to reach out to him. Instead I leaned closer, my side pressed against his, and asked, "You didn't drive home, did you?" I wasn't sure whether I was begging him or scolding him for being so damn stupid. If he'd been drinking and driving not only could it be the end of his career, but more importantly he could have killed someone. And it was all because he didn't call me.

"Nah, I walked it. The night air sobered me up pretty fast."

*Thank God.* I let out the breath I was holding, relief winning my emotional tug-of-war.

"So what happened yesterday and today? You just kept drinking?" It was none of my business, I knew that, but I didn't care. I needed to know.

"Something like that," he muttered. This was him shutting down. A noncommittal answer followed by either a subject change or him going quiet, but I couldn't do it. I needed him to be able to talk to me.

"Look, I'm not going to push you, but maybe it'll help if you spoke about whatever is bothering you. I'm here. I'll listen, and I'll do my best to help, but I can't unless you talk to me. If not me, then pick someone else. I'm worried about you."

"Some bad shit happened when I was younger. This time of year always drags it back up, but I'll get through it." He paused and added, "This—walking and being outside, spending time with you—it's helping. *You're* helping."

I smiled softly and squeezed his shoulder, letting my hand drop after I'd reached out to him. I liked touching him, liked showing him that he was important to me. The silence stretched out between us for a moment, and I figured he could use a break from talking about himself, especially if whatever his memories were, were painful. "I got another job this morning. One of Brad's construction crew had a baby a couple of months ago. They want me to do a family shoot for them with their dog. They're booked in next week. I've never done one before though. I'm a little nervous about getting it right."

Trent smiled, and this time it reached his eyes. "That's great, Angelo. You deserve it." He motioned to the street bordering the park. "How about we try to make it two jobs in one day? Let's go visit this gallery and see whether you can get some of your landscapes in it."

His words lit me up from the inside out, warming me like butter melting on soft bread straight out of the oven. I'd only known him for a short time, but Trent was one of the good ones. He wasn't perfect—none of us were—but he'd quickly become the most important person in my life outside of my family. His friendship meant everything to me.

Dodging pedestrians and traffic on the busy street, we made our way to the gallery. Bold paintings and photographs of spectacular scenery were hung tastefully on the walls, each one having its own space. It was more than just an artwork store. High-end tourists would be their main clientele—exactly the crowd I was aiming for—but the works were varied enough that I could have been wrong.

I wandered around, taking my time to look at the composition of the images while mentally assessing my own photographs against them. Some of mine were better, but there were many that outmatched my art, the photographers beautifully capturing the moment.

Trent followed me around the gallery, his distraction not lost on me. He stared unseeingly at some pieces and wandered by the most impressive ones as if he hadn't even noticed them. I couldn't focus on him though, because the manager approached looking to make a sale. As I spoke to her about supplying them with one-off pieces, I watched Trent out of the corner of my eye. He was focused on something happening across the road and kept shifting so he could look out the door. When the manager went behind the counter to get a business card, I moved over to him and quietly asked, "You okay?" That same sadness I'd seen written in his features earlier was back. Mouth turned down, he had a faraway look in his eyes, but his gaze never wavered. I followed his line of sight and didn't see anything at first, but then I spotted them. I couldn't tell whether the person was a man or woman, but they were old and frail and sitting on the cold concrete. The threadbare blankets wrapped around their shoulders wouldn't keep out the winter cold, especially with overnight temperatures dropping down to near freezing. Huddling against a dumpster wouldn't be enough shelter from the cold winter gale either. My gut twisted knowing that the person would likely spend another night out in the cold, and more beyond that.

Trent didn't answer my question before the manager returned. Instead he wandered off. It was a strange reaction, but I couldn't ponder it without being unprofessional. I took the proffered card with the gallery's email address, and the manager said, "Send through a few examples of what you'd propose we stock, and we can talk, Mr. di Pasqua."

"Thank you." I smiled, shaking her hand and bidding her goodbye. I looked around the gallery but couldn't see Trent. It wasn't until I walked outside, my eyes drawn back to the homeless person near the dumpster, that I saw him. Crouched down, he was talking to them, holding their undoubtedly frail hands in his strong ones. As I crossed the street to him, he pulled something out of his jacket pocket. Halfway into the alley, I realized he was talking to a woman, and he'd given her his gloves. He slid them onto her hands and pulled out his wallet. *What's he doing?* I paused, watching them quietly from a few yards away. Trent pulled something out and handed it to her. They spoke, her crying and him nodding and soothing her. It wasn't until she shifted to pocket the note that I got a look at it. Unmistakably red, it meant one thing—he'd given her a hundred dollars.

I was floored. The homeless were so often invisible. People never knew how to react, me included. Did you smile? Would that be misread as you laughing at their misfortune? Did you show them pity? Homelessness might be a sight better than where they came from, but people rarely asked for it. Did you give them money? What if they were drug addicts or alcoholics and you were just making things worse? Most people simply ignored them. Walked past as if they weren't there. But not Trent. He'd gone out of his way to speak to her and help her where he could. Even the way he held her hands showed how much he cared. He'd literally given her his own gloves to help keep her warm. My breath caught in my throat, and I closed my eyes, thanking God for giving me his friendship.

By the time Trent made his way back out of the alley, I'd returned to the sidewalk and was browsing the kitschy display of tourist knickknacks in the windows of the nearby store. "Hey, I was wondering where you'd gotten to," I mused. I was sure Trent saw right through my façade, but he didn't call me on it, in the same way I didn't say anything more about the lady he'd helped.

---

IT WAS WEIRD TO DAYDREAM, WASN'T IT? I'D BEEN SITTING AT the desk in Riccardo's lounge room, my Mac in front of me, with the final edits of Brad and Jenna's wedding photos spread open. Ricky had long ago gone to bed, and I should have done the same, but I wanted to get the album finished. Except that I hadn't touched the images for an hour. I was distracted. I couldn't focus on anything except Trent crouching down in that alley helping the woman. Giving her a lifeline. My friend, the same one who had something going on that was eating him alive, had stopped to help her. He hadn't hesitated either. Then when I hadn't questioned him on it, he'd looked relieved, like a weight had been lifted off his shoulders. *But why?*

My cell pinged, an incoming message from my sister, Gabriella. She was visiting her boyfriend a few hours away from our parents.

**Gabriella: Are you around?**

I opened up Skype and dialed her, waiting for her to connect our call.

"*Ciao*, Ang," she greeted when her face appeared on the screen. She looked radiant, her dark hair glowing and her tan a deep golden color. We all had the same eyes—hazel—but hers were a vibrant green this time. She was happy, and my heart warmed seeing her like that.

We spoke in Italian, my brain heaving a sigh of relief at no longer having to translate my thoughts into a foreign language before I spoke. "Hey, beautiful."

We caught up on the goings on, and I broke the news from earlier in the day. When I'd arrived home, I'd emailed the gallery and the manager was impressed. She'd have to speak with the owners but was going to recommend they purchase a few of my images as exclusive one-off pieces and others as prints that could be supplied on demand. That combined with the family portrait shoot had me confident I'd one day be able to make a living from my photography gig.

She was telling me about her stay, about how her boyfriend wanted her to move in, but I was only half listening. "What's wrong, Angelo? You're off with the fairies. I've been quiet for a whole minute and you haven't even noticed."

"Sorry, it's late here," I hedged. "Had a busy day."

"Old man," she teased. "Are you sure that's all?"

Sighing, I admitted, "No, I've got a bit on my mind. I'm worried about my friend, Trent. Something is bothering him. He's had a rough few days from what he told me, but then today he did something that I can't get out of my head."

"What?" she asked, her head cocked to the side like she often did when she was curious.

"I told you he's a mountain rescue paramedic too, didn't I?" I continued without waiting for her to answer. My sister had gotten her accreditation in specialist first aid only the year before. "Anyway, I suppose it's not strange that he'd help people, but he was down today. I wanted to make him smile, you know? We went for a walk together and even though he's got a lot of shit going on, he still took the time out to help a homeless lady. He talked to her, gave her his gloves and money. Not just pocket change either. I can't get it out of my head. I've been sitting here replaying it over and over."

"You like him," she said with a small smile.

I paused, confused. "Of course I do. He's my friend."

"No, you *like him*, like him." Her smile grew and I scoffed at her, laughing at the ridiculous notion that I was crushing on my friend. There was no way. It was ridiculous. But at the same time, the way he made me feel…. No. Impossible. Wasn't it?

"What are we? Fifteen? And anyway, I'm straight."

"Are you?" she asked without missing a beat. "You've told me yourself that you've never lusted over anyone, you've never been sexually attracted to anyone before. It's one of the ways you figured out that you're asexual. Maybe you haven't connected all the dots yet, but it's not outside the realm of possibility that you're falling for your friend. Remember, sexuality is a spectrum. You might fall at a different spot than you thought."

"Yeah, but what's the likelihood of having two people in one family 'on the spectrum' as you say." I added the air quotes in as I spoke. "Riccardo's pan. I'm gay, or bi, or whatever now?"

Gabriella shook her head and gave me a patient smile, like she had all the time in the world. "You do realize you're already on the spectrum, don't you? Asexuality is just as much a sexuality as homosexuality or heterosexuality. Bisexuality, pansexuality. You get my drift. And come on, after our upbringing does it surprise you that we accept sexuality isn't as easily defined in society's nice little boxes?" Our very Italian, Catholic parents were swingers and had an open relationship during their entire twenty years of marriage. They were divorced now, but when they were together we would often have sleepovers at Nonna's. Turns out date night for them was swapping keys or visiting their latest girlfriend, boyfriend, or both. As we got older, they were more candid about their preferences, letting us see that while unconventional, their relationship was solid. Then they simply outgrew each other. Papà wanted to move in with his girlfriend, and Mamma was happy hooking up with her men—two bisexual guys in a committed relationship who were voyeurs and exhibitionists too. They liked to bring her in —the sexy cougar—as a third member. It wasn't hostile in any way and Mamma and Papà still apparently got together when the urge struck, but mostly they were just friends now.

"No, I suppose not. But regardless, I'm not into him."

"All I'm saying is maybe he's someone special to you."

I nodded and agreed, "He is special to me. He's my friend. Nothing more, Gab."

"Okay," she conceded. "You obviously know your own feelings."

We wrapped up the call soon after and I turned in for the night. Crawling into bed in sweats and an old T-shirt, I pulled the covers up to my neck and closed my eyes. It took me a long time to wrangle my thoughts into line. Gabriella had gotten to me. She had me thinking things that I didn't want to. I wasn't crushing on him, and if I kept telling myself that, the stupid nagging voice in the back of my brain would finally shut up and listen.

SUNLIGHT PEEKED AROUND THE OUTSIDE OF THE WOODEN timber slat blinds that adorned the windows in the room I was staying in. I had no idea what time it was, but I couldn't smell coffee. Either it was really early—which by the look of the amount of light coming in, it wasn't—or it was late and Riccardo had long ago left for the workout he did at the ass crack of dawn every Sunday morning.

I stretched, my hard length tenting the covers even more as I arched my back. It'd been a while since I'd had an erection, months since I'd jacked off last, and it felt good to be hard. I closed my eyes again and relished the heat, the stretch of taut skin over my dick, the soft fabric of my sweats brushing against my nerve endings. I palmed myself, squeezing myself over the material, and moaned quietly.

I wanted to feel, wanted the release.

I didn't have lube handy, but I didn't care. Pushing down my sweats, my feet flat on the bed, I closed my fist over my hardness and stroked slowly. Up and down I moved, and heat pooled between my legs while a natural high flooded my body. Every part of me tingled. I sped up, using the drop of precum to ease the movement of my hand and rocking my hips in time. Images flashed before my closed eyelids. Hands cupping and touching, soft brushes of skin against skin. Facial hair against my palm, thick legs, and a spicy scent. The curve of firm muscle, peaks and valleys of abs and the dark happy trail below his navel leading down to the waistline of his loose-fitting basketball shorts. The V that followed the same path, pointing to his package hidden away. His pecs, and the hair on his chest. I gasped as my dick pulsed in my palm, my imagination telling me exactly what I wanted to happen next. Trent's warm hands, big and strong yet gentle, pulled me closer, and our mouths joined.

Lips pressing together, our tongues softly sought each other out. Moans and gasps as he drew me closer, aligning our bodies, every inch of our naked skin touching. Our legs tangled together, and arms wound around each other. His warmth blanketed me, his solid body sheltered me, but he was vulnerable too. Hurting. I cupped his face and pulled back to look in his eyes. I didn't see pain there anymore. I saw love. Contentment. Desire. He smiled and my heart fluttered. I'd done that. I'd given him peace. I'd made him happy. He whispered my name, his voice husky with desire, and it sent me over the edge, my climax washing over me. My seed spilled onto my stomach and I gasped for air as I rode the high. Orgasms were never powerful and all-consuming for me, but this one was different. It was longer, harder.

Breathless, I lay there, holding my softening erection as I realized what I'd done. I'd thought about another person while I was jacking off. It wasn't just any person either. It was my friend, my male friend. Gabriella's words came back to me, *"Maybe he's someone special to you."* He was. But I couldn't be falling for him. Like Gab said, I'd never been attracted to anyone, male or female. His gender didn't bother me. The fact that he dated women did. I couldn't be that clichéd, could I? The one person who had made me even think of touching another sexually was straight? Completely out of reach? *Fuck. I'm screwed. But maybe not. Maybe I'm only thinking of Trent because Gab mentioned it. Like she planted the seed and in my pre-caffeinated state, my body is using the last thing I thought of before I slept as inspiration.*

I chose to ignore the voice in the back of my mind reminding me that going to sleep thinking of Trent and waking up with him there too meant something more. He was my friend. As long as I kept reminding myself of that, it'd be true. I hoped.

I DIDN'T SEE MUCH OF TRENT OVER THE NEXT FEW DAYS. HE pulled a few extra shifts to make up for the ones he'd missed the week before, and the one night he had free, I had the family photo shoot scheduled. I was looking forward to Thursday night with him watching the rugby match on the big screen at the sports bar. He'd been invited to go with a group of friends, and he'd asked me along too. I was nervous, but I didn't want him to know that. I stood in front of my closet, wearing only my briefs with three discarded changes of clothes on the floor and countless shirts tossed on the bed. I was going out of my mind. I wasn't comfortable in anything casual. T-shirts and sweaters made me antsy, and while I didn't want to go too formal, I knew I wouldn't be able to settle in a large group of people until I was at ease in my own skin. But if I didn't pick something, I'd be late, and that was even worse. I settled on black jeans and a pale purple checked shirt with a gray waistcoat.

I looked over my reflection once more, fixed my hair, and snagged my wallet, cell, and keys off the nightstand before jogging down the stairs. My heavy coat lay on the sofa, and I snatched that up too. The drive to Trent's house only took a few minutes, and as I parked in the drive, I took a deep breath, hoping that I wasn't so overdressed that I stood out like a sore thumb.

Trent must have seen me pull up because the next moment he was out the door, walking toward me. Blue jeans, a black button down, and his black leather jacket gave him a dark edge that made him look mysterious. His eyes, his strong jaw, and those muscles combined with his lips and the air of what I was coming to realize was sadness, made me want to photograph him. Black and white, stripped of anything but a gray background. I wanted to peel back the layers, rid him of the background noise—and his clothes—so the world could see him the way I did. He was beautiful.

He slid into the passenger seat, looked me up and

down, and grinned. "The guys are gonna think you're a Storm supporter." When I raised my eyebrow at him questioningly, he laughed and added, "I love how clueless you are about this."

I probably should have been annoyed by the smart-assed remark, but instead I laughed. "Fuck you." I gave him my middle finger and grinned. "You try moving to the other side of the world and be an overnight expert." That comment had him chuckling again, and I smiled at his easy laughter as I reversed out the drive and headed back toward the center of town and the sports bar we'd become semi-regulars at.

The door hadn't even swung closed behind us when I wanted to turn around and leave again. I knew the group as soon as I saw them—loud and obnoxious all wearing the home team's color: black. My purple would stand out like a lighthouse beacon, and worse still, was the color of the opposing team. *Shit.*

"Come on." Trent nudged me in their direction with a hand to my lower back and flashed a small smile at me. "They'll give you a hard time, but they're all pretty good guys." His reassurance only made me more nervous, but it was his touch that had me sucking in a breath.

Trent made the introductions, and I shook a few hands and nodded at a couple of the men on the other side of the round bar tables cobbled together into a line. Stools were pulled up and a pitcher of beer put in front of us. I waved it away, not wanting to drink while I was driving. "I'll get your drinks tonight," Trent said from next to me. Before I could object, he was off his stool and walking to the bar. I watched him go, watched the way he moved easily through the crowd, greeting people as they recognized him. I turned back to the table and saw everyone busy in their own conversations. I was people-watching like I often did, looking at the way they held themselves. Individuals stood out to me.

There was one woman a few tables over who captured my attention. She was fascinating. With soft features and a slim build, she moved like a ballerina. Graceful and almost feline. At another, there was another woman who had a hearty laugh. Warmth radiated from her. At our table, two men who were deep in conversation looked like they'd come straight from work. Dressed much like me, it was clear they were in business, but it was their heads close together that made me wonder whether their conversation was about work or something else.

None of them held my attention for longer than a few moments though, and I found my eyes drifting back to the man at the bar. I watched his lips move as he chatted with a woman, casually leaning against the black timber bar while my soda water and lime and his drink sat untouched next to him. Trent tilted his head over in the direction of our table, and the girl held her hand out. He didn't hesitate, handing over his cell. I watched as their hands connected, but it was his that I was focused on—big and strong, but gentle too. I'd seen with my own eyes how caring those hands could be.

"Look at that bastard, getting another number," Jason, the man beside me, huffed with a laugh. "Lucky prick."

Trent took back his cell and smiled at the woman before pocketing it, picking up my drink, and coming back to the table. Our eyes met across the room, and he smiled. My heart beat faster, and I yearned to reach out to him, but I pulled away, forcing the connection to be severed. Disappointment surged through me, but I ignored the sensation. I wasn't going to do this. Not here. Not now. Not ever.

"Another admirer, Trent?" Jason asked.

He shrugged, but the satisfied smirk gave him away. There was no doubt she was sexy. Curvy and voluptuous, with a shock of red hair down to her waist. Jason's elbow hitting me hard in my shoulder snapped me out of my musing. "Keep staring at him like a faggot and you might get your teeth knocked out in this bar, but you'll learn the secret to getting laid, won't ya?" His question, spoken as a statement, made my skin crawl. But it was Trent's reaction that made me wish I was anywhere but there.

"Nah, man. Angelo's no homo."

I shook my head and scoffed at the idea, the whole while thinking Gab was right. I wasn't as straight as I'd assumed, and I couldn't deny anymore that I liked him.

*I'm screwed.*

# CHAPTER 6
## ANGELO

## THREE MONTHS LATER

It'd taken me six months to get enough work booked to be able to afford my own place. Riccardo insisted that I should stay with him, but I'd already sponged off him for too long. The board he would accept wasn't enough, and I hated feeling like I wasn't pulling my weight. That, and he'd begun dating a woman who seemed to be his perfect match. They'd started to get serious pretty quickly, and I didn't want to be in the way when they decided to take it to the next level.

I'd started to venture out farther and farther into the hills and mountains surrounding Queenstown, trying to get a few more of the unique pieces that always sold well in the gallery, and it was working. They were selling, and I was getting enough commissions coming in to make the move. The only problem was that between clients, editing photos, promo work, and my hikes, it hadn't left me much time to look for an apartment. But I was on my way out to look at a rental that had just opened up. Competition for affordable housing was fierce, so if it was even remotely livable, I'd sign the lease on the spot.

I pulled up in the street and smiled. I could see myself living there already. Queenstown in the dying days of spring was just as beautiful as in the winter. I closed my eyes and let the warmth in the breeze ruffle my hair. Opening them, I looked up at the vibrant blue sky. Dappled sunlight filtered through the tall canopy of trees casting shadows that danced on the street. Wide sidewalks encouraged people to get out and about, and there were people everywhere. An elderly man and a younger woman spoke to each other from their driveways, and a couple of young kids walked their dog. The park across from the building was bathed in sunshine. A basketball court and skate bowl there were both full of teenagers, and, on the small patch of grass, a young family played.

The sharp lines and shadows of the concrete snagged my attention immediately and I itched to get my camera. The lighting was near perfect. I bit back a frustrated groan because I knew I couldn't be late to the showing. Agents around these parts would happily give the rental to someone else if I wasn't there on time. I did the responsible thing and jogged across the street, heading up the sidewalk to the complex. The street was a mix of apartments, charming little houses, and a few townhouse-style buildings with two and three homes joined under the one roof. Literally around the corner from Trent's townhouse and only a two-minute drive from the main street, it was close to everything but quiet too.

Christmas was getting closer—only five weeks away—and there were a few houses already decorated, tinsel hanging in many of the windows and lighting displays on more than one of the balconies. It was strange; the warm weather and decorations didn't go together. I'd only ever experienced a white Christmas; Santa Caterina di Valfurva was always under a few feet of snow when December rolled around, and seeing greenery and people wearing short sleeves and swimming in the lake were strange to say the least.

Trent waited for me, and I joined him in front of the circa 1980s squat apricot-colored building. Designed in a U-shape with a courtyard in the middle and the office to one side, the building was ugly. But I'd been assured that the fourth-floor apartment had been renovated. Anything had to be better than the depressing look of the outside of the building.

Still dressed in his navy blue paramedic uniform, Trent must have come directly from work. His uniform reminded me of the dangers of his job every time I saw him in it. He came across drugged-up and violent patients far too often for my liking, and he was still sporting the black eye he'd received from the partner of a domestic violence victim.

"It's a nice street," he said by way of greeting. "How are you, bro?"

We shook hands and gave each other a one-armed, back-slapping hug before pulling back. I breathed him in and for that moment, held him close. Gone after barely a second, the memory of him in my arms had to sustain me until I could touch him again. I couldn't help myself; I needed those brief moments more than ever.

Being away from my sister, who couldn't have a conversation without a hug or linked arms, meant that I was starved for affection too. Hugging him hello in that bro-y way was, apart from when I saw my brother, the only touch from another human I ever had. Even though he always pulled away quickly, I knew it was a concession Trent gave only to me. None of his other friends were ever privileged enough to get as close as I did. But I still wanted more.

I was lonely.

I had it all: my circle of friends was small—really only my brother, Trent, Ford, who I'd gotten to know through both Ricky and Trent, and Brad, the groom from my very first wedding—but it was solid. My career was on the up, and I was finally going to get set up in my own place. I'd tried dating a bit too, but it didn't go anywhere. I'd managed two dates with a woman before she flat-out asked me why I hadn't made a move on her. When I tried to explain that I was asexual, she basically shut me down, saying, "Thanks, but no thanks." It was even worse with the man I'd tried hooking up with only a few nights earlier.

*"You visiting or a local?" the stranger asked me as I sat at a barstool at Truth, the only gay nightclub I'd visited in town. I turned to him and checked him out, sipping my whiskey to delay answering him until I'd gotten a good look.*

*"Local, but new," I replied. He was good-looking. Sandy hair with long bangs that covered his eyes. He flicked his head sideways, and I saw his eyes. They were dark, but I couldn't make out the color. His lips were on the thin side, but he had a broad, friendly smile that I liked. He was muscular too—thick arms and wide shoulders with a narrow waist highlighted in a light, short-sleeved, button-down shirt. When he licked his lips at my perusal, my face heated. I'd been busted, but I needed to try*

*again. I'd been celibate for years now, with nothing except my hand to make me come. Usually that was fine, but not that night. Not the night when Trent was out on his third date with the same woman. It was the longest he'd dated in a while, and he got that stupid smile whenever she messaged him. He was genuinely interested in her, and there I was, still stuck in the same rut I'd been in since college. "You?"*

*"Let's not talk about me," he purred before picking up my drink and downing it like a shot. I was pissed, but he'd leaned in, wrapped his hand around the back of my head, and pressed our lips together. "Wanted to know how you'd taste."*

*"You owe me another."*

*"I'll pay up in an orgasm." He motioned for me to follow him, and all rational thought fled. It wasn't desire coursing through me though, but grim determination. I want this, I thought. If I repeated it to myself enough, I might actually believe it. He walked through the club and down a darkened corridor toward the ladies' bathroom. There weren't any bachelorette parties on that night, so the ladies' was almost deserted. I didn't really care anyway. I wanted this over and done with. I wanted my dick in his mouth and my cum sliding down his throat. But even as I imagined it, I knew it wouldn't happen. I could barely stand the thought of having another person's hands on me instead of the man's I truly wanted.*

*He pushed me against the wall and captured my mouth with his. Sliding his tongue into my mouth, he rocked his erection against my leg, and I forced myself to move. I slid my hands along his back, and his muscles rippled under the thin cotton of his shirt. I kissed him back, but there was nothing there, not even the slightest of sparks. I was embarrassingly flaccid and grateful that his hands, which were like octopus tentacles, hadn't found the front of my dress pants yet.*

*I breathed him in, practically begging my body to get stimulated in some way. But he smelled all wrong and I was already out of time. He brought his hand around to cup my groin and pulled back the instant he felt that I was soft. "Bro, nothing?"*

*"I'm sorry," I started, but he held his hand up.*

*"Look, you want this or not? I want your cum but I'm not sucking a soft cock. You either want me or you don't."*

*I sighed and scrubbed my hands over my face. "I'm asexual and I'm totally hung up on someone else. I don't... I don't know if I can even get hard like this."*

*He raised an eyebrow at me and huffed out a laugh. "Fuck me," he muttered under his breath and shook his head. I couldn't hear him, but the movement of his lips was clear. "Yeah, I think I'm good. I'll see you round." He took two steps away but paused. "Look, sorry if I sound like a prick, but I'm only recently single—"*

*"No need to explain," I assured him. "It's a lot even without the whole 'other person' thing."*

*"Yeah." He nodded. "Good luck." With that he turned away and I was left standing there wondering if I would ever be anything but lonely.*

*Or stupidly mooning over a man I could never have.*

I snapped back to the present when Trent waved his hand in front of my face, laughing at me. "Bro, you totally spaced out on me. You okay?"

I forced a smile. "Yeah, I'm good. You?" I asked, then cleared my throat when my voice sounded far too high-pitched. It was as if I was screaming out "I'm lying!"

He nodded and grinned, his eyes twinkling with mischief while I mentally cringed. I knew what would come out of his mouth next. "Pretty fucking fantastic—"

I cut him off, holding my hand up. I couldn't listen to

him give me the rundown on how his date with Margarida went. Ever since that night months ago—the one where he said I wasn't a homo, right when I was realizing I was falling for him—I'd tried desperately not to hang off him. I didn't want to be one of those pathetic losers who were all heart-eyed and gazey, but I couldn't get him out of my head. Hearing about his sexcapades, especially after my own clusterfuck of an attempt, was more than I could manage at that point. He'd rarely asked me about whether I dated or hooked up, and I honestly wished it was something we just didn't speak about at all, but Trent enjoyed sex and wasn't afraid to admit it.

"Tell me later. We're gonna be late. Better head in. Don't want to keep them waiting." I pulled open the door before he could protest and held it for him as he walked inside.

After introductions, the agent took us up to see the apartment. Everything was brand-new and sparkling clean. It was also the pokiest little place I'd ever seen. While the combination of white- and dark-colored tiles in the bathroom and the almost black kitchen cupboards was striking and exactly my style, it made the place look even smaller. I'd be lucky to get a tiny two-seat sofa in the living room, and if I pushed it right up against the wall, maybe a double bed and a nightstand in the bedroom. *Dammit.* I'd been looking for weeks and there was so little available that wasn't holiday accommodation. Most people wouldn't even sign six-month leases so they could short-term let during the winter season and make some extra cash. Finding a place where I could sign a long lease was hard.

But this?

I honestly didn't know whether I could live there and not be tripping over my own feet all the time. I had no idea where I'd store my camera equipment and do my editing either. Maybe if I repurposed part of the kitchen—instead of a table in there, could I have a desk? Or maybe elevate the bed? I walked back into the bedroom and tried to picture the space. Leaning against the doorway, I closed my eyes and sighed.

"You're not seriously thinking of it are you?" Trent asked from behind me.

"It's clean, brand-new, and within my price range."

"True. But it's tiny." He paused and suggested, "Move in near me." When I whirled around to face him, my brows drawn together in confusion, he added, "There's a three-bedroom townhouse opening up in a couple of weeks in my complex. Ataahua, the lady I check up on, is moving out. She needs to go into a care facility. The landlord told me they're changing the flooring, then it'll be good to go."

I perked up at that. Trent's place was affordable. Maybe a three-bedroom townhouse in the complex would be too. I'd also be walking distance from him. That alone made it worth it, even if I was pushing the budget. "Yeah? That could work."

"And if it's too expensive, we could share it. Unless you think that's too gay." I blinked, trying to take in the words that had just flown out of his mouth with only the barest of pauses between them. Then what he said sank in. We could live together, unless it would be too gay. Like gay was the antithesis of what he'd like to be. He had no idea what he did to me, but every time he said things like that, it was as if he cut my heart out with a rusty knife then stomped all over it. I gritted my teeth and hardened what was left of my shredded heart and my tattered dignity. Why did he do that? Why did he use gay as an insult? Why did he keep hurting me like that? And why did I keep coming back for more? "No," I spat back, my tone sounding defensive even to my own ears. "It's not gay."

"Good," he replied happily, seemingly blissfully unaware of my wound. "We could use the spare room as your studio or office. You'd have plenty of space."

"Why would you move? You're comfortable where you are."

"Figured we've known each other for a while, and my lease expires soon. If I was gonna live with a mate…." He shrugged and looked away, stuffing his hands in his pockets and seemingly turning in on himself. He only ever did that when he was afraid to admit something. When he tried to protect himself against being disappointed, as if he was planning an escape in case I shot him down. He'd never admit it openly, but I knew him well enough to know that he wanted this. His comments were giving me whiplash. One minute he was questioning whether being roommates was gay, and the next he was asking to share— oh. *Oh.* He wanted a roommate but didn't want to ask for one in case people took it the wrong way. No one would blink an eyelid if we moved in together. He was the jock and I was the weird single friend who wore bow ties with suspenders or vests and carried around an old-school looking SLR. "Never mi—"

"No," I blurted out, this time sounding panicked. "No, not never mind." I stepped closer to him and crossed my arms to stop from reaching out for him. Was it the right thing to do? There wasn't really a question about it; I couldn't ever fathom saying no to Trent. I was a masochist; I had to be. I hated hearing about his sessions with women, and I was contemplating moving in with him? Not only would I hear *about* them, I'd probably hear them. "You don't think you'll get sick of me banging around in the kitchen?"

"I'll always eat whatever you're cooking." He smiled and my world lit up. Warmth curled through me, and I rocked on the balls of my feet, pulling myself back from taking him into my arms.

"Will whatshername or many other girls be spending the night much? Do I need to soundproof my room?" I blushed. God, I was such a prude. Just thinking about sex made my insides squirm around. But this time, it wasn't in a bad way. My heart thudded in my chest at the realization, and I sucked in a breath when my cock thickened. I wanted to hold him and show him just how good I could make him feel. I would explore every inch of him. I'd make love to him. For the first time in my life, my body demanded that I satisfy its cravings. The flood of heat through me was overwhelming.

I was hungry for him.

Starving.

Warning bells, like the cacophony of chimes from the steeple in the church in Santa Caterina di Valfurva, sounded in my mind. Maybe it was my heart instead, scared of getting stomped on and being left broken and bleeding. But I paid no heed to the warning. I couldn't. Whatever it was flowing through me demanded I get as close to him as possible. I'd never have the relationship I craved with him, but getting to wake up and have Trent be the first person I saw? Or do everyday domestic things like spend quiet nights at home? Even if those twilight hours weren't filled with lovemaking, how could I say no?

Trent watched me as I struggled. I could feel myself swaying toward him, and I straightened, trying to shake myself out of my stupor. I wet my bottom lip and swallowed hard when Trent replied, "Taking a break from dating for a while. Me and Margarida decided not to keep seeing each other, but it's okay. At the moment, I'm happier being single."

I was a shitty friend, a shitty person for wanting something when he might have been hurting. This time I didn't hesitate, reaching out and half hugging him, I laid my palm on his lower back and guided Trent out the door. The manager was waiting outside for us and locked up as we exited.

"Thanks for showing me. As nicely as it was finished, it's not the apartment for me," I explained before shuffling Trent to the old elevator. "You got anywhere to be now?" I asked him as the doors closed.

"Nope, I'm free for twelve hours until my next shift starts."

"Good, let's go to yours, get a lease signed up, and then we can go fishing. If we catch anything, I'll make you my mamma's baked fish."

Trent laughed, and when I questioned him, he replied, "I'm okay, but I appreciate you trying to cheer me up with food. Like I said, I'll always eat." I rolled my eyes and bit back a smirk. So I was predictable. Sue me.

A few hours later I sat on the end of the rickety pier with Trent, our bare feet dangling over the edge and a cooler between us. Tranquil waters lapped at the pylons. The shadows began lengthening in the afternoon light, and the golden glow cast over the water was magical. Insects buzzed around the surface. A fish broke it looking for a meal, the water rippling outward in ever-growing concentric circles. I breathed in deep and enjoyed the peacefulness between us. These moments where it was just us were perfection.

Trent cast his rod and waited for the slack in the line to be taken by our dinner. I'd had no luck, only catching a few trout that were far too small to keep. I wound my line in and laid my rod down, picking up my camera instead. I took photos, capturing the scenery around me, a leaf floating on the water, a shaft of sunlight through the trees onto the lake, and Trent. He stoically ignored me, intently focusing on the fishing rod. I grinned and snapped more shots, some close-ups of him and some of the line bobbing in the water. The aged timber on the pier against the glass-like clarity of the water was a beautiful contrast in the failing light too, so I moved around, getting the best composition in my viewfinder.

Barely ten minutes later, I heard Trent exclaim, "Oh ho, now I've gotcha!" I jogged back to him and watched in wonder as his rod bent at an acute angle. He worked it, pulling the rod up and winding the reel as the tension let off. He'd only cast a hundred or so feet into the lake but the fish fought him for every inch of line. It was a good five minutes before he could get it close enough that we could see a flash of silver on the surface.

I emptied the cooler of the remaining drinks and

grabbed the net, readying to reach down and catch it as he reeled it in. "He doesn't want me to bring him in," Trent pondered as he handled the rod with practiced ease. In the last few feet, the fish tired, and I reached down with the net, bagging it. At just over a foot long, the beautiful rainbow trout would be good eating. Trent's broad smile matched my own, and when he aimed it at me, my stomach swooped. I loved making him happy. His smile lit up the world around him, and my heart beat harder seeing it. His face was flushed. The sun's reflection off the water had deepened his already tan skin, which was uncovered by his loose wife beater.

"It's a keeper," he exclaimed happily as I held the net steady and he reached in for it.

"Don't cut the head off," I instructed when he held the wiggling fish on the cutting board and pulled his paring knife from its holster. "Just clean it, and then I'll cook the fish whole."

He didn't hesitate, gutting and cleaning the fish before placing it on ice in the cooler. We packed up, gathering our things and heading back to my car.

It was a few hours later when I was back at home that I got a Skype call from Papà checking up on how my apartment hunt was going. Gabriella was visiting him and soon overtook the conversation. "*Sì*, I have one," I explained in Italian. "It's three bedrooms in the same complex as Trent. Once the new timber floors go down, we'll be able to move in."

"We?" Gabriella asked as Riccardo flopped down on the sofa next to me and asked the same question.

"Trent and me. We're going to be sharing the house." I shrugged, trying in vain to downplay the magnitude of my decision. Gabriella knew about the complex, confusing torch I held for my best friend, but Riccardo was clueless. He'd heard Trent's offhand insults before, and I'd begged him to leave it well alone, but he'd never forgiven him. Riccardo couldn't understand why someone like me—queer—would be friends with a homophobe. I wasn't exactly proud of the fact that I didn't stand up to him, but I couldn't walk away either.

"Is that a good idea, Angelo?" Gabriella asked in rapid-fire Italian, and I knew she was referring to a whole lot more than Trent's odd insult. I nodded, trying to assure her that I'd be fine, even though I wasn't sure I would be when Trent decided to take up dating again.

"You know you can move back here anytime if things don't work out, right?" Ricky assured me, wrapping an arm around my neck and rubbing his knuckles over my hair. I pushed him away and laughed before running my fingers through my bangs again, pushing my hair off my forehead.

"Thank you, but you and Mary-Ann seem to be going full steam ahead. Wouldn't want to intrude."

He huffed out a laugh, but it held no humor. "You have nothing to worry about there." He shook his head and pursed his lips. "We're over. I came out to her, wanted to be upfront about partners and my orientation. We've only been together for a couple of months, but we were talking about being exclusive—not that either of us have been seeing anyone else—so before we made that move, I wanted her to know. You know, for it not to be a surprise if we run into a man I've dated before."

"She didn't take it well," Gabriella surmised.

"No. Not at all. I don't know what made it worse—the fact that I told her I'm pan, or that I've been with men before." He blew out a breath. "She flipped out. Told me it wasn't something she was comfortable with and then she got up and opened the door for me. When I asked her what was going on, she asked me to leave and lose her number at the same time." Riccardo scrubbed his hands over his face and sighed. "Apparently, *my* being pan increases *her* risk of contracting HIV because I can't make up my mind who I want and if I can't do that, there's no way I could stay faithful."

"Bitch," Gabriella muttered, while I reached out and wrapped an arm around Ricky's shoulders. He groaned and shook his head.

"I liked her, you know?"

"Yeah. I do," I murmured. Trying to lighten the mood, I quipped, "At least she doesn't think you've got a fetish for pots."

Riccardo barked out a laugh and playfully punched me in the side. "Shut the hell up. You know I prefer pie dishes."

We stayed talking like that for another hour until I was practically asleep on Ricky's shoulder. He nudged me and told me to say goodnight to Gab while he locked up. Rubbing my eyes, I yawned and looked up at her. "You love him, don't you?" she asked, although it wasn't really a question.

I nodded and pursed my lips. "I can't help it, and I don't know if I'm setting myself up to be destroyed, but the thought of saying no when he asked…." I shook my head. "I couldn't. We'll never have the relationship I want, but I can't be without him either."

"Maybe coming home over Christmas and having some time apart would be a good idea."

I looked down, unable to look her in the eye when I made my admission. "He's not close to his family. Never mentions them. I don't think he talks to them at all. He was going to be alone over Christmas, and I couldn't let that happen."

"You're not cancelling your trip, Angelo," Gabriella warned, but she didn't have to.

"He's coming with us."

Her stunned silence would have been laughable under any other circumstances.

"He's your person. It's not just puppy love. It's the real thing, isn't it?" The sympathy in her voice had me reflecting on what a sorry sap I was. God, I must have made a sight. I was pathetic, falling in love with not only a man I could never have, but one who'd spurn any advance I'd make with derision.

"Yeah. Yeah, he is. You wanna know what makes it worse?" I huffed. "I want to have sex with him. I want to get naked and," I waved my hand at her, "do everything together. I've wanted it for a while, but today I knew without a doubt."

"Jesus, irony is a bitch, isn't it?" she sighed. "The one man you can't have, and you're turning into a horn bag over him."

I ignored her quip but couldn't help my smirk. "I don't think I'm asexual. I think I'm more demi. I've been thinking about him a lot. Dreaming of him too. Every time I do, we're in bed. I thought maybe I was just lonely or horny. I tried to hook up again. I figured it might help. There's this gay bar here and a guy hit on me. He was good-looking and he wanted it, but I couldn't. His touch was all wrong." My shoulders dropped and the hopelessness of my predicament hit me square on. "I'm fucked, aren't I?"

"I don't know what advice to give you, Angelo. I want you happy, and he makes you happy, but he's also hurting you and you're hurting yourself. Moving in together just seems like a way to make it worse, and a secret like that will probably destroy your friendship, especially if he's... intolerant."

"Yeah, I know. I'll let you tell me you told me so when all this goes to shit." I gave her a small smile and waved to her, wishing her goodnight. Gab blew me a kiss, and in that moment, I almost wished I'd never moved here.

I was comfortable at home. Queenstown had been a roller-coaster of a ride so far, but the tunnel ahead scared me. I wasn't sure whether it would branch off and become the adventure of a lifetime, my very own Eden, or whether I would descend into some nightmare. Maybe I was over-reacting. Maybe it wouldn't end badly. But even with the knowledge that I'd probably end up hurt, I couldn't walk away. Having Trent as a friend would always be better than not having him at all. I just had to be strong. I had to make sure I never crossed that line, because losing our bond was a risk I wasn't prepared to take.

# CHAPTER 7
## TRENT

My life had changed so much in a decade that it was unrecognizable. I didn't know if I was even the same person anymore. Sitting around a pub in a little village in the mountains of northern Italy on Christmas day, while snow fell outside and a fire blazed inside, was surreal.

The only customers in the pub that day were Angelo, his extended family, and a select group of friends—Alfonso, the owner of the pub, Ford, who had just started working with Gabriella as mountain rescue on the nearby slopes, and me. But I felt like an interloper into Angelo's close-knit family. As the matriarch of Angelo's family, his mom, Palmira, ruled the roost with a heavy rolling pin and laughter. Wrong her or her family and you'd find yourself at the business end of the implement, but do something right and she'd cook you one of her traditional recipes that had to have been handed down over generations. Luckily for me, she was being generous and letting me hang around.

Christmas was apparently the only time of year

everyone and their plus ones were together. Both Angelo and Ricky were ordered home and wouldn't dream of disobeying. My invite had been more of an insistence by Angelo than a question, and the whole family had welcomed me into the fold immediately. But I still couldn't figure out why. I must have done something right in a former life to deserve a spot at that table—it certainly wasn't anything I'd done in this one.

I was a fraud.

These people thought I was a good person, but they didn't know me. Not even the man sitting next to me, who I'd been drawn to from the moment I'd met him, really did. I was proud of who I'd become, but I'd also done the unforgivable. My stupidity as a teenager tore my family apart and sent me to hell. I'd clawed my way back, but I hadn't really left purgatory. Saying I was gay was a mistake. An incredibly stupid one.

I wasn't.

There was no way I could be, and I knew that now. My godfather was just helping me see the truth that night. I'd hated, no, *loathed* every second of what he'd shown me, and to do that, he'd had to become something he wasn't either. He was so angry at my mistake that he'd taught me I was wrong the only way he knew how—by a hands-on demonstration. Whatever his intentions, his methods were wrong and not something I could ever forgive. I'd been scared and broken my parents' hearts too. I'd left, walked away, never to go home again. It was inexcusable. What I'd done to them haunted me every day.

I wished I could have gone home to see them even just one more time, but it was too late now. Too much water had passed under the bridge. They'd never want to see me again for what I put them through. But it was times like these—Christmas and birthdays—that I really missed them.

Since I'd left, I'd spent every holiday at shelters, the first as one of the people receiving a meal, and the rest as a volunteer. I'd served tens of thousands of meals and handed out so many packets of essentials that I'd lost count. I'd never had family surrounding me, but as I watched Ricky and Ford clink their beer steins together, Gabriella pass a bowl of peas to Angelo, and Frank, Angelo's father, kiss his ex-wife on both cheeks to say thank you for the meal, I wanted more than anything to be accepted into this one.

The conversation flowed as the plates were wiped clean. Even second helpings barely made a dent in the mountain of food in the center of the table. Most of the talk was about people I didn't know. Relatives perhaps, or family friends, people in the village possibly. I wasn't sure, but it didn't matter. Watching Angelo in his element made me smile. He spoke with his hands, using them to express himself as much as he communicated with words. And that Italian accent of his... even I could admit it was sexy. His million-mile-an-hour conversation with his father sounded like a heated argument when he spoke in his native tongue, but then they both laughed and Frank clapped his son on the shoulder. Angelo and his sister were close too, sometimes communicating with nothing more than a look between them.

Ford caught my eye and nodded at me, a smile crossing his lips. "You wanna come to Bormio tonight, Trent? There's a club that's just opened."

I looked to Angelo to ask what he had planned for us,

and a pang of disappointment shot through me when he encouraged me, saying, "You should go."

"You won't come?"

He shook his head and looked down. I wanted to reach out to him and lift his face to mine once more. To have those warm hazel eyes that sparked with life focused on me again. It sounded gay, but I loved it when he looked at me. It was like nothing else in the world mattered. As if I was the most important person in Angelo's life when he did it, and seeing that made me feel a little more like I mattered to someone significant. So whatever he was feeling to make him look away like he was ashamed or sad, I wanted it gone.

"You know me, I'm not really into the hookup scene," he replied. "But it's okay. Gab and I have a Christmas tradition too."

I saw the flicker of surprise cross Gabriella's face before she schooled her features. Was she shocked that he'd mentioned them having a tradition? Or was it an excuse because he didn't want me hanging around? We *had* spent almost every minute together for the last week since we'd left New Zealand. I supposed that he'd want to spend some time with his sister. After all, he hadn't seen her in months. Maybe I should give him some space. I looked across to Ford and Ricky to see Alfonso nodding in agreement, and I plastered a smile I wasn't feeling on my face. If I were being honest, I would have preferred to stay in the quiet pub all night, sitting on the sofas over by the fireplace.

"Yeah, okay. I'll go."

"You aren't leaving until we've had dessert and the rest of the presents are opened," Palmira warned. "And you'd better be safe on those roads. It's a long drive at night when it's been snowing."

"Wouldn't dream of anything else, Mamma," Ricky crooned, getting up to kiss his mom on the head and pour her another glass of red wine.

It was less than an hour later that the dishes had been cleared and platters of desserts lined the table. I couldn't fit another thing in even if I tried, but I wanted to taste everything. It was something I didn't think I'd ever get used to. The excess was so different to the modest meal I'd served so many years in a row. Every time I walked into one of the soup kitchens as a volunteer, I was grateful to have a home to go to when my shift ended and not be reliant on the food they were providing for my day's meal. I'd been on the other side of the table, and that dinner was often the only one for the day. It'd certainly been like that for me for months.

Sitting down on the sofas, relaxing after a meal unlike any other I'd ever had, I watched the flames dance in the stone fireplace. The fairy lights on the huge pine, decorated with tinsel and every sized bauble imaginable, twinkled. The tree, the fireplace, and the love of a family, even if it wasn't my own, made me realize how content I was. I was at peace. I wanted to file this moment away forever and relive it over and over. Looking around, I caught Angelo's eye and held his gaze, mentally thanking him for insisting I take this trip with him. He'd given me something I hadn't had in a decade—family. I grinned, and he blushed, which only made me smile harder. He did that to me often; made me laugh more than anyone else. He looked away first, and I smiled wider, warmth flooding my chest knowing I'd made him happy.

"Okay, we've all been patient long enough. Presents!" Frank clapped his hands together and rubbed them while Gabriella hopped off the sofa and kneeled by the tree, reaching under it to pass around the presents. One by one they were unwrapped, until she called out my name. I sat there, stunned. Angelo and I had agreed that it'd be painful to carry anything back with us, so we weren't buying each other presents. Who else would get me one?

I had my answer soon enough. A box, half the width of a shoe box but just as long, was tossed at me. The gift card, addressed from "your pain in the ass boss," had me shaking my head at Ford.

"What did you get me, dude?"

"Open it." His wicked grin had me more curious than nervous, but I felt the blood drain from my face and horror claw its way up my throat after I tore open the wrapping.

Inside was a boxed dildo—a giant, black, dick-shaped dildo.

*He knows. Oh fuck, he knows. But I'm not gay. It's impossible. I'm not. It was a mistake. I'm not.*

Stars flashed before me, and my lungs burned. I gasped in a lungful of air, and the oxygen rush after holding my breath made me dizzy. My hands were clammy, and I couldn't get that thing away from me quick enough. Pushing it away, my first instinct was to run and hide. But I lashed out instead, taking out every ounce of anger and hurt that I still felt a decade on out against my supposed friend. I was halfway out of my seat, grinding my teeth together and about to beat his face into a pulp, when Palmira's hand landed on my arm.

"*Grazie,* Ford! It was a stupid prank to play on Trent, but a nice thought for you to get me the toy I wanted."

I stilled at her words. *A prank? It was for her?*

I looked at Ford, staring daggers at him, and his gaze bounced from Palmira to me and back again. "Ah, yeah," he stuttered. "Just a stupid prank. Merry Christmas, Palmira." He looked to me cautiously and added, "Sorry, mate, just a stupid prank."

I almost fell back into the chair, all the air leaving my lungs in a rush and taking my last vestiges of energy with it. I sat quietly after that, my thoughts overwhelming me. I was kidding myself if I thought that I was over what Ryan had done. Yes, he'd taught me that I was wrong in my assumption, but the way he did it was something I didn't think I'd ever get over.

In that moment when I'd opened the box, I'd been powerless to stop the rush of emotions attacking me. I was the victim again. The same one I was during the Friday night football match when I was sixteen, bloodied and bruised and being pinned to the kitchen countertop by a man I trusted as he emptied himself inside me. I'd frozen that time, scared of him, terrified for my life, but this time I didn't. Like a cornered wild animal, I was ready to strike and protect myself. No one would ever hold so much power over me again.

---

NIGHT ROLLED AROUND, AND WE WALKED THE FEW BLOCKS back to Palmira's house. The freshly fallen snow glowed under the light of the streetlamps, the flashing lights of Christmas displays along the street and the odd laugh coming from inside the homes creating a magical moment. It was oddly romantic walking with Angelo. The quiet of the night seemed to close in around us, and I could imagine for a moment that we were the only two people in the world. I could happily live out my days just the two of us. Rooming with him over the last few weeks had been comfortable. We'd gelled with barely a hiccup. It was easy, easier than I'd imagined possible.

Angelo's childhood home came into view, and I slowed my steps, stuffing my hands deeper into the pockets of my woolen coat. My beanie was pulled low, covering my ears and my scarf covered the rest of my face. All except my eyes. It was cold out, but I didn't want the moment to end. As if he could read my thoughts, Angelo slowed too, and we meandered home. We didn't speak, but the faint brush of his arm against mine said enough for me. He was here. We were together. Friends stuck by each other, and I loved him for that.

Walking inside, we toed off our boots, called out our greeting to Palmira, and headed upstairs into the same bedroom Angelo and Ricky had shared as children. Two twin beds pushed up against opposite walls, a window above, and a nightstand between them almost filled the room. There was barely enough space for the heavy timber closet. When Rick had moved out, Angelo replaced the beds with a double, but he'd sold it when saving to move. Now, back to the original furniture, it was cramped but homely and gave me an insight into Angelo's life in Italy and abroad. There were black-and-white photographs of people and places ranging from the Eiffel tower to Disneyland, the three siblings as children, and an elderly lady making lace. Each one was beautiful, and I'd spent way too long staring at them and thinking about the stories of each of the people and places that went with the images.

Angelo stripped off his socks and sweater before rifling through the closet. He pulled out a pair of navy blue and white striped flannel pajamas while I stood by the open doors on my side. My motivation levels to go to the club were at zero, and not just because my best friend wasn't going to be there. I'd made the remainder of the family Christmas uncomfortable, unable to get out of my head. The other two presents I'd been given had floored me—an antique stethoscope from Gabriella and thermal socks from Palmira. They were thoughtful, kind presents, and the guilt at losing my shit ate at me the longer I'd sat there.

Even though I didn't want to go out, I forced myself to choose something. I heard the shower start and stop while I dressed in a button-down shirt, jeans, and a clean pair of socks. I was still sitting down, one sock in hand, when Angelo came back in. The ends of his hair were wet and curled outward, giving him a boyish appearance that added to his attractiveness. There was no denying it. Always so put together, dressed sharply with his hair perfectly styled and his face shaved clean, it was a wonder the girls weren't falling over him. Maybe they were, but I hadn't seen much of it. He didn't flirt and absolutely hadn't hooked up while we'd been living together. He was polite to everyone he met, but I could tell it took him a while to warm up to new people. It was funny—we were never like that. Even from that first moment, it was as if we'd known each other for years.

I realized I'd been staring at him in loose-fitting pajamas and bare feet when he asked from the open doorway, "You ready?"

"Yeah. The others will be here soon," I responded quietly.

Angelo stepped into the room and shut the door, standing so he was blocking my exit. I knew what was coming next, and I cringed when he said the words. "I know what your answer will be, but I just wanted you to know that I'm here if you ever want to talk about what happened before." I opened my mouth to interrupt him, and he held up his hand. "Don't tell me nothing's wrong. I have eyes and I *know* you. I know that your reaction was...." He trailed off, and when he looked at me I saw the pain in his eyes. I expected to see pity, but it wasn't that. Hurt seemed to linger in his gaze. "Something happened back at the pub, and I know you well enough not to expect you to talk about it, but one day if you're ever ready, I'll be here."

"Thank you," I whispered, unable to say more with the lump in my throat.

When the silence stretched on for a beat too long and it bordered on uncomfortable, Angelo opened the closet and pulled out a small black bag that looked like a bigger version of a shaving kit. "Um," he started, pausing like he didn't know what to say before holding it out to me. "I know we said we wouldn't get anything for each other, and I know you haven't gotten me anything, but I kind of wanted to do something for you for Christmas." He dropped his hand as my brow knitted and I reached out for the bag. "It's not strictly a present for you. It's just something I thought you might appreciate." He handed the bag over to me and I turned it over in my hands before unzipping it.

I tipped the contents on the bed and couldn't help but wonder why he'd given me what looked like an emergency kit. Wet wipes, toilet paper, toothbrush and paste, deodorant, a bottle of water, foil blanket, and rain poncho, as well as tampons and sunscreen. When I looked at Angelo curiously, he sat on the opposite bed and inter-twined his fingers, resting his elbows on his knees. "I made up a hundred of them and took them to the soup kitchen you volunteer at. Anyone who goes there today is getting one."

I opened my mouth and closed it again, words escaping me. I blinked and tried again but nothing would come out. He'd floored me. I was speechless. No one had ever done anything like this before. It was the most thoughtful gift anyone could have ever given me. He'd never said a thing about it, but I knew he saw me trying to help when I could. He didn't know the whys. He didn't know my story. But neither of those things mattered to Angelo. He did something this thoughtful because he'd figured out helping the homeless was important to me.

I sucked in a breath and held it, not wanting to let the tide of emotion drown me. Being out there, sleeping on the ground and not feeling safe for one moment was terrify-ing. Especially for a boy like I'd been. Tragically, it was a reality far too many people had to face. There were never enough beds in shelters. Never enough resources to feed and clothe people who desperately needed it. Never enough help. My hands were shaking and my vision blurred as I exhaled slowly and breathed again. It didn't work though. Angelo's, "Shit," barely registered as he pulled me into his arms and held me while I trembled, full body shudders wracking me.

His hand on my back, rubbing up and down, and the soft fabric of his pajamas against my face held me grounded, while his scent—fresh and woodsy—

surrounded me. I burrowed in, holding tight. His murmured words rumbled through his chest and the indescribable need to get closer to him overwhelmed me. I wanted to surround myself with him. To really feel him. Touch him. Skin on skin with no barriers between us. I wanted to kiss him.

*No.*

Like a bucket of iced water being dumped on me, whatever the hell was going on with my crazy brain shut down and I startled, pulling back and putting some distance between us. I cleared my throat and forced a smile. "That was…." I hesitated, trying to find the right words. I couldn't brush this off. It meant something to me. More than something, if I were being honest. I wanted Angelo to know that. But, God, I was confused. Why did I get the insane urge to kiss him?

"No one's ever done anything like this for me, Angelo. I… Thank you." I huffed out a sigh and shook my head, frustrated that I just couldn't get the damn words out. He reached out and squeezed my forearm, his gaze fixed on the point where his hand met my arm. I watched him and returned his stare when he looked up. "It means more than you could ever know. Thank you."

"Will you tell me one day?"

I shook my head and reached for the hand he had on me, brushing my thumb over his skin to soften the blow. His warmth seeped through me, and in his touch, I didn't feel so alone in the world. I hated that I disappointed him when he'd given me so much, but I didn't talk about my past. I wouldn't. I'd never let him be tainted by it, and I sure as hell didn't want to revisit those days. My history was better off remaining buried where it couldn't hurt me anymore.

"Trent? You coming?" I heard yelled from downstairs. I pulled my hand away at the same time Angelo did.

"I'd better—"

"Yeah." Angelo nodded and stood up, backing away. Even that small distance between us suddenly felt too much, but I needed space. I needed to get my head on straight, and a night out with the boys, a few drinks, and a hookup with some hot Italian girl was exactly what I needed. But as I trudged down the stairs, the desire to turn around and stay with Angelo hit me like a force of nature.

---

THE CLUB THAT WE PULLED UP AT A COUPLE OF HOURS LATER had an industrial vibe from the outside. Its dark, square block walls and flashing neon martini glass sign stood out starkly against the snow-covered gables of the more traditional shops and apartments along the normally busy road in Bormio. Located on a corner, the only signs of life around were cars parking nearby and people gathered around the entrance, queuing up to show IDs to security. The two burly guys looked bored, but studiously checked each of the cards against the faces that presented them, the line flowing slowly as they did their job.

The beat of music I couldn't make out the lyrics to pulsed through the building, reverberating through us as soon as I entered. Flanked on either side by Ford and Riccardo, we checked our coats and I followed them through the black swing doors into the club proper. I expected it to be dark—a nightclub—but the room we were in was more like a sports bar. A bank of TVs ran along one wall, and a collection of high-top tables faced them. There were more people than I expected in there too, most either playing pool or gathered around the tables talking and drinking or watching the sports report on the screens. The black bar that ran most of the way down the opposite wall was lit with neon blue from underneath and had only a handful of people queued up waiting for service. Ford motioned to a table that had just freed up, and Rick pointed to the bar, then to Ford and me. I nodded before saying, "Whiskey. Thanks, man," and our other companion agreed.

Alone with Ford, I guessed he'd want to talk about what went down over lunch, but it was the last thing I wanted to do. I was still kind of pissed at him. Who did that shit? Buying a dildo for another dude was downright offensive. I stared at the TVs, avoiding his gaze, and he soon got the message, turning his attention to the sports report. I looked around, taking in our surroundings. I couldn't see the source of the music, but the flashing strobe lights from what looked like another room in the club hinted to more than I could see. Turning my attention back to the TVs, I watched Ford out of the corner of my eye. He tapped his hands on the table in time to the drum beat and bobbed his head, seemingly enjoying himself.

Even if I could have heard the TVs, I couldn't under-stand what was being said about the aerial snowboarding they were televising. From what I could gather from the pictures, it looked like reruns of an earlier competition. The talking head did what appeared to be a wrap up of points in the world championship circuit, a leaderboard of the top ten men's competitors flashing up on screen. Once the talking head was on screen again, an inset appeared of a man's face. He looked carefree, his dimpled smile broad. The top half of his face was covered by reflective goggles, and I could see a hint of sandy blond hair peeking out from under his beanie. I had no idea who he was, but Ford sure did. "This guy's brilliant," he stated reverently and pointed to the screen. "Reef Reid. I could watch him jump for hours—"

"Sounds like you've got a boner for the dude," I muttered petulantly, my mood taking another nosedive.

I didn't think I'd spoken loud enough for Ford to hear, but his bark of laughter followed by a nod had me looking twice. "Don't you? You can't argue that he's good-looking. Even a blind man could see that, and he's got more talent in his little finger than most of the other snowboarders combined. I guarantee you, he'll be world champ one day."

Rick slid two beers and a tumbler of whiskey on the table and motioned to the TV. "He's got to beat Caden Lambert first, and that's not gonna be easy."

The two of them continued their conversation but I was stuck on the other dude—Reef. He *was* attractive. His smile, the dimple, his perfect teeth made him look pretty in a masculine kind of way. *But he's not my type*, the voice in my head helpfully interjected. No, he wasn't. *He* was a man. *I* was straight. But then whiskey-eyes, dark, swept-back hair, and olive skin flashed in my mind's eye and my body reacted instantaneously. My breath hitched and my heart beat faster. I yearned to reach out to Angelo, to be in his arms again. But that want, that desire pissed me off. I had to be strong. I had to resist. I had to blot him out. I tipped my glass up and downed my drink in one long swallow. It went down easily, but I needed another few if I was going to be able to hook up.

Rick and Ford were nursing their beers and debating something. I tried to focus on what they were saying but my eyes were drawn to Rick's. His were the same color as Angelo's; the same golden brown. It had to have been Angelo's present that had me thinking this way. Something so kind and thoughtful that spoke volumes about the giver had upended me. It'd blown away my carefully constructed fortress like tumbleweed in a breeze. Emotion had swamped me, and I was reaching out again for the comfort he'd given me.

That had to be it.

I ground my teeth together, disgusted at myself for not being stronger. For not being able to see that men were only for being mates with. How could I be thinking I wanted more than that? It wasn't me. My godfather had shown me, so why the hell couldn't whatever idiotic body part of mine that was thinking about Angelo in that way get with the program. I tried to concentrate harder on what Rick was saying, but the line of his brows and the curve of his lips as he smiled looked so familiar that the same pulse of want speared through me. *Jesus H Christ, I'm fucking pathetic.* Never mind needing something stronger to hook up. I needed it to shake out of this crazy talk.

I didn't think Rick and Ford even noticed when I walked away from the table, heading to the bar for another round. I swapped to tequila shots, and as the three glasses hit the bar and the clear liquor was poured into them, the feeling that I shouldn't have even been standing there at that club hit me.

*I should be with Angelo.*

It was Christmas and it was the first one I'd shared with someone I considered my family in a long time, but I'd done the same thing to him as I did to my parents. I left him.

*No, he told me to go.*

I was going around in circles, my thoughts getting more confused with each revolution. I kept thinking of Angelo, but I didn't want to. He was my friend. That was it. It was how it would always be, and the way I wanted it to be.

*No, you don't.*

I mentally head-slapped myself and tipped back one of the shots of tequila. It burned all the way down, my thoughts consumed by the feel of the liquor sliding down my throat. I brought the second and third glasses to my lips, downing them too, and waved the bartender over for another round. The alcohol warmed me, and the buzz unfurling through my body dulled the tension I was carrying. It wasn't enough though. When I closed my eyes, Angelo's face popped into focus.

He was beautiful, so much *more* than the Reef guy. And being in his arms like I was earlier that night had me wanting more, wishing for more. I shook the thoughts out of my head, wishing that the next round was in front of me. The only way I was going to get him out of my head was to get drunk and get laid. I tapped the pocket of my button-down shirt, feeling for the little blue pill there. My vitamin V. It was times like these I was grateful for knowing which of the doctors would issue prescriptions without asking too many questions. The last thing I wanted to admit was that when I needed to fuck the most, I had trouble getting it up. Curves and tight, wet, willing pussies were what I should crave, what I wanted to crave, but my dick rarely wanted to get in on the action. Much like whatever body part was thinking of Angelo.

Fresh drinks were placed in front of me, and in a haze, I paid and reached for them, taking them over to Ford and Rick. I lifted mine up in a toast and sucked down the shot. The familiar burn had me exhaling, loving the numbness and loss of inhibition creeping in.

The music beckoned. The bodies writhing and grinding together called to me. I clapped Ford on the shoulder and motioned with my head to the other room of the club. "I'm gonna go get laid. You fairies comin'?" The room spun when I stepped away from the table, but I righted myself and reached for my pill. Swallowing it down with another shot, I hoped that there was at least one woman there who'd make my night. I wanted to laugh hysterically, but I was too fuckin' cool for that. Instead I raised my hands above my head like a general calling his troops to battle and shouted out my war cry. "Pussy!"

"Think you've had enough to drink, mate," Ford chastised me, looking between me and the table. "How many of these things have you had?" He raised an eyebrow at me, but I didn't care and didn't want his lecture. I downed the last shot, turned my back on him, and stumbled toward the dance floor.

When I pushed through to the back of the bar into the nightclub section, I saw what I expected when I initially entered. Pulsing lights and a beat that was deep enough to shake the walls had me moving toward the dance floor and the bodies sweating and moving together as one. Grinding on each other. Skin touching, the contact intimate in its own way.

I didn't stop at the edge of the mass of bodies. I worked my way in deep and found what I was looking for after only a moment. Three girls dancing together. They were cute, and from the way the one with shiny black hair checked me out, I knew I wasn't going to be kicked to the curb if I joined them. I moved over to them, Ford and Rick on my heels, and we danced. "I'm Trent," I shouted to the girl who'd eyed me. Her red dress was short, and her cleavage spilled out of the low neckline. Curvy with sky-high heels, she was undoubtedly sexy, but my blood didn't pump harder at the sight of her. It should have, and the lack of desire flowing through my veins frustrated me.

"Theresa," she yelled back, stepping closer to me and slipping one leg between mine, her other straddling my thigh. She wound her arms around my neck, and I palmed her ass, pulling her close. Her perfume was spicy, and I breathed deep. I liked that smell. It was almost manly, a lot like Angelo's. That thought—she smells like Angelo—on top of everything else, confused the hell out of me. I wanted him, but I shouldn't. I couldn't. She wanted me. I could have her easily enough, but—and here was the kicker—should I? Of course, right? She was keen; I was going to get hard. My little blue pills always took care of that. But I'd failed to even dim thoughts of Angelo with the tequila I'd drunk. That meant something, didn't it?

For the first time in years, I thought of my life as a façade, and that lie was starting to crumble. Thoughts of "I'm gay" were creeping back into my psyche, but I didn't want them to. I really didn't. God, I couldn't go there again. But now I felt like I was running straight into trouble. I was drunk and I had a girl in my arms who was riding my leg like a randy dog. My brain told me to fuck the doubt out and prove that I was straight. I needed to get off and I needed the affirmation even more. I was desperate for a reminder of why I chose women, but that damn voice in my head was like a fly I couldn't swat away, telling me "no" at every pass. Begging me.

Talk about an existential crisis in the middle of a damn dance floor.

# CHAPTER 8
## ANGELO

Gabriella topped off the two glasses of Campari with a dash of gin and set the bottle down on the coffee table. We'd been drinking since she arrived, and I was warm and fuzzy from the liquor, loose-limbed and lazy. The warmth of the potbelly fireplace cocooned us. Like old times, we cuddled on the sofa, our feet on the old timber table and a blanket wrapped around us. I missed her. I missed my life here too, but I'd found something special in Queenstown. Striking out on my own and finally feeling grown up, it was like an adventure. My sister may be the youngest, but I'd always been the baby of the family. I was the closest of my siblings to Mamma, and I'd lived at home for the longest too. But I'd been bitten, and the itch wouldn't leave me. I had a yearning to set myself free and see if I could make it on my own. Succumbing to the siren's call, I'd followed it to Queenstown. Something pulled me there. Something in me knew I would call it home the moment I saw those mountains. I didn't realize until later that it wasn't the town calling me. It was the man who'd left here a few hours earlier.

As if she'd read my thoughts, Gabriella asked, "You miss living here?"

"I miss you and Mamma. My friends. But no, I don't miss the place. Queenstown is home now." I picked at the frayed wool of the blanket edging, wanting to say more but not knowing how to put it into words.

"I don't think it's Queenstown that's home. I think it's Trent." She grasped my hand and held it tight and I looked to her. She must have seen the truth in my eyes, the emotion I couldn't hold back.

"I love him," I whispered back, barely able to get it past the lump in my throat. "It's been good living together, but it's hard too. I look at him and I want to reach out for him. Hold him. He gets down sometimes, like he's a shell of a person. It's as if he's missing a part of himself. I want to help him, but I don't know how."

"I think you do help him. He looked happy today. He was smiling at you all the time."

"He was happy, wasn't he?" I smiled, remembering all the glances back and forth we'd shared during lunch. But then I thought about the present Ford had given him. My initial instinct was to laugh, but then I'd seen Trent struggling with it.

"Why didn't you go out with them tonight? Maybe you could have carried on the smiling."

"No. I think he needed some space. Ford's present...." I didn't even know how to describe the emotions I saw crossing Trent's features when he'd opened the package.

"Yeah, I saw." She nodded and slowly sipped her drink. "Will he be okay?"

"I hope so," I mused. I shifted on the sofa, resting my head back against the old cushion, and sighed. Hopelessness and helplessness filled me. I wanted to be there for Trent, but I had no idea how. I had no clue about what he needed or why it'd affected him so deeply. "He drinks sometimes, you know?" Without waiting for Gab to respond, I continued. "He gets down and pulls out a bottle of tequila. He'll take shot after shot until he staggers into bed and passes out. It worries me that one day he won't want to fight anymore."

"You two fight?" Gabriella asked, the horror in her voice obvious. I knew what she was implying, and it wasn't whether he was angry. It was whether he took it out on me.

"No, never." If there was one thing I knew about Trent, it was that he didn't have a violent bone in his body. He was a healer, a carer down to his core. He'd never hurt a hair on anyone's head. "I worry that he won't see what he has to live for anymore."

"Oh, Angelo." The sympathy in my sister's voice broke my heart. She leaned her head on my shoulder, and I inhaled on a shudder.

"I know I can never have him, but I couldn't bear losing him."

We sat there like that, sipping our drinks. I was lost in thought, and Gab seemed happy to just sit with me. I found myself watching the clock, its hands ticking slowly away into the early hours of the morning. I wondered what Trent, Ford, and Ricky were up to. No doubt Ford was hooking up with a pretty girl. He loved to love, but he didn't lead women on either. They knew he was only in it for one night with them. He was a playboy and he was drawn to playgirls—the perfect match for him. Ricky could go either way—hooking up or staying solo—and honestly, I'd rather not imagine him doing anything. Then again, if it meant I wouldn't picture Trent with someone else, I'd change my mind. I wanted to believe he'd had a few drinks, possibly danced for a bit, but it was wishful thinking. I'd seen him drunk and partying enough times to know that he'd welcome the press of breasts against him, the heat between a woman's legs. My stomach soured, and I put my drink down, unable to stomach another sip.

Gabriella yawned and stretched, and I took it as my cue to leave. "I'm going to head to bed." I slipped out from the blanket and kissed her forehead. "Goodnight, Gab. I missed this."

"Goodnight, Angelo. And so did I, but I'm glad you left. I'm glad you've found him, even if things aren't exactly how you want them to be."

"Me too." I nodded and headed to the bathroom to brush my teeth before turning in. I stripped off my shirt and slid between the sheets before gazing at the empty bed next to mine, wishing that things between Trent and me could have been different. I wasn't lying to Gab though. I'd gratefully take what I could. His friendship meant the world to me, and while I couldn't love him the way I wanted to, being his friend would always be enough.

***

THE BED SHIFTED, AND I WOKE WITH A START. HEAT FROM THE hard body pressed against me had me stiffening and not in a good way. But when Trent wrapped his strong arm around my waist and pulled me back against him, I melted into his embrace. His lips skimmed across my nape and he kissed a line up my spine to my hair before he took a deep breath. His hand splayed low on my belly had my dick instantly reaching up to greet him. "Trent," I moaned on a breathy gasp.

"Shhh," he whispered. I could smell the liquor on his breath, and when I turned my face to his I got a whiff of a spicy perfume.

"You're drunk, and you smell like whoever your hookup was." I kept my voice soft, trying not to sound too harsh, but I disentangled myself from his grip, pushing his arm away and moving as far out of his reach as I could on a single bed. He was a grown man and I had no right to get jealous, but there was no way I was subjecting myself to being his seconds. I had more self-respect than that.

He laughed, but it held no humor, and when I looked at him, I saw the true Trent. His walls were down and he lay there before me open and vulnerable. The raw honesty in his gaze held me captive, and I was unable to look away even if I'd wanted to. His words were slurred when he spoke. "I tried, but I couldn't. All I could think about was you." Trent closed his eyes, breaking our connection, and the pain in his voice slayed me. He reached out for me again, pulling me close once more, and I let him do it. I had no idea whether he didn't want to want me, or whether I was reading something more into what he'd said. Either way, it didn't matter. Deep down I knew that this would be the only time I'd have him so close.

"You were thinking about me?" I whispered, something dangerous wanting to unfurl in my chest. It was hope, but I dared not hold out for it. I knew I wouldn't get a response from him, and even if I did it probably wouldn't be the one I so desperately wanted, but I waited for him anyway, wishing that he'd reaffirm what he'd said. But it never came. Trent's breathing had evened out and he was fast asleep, curled around me as he held me close.

Tomorrow I'd deal with the fallout—the *what the hell?* and the *I'm not some fairy* when he was sober enough to erect the fortress he held around himself again. Until then, I'd cherish every moment I could with Trent's arms around me, his solid chest pressed to my shoulder, the bulge at his groin nestled against my ass. I lifted his hand and brushed my lips against his knuckles in a whisper soft kiss. *I love you.* I closed my eyes, committing his touch to memory. The gentle way his arm wrapped around me, and the strength in his hand splayed against me. Those same hands could save a dying man or bring new life into this world, and he chose to caress me with them. The warmth of his breath against my nape as he exhaled, and the ghosting of his lips against my own skin made me want to stay in this moment for an eternity.

All too soon the sun's rays kissed the sky, waking me from a deep sleep. I was tangled in Trent, our legs and arms wound around each other. We'd rolled over during the night and now I spooned him, my arm holding him to me as I breathed him in. I could feel his heart beating under my palm. Strong and steady beats. Instinct had me wanting to nuzzle him, but my morning whiskers were sharp and I didn't want to startle Trent awake. I pressed a soft kiss to his broad back and unwound myself. I stifled a groan, my head thudding like a bitch. My hangover pierced my skull with every movement I made, but as much as I didn't want to leave the warmth of our cocoon, I forced myself up. I needed a piss and Tylenol too.

Leaving the bed without waking Trent up was harder than I thought possible. I had to scoot down to the foot of the bed before I could climb off, and doing it shirtless was bloody freezing. I slipped into the flannel shirt and padded out in search of painkillers and water to fix my cottonmouth.

"Good morning, Mamma," I mumbled as I stumbled into the kitchen and poured a glass of water from the faucet. Blindly, I opened the cupboards in search of painkillers and groaned when I couldn't find where she'd moved them to. When I turned to ask her, she held out the packet to me. I downed a couple gratefully, refilled the glass, and took it and the pills back into the bedroom.

Trent was sitting up, rubbing his head when I entered, and my breath caught at the sight. He was warm and sleep rumpled and in my bed. I bit my lip, resisting the temptation to touch him. His hair was sticking up in patches and flat in other parts, and his stubble was longer this morning. He usually kept it short, but I liked this look on him. I wanted to know whether it was as soft as it seemed. Would he finally welcome me if I reached out and cupped his cheeks, pulling him to me and kissing him the way I'd wanted the night before? He was bare chested, and I admired the curve of Trent's muscles. Not as built as a body builder—he was still far bigger than me. Where I had height and a lean build, he had size. My olive complexion courtesy of my Italian heritage was so different to his light brown skin. It had me wondering whether he had a Maori background. I couldn't ask about his family though; the subject was an unapproachable one and I wouldn't ruin the morning by asking. Trent scratched his chest, drawing my attention to the soft hair there. I wanted to curl up on his lap and rub myself against him like a cat.

"Morning," I greeted him, still a little groggy but my headache forgotten at the sight of him. I hoped that my loose pajama bottoms hid the wood I was sporting. There was nothing hotter than Trent with my rumpled covers pooling around his slim waist. He wore only underwear, tight-fitting boxer briefs that I wished I'd gotten a thorough look at. He had a good ass—a great one in fact—and I really wanted to get a look at it in those boxers.

"Oh, thank God," he mumbled when he saw what I was carrying as he clutched his head. "I feel like shit." I placed the glass on the nightstand and popped two pills into his outstretched hand, inhaling sharply at the briefest brush of our hands.

"How much did you drink?"

"Too much." He downed the pills and drank the water and looked around the room, his brow furrowed. "Apparently when I'm drunk I don't know which bed is mine."

I smirked and cleared my throat inwardly, cursing at the excited jump my cock just made. "I didn't mind."

"At least you weren't asleep when I got here. How gay would it have been if we'd shared a bed?"

I opened my mouth to correct him but shut it again, turning toward the closet to hide the emotions I couldn't control. I wanted to cry. I wanted to rage and scream at him. Why was it that he would pull me into his arms and hold me like a precious lover when he was drunk, and when he was sober, he did shit like that. He hurt me more with his careless words than anyone else had done before him. I guess it was because I wanted him to want me as much as I did him. Instead I'd gone and fallen for a homo-phobic asshole.

I did the only thing I could. Chin up, I pulled a change of clothes out and walked away from him, going to take a shower without saying another word to him.

---

I DON'T KNOW IF I WAS BEING CHILDISH, BUT I DIDN'T REALLY care. I'd managed to ignore Trent for most of the morning, but Mamma was calling us for lunch, and I'd have to at least be civil to him. She wouldn't stand for us fighting when we came together for another feast, this time to make a dent in the leftovers.

Gabriella had picked up on the tension between us, but I'd waved off her concerns. I didn't want to talk about it with her. It'd only hurt worse to admit that I'd gotten my hopes up despite knowing he was drunk and not thinking straight. I was an idiot. A fool. And I was pissed about it. I slammed the door to the cupboard shut and made my way back to Mamma with the tea towels she'd asked for.

"I take it you haven't finished being shitty yet?"

I stopped in my tracks and whirled on him, grinding my teeth together before hissing, "What did you just say?"

He puffed out his chest and took a step closer to me, coming face-to-face. "I said, you haven't finished being shitty yet."

Before I knew what I was doing I'd thrown the towels on the floor and grabbed his sweater, pushing him against the wall. "Fuck you, asshole." I shoved him again and stepped back, but Trent had fire in his eyes. He wasn't finished, and neither was I.

He laughed coldly and pushed me back, making me stumble. I fell against the wall and used it to brace myself, stopping me from landing on my ass. "Little limp-wristed there, Angelo. Want me to show you how a real man fights?"

Seething, I clenched my fists by my sides and stepped up to him again. I wanted to hurt him as much as he was hurting me, to make him regret every moment since he'd opened his mouth that morning. Or maybe I wanted to punish myself for being so damn stupid to think that he was anything other than a homophobic bastard. And I was even more of a fool for being friends with him. In that moment I despised him, but I knew I couldn't hurt him. Not intentionally. I could never do it. I wasn't that sort of person. The fight left me, and I looked down into his eyes, searching for something I knew I'd never find. What I did see eviscerated me, and I knew the answer before I'd even asked the question.

"Why is it so bad to be gay?" I whispered and shook my head, knowing that in his mind it was something to be reviled. Without waiting for an answer, I turned and walked away collecting my coat and boots from the mudroom and leaving through the front door. I closed it quietly behind me and walked away from my childhood home, my family, and the man who'd broken my heart.

The weight of the world sat atop my shoulders as I trudged up the path leading to the lookout. It was closed at this time of year, but it wasn't exactly a high security entrance. The lone chain across the walkway and a sign that said No Entry in my mother tongue were easy to ignore. I knew this place like the back of my hand. I'd traversed it hundreds, perhaps thousands, of times, going there whenever I needed a timeout. It was midsummer the last time I'd gone, and it looked very different from that day but no less beautiful.

Pristine white snow a couple of feet deep covered the path that snaked its way up the steep slope. The branches of the large trees, heavy with the fresh Christmas Day falls, gave me enough purchase to haul myself up through the knee-deep icy clumps, but I ended up covered in heavy chunks that had shaken onto me. Even though it wasn't a long way up, it was still challenging in the snow, and I was grateful to finally reach the rocky outcrop. A chain-link fence spanned the open space at the highest point of the lookout, and I leaned against the attached iron railing to catch my breath.

Overlooking the village and the mountains surrounding it, I was in awe every time I saw it. Stunned by the perfection of nature. A cerulean sky painted a perfect contrast to the blanket of white covering the ground below. Towering conifers rose up and stood at attention like silent sentinels. Without a breath of wind in the air, their branches were still. Undisturbed.

I used to find peace in this place, but not that day. Anger and frustration swirled around me while sadness hung over me like the blizzards that would roll over the mountaintops surrounding this place. My mind raced, and yet it could have been on a loop, the same thoughts repeating over and over again. I'd laid a hand on my best friend. I'd pushed him and wanted to hurt him. It was irrelevant that he'd done the same to me or that I knew he could defend himself. I wasn't that person.

Shame washed over me. I owed him an apology, but would he even want to hear it if he knew what I was?

Surely from my question he'd figure it out. Then again, did I even want to remain friends if he truly hated an undeniable part of me? I'd have to move again, probably back in with Riccardo. I was at a crossroads, unsure of which path to take.

A chill passed through me, and I pulled my coat tighter around my body. Was the sudden biting breeze a foreboding sign of what would come?

I didn't know how long I stood there, staring out at the view while I tried to make sense of my jumbled feelings and plot a path through the mess. The sun inched toward the ridgeline, and I knew I should head back. Light didn't last as long this far north, especially surrounded by the towering mountains. I'd walked out on Mamma and my family without a word. I'd ignored Gabriella's calls when she'd come rushing out after me, and I didn't have my cell. They'd probably be starting to worry. I sighed and turned to leave, but I stopped in my tracks when I saw him. Trent stood before me, breathing hard and looking around frantically.

"Oh, thank fuck," he cursed when he saw me, rushing to me with a blanket outstretched in his arms. "Get under this, you crazy bastard. I've been worried sick." His words had an edge to them, but the care he took in wrapping the blanket around my shoulders and tugging it together reassured me that he was happy to see me. With his gloved hands, he cupped my face and tilted it down to his, inspecting me. When he pulled me into his arms, I stood there unmoving, unsure of what I should be feeling.

"Trent—"

"I'm sorry, I was an ass. I can't tell you how much I hate myself for saying those things, for even thinking them." He sighed and squeezed me tighter. "Please don't leave like that again. People die in these conditions, Ang. You just left, and I had no idea where you went and then you didn't come back and I was going out of my mind. I've been looking for you but I didn't know where you'd gone. You've been out here for hours. You're probably hypothermic and, Jesus—" His words ran together the more worked up he became, barely pausing to take a breath.

"Trent." I pushed away from him, surprised at his concern after our run-in earlier that day. "I'm fine."

"No. You're not and it's because of me." His tone was gentle, remorseful, as he reached up to brush a stray bang from my forehead. "You're shivering and your pants are soaked through so you're only going to get colder. The sun's setting too. I need to get you inside and warm you up. Will you let me take care of you? Please?"

I closed my eyes and nodded. I owed Trent an explanation and an apology as much as he owed me one. When he wrapped me in his embrace again, I sank into him. Having his arms around me was like coming home. I could never give that up. I never wanted to. Whatever our differences were, we'd just have to make our friendship work.

A full-body shudder ripped through me. I hadn't realized how cold I was, but now he pointed it out I could feel it. Trent pulled back a little, holding me by my waist, and I was glad for his solid presence. My legs felt like Jell-O as I walked down the path with him. He didn't let go of me the whole way home.

He waited until we were around the corner from Mamma's house before he spoke again. "Your sister's meeting us at home. She's probably gonna want a word." I cringed and hated myself even more for making everyone worry. I'd needed space, but that was no reason to walk away. "She'll be happy to see you. Everyone will."

"Everyone?"

"Gab, Rick, and I have been out looking for you. Your mom stayed at home in case you went back there." At his answer, I let out a sigh and shook my head before running my fingers through my hair. "I can run interference if you like."

"I'd love you to, but I owe them an apology too." Mamma's front door was a few feet away, but I stopped short. "Listen, before we go inside...." I let out a shaky breath and pursed my lips, nerves suddenly coursing through me. "I'm sorry, Trent. I shouldn't have treated you the way I did. I had no right to do that."

"I was a jerk and what I said wasn't fair. You don't need to be sorry for reacting to that, but honestly, I really just want to get you inside." He ushered me through the door, and Mamma was waiting on the other side of it, hands on her hips, wearing the same expression she'd use to scold me as a child.

I put up my hand to halt her tirade before it started and opened my mouth to speak, but Trent interrupted me. "Palmira, he's safe. I want to examine him. Do you think while I do that you can get those hot water bottles organized and some of that soup?"

"*Sì,*" she muttered, nodding before her gaze cut to mine. Her expression was filled with relief. "You know better than that, Angelo. You had me worried. All of us worried."

For the first time since he'd found me, I stepped out of Trent's arms and hugged her tight. I towered over her, having to bend to kiss her hair. "*Sì*, Mamma. I won't do it again."

An hour later, showered, dressed in sweats, and sitting under the thick covers of my bed with an empty bowl of soup on the nightstand, I yawned. It was too early to sleep, but my energy levels had bottomed out. Trent's hovering, treating me like a patient who could break at any moment, unnerved me. I needed him to relax as much as I needed it myself. "Wanna watch a movie?" I asked, reaching for my iPad.

"Sure." He smiled and checked my temperature again. He motioned to the thermometer and added, "You're all good."

"I've been the same temperature since I walked inside. Don't worry so much." He glared at me for a moment before I shifted to one side. "Sit your ass down and watch a movie with me, Trent. Your pick. Here."

He scrolled through, and I found myself leaning into him to check out what movie he'd pick. His spicy scent filled my senses and I breathed deep, wanting to get even closer. Reality slammed into me when Trent shifted and I realized how close I'd gotten.

*Shit, he's uncomfortable. What straight dude wouldn't be when he had another man all up in his personal space and leaning on him like a creeper?*

"Sorry," I muttered and sat up straight. He shocked the shit out of me when he wrapped an arm around me, pulled me closer, and set the iPad on his lap. I couldn't help myself and snuggled into him, resting my cheek against his shoulder. My eyes were heavy, and I closed them waiting for the movie to start. I hadn't even realized we'd gotten past the opening scene before I felt the bed shift. I reached for Trent, but there was only cold air in his place. I knew before I'd even opened my eyes that I'd be waking up alone in my bed and the other single in the room probably wouldn't have even been slept in. It was uncanny how quickly I could get used to him next to me and how right his arms were wrapped around me.

I couldn't hope for something hopeless. I had to be satisfied with what I had, and I was. But I could still wish for those strong arms to remain around me for just a little longer.

# CHAPTER 9
## TRENT

## THREE AND A HALF YEARS LATER

I hated this time of year. I despised this day in particular. But I was determined not to let the memories overwhelm me. Angelo knew I found it hard. He'd figured out after years of knowing me better than any other person that there was something fucked-up in my past that pulled me down every year. Even though I'd managed to avoid giving him any real details, he always told me he'd be there whenever I was ready. Then he'd save me from myself when I was drowning. Whether it was telling me to chill, taking me out to do some random activity that he'd concocted—lawn bowls was yesterday's spur of the moment thing—or serving me his Mamma's famous pasta recipes, he always lifted my spirits. He helped keep the memories at bay by giving me the most important thing he could: his time. It was easy to smile around him, and I'd done a lot of it in the years that we'd been living together.

There was only one thing I would change about us—

I'd be honest with him. But it could never happen. He knew the person I was now; he knew Trent. He didn't have any details about my past. About Keir. I'd keep my secrets locked down in a vault that made Fort Knox look like child's play. But his knowing my mistake and what my godfather had done, and then what I'd put my parents through would be the end of our friendship. He was the best kind of man: generous, thoughtful, and loyal to a fault. He valued family above everything.

I didn't deserve him, not after all the shitty things I'd done.

He was my sounding board, the reason to my hot-headedness, my strength when I was weak. So I wouldn't tempt fate. I wouldn't confess and risk the way he looked at me changing. The softness in his eyes and the shy smile he reserved especially for me would disappear. He'd walk away, just like I'd done. It was what I deserved, but I was too selfish to let it happen. I'd lived nearly half my life without once divulging my secrets. I would keep them for decades longer if it meant keeping Angelo.

That morning though, it wasn't Angelo I was meeting. It was Ford. He'd just been released from hospital and, with a busted-up knee, was probably surviving on tea and toast. Avalanches were a fact of life with any area covered in snow, but there was one ridgeline that the back trail skiers liked to use that posed a higher risk. Ford had gone heli-skiing to inspect the ridge from afar and somehow got caught in a freak blizzard. It came out of nowhere and we were all unprepared. Ford and his charge were caught out there and sought shelter in a ranger's hut I hadn't known existed while we nervously waited it out by the emergency radio. It was three days before we could get a chopper up to look for them, and Rick was the first pilot to volunteer. I was the first paramedic.

Ford and I had had some run-ins. We'd clashed, and he was a pain in my ass most of the time, but he was a damn good boss and a good friend. So I supposed, with everyone else working, I should take him some food. It was the least I could do to repay the favors he'd done for me when I'd struggled. Instead of firing me on the spot like he should have all those times I'd gone to work still lit, he'd forced me to do a breath test, then put me on the next bus back to Queenstown. No one else would have done that, but he'd protected me from myself, much like Angelo did.

When we'd received the call that Ford's emergency beacon had been activated, we hauled ass over to him. The injuries he'd suffered from getting caught in the avalanche were minor, but he couldn't walk on his bruised knee. We found him and the tourist safe and sound at the ranger's hut. Only in Ford's world would that tourist end up being the dude he'd been a fanboy of for years—pro snowboarder, Reef Reid.

Pulling my beat-up 4x4 to the curb in front of Ford's house, I grabbed the breakfast burritos off the passenger seat and headed up the drive. I didn't recognize the SUV parked there, but at a guess, I'd say it was probably his cleaner or a nurse friend checking up on him. The front door was this heavy timber thing, so I knocked hard a couple of times and waited for him. The snick of the lock on the other side preceded the door opening, and Ford stood there wearing only a pair of unbuttoned jeans. "Trent, hey."

He was still sleep rumpled and trying to balance on

one crutch. I didn't want him to fall on his ass or freeze in the chilly wind buffeting my back, so I pushed past him and held up the food I was carrying. "Dude! Brought over some breakfast burritos to heat up. Figured you'd be starving if you can't cook."

"Thanks. I, ah, don't want to sound ungrateful, but now isn't a good time." I looked around the house for the first time, but nothing was out of place. Whoever was parked in the drive wasn't even around. Then it occurred to me. She was in the bedroom. Ford had hooked up and they'd gone back to his house. How he managed to do that was beyond me.

"Pity sex?" I scoffed. "Nice. Who'd you score with?"

"You're a pig." Ford's anger surprised me, especially when I was only fucking around with him. Movement in the doorway to Ford's bedroom caught my attention, and in one fell swoop, the floor fell away from me. Tall, lithe muscles, and blond hair. Reef Reid was there, and completely naked. My heart slammed against my chest, and my breath caught like my lifeblood was being drained straight out of me.

Panic seized me. I was suddenly right back there.

In my nightmare.

My sixteen-year-old self owning up to my greatest mistake and Ryan teaching me a lesson. One I could never forget. But this time terror didn't take hold of me. It was disbelief. Disbelief that Ford, my mate, would do that. That he'd experience the one thing I'd wanted but could never have. Still couldn't. I'd only admitted that desire to one person and look where it had gotten me. I'd learned my lesson, but Ford hadn't been told.

Hatred, as vile as the part of me that was so wrong and

as fierce as the blizzard that had enveloped our town for days, slammed into me. I was thrown in a whirlwind of swirling ice and gale-force winds.

I was disgusting. I was an abomination.

I was dirty.

Wrong.

I wasn't gay.

But I was. I always had been, but I'd tried to forget. I'd tried to change. I'd tried to fight off the need for a man's touch. With every punch of my godfather's hips against my broken and bruised body, he'd pushed me farther and farther away from wanting to admit my truth. He'd spewed venom, and I'd been poisoned by it. I wanted to scream and shout, to stop him. I had to stop him. I had to save myself.

I lashed out, disgust in my voice. "What's he doing walkin' around naked in your house?" Ford spun around to see an undressed Reef staggering toward the bathroom, still half asleep. There was no doubt they'd been in the bedroom together. Jealousy and revulsion at myself and what I was spurred me on. The venom pumped into me by my godfather poisoned me all over again and I spat out, "You're a faggot? Are you fucking kidding me?"

"What? No, no," Ford answered defensively, looking like he wanted to punch me. Good. If he did, the physical pain would match the soul-destroying agony inside my heart. "He's… nothing. Never mind."

The moment he uttered the words, I saw his whole demeanor change. He went from defensive to panicking, and in that instant, I knew this was no one-time thing for him. Here was Queenstown's ladies' man who'd gone and lost his heart to a man, and the knowledge that Ford was free to do that sent another jolt of self-loathing through me.

Reef said something and walked away, but the words didn't register. It was taking everything in me to stop the gut-churning nausea pulsing through me from making me hurl. Ford stepped forward so we were standing chest to chest. He didn't need to speak in more than a whisper and I could have heard him. His voice though, was a hiss, like a pissed-off snake ready to strike the lethal blow. "What the fuck, Trent?"

*I hate myself. I'm jealous and horrified and angry. I make myself sick.* "You make me sick."

Ford got all up in my face and glared. He was an intim-idating fucker when he was pissed. I couldn't help but flinch when Ford narrowed his eyes and growled at me. I'd seen rage like that in someone's eyes only once before. Ryan.

"Sit the fuck down and shut up, I need to see him out. Then we're gonna have a word about showing some fucking respect while you're in my house." Ford turned and began hobbling over to the bedroom as the front door slammed shut, the noise reverberating through the quiet house. Reef had just left. Ford didn't hesitate, following him. He shouted at Reef to wait as I pivoted on my feet and walked out, pushing past him.

"I never pinned you as a fairy. Yet, you're out here weeping like a fucking girl over your boyfriend getting all pissy. I knew you two were goin' at it when we busted into that cabin. I'm just glad I didn't have to see you sitting on his dick." *Oh God, stop. Please, shut your mouth and get out of here.*

"Who the fuck do you think you are? Get the hell off my property and don't come back."

I wanted to stop my mouth from running, but I couldn't. I was so far beyond controlling myself that I was back to that sixteen-year-old dick I used to be, and my next words proved it. "Aww, the little princess has had her feelings hurt?"

"Grow up and fuck off." Ford elbowed past me to get in the door and slammed it in my face while I stood there. In an instant my world had shattered again. My anger boiled my blood, but the revulsion in myself won out. I made it to the gray picket fence along the front perimeter and vomited in the bushes. I wished I could purge the loathing and the memories as easily as my morning coffee, but that could never happen. They say sometimes when the body has a traumatic experience it blocks out the event so it can heal. Why did I have to be different? Every second of what happened was burned into my memory. Imprinted on me so I could never forget.

I wiped my mouth with the back of my hand and stepped through the gate before walking out to my truck. I drove home, giving a one-fingered salute to more than one person on the way, and skidded into the drive.

Slamming the front door shut, I stomped across the living room toward my bedroom. I had no idea what I was going to do but pounding the shit out of the pavement sounded good right about then. My footsteps were heavy against the floor, and before I could get in there to change into sweats and hit the road, Angelo was in front of me. In my face. I couldn't deal with him. I had to keep my distance. His concern would only piss me off more, and I needed to protect him from me.

"What's wrong?" he asked, putting a gentle hand on my chest and stopping me in my tracks. I looked at him and saw beauty and love. A pureness about him that I'd never have again, perhaps never had in the first place. His eyes always captivated me. Whiskey with bright flecks of green and brown. Warm fall colors, as if he alone could keep the harsh winters at bay. So kind and caring. His furrowed brows and pursed lips told me he was worried about me. His hand on my chest seared me with the love of his friendship. It had me wanting to fall into his arms. Instinct told me to pull him close, but I couldn't. I wouldn't. I'd just spewed the same vile hatred that my godfather had spat at me. I wouldn't taint Angelo. He was too good for that. Too good for me.

"Don't, Angelo," I warned, shaking my head, trying to protect him. I was walking a fine line, and the tether holding me was about to snap. Anger, pain, and loathing for myself and the world I lived in would swallow me whole. I was already engulfed in the firestorm. I'd be scorched alive. Then when I fell, I'd be lost in an abyss. I'd fall into the flames of hell like I should have that day on the bridge when I met him.

He didn't move. Like a stone bastion, he was unyielding. Angelo planted his feet shoulder width apart and squeezed my arm. "Whether you like it or not, I'm here for you. I'm not going to walk away, and you sure as hell aren't going to be alone with whatever it is that's eating at you."

"No—"

He laughed as if I was being ridiculous. "You know me well enough to know I'm stubborn. I'll stand here and wait you out if I have to, but just so you know, we're going to the gym and you're going to beat the shit outta the punching bag I'll be holding."

I looked at him then. Gazed into his eyes, and I saw compassion there. He may not have understood why I was so worked up, but I knew that to him it didn't matter. That was the kind of friend he was. Loyal, with an unwavering strength. When he eventually found out what I'd said, he'd rip me a new one. I had no doubt about it. He'd never let my bigoted comments stand. I appreciated that about him too. He was no pushover. He'd never let me get away with shit he didn't like. He'd always have his say. He was blunt and honest.

When Angelo raised his hands to my shoulders and squeezed them, I nodded, not trusting myself to say anything at that point. "Go and get some sweats on. Then we'll leave. Whatever happened, we can get through it, okay?"

In my bedroom I paced. The doors to the walk-in closet were drawn open and I was between it and the bed. Frustration stirred within me. Why did my godfather still have so much control over me? Why did the events of a decade and a half ago still make me crazy? I shouldn't care who Ford was fucking. I shouldn't. But I did. The knowledge that I'd once made the same mistake and had been taught a lesson for it played on me until I was seething with anger. Gritting my teeth, I fought the urge to throw a punch at the mirrored doors and pulled the first random set of clothes I could find on. I had to get out of there.

Angelo was waiting for me when I walked out, handing me a bottle of water but keeping the boxing gloves he'd grabbed from the garage. The drive wasn't long—nothing was in Queenstown—and soon I was attacking the bag he gripped. He'd taken me into one of the quieter training rooms, and for that I was grateful. I let loose, every ounce of frustration and injustice and anger pouring out of me with each punch into the bag. Every hit I landed sent Angelo stepping backward, until he braced himself with all his bodyweight pressed up against the bag. My form wasn't perfect; it probably wasn't even good. But I needed this more than I could ever have known.

With every punch, I pictured his face. The one I'd never been able to forget. Contorted with rage, I remembered him more than I did my parents. I relived the pain, the scars he left me with opening again. I fought against the endless months I spent sleeping on the cold, hard ground and railed against the beating I took the final night that I'd slept behind the shopping mall. The same night that Edith, the lady I'd slept next to for months, had been raped in front of me while I fought to get free and help her. But the disgust I felt for Ryan and those men who'd ganged up on us was nothing compared to what I reserved for myself.

The picture in my mind's eye morphed into me. Distorted, it was hideous. As if my corrupted and warped soul had taken corporeal form and the monster staring back at me was the embodiment of that. I hated the vision. I hated myself. I wanted to erase it off the face of the planet. I wanted to erase myself.

My eyes stung and I couldn't catch my breath, but I kept punching. The pained cries didn't sound like a noise I'd make, but I knew it was me. My throat was raw. I was gasping for air. My lungs were burning, my heart pounding in my chest. My arms were so heavy that I could barely lift them anymore. My strength was entirely sapped. I didn't know how long I'd been hitting the bag, but exhaustion permeated every part of me.

Angelo wasn't holding it any longer either. He didn't need to. I didn't have the strength to push it far enough that it'd do anything more than sway gently. He was beside me, calling my name, but I couldn't stop. His hands on my shoulders pulling me away forced me to though, and I felt myself falling. Collapsing until I hit the rubber mats. I was in a crumpled heap on the floor and I couldn't breathe. My lungs were closing down, my vision going hazy. Panic set in, and I grasped fruitlessly at the loose singlet around my shoulders, trying to get the constriction off my chest.

I had to get it off, but my gloves were in the way.

I had to get them off. I couldn't breathe.

*Oh fuck, I can't breathe.*

Angelo was on his knees in front of me, and I reached for him, needing him. He cupped my face and drew me close, murmuring softly in my ear and rubbing my back. I couldn't understand what he was saying, but his words kept me grounded. Stopped me from spinning entirely out of control. They brought me back into myself.

I clutched at him, never wanting to let go, and he wrapped his arms around me, holding me close. I breathed in his familiar scent. Took comfort in the steady heartbeat against my cheek as I pressed it to his throat. He was rocking me, and I was crying. Grieving for what was and what I'd turned into. I'd been down before. I'd felt the darkness envelop me so thoroughly that I never wanted to escape, but this was the first time it'd hit me like this. The release was cathartic.

Angelo's hands loosened around me, and I pulled him

tighter, not wanting to let go. "Shh, it's okay. I'm just taking off your gloves," he crooned. The constriction of the band around my wrists loosened, and cold air wafted over each of my hands in succession as he pulled the gloves off and tossed them aside. I curled my hands around his back again and held on to Angelo for everything I was worth. In his arms I was safe. I wasn't that lonely teenager, scared out of my mind and wishing that the darkness would finally envelop me. I was just me. Broken and scarred, but he made me feel important. Like I was strong enough to pick myself up and dust myself off.

"You're always here for me," I whispered. "Why?"

"Because I could never be anywhere else." Angelo threaded his fingers through my hair, and I lifted my gaze to his. He'd been crying too, and the despondency in his eyes broke me.

"Can we go home?" I rasped, my throat feeling like I'd swallowed knives. Angelo nodded and pulled away to pass me a bottle of water. I guzzled it down while sweat dripped off my brow and stung my eyes. My shirt was soaked through, but Angelo didn't seem to mind. He helped me stand and wrapped an arm around me to guide me out. I was grateful for the support. My legs were like jelly, but more than that, I needed him to feel grounded. Tethered.

Angelo led me straight into the main bathroom when we arrived home and turned the hot water on in the tub. He added bath salts and a few drops of something that reminded me of warm tropical nights on far away beaches, and it wasn't long until the room started to steam up. "You right to get in?" he asked, then looked at me, shook his head, and blew out a breath. He mustn't have been impressed with what he saw, adding, "Let me help you." He was on his knees undoing the laces on my trainers before I could object, and he pulled each of my shoes and socks off.

When he rose, he slipped off my shirt and tossed it into the hamper in the corner. I swayed on my feet, not because I was unsteady, but because I wanted desperately to get closer to him. I had to fight down that instinct. It wouldn't get me anywhere, especially not after this morning's shit went down.

"You got the rest?" he asked. When I nodded, he busied himself with getting out a fresh towel for me from the cupboard. I had one in my bathroom, but I had a feeling he wouldn't have left me alone even if I'd insisted on it. With his back turned, I slipped off my shorts and sank into the foamy water. It wasn't deep yet, but I knew he was giving me whatever privacy he could in the confines of the small room.

I sighed as I sank down and rested my head against the porcelain. "Look," Angelo started, hesitating as if he wanted to choose his words carefully. He sat down on the side of the tub, still not looking at me. "You've made it pretty clear you won't share this stuff with me, but you need to speak with someone. I want you to get some help, Trent."

I wanted to resist, but I knew it was futile arguing with him. He wouldn't give up until he took me to see a counselor himself. "I know," I croaked. "I will."

"Don't just say it and not mean it." He turned to me then, and in that moment, I would have done anything for him. He was as broken as I was. He was hurting just as much. His eyes, red-rimmed and puffy, were dull. Their usual spark nonexistent. His lips were turned down and his shoulders slumped in defeat. I caught myself reaching for him and pulled back, dropping my hand back into the water. He flicked his eyes to it before hanging his head low. His reaction to that simple move solidified my promise. How could I keep hurting him?

"I will. I'll get help." The resolve in my voice must have satisfied him. He nodded and stood, keeping his back to me.

"I don't want to lose you, Trent, and every time this happens it makes me think I'll be burying you. I can't do that."

This time I didn't hesitate. I reacted on instinct and reached for his hand, clasping our palms together. I squeezed hard, trying to reassure him. "Some shit happened when I was younger. I don't like to relive it, but I do. The memories… they're not good. I don't want to…." How did I put into words that I didn't want my memories to taint him? That I didn't want him to look at me differently? I couldn't risk losing him. "I promise I'll speak with someone. I will."

His only response was to squeeze my hand and sit back down. We stayed like that for a long time, the water turning tepid before I could will myself to move and break our connection. It'd been a long time since I'd dated—years since I'd had more than a one-night stand—and the loneliness had crept in.

The only thing that'd kept it at bay was my friendship with the man sitting beside me. The hole in my chest never felt as big when he was around. It was never as deep and dark. I'd had hookups, but they were meaningless. A way of fulfilling a basic human need with a warm, willing body. I never had the slightest hesitation when it came to walking away. But with Angelo sitting there with me, it was different. His warmth soaked into me and his calm steadied me. We took comfort from each other, reaffirming the rock-steady bond of friendship we had. Only once before in my life I'd had a friend like Angelo—Jake, my teenage best friend who'd risked everything to give me clothes, money, and food.

"You're coming out with us. Go get dressed," Angelo ordered as he buttoned up his dark gray vest. He'd paired it with a matching pair of suit pants and a pale blue button-down shirt. With his shirtsleeves rolled up his forearms, he looked damn fine. Add on the black woolen coat and dark gray scarf and he would catch the eye of every woman in the place. He barely even glanced their way though. He'd smile and talk to them but rarely even showed any hint of being interested. It amazed me that a man like him was still single.

"I don't think so," I muttered. Ricky had organized drinks, but I knew Ford would be there with Reef. He wouldn't want me to go, and if I were being honest, I'd rather not be there either. A few weeks earlier when I'd seen them together, it'd been enough to send me spiraling. I didn't want the same thing to happen again, and frankly, I figured I'd be lucky to survive the night without a fist to my face.

Angelo looked at me and pursed his lips, looking disappointed. "Please?"

I sighed and nodded. I couldn't turn him down, even if I knew it wasn't going to be a happy ending.

"I wouldn't mind a night out." I smiled, hoping it didn't look too forced, and went into my bedroom to get changed. I wanted to look good. For him? For me? I had no idea. It didn't really matter. All I hoped was that the night didn't turn into a total clusterfuck. Probably too much to hope for, but hell, I deserved one night, didn't I?

I picked out a pair of dark jeans, a white button-down, and pulled my suit jacket out of the closet. In fifteen minutes I was ready, and I refused to stall. I was either going to jump in headfirst, or chicken the shit out. You'd never know it with my history, but I hated confrontations. I was nervous, both as to how I'd react and how Ford would.

I saw Ford and Reef enter before they saw us. I'd positioned myself closest to the edge of the booth when they spotted us and started making their way over. I downed the scotch I'd bought and swallowed hard. They came closer and my heart rate spiked. My throat constricted.

But it wasn't fear. It was shame.

What sort of person reacted the way I had when they saw two people together, no matter who they were? What sort of man was I when I hated myself so much that I took it out on them? I didn't even deserve to be sitting at that table with my friends. They were far too good for me. I stood, resigning myself to leaving, when Ford stopped in front of me. He eyed me, and I tried to hold his gaze and apologize without words, but I couldn't.

Humiliation swamped me, and I knew that the right thing to do was walk away. If I stayed, I'd ruin their night. If I left, they wouldn't even miss me. I closed my eyes and begged Angelo for forgiveness in my head, then turned and walked away. I only got as far as the bar. I needed something to wash down the bile making its way up my throat.

I barely choked out what I wanted before I had to suck in a few deep breaths to stop myself from puking. It was a bitter pill to swallow, knowing that I'd disappointed my friends so much. The end of the night couldn't come soon enough. But I knew when it did, I'd have to contend with Angelo and what would be a difficult conversation. It'd also be entirely one-sided. How could I explain everything —or anything—to him?

I left early but waited up until Angelo arrived home before I headed off to bed. I couldn't bring myself to go to bed without seeing him. I didn't know why, it was just one of those things that I apparently did. The more I thought about it, the more I realized I did it every time he was working or went out. I needed to know he'd come home safely before I could sleep.

The half-empty bottle of tequila sat next to me on the side table. I'd drunk most of it since getting home and it still hadn't dulled the pain sitting heavy on my chest. Contempt and humiliation, shame and yearning all mixed together, sloshing around like the potent liquid I'd swallowed, relishing the burn as it flowed down my throat. I deserved nothing less.

The snick of the lock on the door had me zeroing in on it. I watched silently as the handle turned and Angelo entered. He looked tired. As if he had the weight of the world on his shoulders. He didn't say a word as he tossed his coat carelessly over the sofa and reached for the bottle. He took a swig from it and winced.

Standing over me, he asked, "You want to tell me what the fuck happened tonight?" His cold voice, devoid of its usual warmth, cut me like a knife. But it helped maintain the walls I was desperately trying to keep from crumbling. I couldn't let them fall. I wouldn't. I'd lose Angelo if the truth of what I'd done came out, and that wasn't an option.

"Nope," I muttered mulishly.

"Of course not. You never fucking do." Angelo scrubbed a hand over his face and started pacing. "You hurt Ford tonight. Reef didn't know what the hell to do. Ricky thinks you were acting like a child, and you put me in a position you are *never* to put me in again."

My posture remained relaxed. I was sprawled out on the sofa, one leg kicked over the armrest, but every muscle in me tensed knowing the blow he was about to wield with his words. It could break me. I held my breath, waiting for him to continue until he faced me again. He stood there, legs shoulder width apart, arms crossed in front of his body, and his jaw set. Anyone else who looked at him would have seen aggression. I saw him trying to protect himself. His arms were a shield. I knew I'd hurt him before I asked, my tone more caustic than I had intended, "What position's that, Angelo?"

"You made me choose between you, my brother, and our friends. Don't you get it, Trent?" He spoke with his hands. He always did, but this time he pointed at me, his voice raised in a passionate cry. "You're as much my family as they are, and you made me choose."

"You chose them," I yelled, surging up off the sofa. I stood before him, chest to chest, almost daring him to taunt me more. I waved at the front door, as if he could tell I was talking about the others who were probably in their own homes by now. "You didn't choose me. You fucking chose them!"

"No!" He grabbed my arms and squeezed them, as if he was reassuring me. "No." He shook his head and this time, lifted his hands to my face, cupping my cheeks. His warmth seeped into me and unfurled something that had long gone dormant. His voice was barely more than a whisper, uttered quietly just for my ears, when he said, "I love you, man. I'll always choose you. Always. But you needed space."

I closed my eyes, wishing that he meant something entirely different than the love between friends. Wishing his touch didn't feel so good and that I didn't want to lean in a fraction more and kiss him. I had no idea whether he'd welcome it. He shouldn't, especially not from a worthless piece of shit like me. I shouldn't want it either, not after the lesson I'd been taught, but it was getting harder and harder to keep denying the side of me I'd buried.

Seeing Ford and Reef that night, dancing together wrapped in each other's arms. Making out. They were beautiful together. Lovely. Sweet in a way I'd never thought two men together could be. Jealousy had burned through me that they could express themselves like that. Longing had overtaken me, and I couldn't deny who had been in my thoughts. That was when I had to get out of there. I couldn't watch them any longer without forgetting every lesson I'd learned that terrible night. I sucked in a breath and pulled away from Angelo. When I opened my eyes, I saw heartbreak in his. They were glassy, like he was about to cry.

"You never talk to me," he murmured. "You never open up. I wish you would."

"I can't."

Angelo ran his fingers through his hair and sighed. "Can't or won't? You're fine speaking to a counselor. A stranger. But not me."

I wanted to reach out for him, to comfort him like he'd done so often to me. I wasn't sure whether it was the liquor loosening my inhibitions, or that inner part of me attempting a jailbreak, but I was powerless to stop myself from wrapping my hand around the back of his neck and dragging him into my arms. I held him close and he nuzzled his face into my throat. Longing, yearning, and love flittered around in my chest like a kaleidoscope of butterflies, lighting me up inside with all the colors of the rainbow.

I voiced my deepest fears to him, slicing myself open and laying it all out there—another product of too much tequila. "My therapist's opinion doesn't mean anything. Yours does. It means everything. I can't lose you, and that's what would happen if I told you."

He pulled back just enough that he could look into my eyes. "You underestimate me. I'd always choose you." My heart thudded in my chest and those butterflies took flight again.

My gaze roamed over his face, and I marveled at how handsome he was. His eyes, the brown and green flecks in his irises contrasting against the rich whiskey. His almost black hair, which was ordinarily brushed back in a perfect coif, was messy. It was as if he'd run his hands through it until the style he meticulously applied had completely disappeared, the fine strands falling to the side of his face, kissing his cheekbone. His straight nose and smooth jawline framed his perfectly pouty lips, tinged with pink. I sucked in a breath when his tongue darted out to wet his bottom lip, and he kept them parted as his breathing became heavier. He trembled in my arms, and I held him tighter, splaying one hand low on his back as I rubbed my thumb along his nape. Soft skin and silky hair met my touch, and I leaned in closer, wanting to taste those lips, needing to sip from them like a man dying of thirst.

A puff of his breath echoed along my cheek and he pressed his fingers into the curve of my spine, this time making me shiver. My gaze snapped back to his as I swayed closer still. His pupils were blown, his eyes darkened with what looked a lot like desire. Knowing it was me that he wanted in that moment was enough to make me soar among the eagles.

But the whisper of long-ago words danced in my head and doused the desire playing through my body, tossing me back to earth like a limp rag doll. *"No boy of mine is a good-for-nothing faggot."* I pulled back from Angelo, putting some distance between us, the spell we were under broken. He blinked and turned away, but I didn't miss the flush that colored his cheeks. He picked up his coat and slung it over his shoulder, walking away from me without another word. I tried to call him back. I tried to reach for him. But I was paralyzed. Rendered mute by the horror of what I'd nearly done. How could I expose Angelo to that? To me?

IT WAS LATE WHEN THE MOST RECENT EMAIL FROM FORD popped up on my screen. He'd been gone for months, leaving Queenstown just after the night from hell at the club. He and Reef had come out to Angelo and Rick, and I'd flaked out, unable to be near them. He was due back soon, having worked another winter in Santa Caterina di Valfurva, but I hadn't spoken to him since I'd first seen him and Reef together.

I hadn't been able to swing time off work to travel there for Christmas too. Rick had gone home, but Angelo insisted on staying with me. It was nice, just the two of us waking up in the morning and having a quiet breakfast together before we hit the soup kitchen. We didn't serve food this year, instead giving out the care packs we'd spent days putting together. This year we'd included the kids, giving the older ones coloring pencils, books, and notepads while the younger ones got teddy bears.

I closed my email program down without looking at the one from Ford. I'd read it when I could focus. I'd been distracted all day—not surprising given the date. April 18. It was my mom's birthday. I missed her, even more so on this day every year. I wished I could bridge the gap between us, contact her and let her know I still thought about her, but too much water had passed under the bridge. I wanted it more than ever, but I'd hurt them too much for them to ever want me back. I'd waited too long, too insecure and scared of my godfather to even seek out my parents. I wondered, not for the first time, whether Mom and Dad had entered the age of technology and signed up for social media. I hadn't. I kept off it, never wanting my image to be tagged and someone from my old life to recognize me. Probably a stupid precaution, especially because no one could forcibly send me to see Ryan, but old habits died hard.

Angelo's iPad was on the coffee table where he'd left it, and I sneaked a peek at Facebook. I hadn't used it before but quickly found the search bar. I didn't know if I could just randomly find someone, but figured I'd try. I typed in Mom's name and within seconds, I was staring at a profile that was unmistakably hers. The picture that was her avatar was of me as a teenager—my school photo taken only a few weeks before I ran away. I pressed the link with shaking hands, and a profile loaded that seemed to be locked down. I couldn't see anything except a post from that day:

Missing. Lost. Vanished without a trace.

Leaving behind broken hearts and love eternal.

Wherever you might be, our son, know our love is with you.

When the dawn breaks, we think of you.

As the moon and stars light the sky at night, and every moment in between.

We wished just to see your face once more, but silence has met our prayers.

Another year passes for us, so many more days without you.

Now we hope that your soul flies free, our boy,

Until one day we meet again.

The picture they'd posted was one of the rare ones without Ryan. Just the three of us there, grinning at the camera. I was flashing a peace symbol, and Dad had me in a headlock, laughing. The picture went blurry and I swiped at the tears welling in my eyes and trailing down my cheeks.

Pain lanced through my chest, piercing my heart. They thought I was dead. They'd grieved for me and given up any hope.

I imagined them burying an empty coffin and had a glimpse of the gaping wound that my parents would have suffered through not knowing—never knowing—what happened. I was worse than worthless. I was callous. Heartless and selfish. I'd put them through hell because I was scared. Afraid that I'd get punished again for something I'd realized pretty quickly I'd been mistaken about. I couldn't deny the attraction I had to men, but it didn't mean I ever needed to act on it. I'd learned that lesson with a one-time fuck. As soon as I'd figured it out, I should have gone home. Not waited for fifteen years. Now, at least, they had some closure. They believed me gone. It really was too late. Going back would just reopen their wounds and make them hurt all over again.

But that knowledge broke me. Deep down, I'd always held out some hope I could return. That one day I'd be able to see them again. But it was an impossible dream.

My therapist, working with what little information I could force myself to give to her, told me that writing down my feelings, penning an old-fashioned letter with what I wanted to say, would help me deal.

So I did.

I dug out a notepad and a pen and wrote. The words didn't flow easily. I'd spent so many years bottling up my feelings that expressing myself was harder than I ever imagined. But I kept going. I pushed myself to share more than I ever had before. I told them about those early nights in the hotel—how I turned my nose up at the stucco falling off the walls but that it was five-star luxury compared to some of the places I'd laid my head. Then about the job washing dishes and how it was supposed to give me an opportunity, but instead they'd just been using me. They'd ripped me off, never paying me a dime for the work I'd done. I told them about the paramedic who'd given me a shot at a better life after Edith was raped.

But I couldn't share my friend's story. It was too personal. Too close to my own.

I told them what I was doing now, how I'd found family with Angelo. How I loved him for saving me, for being protective and loyal. And even though my apology would never be enough, I said sorry for putting my parents through hell. For making them believe I'd died somewhere, somehow, and was gone. I begged them to forgive me for never being brave enough to go home and in turn making them wait so many years to never really get closure. I couldn't bring myself to explain why I'd left, only that it wasn't their fault. They had never done anything but love me. They were the innocent victims caught in the crosshairs. It sounded stupid when I put it on paper, but I'd tried to save them from getting hurt, only to have hurt them worse in the process.

I signed the name they'd given me—Keir—instead of my middle name, the one I'd been using since I left. I'd grown into Trenton over the years, so the other name felt foreign on my tongue and at the end of my pen stroke now. But that's how Mom and Dad knew me. I tore off the sheets and folded them up, ready to stuff in a drawer somewhere never to see the light of day again, when Angelo surprised me. He opened his door, and like a kid caught with his hand in the cookie jar, I hid what was in mine, stuffing the pages down between the sofa cushions as he staggered out into the light. His hair was mussed, a sleepy, sexy bed head, and he was dressed only in loose boxer shorts that hung low on his hips. I could see the top of the dark curls that framed his shaft and the beginnings of the sexy V that framed his groin. I swallowed. Hard. Damn, his hip bones, his long lean body, and that hair were sexy as fuck.

Wincing from even the soft glow of the lamp, he looked at me, confused, and rubbed his eyes.

"You're still awake? Why?" he croaked.

"Just checking emails, but I was about to head to bed. You need something?"

"Water," he mumbled, still standing there looking a little lost.

I made my way over to the kitchen and smiled at him. "I'll get it. Go back to bed. I'll bring it in." Angelo yawned and nodded as he turned and stumbled back into his darkened room. He left the door open and looked like he'd already passed out again on his bed when I took the glass in and set it on his nightstand. As I was leaving, he grasped my arm.

"I'm lonely, Trent. Can you stay with me?" His quiet mumble shocked me still, and I sucked in a breath, wanting desperately to say yes, but at the same time having everything in me screaming no. I was lonely too. It'd been a long, hard night, and I wanted for a moment to just forget who I was. Before I could talk myself out of it, I stripped off my shirt and unbuttoned my jeans. Letting them fall to the floor, I stepped out of them and tugged off my socks. The cool fall air had a bite to it, and I shivered before Angelo lifted the covers next to him and I slid in. He didn't give me much time to get settled, pushing my arm up and resting his head on my shoulder as soon as I was prone. His legs tangled with mine, and he wrapped his arm around my waist. With anyone else I wouldn't have been able to lie there, and admittedly it did take me a moment to adjust to having him so close. But I breathed deep and held it, trying to stop the fear and self-loathing from taking over, actively talking myself out of instinctively pushing him away. Then his warmth seeped through me. It comforted me as much as I filled the ache of loneliness for him.

"Why don't you date, Ang?" I asked once he was settled. "You deserve to be happy."

"I'm waiting for The One," he mumbled, nuzzling closer. His fingertips traced the line of my boxers near my hip, and I bit back a moan. It was an innocent touch. Something someone did when they weren't thinking, just feeling. But it left pinpricks of awareness piercing the armor I'd fortified myself with.

When his words sank in, I scoffed at him. "You'll never find her unless you look though."

"I already have." He sighed, and my brain went numb. By the time I regathered myself, I knew he'd fallen asleep. His breathing was deep and his arm a solid weight on my belly. I touched him then, bringing my arm around him and pulling him closer. Feeling the smooth skin of his back against my palm. I kissed his forehead and closed my eyes, wishing that whomever he was in love with would wake up. Would see what I saw in him. The love that he gave so freely. His loyalty. His friendship. She would be his entire world, and he'd go to his grave loving her. The lady who received the gift of his heart would be the luckiest woman on the planet. I just hoped that she realized it too, because he deserved nothing less than being the center of this woman's universe. Angelo was one of a kind. Truly a beautiful soul.

I ran my fingers through his hair and ghosted them along his cheek before trailing them down along his arm stretched out across my middle. I wanted to hold his hand. To touch him and kiss him properly. I wanted to make love to him.

For the second time in as many moments, my body tingled with an awareness that it hadn't understood before. I opened my eyes to the darkness, and my heart slammed into my ribs. Time stood still and sped up all at the same time. I was light-headed and giddy and impossibly alone all at the same time. He was my home. He was my best friend and always would be. But in that moment, something clicked. Like a doorway to a secret chamber had been opened, I realized that it was so much more. I loved him. *I love him.* I think I always had.

But he loved someone else.

He'd already found The One.

I wished he'd fallen for me. I wished I could be the one to deserve him. The one to love him. Even if he was into men, I'd never be good enough. I'd never be free enough of my hang-ups, of my past that still haunted me.

# CHAPTER 10

## ANGELO

I woke with the heat of a body pressed against me and vaguely remembered staggering out of my bedroom in the middle of the night. Alone. I should have been alarmed that there was another person in my bed, but fragments of my conversation with Trent were coming back to me anyway.

My cell had dinged with an incoming message and I'd woken. Too thirsty to go back to sleep, I'd gone to get a drink. He'd brought me water, and I'd asked him to stay. It was the first time I'd had anyone in my bed since our first Christmas together years ago, and being held in another's arms was far too comforting and rare for me to give it up. Even if he'd reacted badly the last time it happened. Christmas three years earlier was a night that held bitter-sweet memories for me. I'd hoped, after Trent admitting he'd thought about me at the club, that he'd be open to testing the waters of a new relationship. But it'd backfired spectacularly. I'd waited years to hold him again, and the next time it was when his world was falling apart. Ford had danced around the issue, but it didn't take a genius to figure out that Trent had lost his shit when he'd found out Ford was dating Reef.

Any hope of Trent one day accepting my sexuality had been dashed years ago, but the final plunge of the knife was seeing his reaction that night with Ford. Then, when he'd agreed to speak with a therapist rather than opening up to me, he'd shattered the remaining pieces of my heart. All I wanted was to be there for him, but in our years of friendship he'd rarely let me. It was hopeless. I'd never get past the friend zone. Deep down, I'd always known that, but when we were alone and he let his guard down I thought maybe things between us could change. But they never would.

Trent moved behind me, beginning to wake up, and I tried to put a bit of distance between us. I didn't want him to freak out on me this morning. But he wouldn't let me. He hummed low in his throat and pulled me closer, mumbling, "Mornin'," as he nuzzled the nape of my neck.

"*Buongiorno*," I replied in a voice still scratchy with sleep.

"You remember asking me to stay?" he asked, a little hesitation in his words.

"I do. Thanks for being here."

"Always." He sighed but made no move to get up. After a moment he added, "Your bed is comfy."

"So stay in it," I teased.

I didn't think for a moment he'd say yes, but he shocked me with his response. "Think I might." He rolled over onto his back and I followed, mirroring his position and moving over to my own side of the queen bed. When he stretched his arms above his head and arched his back, I nearly swallowed my tongue. Dark hair under his arms was matched by shorter curls covering his pecs. A happy trail ran from his navel, disappearing below his dark gray boxer shorts, the same ones I remembered fingering the material of the night before. They were the fitted type, and they were silky and warmed from his skin. The way they snugly wrapped around his package made me want to reach for him. But I never would. I'd never cross that line, no matter how much I wanted it.

"What's on the cards for today?" His words snapped my attention back to his face.

I could feel my cheeks heat under his scrutiny and let out a nervous laugh. "Well, you know how I mentioned last week that I had a new client and she wanted me to do a photoshoot for a book cover? That was supposed to be today, but the model canceled last night. That's what woke me up. I was hoping maybe you could do it instead?"

"You want me to model for you?" he asked, obviously wary of what I was asking.

"It's torso shots only. I won't take your face, so no one will know it's you. And I'll pay you for it."

"I don't want your money, Angelo." He shrugged. "No one would want me on their book. I'm not exactly model material."

I outright laughed at that. He was beautiful. Mysterious dark eyes that were fathoms deep. His short hair was perfectly messy all the time; even his bed head was sexy. Stubble that looked as if he'd spent hours shaping it, when in truth it simply grew naturally like that. But it wasn't only his facial features that made him gorgeous. His body was a work of art. Broad shoulders with thick biceps and a narrow waist. He didn't work out much, but it was enough to be toned. He wasn't a bodybuilder by any stretch of the imagination, and he didn't have a perfect six-pack, but he was still extraordinary. "Let me photograph you, Trent. You'll surprise yourself at how sexy they turn out." I cocked my head to the side, framing the picture in my imagination. "Actually, stay exactly like that. I want that shot."

I scrambled out of bed and ran into my office, plucking my camera out of its bag and getting the flash umbrella too. After I'd set up the umbrella, I adjusted the settings for the lower light and the close-ups I'd be taking. I snapped a test shot and checked it on the screen, making a few more adjustments to the filters and the flash settings. I took another photo, and this one turned out exactly how I'd pictured it. Soft lighting, rumpled sheets, and a hard body. It left enough to the imagination that every dirty fantasy possible played out in your mind, yet it was inti-mate too. Those dirty fantasies could just as well include breakfast in bed and slow lovemaking. "Look at this." I smiled, flipping over the camera to show Trent. He stared at it for a moment, his eyebrows jolting up in surprise before his gaze flicked back to mine.

"How did you make me look like that? I look... sexy." He scrunched up his nose and looked adorably innocent. "Is that weird to say?"

"No." I shook my head. "This is how I see you, Trent. You're beautiful. And I don't just mean what you look like. You know that, right?" I placed my hand on his chest, right above his heart, and said, "It's this. Your heart loves harder than anyone I know. And you're incredibly smart. You're so much more than you give yourself credit for." I grasped his hand and ran my fingertips over his palm.

"These hands save lives, Trent. They help people. They heal them. This picture"—I lifted the camera and set it out of the way—"it's just capturing what I see every day."

"That's not true," he answered, and cleared his throat. "You love harder than anyone else."

I smiled at him, feeling shy, and he smiled back. My heart flip-flopped in my chest, and I wanted to giggle. Instead, I snapped another round of photos of his face, the smile slowly slipping from it as he watched me. In that moment it was as if I was looking into his soul. He was stripped bare, vulnerable and trusting.

I moved the camera to take more pictures of his body and directed his movements. "Stay partly covered up but show me a bit more leg." He did, and I touched his hip. "Turn a little more onto your side and rest your head on your hand." He moved, and I lined up the frame. "That's perfect. Okay, now think about being in bed with a lover. Seduce them."

He stared at me again, and the intensity took my breath away. I wished he would really look at me like that rather than it being an act. Having the focus of his attention squarely on me had my heart beating harder—a thud, thud, thud as it knocked around in my rib cage. My palms were sweaty, and I flushed with heat. My cock swelled. There was no hope hiding it. It would quickly be tenting my boxers if I didn't get myself under control. But then Trent hooked his thumb under the waistline of his boxers and tugged them down an inch.

I was a goner.

His trimmed pubes were just visible, and I had the uncanny urge to lick his skin. To taste him. When he bit down on his lip, I depressed the shutter, taking a series of photos. "Arch your back a little," I instructed, and he obeyed, pressing his head into the pillow and slipping his fingers up to the second knuckle into his boxer shorts. I bit back a moan and snapped more photographs.

He moved, kicking off the covers altogether and lifting his knee up. His arms, stretched up near his head, showed off the curve of his lat muscles, and he played with his bottom lip. My semi had become a full-blown erection. There was no way he'd miss it in my loose boxers.

I stood on the bed to get a better shot and hovered over him, clicking away. I wanted the opposite angle too, so I stepped up to his head and took the photo looking down his body. These ones didn't have his face in them, but I wished I could get more close-ups. He moved naturally, shifting positions slightly to give me just the right view.

"Want me on my front?" he asked, his voice rough as he looked away from me. I palmed my dick and hissed softly from the pressure on it. It had been a while since I'd been like this. Wanting. Needy. But I was raring to go now.

"Yeah. Roll over." I guided him, hoping he didn't see me touch myself as he turned.

The view from the back was just as sexy. A dip in the muscle followed the length of his spine, disappearing under the waistline of his shorts. And damn those shorts. They hugged his ass like a second skin. They sat low on his hips and at the same time exposed just enough of his cheek to entice. His skin was a temptation, taunting me to do the unthinkable and lick along the crease between his quad and his ass. I wondered what the fine, dark hairs that dotted his legs would feel like against my tongue, and I squeezed the base of my dick to stop myself from blowing on the spot. It took every ounce of willpower I had to remain professional and photograph him.

The first shot wasn't perfect, but I knew what would make it so. "Bring your arms up to your head." He did, resting his head on his hands, and I clicked away, capturing his beauty with my camera. "Bend your knee for me?"

Trent moved his arms too, burying his face under his bicep and bringing his other arm down underneath him. I could imagine him cupping his package. Stroking.

It was a ridiculous fantasy, one that was an impossibility, but imagining that he was turned on enough to be unable to resist touching himself was wildly erotic. Every dirty fantasy of mine sprang to life. Would he like his balls being played with in that position? His ass? Would his dick be bent down so I could lick the tip?

I gritted my teeth and sucked in a breath, trying to control myself. But when he rocked his hips, his ass cheeks clenched, and the movement was one I could all too well imagine being on the receiving end of. I couldn't help my soft moan. Trent stilled, then did it again, and I moved in close, capturing the heart shape his ass made as he tightened the muscles there. The rippling of his back and the curve of his spine as he rubbed himself on the sheets had me filling my camera's memory card all too quickly.

"Shit," I swore under my breath. Each time I tried to depress the shutter, an error message popped up in my viewfinder. My words were enough to break the spell Trent was under, and he looked up at me in a daze. "My memory card's full. I, ah—"

"Oh, okay. Yeah. Cool," he stuttered. "I'll just, um." He paused, then blurted out, "Are we finished?"

"We can be if you've had enough. I've got all the shots I need here." I motioned to my camera and stepped away from the bed. I suddenly felt awkward, not really knowing what to do with myself. But I did know one thing. I had to get out of there. Mortification filled me. The boner I was sporting was all too obvious. I motioned out the door and added, "I'll just go and, ah, give you some privacy."

"Yeah, thanks." Trent cleared his throat, and I realized I was still staring at his ass. Knocked out of my daze, I made the quick retreat into my office and busied myself with taking out the memory stick and putting away my camera. I downloaded the images to my computer, separating out the wedding I'd attended the day before from Trent's photoshoot.

I didn't hear him leave my room, but I did hear the shower in his start and stop a few minutes later. I took the chance and went into my bathroom to get ready for the day too, delaying the inevitable awkward exchange between us for a few more minutes.

It'd been six weeks since the session with Trent, and I'd finally managed to edit the images I'd taken of him. The author I'd done the job for had picked one of the first shots I'd taken, and it was currently being made into a cover. I was looking forward to seeing the finished product, but in the meantime, I wanted Trent to have the others. I wanted him to see what I saw: his beauty, both inside and out.

Awkwardness had pervaded our interactions since the photoshoot. That was on me. He was trying to get me to talk, to get me to go back to being the friend who'd always been and always would be there for him. Something had changed in our interactions since the session, though—me. I'd always sworn friendship would be enough, and it would be—it was—but getting the picture of him rolling his hips and rubbing himself against my bed out of my head was harder than I'd ever imagined. I'd loved him for so long that the sight of him letting go and being so sensual had flipped a switch in my head, and I hadn't yet found where the mute button was.

The smell of him on my sheets had lingered for days afterward, and that had only served to make the highlights reel replay in my head even more. I'd relived those moments while imagining what I'd really wanted to do with him so many times that I couldn't count. I'd jacked off every time too. I was liberated, free to explore my attraction to him, even if it was a freedom that only existed in my head. That freedom was terrifying too, and hope-less. I wanted him, but having him was impossible and going back to our pre-photoshoot selves was taking a bit of adjustment. I'd had a taste of an experience with him and now had to live with the knowledge that for him it was just a few photos. The attraction, the lust, it was all one-sided.

Seeing him every day, and especially when I was still floating around in a cloud of post-orgasmic bliss where I'd jacked off to mental images of him, brought me back to reality with a resounding thud. Guilt slammed into me, knowing that I'd been dreaming up all the ways I could love on my best friend without him even knowing I was lusting after him. I felt like I was betraying him. I second-guessed every interaction we'd had too, questioning whether they were for his benefit or mine. Had I tricked him into my bed that night? Would he feel used if he knew the part of me I'd kept on lockdown? Had I asked him to do the photoshoot so I could lewdly stare at him, instead of what I'd told myself—that I wanted him to see what I saw?

I knew he thought he'd done something wrong, but I was having trouble working through the quagmire of my thoughts. My libido wasn't helping things either. Seeing him wake up each morning, sexy and tousled, and walk out of his bedroom wearing only oversized pajama pants that sat so low on his hips I could often see the top of his trimmed pubes, bed hair, and a few days' growth had my cock straining. Every. Damn. Time. I was acting like a horny teenager, and the last thing I wanted was for him to call me out on sporting a boner for him. Calling someone gay was about the biggest insult he used. The thought of him being so disgusted in me that he'd direct those hate-filled words at me was a fear I couldn't simply disregard anymore as being unreasonable. I wasn't gay, but a response of, "No I'm not gay. I class myself as homoromantic demisexual. I'm only attracted to you, not other men," wouldn't exactly go down well with him.

I was going to show him the photos that morning though. I was going to put on my big boy pants and finally run him through what I'd been working on. He deserved to at least see the edited photos. But before I called him into my office, I needed a shower and some clothes. Sitting behind my desk in only my underwear wouldn't make for a good impression if I was sporting wood.

With the towel still wrapped around my waist from my shower, I was in the kitchen when my stomach rumbled. I popped some bread in the toaster, then slathered it in butter when it was golden brown. Carrying a plate in one hand and my espresso in the other, I hummed a Maroon 5 tune and absently headed back to my room to get dressed. I wasn't expecting Trent to be barreling toward me when I rounded the corner. Coming face-to-face with him after so many tense weeks, while I was dressed only in a towel loosely secured around my waist, had me gasping. "Oh, shit."

"Whoa." Trent skidded to a stop and held his hands up, pressing them against my chest as I tried to avoid crashing into him and spilling my scalding hot coffee on his bare skin. His eyes flicked to my toast as he smirked. "In a rush, are we?"

"Just finished something I've been working on. Give me a few minutes and come into my office so I can show you." I sounded out of breath, but it was nerves more than anything else.

"Sure." He nodded, and my eyes widened as the towel slipped half an inch. I froze like a deer in headlights. I knew what was going to happen, and worse, I knew I couldn't stop it without dropping at least one thing that I was holding. Another slip and I reacted, but my movements were so slow I could have been swimming in treacle. I swallowed hard as the tucked in corner of the towel came entirely loose and fell, spiraling down my legs. I wasn't embarrassed by my nakedness, but with the discomfort between us and my cock reacting every time I set eyes on the man standing only a few inches away from me, I knew flashing him my dick would only make things uber uncomfortable.

My toast shot off the plate, skidding across the floor and coming to a stop under the sofa as I lunged for the towel, trying at the same time to keep my espresso upright. I caught the other end of the terry cloth and held on to it for dear life, trying desperately to pull it up and around me singlehandedly. It didn't work. Instead, all I'd managed was to spill my coffee, send my toast flying, nearly drop the plate, and bend over, completely naked, in front of the man I'd been avoiding for six weeks while trying to cover my junk. Mortification burned my cheeks scarlet, and I wished the floor would open up and swallow me whole. Instead, Trent's snort of laughter drew my attention.

"Dude, you couldn't have screwed that up any more if you tried."

"Yeah, thanks," I muttered, handing him my cup and the empty plate so I could get the towel around me again. When I finally looked at Trent, my face still flaming, our eyes locked and the intensity stole my breath. He didn't waver. He just stared me down. His breathing was heavy, nostrils flared as he sucked in breath after breath. Lust exploded through me. I couldn't look away.

He pinned me to the spot, with blown pupils in eyes so impossibly black that I could fall into them and never climb out. My mouth went dry and I swayed toward him, caught in his magnetism. His lips parted, and his tongue crept out to wet his bottom lip. There was no camera between us, no instructions from me to seduce someone with those bedroom eyes framed by perfect, long lashes.

This was him and me.

Sparks. Chemistry. Fire burning me up.

I wanted to reach for him, to pull his hips to mine and see for myself whether he was as aroused as me with a simple look. But I didn't. I dared not move in case I broke the spell.

My breaths were shallow. My heart thudded fast, the rhythm reverberating through my chest. Wanton need flared through me. Desperation. Desire. I'd loved him for so long. I'd do almost anything to pull him into my arms. To touch him. To hold him. To worship him. A strangled noise escaped from the back of my throat, and that was all it took. Trent jerked like I'd slapped him, turning his face away. I caught the flush that colored his skin as he spun on his heels and stalked back into his room, shutting the door with a resounding thump.

I stood there in the same spot for what could have been a minute or an eternity. Rejection sunk its bitter claws into me, and my shoulders fell. I closed my eyes, and shame washed over me. I was so affected by him that I couldn't think straight anymore. I hadn't seen heat in his eyes. I couldn't have. Not that I'd even know what desire looked like. I was so pathetically naïve.

What was left of my coffee had turned cold in my hand, but the thought of eating anything soured my stomach. I collected my toast from under the sofa and dumped my breakfast in the trash before trudging back to my bedroom. I wanted to wallow. The idea of crawling back into bed and staying there for the rest of the day was tempting, but I had a meeting with a potential client in a few hours. The one disadvantage of being a wedding photographer was when my relationship—or lack thereof—sucked I couldn't avoid seeing people with love heart eyes mooning over each other. I set my alarm, ditched the towel that was still securely tied around my waist, and crawled beneath the covers of my bed.

I closed my eyes, hoping that if I fell asleep quickly enough, I'd forget how humiliated I was. Better yet, I'd somehow transport myself back in time so that I was wearing a pair of sweats or dress pants with the suspenders I often wore for work. Anything else really, as long as it didn't fall off me. I thumped the pillow and groaned. *Damn it. Now how will I face him?* I had another thing to apologize for.

I didn't think I'd slept, but the warmth of my covers and the comfort of my bed must have lulled me under, because the next thing I knew my alarm was dragging me back to consciousness. Bleary eyed, I stumbled over to my closet and searched for something suitable to wear for work. Dressing in light gray slacks and a matching vest paired with a lavender shirt and dark mauve bow tie, I headed to the bathroom to tame my hair into some semblance of style. After twenty minutes I had my messenger bag, keys, and wallet by the door, ready to go. Then I heard it.

A cry.

It wasn't a sob. It sounded like pain. *Trent.* Blood turned to ice in my veins, but instinct kicked in and I ran for him. I had to help him, to fix whatever it was that was hurting him. What was it? What was wrong? I'd been asleep for hours. Anything could have happened in that time.

"Trent," I called through the door, the panic in my voice making it waver. When there was no answer, I banged on it and said his name louder, this time not waiting for a response. I crashed through the door and looked for him in the modest space, ready to run to his aid.

But what I saw knocked me flat on my ass.

The two men fucking on Trent's television barely registered, but the black dildo Trent was trying to impale himself on did. In the split second after I entered, I stared dumbfounded while my brain tried to register what my eyes were seeing. Trent naked, porn playing in the background. Not any porn, but gay porn. He was on his knees on the bed, his legs spread as he tried to sit on a dildo that would be too big even for a porn star. I opened my mouth, but nothing came out. Trent's gaze shot to mine, and he reacted like he'd been electrocuted, scrambling off the mattress and pulling the covers up to cover himself. The dildo lay discarded in the middle of the bed, and I looked between it and him, trying to process everything.

"Wha—" I started, but Trent's scream cut through me, halting me in my tracks.

"Get out!" His voice was unusually high-pitched, panicked.

I opened my mouth to say something, anything, but nothing came out. The words couldn't form. My brain had short-circuited, still trying to make sense of what was happening. I snapped my mouth shut, looked to him again, and saw the abject horror in his eyes. It quickly turned to what I could only assume was anger.

He clenched his jaw and his eyes turned wild, his body stiffening, and he looked like he was readying to pounce. He didn't want me there; that much was obvious. But I was glued to the spot. Everything kicked into gear though when he yelled at me to leave again. I fled, barely pausing to collect my things at the front door before I burst through it and out onto our tiny front lawn. My heart thundered in my chest and my palms were clammy, my breaths coming in staccato pants.

We'd always had an unspoken rule in our house—never go into each other's bedroom unless invited. I'd blown that rule right out of the water and just when Trent was doing… whatever the hell he was doing. The picture my eyes had painted made no sense to me. He was straight. Straighter than straight, if what I'd thought for years was true. But then, why? Was he experimenting? Just trying it out for curiosity sake? Bored?

I was confused. Angry with myself. Shocked.

I closed my eyes, and the picture on the television screen popped into my head. Why was he watching gay porn? It was one thing for him to watch straight or lesbian porn. I'd heard all the guys in high school brag about that. I'd witnessed the jerks in college trying to hook up with the lesbian couples so they could participate in a three-some where the girls got it on. Trent was one of those guys sometimes—vocal and ignorant, homophobic—but… what, I had no idea.

My gaze wandered back to the front door of our town-house. Everything was normal. Nothing had changed. Visually, everything was still the same. But inside the house, everything had shifted. It'd been flipped on its head. There were so many questions flying around in my head that they were making me dizzy, and I didn't know what the answers to any of them meant for me and Trent.

I slid into the front seat of my car and found myself shaking. Regret barreled through me. Why did I act without thinking? Why did I barge in on him instead of giving him the privacy he deserved? Fear. Love. Concern. Hell, it was all those things, but that wasn't good enough. Trent was a private person. He had walls around him so high and so thick that I didn't think I'd ever break through. I'd always hoped that he'd open up when he trusted me enough. But now… I'd ruined everything.

DAYS HAD PASSED AND I HADN'T SEEN HIM. I DIDN'T THINK IT was a matter of our schedules not meeting up. Trent was avoiding me, and who could blame him? I'd spent six weeks doing exactly the same thing. I wanted to apologize, but after everything that had gone down, I wasn't sure if I was apologizing for me or for him. The last thing I wanted to do was make things worse between us. But as I sat at one of the stools along the kitchen counter sipping my espresso, my decision was made for me. Trent opened the front door and stepped inside, scanning the room. I looked to him and he tensed, visibly on edge. I'd hurt him so much that he wasn't even comfortable being here anymore. That move, that thought shattered my heart. I really had ruined everything.

"So… eating breakfast?" he asked after a beat of silence that went on for too long.

"Just coffee," I mumbled. "Feel like one? I could make it for you." I sounded so damn eager. Exactly like a puppy. It was kind of pathetic, but this was Trent. I'd do almost anything to keep our friendship intact.

He slid onto the stool next to me, and I sat there silent and still. I'd gone from a puppy to being scared to spook him. I had expected him to politely refuse, or maybe even ignore me in favor of his bedroom. But this felt like a second chance. Hope bloomed in my chest and I had to tamp down my eager smile when he answered, "Coffee would be great, thanks."

I hopped off and practically floated into the kitchen to make him a pod of his favorite. Steaming mug in hand, I slid it across the countertop to him and stayed there watching as he wrapped both hands around it and took his first sip. Eyes closed, he sighed, and I could see the tension draining from him.

"Trent, I—"

"Please don't, Angelo," he whispered, his voice broken. "I'm not ready."

I slumped against the cupboards, grateful to be able to lean on the countertop. "Will you be? One day, maybe? Or have I broken us?" I couldn't look at him as I whispered the question. I couldn't stand to see rejection in his eyes. I didn't realize how hard I was wringing my hands together until he closed his over mine. They were warm and full of comfort, and I soaked up the piece of him he'd given me.

"The last couple of months has been tough, hasn't it?" I nodded, and he continued. "It's on me though, not you."

My gaze shot up to his, my brows furrowed in confusion. "What do you mean? How is it your fault?"

He shrugged. With anyone else I would have assumed it was no big deal, but Trent's grip on my hands told me otherwise. "I made you uncomfortable after the photoshoot. You've barely been able to stay in the same room without getting embarrassed."

"I wasn't embarrassed. I was self-conscious." I took a deep breath and tried to explain what I'd wanted to tell him for years. "The session was hot. My reaction...." I trailed off, the words not coming out.

"We're as bad as each other, aren't we?" It was a question, but not one at the same time. He was right—two peas in a pod. Completely incapable of communicating with each other like adults and now so tentative around each other it was starting to get ridiculous.

My cell pinged with an email, but I ignored it. This fragile bridge we were building was far too important to fob off. I huffed a laugh out that held no humor. "Maybe one day we'll be normal."

"Normal is overrated. But talking to my best friend again without walking on eggshells might be nice. Can we hit Pause and try to get back to normal for a while?" He squeezed my hands again before letting go, smiling tentatively. "I don't want to lose what we have."

"Neither do I." I shook my head. Breakfast was our thing; we cooked together often, and my appetite was returning with a vengeance. I couldn't remember the last time I ate a proper meal, and if Trent's hollow cheeks were anything to go by, he hadn't had much either. "Want to help me make breakfast?"

He nodded and this time gave me a genuine smile. "I'd like that."

# CHAPTER 11
## TRENT

"You never checked your email," I remarked, noticing his cell flashing.

"Eh. It's Sunday. Whatever it is, it can wait." I could see the twitch in his eye. It was an effort for him to hold off. He wasn't a workaholic, but he did work hard. Often long hours too—there was no such thing as nine-to-five with a wedding photographer. I appreciated that he was prioritizing us; he didn't need to, but I did appreciate it.

I had a scoop of vanilla ice cream at the ready while Angelo finished spooning cinnamon-infused apples onto our crepes. He folded the thin layer over, somehow managing to divide it right down the middle. It didn't surprise me that he cooked like a boss; his mom was a queen of the kitchen, but from the aroma I was salivating over he'd outdone himself this time. I couldn't wait to taste it.

I dropped the scoop into the middle of the plate and added a second before picking up his cell. "It'll drive you insane." I went to hand it to him, but he shook his head, waving me off, concentrating on the second plate. "I know you want to," I teased. "You get this nervous tic in your eye." I reached out and brushed my thumb against his temple before I realized what I was doing. He went as still as a statue, and I couldn't let go, but logically I knew I couldn't keep my fingers curled against his cheek either.

His soft skin against mine had me closing my eyes, sinking into the feeling of him. It was the barest contact, but it was enough to have longing well up within me. It wasn't desire, although that was certainly there. It was an ache. For freedom. A wish that I could step out into the open and spread my rainbow wings. To soar, rather than skulk in the background. It was becoming harder to resist him because I'd realized I didn't want to. I wanted to give in and experience love. I'd never had it before, and the likelihood of having it with Angelo was remote—I didn't even know whether he swung that way and he'd already told me he wanted someone else—but it wasn't so much the sex that I yearned for.

It was intimacy. Trust. A simple touch, like the one I was experiencing at that moment.

Angelo straightened slowly, and I let my hand fall away as we came face-to-face. I'd never get sick of looking into his eyes. Soft and full of affection, they held a warmth that made me want to sink into them. This time, I knew mine reflected that same affection. I loved him, and yet almost since the moment I'd finally understood it, our relationship had been fucked-up. The last couple of months had been torture. "Trent—"

"You should check this," I deflected, knowing I'd give him whatever he asked for in that moment, including my deepest secrets if that was what he wanted. I handed him his cell and he scanned over the email, a look of resignation crossing his face.

"It's nothing. I'll have to send a quick reply after breakfast, but it'll only take me five to do it." He blacked out the screen and dropped it on the countertop before getting back to the crepes.

"Everything okay?" I asked, my question tentative. He didn't look happy. Not angry, but frustrated perhaps? Disappointed? I wasn't sure.

"Yeah, that author I took the photos for was asking whether I could get some more photos but with two men in them. But it's not gonna happen. Not with the model she wants, anyway." He dropped the empty bowl onto the countertop a little too hard, the clang making him flinch.

"Who does she want?" I asked, my gut telling me exactly who it was.

"You." Before I could interrupt him, he held his hand up, silencing me. "The last time we had a shoot, it nearly fucked-up our friendship. I'm not letting it happen again."

"What if we agree it won't?" I asked, propping an elbow on the counter. "It's not like…. I don't know. Surely it's not going to be porn-worthy." At the mention of what I was doing when Angelo walked in on me a couple of months ago, my face flamed and I gulped. Would he bring it up? Would he continue letting me avoid talking about it?

He gazed at me long and hard. "Sure, okay. We can do a test to see if I can take the shots using a tripod and the timer. If it works, we can do the actual shoot whenever I work out the details with the author."

I knew what Angelo was doing, and I didn't know whether to be pissed off or grateful to him. He didn't believe that I'd do it. Giving me a taste of what it might be like so I could back out before he agreed to the photoshoot with this author. But I wanted this. I wanted to break free of the shackles that had bound me for so long.

"Great. Let's eat, then we can get started."

Angelo was quiet throughout breakfast, and my earlier bravado was waning the longer it took me to eat. It was delicious—sweet and spicy at the same time—but nerves churned within. I may want to let go, but the thought was terrifying. The last time I'd tried to do it my world had been turned upside down. I was scared shitless of the consequences of trying to do it again. But I couldn't not try either. Not anymore.

Finally, our plates were empty. I snatched them up and loaded the dishwasher, wiping the counters down as Angelo watched me. I didn't know if I was freaking out, procrastinating, or nervously excited. Perhaps it was a bit of everything, but I wanted it. "Right," I uttered after I realized I had wiped the backsplash for the third time. Angelo was there in front of me, and I swallowed before looking up at him, wide-eyed. I froze. He took the cloth out of my hand and tossed it in the sink before grasping my biceps gently.

"You're pushing yourself past what you're comfortable with. I can see it written all over your face. Don't feel like you need to do this for me. I'm okay with telling her I can't."

"I want to help." I managed to get the words out around the lump that'd formed in my throat, but my voice sounded scratchy even to my own ears.

He didn't say anything in response, but he watched me, studied me. Waiting to see if I gave the barest hint of reluctance. There was trepidation. A hell of a lot of it. But

I'd learned something about myself in these last few weeks. I wanted to give Angelo as much as he gave me. Hurting him, having him avoid me, was hell. I'd wanted to give him space, but the only way I'd been able to do it was to stay away altogether. I'd been sleeping at the station even when I wasn't on shift, because when I was home, I wanted him with me.

Even in my dreams—especially in them—I'd wanted him closer. When I put aside my hang-ups, when I looked into my heart, I saw him front and center. So no, there was no reticence on my part. I wasn't exactly ready to fly the rainbow flag and dance half-naked in the pride parade, but standing next to him for some photos? I could do that.

Angelo apparently saw what he needed from me and nodded. He motioned to his office and I followed him there. He had a stand with a roll of gray paper-like fabric as well as all the camera equipment you could imagine. "We'll do a test shoot against the backdrop. She wants the images silhouetted, so I'll set the big flash umbrella up too. You want to help me with getting this into the living room?"

We quickly set it up, moving equipment and furniture around until Angelo was happy with the lighting. My nerves had subsided—until Angelo clicked the camera into place on his tripod and asked me to stand in front of it so he could line up the shot. Then, the kaleidoscope of butterflies dancing around in my belly were whipped up by a tornado whirling around so fast it made me nauseous. It took everything in me not to run and hide.

Angelo made a few more adjustments and came to stand next to me. He fingered the material of my light sweater and smirked before slipping his hands under it. I gasped at the touch on my skin, my abs quivering. The camera flash lit up the room in bright white light, and I flinched. Angelo leaned in closer, bending down as if he was going to kiss me. I was sure my wide-eyed stare and thumping heart gave away how overwhelmed I was, but he just grinned before tugging on it, pulling the sweater and my tee straight over my head in one fell swoop.

"You're trying to make me freeze, aren't you?" I laughed.

"I am, but you're a big boy. You'll survive."

The laughing and joking around became serious when he cupped my face and stepped in closer, until our bodies were touching. I held on to his hips, unable to break his stare and unwilling too. The flash was lighting up my periphery, but my vision was filled with Angelo.

I sucked in a breath, and with every ounce of bravery I held, I slid my hands under Angelo's tee and flexed my fingers over firm muscle. He let out a strangled moan, and I was empowered. Emboldened to continue exploring. I tugged off his shirt and let it fall to the floor by our feet, then walked my fingers up to his chest. Flashes went off in the background as we stared into each other's eyes. I swayed closer to him and I felt Angelo do the same. My heart thudded in my chest, and my lips were suddenly too dry. I wet them, my tongue tracing the line of my bottom lip, and Angelo's whiskey eyes darkened, his pupils blowing out. His cock twitched against my belly, and my eyes slid closed on a low moan. I waited, I wished.

But the kiss never came.

Angelo shifted, trailing his fingertips around my shoulders as he moved behind me. With one arm over my shoulder and the other under, Angelo pulled me against him and buried his face in the junction of my throat. I dropped my head back against his shoulder and shuddered when Angelo breathed out, his hot breath ghosting over my skin. His hard length pressed against my back, and he dragged his hand down to my hip, holding me there as he rocked gently against me. I hissed out a breath, and he moved his hand so his thumb was caressing my throat, but he didn't stop. He shifted again, his hand gently closing around my throat, and I froze.

Memories crashed over me.

Pain. Anger. Powerlessness.

I tensed, my shallow breaths coming out hard and fast. My vision clouded. I heard a noise that sounded animalistic. Tortured. Wounded. I found myself pushing him off. Fighting for my life. I thrashed, yanking myself out of my godfather's grip. I wouldn't let it happen again. I wouldn't let him abuse me another time. I wasn't the scared sixteen-year-old anymore. I was stronger. I was a survivor. I'd never be hurt like that again.

I could hear my middle name being called, but I didn't know why. All I could focus on was the hand that'd closed around my throat. The one that had held me in place while he yanked my sweats and underwear down and slammed into me dry, pushing past the ring of muscle that was unyielding except for the force he applied. Pounding into me through my screams and cries. Pinning me to him while he rutted against me. Forcing me into submission by cutting off my airway. Hatred, vile and evil spewed from his mouth, poisoning my thoughts and making me detest that fundamental piece of my soul reserved for Angelo.

I couldn't let it happen again. I wouldn't. Angelo was too important. He was everything. I wanted happiness. I wanted love. He wasn't going to take it away from me again.

My throat closed over, and only a sob escaped. I spun and struck out blindly with a roar, my fear and anger strengthening me. My fist connected, and skin and bone yielded. There was a shout and a flash in my eyes.

Everything snapped back into focus, and I froze.

Angelo, not Ryan.

Our living room, not a kitchen.

A camera, not a football match.

My breaths heaved in and out of my chest as I took in the sight before me. Angelo had staggered back and was using the wall to prop himself up. He was clutching his jaw and looking at me with a mixture of horror and fear. What had happened? Oh God. What had I done?

Tears sprung to my eyes and I staggered to him, but Angelo held his hand up, stopping me dead in my tracks. "Don't," he warned. My worst nightmare was coming true before my eyes. I'd hurt him. I'd broken us. I'd ruined the one thing my fucked-up mind was trying to protect.

I couldn't hold myself up anymore, my knees buckling under me. Pain flooded my chest, pulling me under like the swelling of the tide. This time when the animalistic sound came out, I knew it was me making it. I sobbed, grieving for everything that Ryan had stolen from me. That I'd run from.

Angelo's touch was tentative on my hair. He ran his fingers through it and whispered, "Hey. Hey, it's okay. I'm okay."

"I'm sorry," I sobbed. "I thought you were him. Your hand—he did that. I got scared. I'm sorry. I'm so, so sorry." I turned to him and hugged him close, his warmth seeping into the bone-deep cold that had shrouded me. I cried. I couldn't stop the tears even if I'd tried. When he embraced me back, the relief pulled me from the brink of drowning. It let me breathe again. A fresh set of tears fell, and I pressed closer, desperate to hold onto him.

"Who did you think I was, Trent?" he asked quietly after a time. He'd never stopped running his fingers through my hair. He'd never loosened his grip on me. He was the only thing keeping me grounded. The only thing tethering me to earth, stopping me from getting sucked up in a tailspin and losing myself completely.

His question settled on me, and the walls I'd hid behind, the ones I'd tried to protect myself with gave way. Crumbled around me, leaving me amid the rubble. With the walls went any desire to keep hiding. I wanted out of this prison and the nightmare that my life had turned into. I wanted freedom and happiness so badly I craved it. I sensed how close it was. I could almost taste it. And I could finally see the path. I could finally see the light guiding me.

"Him." Angelo's hand stilled in my hair for only a moment, but it was enough to jolt me into action. "My godfather. He hurt me." Those words, the first of my story, weren't hard to pronounce, but I'd never uttered anything more difficult in my life.

"I'm here, Trent," Angelo encouraged. That was all I needed this time. I'd hidden from him. I'd covered up my shame in an armor of bravado and a sword filled with the same poison used on me. I'd hidden from the horrible things I'd done before and after. I was now at a crossroads. The light was pointing down one path, but I could see from its aura the dim opening to the other way too. A rocky track covered with brambles. One that I knew I'd travel alone.

I took a breath and pulled my face away from his tear-soaked chest to look up to him. I needed to see his beautiful face one last time before I confessed to him. My greatest fear had always been seeing Ryan again, but in the years since I'd met Angelo that had shifted. My greatest fear now was losing my best friend.

From the moment we'd met, he'd been there for me, and the thought of him walking away because of my shameful history broke me. But I had to tell him, because that poison-tipped sword had turned on us now. It was going to drag me into the depths of oblivion if I didn't come clean, and in doing so I'd hurt him. I couldn't do that. I wouldn't. If it meant saying goodbye to Angelo now, I'd do that to protect him.

I memorized every inch of Angelo's face. His hair always swooped back, but it was now falling to the side. I wished I could run my fingers through it to see if it was as soft as it looked. His eyes that were always so warm and filled with affection. The curve of his lips I'd wanted to kiss, and his strong nose and jaw. Then I looked down, gathering my courage to come clean.

"He was my first. I was in trouble; he tried to teach me a lesson. I… It wasn't good. I hated it." I took a deep breath and held it, willing the wobble in my voice to subside. When I let it out, I continued, but my voice broke and the tears started again, "He hurt me. I remember it. I wish I didn't, but I remember every single part of that night." Shaking my head, I tried to keep the memories at bay. They always came rushing back when I wasn't strong enough to block them anymore, but I was already on the brink. I didn't think I could handle them assailing me. My next words were nothing more than a whisper. "I never wanted him to do it again. I never wanted anyone to do it again."

The look of horror on his face told me he understood exactly what I was telling him. He knew why I'd kept my past locked down. Why I was so ashamed of my stupidity and what I'd done. But instead of blame, his question surprised me. "How old were you, Trent?"

"Sixteen," I huffed, remembering how grown up I'd felt drinking my first beer in an adult's presence. "I haven't been able to drink beer since." I shook my head. "I only had one. My parents thought I'd drunk all of them, but it was Ryan. He told them I got drunk. They were gonna send me back to him to clean up."

"Was that why you were being punished? Because he said you drank the beer?" Angelo grated out the words between clenched teeth, his hands shaking as he rubbed my back.

"No. I told him my secret. He proved to me I was wrong, but I wasn't. It's still in me." I wiped my cheeks with the back of my hand and sucked in a shuddering breath. Sitting on the floor with Angelo wrapped around me as I confessed what I'd been keeping from him and everyone else for over a decade and a half wasn't how I'd pictured the day beginning, but now it was there, I had to keep following the light. I couldn't give up and let darkness swallow me again.

"He proved it by hurting you?" Angelo asked tentatively, pain and grief in his eyes but tension radiating from his body.

I nodded and looked down, then whispered, "He put it

in me. Held me down and showed me that it wasn't what I ever wanted again."

"Motherfuck," Angelo growled and dropped his arms. He clenched his fists and breathed in and out. Long, slow breaths that seemed to calm him down while I sat there, my heart shattering. I'd shared my secrets twice in my life. I'd told two people, and the fallout was colossal.

A breath hitched in my throat, and I tried to scramble to my feet. I wanted to run again. To escape the pain stabbing me over and over. Angelo didn't want me anymore. He'd seen my damage. He was pulling away. My nightmares were coming true and I couldn't bear to watch it happen.

But Angelo stopped me. He reached out for me and hauled me back to him. Held me tight, his grip bruising as he rocked us gently. I didn't even realize I was crying until he wiped away my tears with his thumb.

"I'm sorry, Trent. So sorry you had to go through that." He repeated it over and over, softly, gently. His voice low, his accent more pronounced. He murmured comfort to me until I'd cried my tears dry and exhaustion permeated every cell in my body. I slumped in his arms and he pulled me tighter.

"Angelo," I whispered, not knowing how to tell him what I needed. Not even knowing what it was myself.

"I've got you," he promised, part lifting me, part guiding me to the sofa. He stretched out, pulling me between his open legs until I was curled up on his chest. His arms and legs snaked around me, holding me close. "Sleep, baby. Sleep."

I closed my eyes, his warmth surrounding me. His scent enveloping me. Safe in his arms, I drifted.

FINGERS RUNNING THROUGH MY HAIR ROUSED ME; A GENTLE kiss on my forehead brought me back to wakefulness. I groaned, my head pounding. "Shh, go back to sleep," Angelo whispered, and I nuzzled back into him. I wanted him to kiss me again. I wished he would. But he didn't. He did hold me close as I drifted again though and that was more than I ever could have asked for.

I floated in warmth, a tight embrace. Firm muscle, the most inviting pillow I'd ever laid on. Fingertips rested lightly along my spine, lips against my forehead. His warm breath in my hair. Angelo's breathing was deep, like he'd fallen asleep too. I wanted to touch him as well, to comfort him like he'd done me. I shifted, and he startled, his arms coming around me tighter as he mumbled hoarsely, "I'm awake, what's wrong?"

"Nothing, Ang." I glided my fingertips over his chest, touching him for the first time. Mapping the contours of his pecs and abs.

He hummed, and I could hear the need in his voice. The want. I didn't realize I'd paused until he grasped my hand and whispered, "Please don't stop. It's been so long since anyone's touched me. I need it." The trauma from my sharing faded as I went back to lazily drawing my fingers over his skin. When I pressed my lips to his throat, he let out a strangled moan and tightened his arm around me. I closed my eyes and breathed him in. The light at the end of the tunnel I'd been travelling down was suddenly a lot brighter. It was Angelo. My guiding light.

"You're lonely, aren't you?" I asked quietly. He gave me the smallest nod in response, and it broke my heart. He deserved everything. Whoever it was he was in love with was a damn fool, and I despised her for hurting him. "You told me you loved someone. Do you remember? You were nearly asleep."

I felt his heart rate spike, thudding against his chest under my cheek, and he swallowed. "I didn't realize. Did I say who?"

"No. But I can tell you, whoever she is she's clueless. She has to be." I shook my head, frustrated that she'd kept her distance from Angelo. Angry that he was alone because she didn't love him back. "Jesus, she's put you through hell. You're in love with her and she's left you hanging for how long? I wish you could get over her. Find someone else."

Angelo shifted then, scooting away from me. I sat up, giving him the space he needed but regretting my line of questioning immediately. He was still facing me, but had curled in on himself. And I was no longer able to touch him. Wringing his hands together, he took a deep breath and let it out, only then looking up at me. "I'm not straight, Trent. I'm demisexual."

"Okay." I nodded, not really sure how that changed anything. Maybe I was clueless… actually, I was. "What does that mean, Angelo?"

"I don't feel any sexual attraction unless I've built up a relationship with a person. Instant lust for someone doesn't exist for me. I can't walk up to someone and want to jump into bed with them. I can't even go on a few dates with someone and want them like that. It's taken me years to feel that."

"And you can't just switch it off and move on," I finished for him. "Does she know? Is she yanking your chain, fucking you around?"

He squeezed his eyes closed and blew out a breath. "It's a man. I'm homoromantic demisexual."

Shock hit me square in the chest. He loved a man.

He. Loved. A. Man.

My mind blanked. Whited out entirely.

Shocked surprise held me fast, my mouth hanging open—catching flies, like my grandma used to say. He'd hidden it from me, let me think that he was attracted to women because of my warped world view. *Fuck.* Shame replaced the shock. Anger at myself replaced the surprise. Disappointment in letting him down, in preventing him from trusting me had me lowering my gaze. I promised myself I'd do better. For him. For me.

Angelo had come out to me, and there was no way I was letting him down again. He'd entrusted me with his truth, and I needed to be there for him. Resolve burned in my veins. No one, especially not Angelo, should be shamed for who they loved.

Then it hit me.

*No one should be shamed for who they love.*

Yet that's what I'd been doing to myself for all those years. Never admitting my sexuality to anyone because of what had happened. My godfather had cracked my foundation with his words, his actions. The fallout from that night was like an avalanche. Picking up speed, the mass hurtled down the mountain collecting everything in its path. Destroying everything.

His words still swirled around in my head, and I fought to block them out. Fought to let the realization that forcing myself into a het mold wasn't the only option. In doing that, in projecting my self-loathing onto everyone else, I'd hurt Angelo. I'd made him hide from me. My best friend had to have been living in hell, not even safe to be himself in his own home. The same man I'd fallen in love with. I reached for his hand and threaded our fingers together, needing to touch him in that moment.

"I'm sorry for being such an insensitive bastard all these years. I've hated myself for so long. Blamed myself for what Ryan did to me. The what-ifs never stop. What if I hadn't admitted it out loud? If I hadn't provoked him until he decided to teach me a lesson? What if I'd just stayed in the closet? Everything would have been fine. But I was stupid. I was sixteen and clueless. Then he showed me what it was like to hate something so fundamentally you have to stamp it out. He infected me with it, and I've spent years projecting it onto everyone else. Onto you without even knowing. No wonder you didn't tell me. I'm surprised you haven't told me to fuck off and never spoken to me again." I paused my ramble at that thought. "Why didn't you? I don't deserve you, Angelo. Why'd you put up with me? Why didn't you kick me to the curb?"

Angelo looked at me, his eyes full of a mix of pain, trepidation, and something else unnamed. "I've told you before. Because I love you. I'll always choose you."

# CHAPTER 12
## ANGELO

The room went silent for the second time in as many minutes. I'd just dropped a bombshell on Trent. Coming out wasn't something I'd planned on doing today or anytime soon actually, but his story, his horror-filled moments that changed the way he viewed himself made me understand him on a level I never had before.

Instead of thinking of him like a badly behaved frat boy when he saw two men together, I finally understood that it was a reminder of the evil his godfather had left him with. The hatred. The self-loathing. Now all I had to do was make him realize that he was perfectly imperfect. He'd survived being raped. Now he needed help—and not just my own, but professional help—to heal from what he'd endured.

When he'd asked me if I remembered our conversation, it'd scared me. Coming out was one thing, but this was too much to pile on him. Yet, when he asked why I was still friends with him, I found I couldn't lie. He deserved to know he was special. I didn't want to build a charade that would inevitably come crashing down. It was now or never. But Trent's silence after my words terrified me. Would I shatter any chance at building our relationship because of what I'd just said? I was me. I couldn't change that. But should I have stayed quiet?

He released my hand and stood, walking away from the sofa I was sitting on. He turned away from me, hiding his expression. I didn't need to see it though. His ramrod straight back, the fists he'd clench and release, and his choppy breathing were all signs I'd seen before. I knew them like I knew the back of my hand.

He was angry.

My hope was snuffed out like a flame starved of oxygen. Like sunlight during an eclipse. This was the end of us. Unless I truly was a masochist, I knew I needed to move on. And living here would eventually kill me. Maybe not literally, but any chance at living a happy life and finding someone who could love me back would die a slow death. His feelings about my revelation were obvious. Any hope that one day he might open his eyes and realize how I'd treasure him and love him was an impossible dream. He wouldn't let me, because he simply didn't love me back. *He doesn't love me.*

I closed my eyes and willed myself not to break down in front of him. Or smash a hole through the wall. I wanted to run and hide at the same time as screaming and lashing out in frustration.

I gathered every ounce of strength I possessed and stood up, ready to walk the long way around the back of the sofa to my bedroom. My keys were there and I needed to get on the open road. Winding corners and steep bluffs with Lake Wakatipu by my side. At least I'd be able to lick my wounds in private. But I didn't have the chance. Trent spun around when I stood and pinned me with his gaze. The emotions running across his face stilled me in my tracks. Anger, loathing, pain. I stepped back, not because I was scared of him—he'd shown me for years how gentle a soul he was—but because I didn't have the strength to face him. I was broken and bleeding inside. He'd flayed me.

"We… I…." He let out a frustrated breath and tried to continue, but I cut him off. I couldn't listen to it.

"You don't have to say anything, Trent. There's nothing more you need to say." I sounded defeated even to my own ears.

"Angelo, what are you talking about? Of course there's more that I need to say."

"No, you don't. I'm not sure where this leaves us, whether we can still be friends." I ran my fingers through my hair, pushing my bangs back off my face as I tried to come to terms with the fact that at some level I knew I would always love him and it'd break me to see him with someone else, but it would inevitably happen. Although we'd always been friends, the idea of staying that way after what I'd revealed seemed like an impossibility now. "Maybe one day, but I think I probably need a clean break. You're angry, and I'm upset. I don't want either of us to say something we'll regret, so let's just leave it."

"Like hell," he huffed, frustration lacing his tone. "I've been sitting here dirty at this woman you're in love with since the day you told me about her. Wondering how she could be so blind not to see you. Not to see how lucky she was. How privileged she was for having your love. And all along it's been me. I've done nothing but hurt you. I say shit you shouldn't have to put up with. I've done things, I still do things that should make you ashamed of me and yet, here you are. Telling me you'll always choose me. That you love *me*. That's what you're saying isn't it? That it's not some random woman you're in love with, but me?"

He paused, wild-eyed and amped up, waiting for me to acknowledge that yes, it was exactly what I was saying. I could only manage a nod because I knew if I opened my mouth, I'd let slip just how hard I'd fallen for him.

"My anger, my frustration, it's not with you. It's with me. Myself. Like usual. I fuck everything up—"

"Don't flatter yourself, Trent. My falling for you isn't a failing on your part," I sneered, feeling all kinds of foolish and frustrated with myself.

"No." He shook his head and took a step closer, getting in my personal space. "My failing is not seeing it earlier. My failing is not telling you that I feel the same. My failing is denying that I was gay for so long that I hurt you. No matter how much I wanted to believe the lie, the truth is in front of me." He reached for my hand and linked our fingers together. The warmth of his grip, the strength in those healing hands momentarily distracted me from what he was saying. "My fuckup is that I've let you think for far too long that you're not everything to me. That I let you think for a moment I don't love you too."

I sucked in a breath and heard a rushing in my ears. Did I hear him right? Did that mean… I wasn't totally wrong, was I? My heart hammered in my chest, sending my pulse skyrocketing. "What are you saying, Trent? Spell it out for me."

"You said you weren't sure where this conversation left us." He brought our joined hands to his lips and kissed my fingers with soft lips. I'd yearned to do that to him or be kissed by him. Now that it'd happened, it left me breathless. "It leaves us right here, Angelo, with me telling you that I love you too. I think I always have." He smiled, a sweet, carefree smile that I'd never seen on him. He looked almost boyish. Innocent. As if he was filled with hope and love, and in that moment I knew he was. He laughed, pure unfettered joy in the sound. "I'm gay, Angelo, and I love you. God, that's the most freeing thing I've ever said. It's like a weight has been lifted."

I grinned back at him, sure I had hearts in my eyes and the goofiest smile on my face. "I love you too, Trent."

We stared at each other, simply leaning into the other's touch. It was as if I was looking at him anew.

His dark eyes blazed with a warmth I'd never seen before. It was life. As if he'd found his spark. With one hand on his back, I brought my other up to his face and ran my fingertips over his stubble. His eyes fluttered closed at my gentle touch, and he swayed forward, coming even closer to me. When he opened them his pupils were blown, desire radiating from them. The smile fell from his lips and he reached up to cup my face, eliminating the remaining distance between us. I sighed when he ran his thumb over my cheek before moving his hand to my nape. The simple act of connecting with him, his hand to my face, was enough to keep me sustained. I could have stared into his deep browns for hours. But the warmth and adoration he was looking at me with made me greedy for more. My eyes slid closed as I brought my mouth down to his and pressed our lips together.

It was an innocent kiss. No tongue or wild clashing teeth, no grinding against each other or stripping off our clothes to race toward the next base. But it was perfection.

The press of pillowy lips against mine. His sharp inhale as I repeated it. His shudder when I ran my hands down his back to hold him close. My blissed-out moan when he held me tighter and kissed me again. I could get lost in him. One day I would. But for now, I had his kiss. I'd waited years for it, and it was worth every moment.

I pulled back and rested my forehead against his. Keeping my eyes closed, I breathed him in and smiled. When I finally opened them, I saw Trent's own smile hadn't faded. I brushed my lips, a whisper of a kiss, against the corner of his upturned ones, and it made him smile wider, a laugh bubbling to the surface. He squeezed me tight and blinked open his eyes. He opened his mouth as if to say something, but his cell chimed from over in the kitchen. It was a tone I knew well and disappointment slammed into me.

"Bugger," he cursed. "I need to go to work."

I brushed my thumb over his stubble again, feeling every rough hair against me. "I'll be right here, Trent."

The rest of the day passed slowly, dragging while I watched the clock like a hawk. Every second that ticked by felt like an hour and every hour a week. Trent didn't finish his shift until the early morning hours and I had a wedding to wake up for, so I couldn't wait up for him. But I still found myself waiting for him to come home. I mentally kicked myself. I'd spent half the day in a daze with my head in the clouds, and I needed to snap out of it. I had work to finish and groceries to shop for.

I started with the album I was compiling and chose the best of the photos to edit then send to my clients. It was from a wedding I'd shot a month earlier and some of the photos made me smile. They were nice people, completely laid-back and filled with laughter the whole day, and the photos showed it. There were a lot of candid shots, everyone with smiles and excitement in their eyes.

I looked at the time after I'd finally wrapped up and understood why I was starving. And exhausted. I'd worked for nearly eight hours solid. My stomach grumbled as I trudged into the kitchen, rubbing my eyes. I wanted something easy, and when I spied the chicken and vegetables, I decided on a stir-fry. Trent would eat during his shift, but whenever he worked nights I cooked him dinner—he did the same for me whenever I was working evenings. So I cooked, putting a bowl away for Trent in the refrigerator and eating mine sitting at the breakfast bar where I'd had my morning coffee.

What a crazy day it'd been. That morning I'd been lamenting barely speaking with Trent, and now we were… well, I wasn't exactly sure, but after years of loving him from afar, he now knew. And he felt the same way too. I sighed happily, but it turned to a groan when I looked at the clock on the wall. I'd barely wasted any time at all. Less than half an hour had passed since I'd walked into the kitchen, and I'd managed to cook and eat.

I cleaned up, then walked around aimlessly, tidying up and putting on a load of washing. I hated laundry but it needed to be done, and I was bored enough to at least start it. Before I started on my bathroom, I called my brother, wondering what he and Mason were up to.

Ricky had been over to the States recently and had come back with a surprise that made me incredibly happy for him. He'd been going out of his mind over two men, falling for both but not knowing how to approach either. Scared that he'd played into every stereotype of a pansexual person—the only thing he hadn't done was fall for his cookware—he held back. Mason and Ricky had stayed here in Queenstown waiting for Caden to call for weeks after he'd left to be with his sister while she had her baby. They'd been worried sick about him when he cut off all contact. It was justified too. He'd gone through hell in the weeks following Gracie's birth. The moment Ricky and Mace found out what he was going through, they were on a plane to go to him. It'd taken something as serious as Caden's life falling apart to push them past the discomfort of talking it out. But as soon as they did, they came together, being there for Caden and each other during the longest winter I was sure Ricky had ever experienced. They'd gone to the US with a mission—to help bring Caden and his adopted daughter home—and their missing pieces were now only a few days away from arriving.

They'd finally be a family. Mason, Caden, and Gracie were exactly what my brother had wanted and never known he needed.

Looking back on all his relationships, I could see why they'd never worked. The dynamic was never right. Ricky was more like our parents than he cared to admit, but I didn't see that as a fault. They loved big and so did he. But where Mamma and Papá were swingers, he was exclusive. He just needed more than one person in a relationship if it was going to last. Ricky didn't smother his partners, from what I'd seen, but he had too big a heart to give it all to one person. Knowing that he'd found three people to give that love to made me happy for him.

I shook my head, unable to imagine being in a triad. It wasn't because I didn't think it'd work or it was wrong; I just couldn't imagine ever looking at another person and feeling the same as what I did for Trent. The goofy smile I was sure I was wearing made me laugh. Excitement pulsed through me and butterflies took flight. I'd kissed him, and he'd kissed me back. I grinned a little harder and those butterflies did a loop the loop. I wanted to pinch myself, but hell if I would. There was no way I was risking waking up from this dream.

Ricky's cell rang twice before he picked it up. "*Buongiorno*, Ang," he answered, audibly out of breath.

"If I've interrupted you just hang up and call me back when you're not naked." I shuddered, not wanting to imagine my brother nude, and then laughed for all the times I had seen him sprint across the house with no clothes on to get his cell.

"No, we've just come back from a run. And be real, do you think I'd answer my cell?" I could hear Mace chuckling and his comment of "Oh, hell no" was mumbled close enough to the speaker that I knew he'd be getting up close and personal with my brother.

"Okay," I answered, sounding as awkward as I felt. "I'm bored so I'm calling you guys. When does Caden get here and what are we bringing?"

"We?" Ricky asked, although it wasn't really a question. "Angelo, I'm not sure about Trent—"

"Look, I know he's had a few issues in the past—"

"Yeah, okay. We'll call losing his shit with Ford and Reef, and the countless times he's tossed out a smartassed insult about something being gay, issues." He barely paused to take a breath. He was on a roll and the sarcasm was dripping from his voice. "Oh, and let's not forget the dildo incident too when he almost went nuclear with even the suggestion of another cock getting near him—"

"You finished?" I ground out. "Because, yes, I remember every one of those—"

"So you understand why I've got an issue with him?" He paused, and I sighed.

"I do, and I know you'll never forgive him."

Ricky groaned, his frustration showing. He was out of patience. "Neither should you, Angelo!"

I ignored his outrage on my behalf and pleaded with him. "Trent… he won't say anything to upset the three of you, okay? He's more than what you think he is. Please, Rick."

He huffed, and I could picture him shaking his head and clenching his jaw tight to stop himself saying what he really wanted to say in that moment. I could hazard a guess, but I knew I wouldn't like the answer. So I waited, hopeful that he'd extend the invitation to Trent, knowing if he didn't, I wouldn't be going either. "Fine. Fine, he can come. But if he says anything even remotely out of line—"

"We're out. I get it."

"No, Angelo. He's out. You're always welcome, no matter what."

I didn't respond to that, changing the subject instead, going back to my original question—what could we take with us. What could I say without revealing way too much about the tentative relationship we were trying to navigate? We hashed out the details and I agreed that Trent and I would bring a pot of Ricky's favorite stew. It was spring, but still cool at night so it'd be perfect to take. I made a list, ordered the groceries online, vacuumed the floors, and put the washing in the dryer before finally giving up the waiting game and heading to bed. Lying there, I knew I was completely gone for him when I desperately wanted to hear his voice before I fell asleep. I couldn't. He rarely took calls during his shift and when he did, they were clipped. He was usually run off his feet, so I sent him a text instead:

**Angelo: Dinner's waiting for you when you get home. Working early tomorrow so wake me when you get in. Night**

I didn't get a response but that was okay. I didn't expect him to even see it until the end of his shift. But when I finally closed my eyes, I did it knowing Trent knew I'd thought of him, and that brought a smile to my face.

My alarm buzzed and I woke to strong arms and heat enveloping me. Trent was spooning me. I silenced the alarm and shifted to look at him, running my fingers over his cheek. I wasn't normally a morning person, but this morning's view was well worth waking up for.

Trent's lips were slightly open, and I could feel his chest rise and fall in deep, even breaths against my side. His face, relaxed in sleep, didn't show any of the stress he normally held. The attitude he portrayed was a shield, a front to ward off people getting close to him. But he'd never done it with me. Still, he'd kept walls up between us; we both had, and I'd only just realized the extent of what he'd been through.

I leaned forward and kissed him gently on his stubbled cheek, and he sighed before his lips tilted up. I hummed, a low satisfied noise, and Trent slowly blinked his eyes open.

"Hi," I whispered, smiling at him. "I'm sorry I woke you up. I was gonna sneak out but I couldn't resist kissing you."

"I'm glad you did." He rolled onto his back and stretched, raising his arms above his head and groaning as he moved. I nearly swallowed my tongue. All that skin, his warmth, displayed like a treat meant just for me. I wanted to love on him, but if I got started I wouldn't even show up at the wedding I had scheduled to shoot that day.

As if he sensed my inability to think straight, Trent reached over and cupped my face, running his thumb along my bottom lip. "You were tired last night. You didn't even stir when I hugged you." He paused then added, "I hope you don't mind that I slept in your bed." He looked a little embarrassed, color tinting his cheeks.

"I never mind." I gave him a small smile and brushed my fingers down his chest, getting lost in the steady beat of his heart against my palm. "Can I kiss you, Trent?" I hovered over him, waiting until he gave me a sign. It came in the form of Trent wrapping his hand around the back of my neck and pulling me forward until our lips brushed together. Soft, gentle caresses like the night before. No tongue, just presses of lips against lips. Mingled breaths and fingertips trailing over warm skin.

"Please, Angelo," Trent begged against my lips. "More."

This time when I kissed him, when I opened my mouth, he did the same. His tongue met mine and I floated in the satin slide of it against my own. His soft lips, his rough cheeks, his smooth tongue overwhelmed me.

I was in heaven.

Electricity didn't spark, tingles didn't race up and down my body. It was so much more than that. It was transcendent. Like the forces creating the universe and the tiny speck of dust we lived on. We shifted, aligning our bodies until there was barely a whisper of space between us, and I kissed him like my life depended on it. Slow and passionate, yet playful too. I nipped his bottom lip and he used blunt fingernails to trail a line down my spine to my pajama pants, making me shiver. I kissed him until I was gasping for breath, and I hoped he understood how long I'd loved him, how much. When I pulled back, his lips were swollen and his eyes kiss drunk, and I knew I looked the same. That made me smile.

"I could kiss you all day," Trent murmured, running his hand over my ass. My response got caught in my throat as I used every ounce of willpower I possessed not to grind against him. His soft chuckle turned into a gasp when I lost the battle of wills and pressed closer, my covered erection sliding against his.

"Fuck," I hissed, knowing I needed to pull back. As much as I wanted him, as much as I wished we could lose ourselves in each other, we weren't ready. We lived together, but we hadn't dated. We hadn't held hands for the first time walking along the lake, we hadn't eaten together, sharing our food, we hadn't cuddled in a movie theater or kissed under the moonlight at our front stoop. There was no way I was skipping that and depriving us of all those moments.

I shifted, pulling away a fraction, and Trent sucked in a breath. His eyes were closed, his brow creased in concentration as he slowly released his hold on me. Blowing out the breath he was holding, he blinked his eyes open and gave me a tentative smile.

"Can we go slow, Angelo? I want to be ready…."

"I want that, too." I kissed his forehead softly, a brush of my lips against the line that still marred his brow and climbed out of bed. "But I still want to sleep with you at night. Is that okay?"

"I'd like that." The smile Trent gave me this time was more genuine. Confident. Relief filled me. I didn't want to screw this up, and taking it slow meant we'd both be ready.

I showered and dressed, double-checked my equipment and loaded my car. Sitting in the confines of the garage, I watched as my window descended and Trent leaned in, pressing a kiss to my lips. "I need a few more hours sleep," he mumbled, rubbing his eyes.

"Go." I smiled at him. "My bed's calling your name." I brushed my fingertips over his cheek as he rested his arms on the door, and I added, "I'll be back late tonight. They want me there for the full reception."

"It's my second-last night shift before I swap to days. I'll be home after noon tomorrow."

I smiled at him and covered his hand with mine. I hated that he worked a string of fourteen-hour shifts. He was always exhausted at the end of it, and it was no different this time. But he'd soon have a few days off to recover. Then he was going back to day shifts for his next set of ten shifts. It was always easier on him; less crazy shit happened and it didn't knock his body around so much either.

"Be safe." I opened the garage door using the remote stuck to my dash, and Trent stepped away, watching me reverse out. I flashed him a smile and drove away, memorizing him standing in our garage in only a pair of blue plaid pajama bottoms.

The wedding was out of town in a picturesque chapel overlooking one of the smaller lakes in the area, Lake Hayes. Surrounded by snowcapped mountains soaring high into the sky, the verdant green of the valley below, and the deep blue of the lake, the scenery was stunning. Combine that with a perfect day with not even a cloud in the sky, and the photos would be gorgeous.

I loved the venue too. An old stone chapel with a towering spire and glass-walled altar overlooked the lake. It was the main attraction, but the stone reception hall and cabins that made up the small resort were no less beautifully built. The stonemasonry was completed by skilled hands and the thick timber roof trusses always drew my gaze upwards. The whole resort photographed beautifully, and having the two brides there—who were already some of my favorite clients—would make it even more special. Laid-back and quick to poke fun at each other, they'd had me snorting with laughter during our consults.

What met me, though, wasn't the laid-back, fun-loving ladies I knew. Cherie looked like she was having a meltdown, panicking and pacing the room in a fluffy bathrobe with her cell glued to her ear. The hairdresser and makeup artist were with Kora, her fiancée, so she should have had her feet up enjoying the breakfast platter and mimosa, but her words were clipped. The look she shot to the woman standing across the room was sharp, and I knew these moments shouldn't be caught on camera.

Before I could back out of the room, Cherie hung up her cell, placed it gently down on the counter, and asked in a deathly calm tone, "Mom, would you like to explain to me why the kitchen is telling me that a last-minute change to the menu was made for both breakfast platters?" When her mother looked haughtily over to her, I could see the feigned innocence as if it were a neon flashing light above her head. The flash of a smirk, which she quickly covered up, was a dead giveaway. "Don't pretend you're clueless. You added a selection of mixed nuts when you know damn well my fiancée is allergic to them."

"I thought it would be lovely to have some nuts with the fruit," she replied matter-of-factly, raising an eyebrow as if to challenge her.

I'd heard enough. I motioned to the door, and when I realized neither of them would see me, I scurried out. There was no way I was getting involved in that. Cherie's mom had been awful from the start, trying to do everything in her power to tear them apart, and now it seemed like she'd stepped it up a notch. I headed to Kora's suite across the homestead and got busy snapping photographs after I warned her away from the platter.

The day went off without too much more of a hitch, but I didn't see Cherie's mother around again either. I'd heard rumors that she'd been asked to leave and hadn't gone easily, but I'd been busy taking photos of Cherie and Kora's kids. The little boy and girl were adorable, and I'd gladly whisked them away when Cherie's brother had barged into the room warning Kora about the platter and explaining what was going on.

By the time I fell into bed that night, exhausted but glad that I'd captured their happiest moments together, all I wanted was to curl up around Trent. It wouldn't happen that night but that was okay. I could wait.

I HATED WAKING TRENT UP AFTER SUCH A LONG SHIFT, BUT he'd asked me to in his note. We were already late to Ricky's house. It didn't matter though; it wasn't like the get-together to welcome Caden, his daughter, Gracie, and his father, Gabe, home was a surprise party. As long as we were in time for supper, it'd be fine. I transferred the casserole I'd cooked to a thick terracotta bowl, covered it, and wrapped it in a towel so Trent could hold it on the drive over. Then I made a coffee for Trent, doctoring it just how he liked it before taking it into him. He was in his bed today, taking the room the farthest away from the kitchen and my office so he could sleep. Six hours wasn't enough, but it was better than nothing.

I opened the door and peeked inside, slipping in before placing the mug gently down on the nightstand. Trent was sprawled out on his stomach, lying diagonally across the bed. The dark sheets pooled low around his waist and contrasted with the threadbare white tee he wore. There was a strip of smooth skin that peeked above the waistline of his pajama pants—this time a gray set—that I wanted to lick. I palmed my semi, reveling in the sexual attraction that washed over me. I wasn't a creeper: it wasn't like I was going to jack off in his room while he slept, but damn, he certainly was something to look at. One arm was up near his face, the other tucked into his side. One knee was bent, his perfect ass right there for me to stare at. And I finally could.

I sat down close to him and ran my fingers through his short hair, then continued on over his shoulders and down his back. He groaned as if he were in pain and shifted, rolling onto his side and curling around me. I leaned down and pressed a kiss to his temple, and this time he hummed, his lips tilting up in a smile. "Second day in a row you've woken me like this," he mumbled before stretching. He groaned again and moved a hand to his back.

"You okay?" I asked, concern lacing my voice as I rubbed up and down his spine gingerly.

"Yeah, long night. We had call out after call out and there was a lot of heavy lifting. My back's a bit sore, but a hot shower'll help." Trent moved, blinking his eyes open and placing his hand on my leg. I smiled at the small move. It wasn't much, but it was huge at the same time. Having him show me any kind of affection made me want to pinch myself.

His wince when I touched a sore spot had me concerned. "If you're not feeling up to going tonight, we can cancel. It's not a big deal."

He turned to face me, his eyes staying open for the first time since I woke him up. "No. Your brother'd like you there, and I know you wanna go. Gimme a few minutes and I'll have a shower, then we can leave."

I shifted, letting him sit up, but he threaded our fingers together and tugged me closer. "Hi," he whispered before pressing his lips to mine.

I smiled and kissed him again, murmuring "Hi" back.

It didn't take long for Trent to have a shower and join me in the kitchen as I plucked a bottle of red from the wine rack. I nearly dropped the bottle when I saw him. Dark blue jeans that hugged his thighs and ass, a plain white Henley, and his black leather jacket paired with a chunky pair of boots. The dark stubble on his chin, which was almost thick enough to be a beard, gave him a rougher edge while his cologne had me swaying closer to him, breathing him in.

He smirked, then motioned to the car, picked up the casserole, and headed out with me following like a puppy dog. Shaking out of it, I plucked my keys, wallet, and cell phone off the countertop on the way and drove the few minutes to my brother's house. As we stood on the front step after ringing the doorbell, I slipped my hand under Trent's jacket, low on his back, and rubbed. "How is your back?"

"Good." He nodded and turned to me, moving out of my reach. He motioned to the dish he was holding and asked, "So what did you make?"

I let my hand drop and answered awkwardly. "Just a casserole. Nothing too complicated—meat, potatoes, and pumpkin. Fresh herbs. Lots of garlic and wine."

Ford opened the door and welcomed us, saying "Come on in, guys. We were wondering where you'd gotten to."

"Worked the night shift," Trent explained. "I slept in a bit. Sorry we're late." He pushed past Ford and headed straight for the kitchen, placing the bowl down gently on the countertop. I stood stock still, suddenly not in the mood to be there. Either I'd misread the signs, or Trent didn't want me touching him in front of our closest friends. When Ford tilted his head, looking at me curiously, I plastered on a fake-ass smile and walked in, letting him close the door behind me.

The night went off without too much of a hitch. Ricky had love hearts in his eyes every time he looked at Caden and Mason and was touching one of them the whole night. Caden's pops, Gabe, seemed great, and I fell in love with

Gracie on sight. She was the most precious thing. It was a competition with Reef, but I held her for as long as he'd let me, and I managed to feed her a bottle. If nothing else, she kept my hands busy. She kept me from wanting to touch Trent. From snuggling up against his side like we'd done in bed. My mind was still going a million miles a minute, analyzing every move each of us made. He kept his distance from me, seemingly deep in conversation with Gabe for most of the night while I caught up with the others. Every time he made a move, I countered, going in the opposite direction to keep as much space between us as possible. I was probably overthinking things, but I didn't think I could cope with him fobbing me off again.

It wasn't until Gracie was fast asleep in her new bedroom and we were all chilling on the sofas eating dessert that I found myself sitting next to him. We were all talking and laughing, and I knocked my shoulder into his, teasing him about landing face-first in the snow when he skied the bowl cut into the mountain at Cardrona. I was too close. It was too personal a move. My gut sank, nerves exploding as I waited for him to pull away. To push me away like I made him dirty. But he didn't. His move in response was subtle but it rekindled my hope. He looked at me and smirked, his eyes sparkling and his cheeks turning pink. When he leaned closer, just an infinitesimal amount, I felt his breath catch and watched as his eyes flicked to my lips then back up again. Still looking at me, he responded, "We could talk about the day you slipped on the green run, you know."

I swallowed hard, resisting the temptation to lean closer. Instead, I pouted as playfully as I could in that moment. "I was lugging around cameras and a bag of lenses though ankle-deep icy slush and trying to take shots of a couple who wanted to run off to their honeymoon straight after they'd said their vows. I hardly had a chance to take any damn photos before they were off again. Who does that? Leaves their photographer in the dust?"

The laughter and conversation still surrounded us, but I drifted into my own thoughts again. I needed to know. I needed Trent to spell it out to me. Uncertainty swirled around me like a whirlwind, questions spinning around in my head. Did Trent want to keep us a secret? Or was he comfortable with us? Was he ashamed of me? Or did he just need more time to adjust? The more I asked of myself, the more arose, leaving me teetering on an edge ready to fall into a vortex that I was a little terrified by. I wanted to go home, but I didn't want to be rude. I wanted to talk, but I feared what he'd say. Being pushed and pulled in every which way, I rubbed my eyes, exhaustion washing over me. But the anxious flutter in my belly didn't let up. When Gabe finally stood up and started collecting the dessert bowls, I didn't hesitate, quickly taking the hint. But I was torn too. Was I ready to face the conversation that would no doubt change the course of our future?

Placing my bowl on the countertop, I looked around the kitchen and bit back a sigh. We couldn't leave it like that. Like he was reading my thoughts, Ricky dismissed us, saying, "Just leave it all. I'll clean up later."

I could have hugged my brother. Without thinking, I placed a hand low on Trent's back and went to guide him out the door. Even through his shirt, he was warm against my fingertips. It was an innocent touch, something I would have done to anyone. At least to anyone else. The second I touched him, I knew it was a mistake. He stiffened, and my gut rolled. I froze. Suddenly the dinner I'd had didn't seem like a good idea. I closed my eyes and blew out a shaky breath. I wasn't good enough to be anything but his secret. He wanted to keep our relationship hidden. To lock it away like something dirty. He was ashamed of me, of us.

I didn't have a chance to drop my hand. He moved so damn fast that he would have given Usain Bolt a run for his money. I sucked in a breath at the sharp pain lancing through my chest before shoving my hands in my pockets.

"We're gonna head off, then," I muttered, trying to hide the hurt. "I'll speak to you tomorrow, Rick."

The drive home was quiet. Trent didn't even look at me, and I didn't know what I would have said or done even if he had. When I pulled into the garage, I didn't bother waiting for him. I got out, closed my door, and went straight to my room, changing into a pair of sweats. He wasn't due at work for over an hour, but when I walked out to make a cup of tea, he was already in his uniform. Keys in hand, he walked by me with his head down, not saying a single word. I reached for him and grasped his hand as he stepped past.

He stopped, his shoulders hunched over and mouth turned down in a frown, but he squeezed my fingers. That simple move—holding my hand tighter rather than pulling away—mended something in me. At the same time it shattered me all over again. I knew he didn't hesitate to touch me because it was just us, but he was still touching me.

I dared another look at him, watching his chest move up and down as he took a breath. Finally, after what felt like an eternity, he looked over to me, and the raw pain etched into his expression stalled the air in my lungs. He'd hurt me, but it was nothing compared to the bleakness I saw in his eyes. I wasn't a pushover—even though it seemed like I was always backing down with him—but something in me told me to let it drop. I forced the words out, squeezing them past the constriction in my lungs. "Be safe, Trent."

"Yeah." He nodded and rubbed his face with his free hand before looking down at our joined ones. "I will." He squeezed my fingers again and gave me a small smile before walking out to the garage. I didn't move. I didn't see him off. I couldn't. I rubbed my chest. My heart hurt. My lungs felt like they'd been caught in a vise. I wanted to curl up and cry. Mourn for Trent's pain. I was hurting, but that paled in comparison to what I'd seen etched into his features. It cut me deeper than my own pain.

Mechanically, I made my tea and curled up on the sofa, staring into space. I shifted the cushions around and tried to get comfortable, but every time I moved, I heard a snap. A crinkle. There must have been something there. I'd look later, but for the moment I ignored it, closing my eyes as exhaustion washed over me.

I napped, tired but too uncomfortable to fall into a deep sleep. I wanted to stretch out, but the best I could do was hang my feet off the edge of the sofa. I shifted and heard the crunch again. The noise was annoying as hell. I dug around between the cushions but didn't find anything until I slipped my hand down the side of the sofa. My fingers brushed against some paper, feeling along the neat fold. I pulled it out, having no idea what I held in my hands, but I could feel the writing pressed through the page. Curiosity got the better of me and I unfolded it, freezing when I saw the words *Dear Mom and Dad* in hand-writing I'd know anywhere.

I folded it back up and smoothed the creases in the paper before placing it onto the coffee table. I shouldn't read it. There was no doubt it was private, and while I desperately wanted to know more about him, I'd never violate his trust in me like that.

# CHAPTER 13
## TRENT

Work had never felt so long. So arduous. My fourteen-hour night shift had come to a close and I couldn't wait to get home. I was about two minutes away from pulling into the drive, but I was scared to do it too. I'd nearly asked Angelo whether he'd still be there when I arrived home. Whether I'd fucked up badly enough that he wouldn't want anything more to do with me, because typical me, I'd managed to ruin things already.

As soon as I'd tensed at Rick's house, I wanted to kick myself. It was a simple touch, nothing like what I'd hoped might happen when we took things to the next level. Now I might never know, and in the process I'd hurt him. Again.

I wasn't ready to do PDAs yet, but we were in a safe place at Rick's house. Hell, if we couldn't be ourselves there, with two bisexual men who were glued at the hip and a second trio of men, where could we? Logically, I knew that, but letting go and exposing that part of myself again was terrifying. Revealing myself to Angelo had taken me half a decade of trust. To then do the same thing only a few days later in front of some people who were relative strangers? It was harrowing. I wished I could be more like Angelo. He was himself wherever he went. He had his own unique style and you either accepted him, or you didn't. But I couldn't be like that. I was scared. Afraid of being judged.

No, that wasn't right... I was afraid of being punished again for being honest.

Once more, logic told me that there wouldn't be a punishment like the one I'd endured at the hands of my godfather, but still. Fear was a powerful motivator to hide. And the closet was safe. I'd been in there for so long that the straight jock costume I wore now fit me like a second skin. Slipping out of it and going to a get-together as the real me was like walking down the main street of town naked.

The crushing pain of knowing how much I'd hurt Angelo again overwhelmed me. But then he'd reached for me. Grasped my hand. He'd given me a lifeline, and I'd latched on. When he'd told me to be safe—the same thing he told me before every shift—I knew we'd be okay in the end. I was going to have to work hard to get over my insecurities, but for him I'd do it. I wanted to live freely. I wanted it with him. The fear I had was eventually going to make me stronger. It had to, or I'd be stuck behind the closet's locked doors forever, and while I could live a life hidden away, I'd never drag Angelo in there with me.

I closed the garage door behind me as I pulled in and hauled myself out into the townhouse. Angelo wandered out of his office as I walked in, and he smiled tentatively at me. I'd never been as relieved, as grateful to see him in my life. Dropping my bag, I strode forward and wrapped him in my arms. He was stiff for a moment. Unyielding. But then he tentatively brushed his fingers over my hair, and I squeezed him tighter. I shook in his arms, overwhelmed with relief, fear, and exhaustion. He held me close and I whispered over and over again that I was sorry. Sorry for hurting him. Sorry for denying him. I wasn't ready to dance in Winter Pride yet, but it was on me, not him.

Angelo held me just as tight. He kissed my hair. He whispered soothingly to me, and when I finally had the strength to pull back, he brushed his fingertips across my cheek and tilted my face up to his, kissing me slowly. "Please be patient with me," I begged, my forehead pressed against his. "I want you. I want us. I want to be free, but I don't know how."

"I'm here, Trent. We'll work it out together. I promise." He ran his fingers through my hair, and I closed my eyes, sinking into his touch. "You need some sleep. You're exhausted."

I nodded. I was weary. Beyond shattered. I was tired at the beginning of my shift, already sleep deprived. It was a crazy shift too. Call out after call out except for an hour six hours into the shift. Instead of resting like my partner did when we had time for some shut-eye, I'd paced. Ruminated over my screwups.

Angelo took my hand and led me to my room, stopping as we reached my bed. He turned and undid the buttons on my green shirt before moving to my belt and undoing it too. He dropped to his knees and unlaced my boots, pulling them off when I lifted my foot. Peeling my socks off, he tossed them toward the hamper I kept in there, missing both times. When he stood, he rested his hand on the side of my face and kissed my cheek, a soft, lingering kiss. I turned into it and took his lips, our tongues sliding and recapturing the moment we'd first expressed that we loved the other. I held him close, wanting there to be no gap between us. I needed him in that moment. Needed him to hold me. To love me.

I whispered the words against his lips again, "I love you," coming more freely this time.

Angelo's response, his murmured "Love you too" meant everything. I closed my eyes and sank into his touch, letting him undress me slowly. I was down to my boxers when Angelo stopped, resting his hands on my hips and brushing his thumbs over my sides.

"Should I run the shower for you?" he asked.

"Mmm, please." I nodded. The only thing I wanted to do was fall into bed, but I needed to wash off my shift. I followed him into my attached bathroom and pulled my dark blue towel off the rail while Angelo fiddled with the water. He squeezed my shoulder, then ran his hand down my arm. "I'll get your uniform in the wash for you while you're in here."

I was a little more awake after my shower. I staggered into my room in just the towel, intending to crash, but what I saw Angelo doing gave me pause. He'd placed a cup of chamomile tea on my nightstand, together with a folded sheaf of lined paper. It was familiar, and his words solidified my knowledge of exactly what it was. "I found this between the sofa cushions. I didn't read any more than to see it was to your parents. I thought you might have forgotten it there."

I took the letter and sat down on my bed, heaving out a

sigh. Angelo ran his hand down my back, and I leaned into his touch. "You okay?"

"Mom's birthday was on April 18. I logged onto your Facebook account and looked her up, then I wrote this." I paused. "Sorry."

"I don't care if you log on as me." Angelo waved his hand, dismissing my concern. He sat down beside me and took my hand in his. "You don't talk about her. Is your mom still alive?"

I nodded. "Yeah, Dad too. I haven't spoken to either of them in years though." I rubbed a hand over my heart, the pain of walking away from them still as fresh as it was the day I'd left. "What I told you about last time? About my godfather? That was just the beginning." I opened the letter, seeing my scrawled words for the first time since I'd written them, and held it out to Angelo. "It's not everything, but it's more than I've told anyone before."

Angelo studied my hand as he held it before taking the papers from my other one, folding them again and putting them aside. "Will you tell me about your parents? What they were like."

I gave him a small smile. "Dad was right into footy. Not your kind, but rugby. He played it for years, and we watched every one of our team's home games together. It was a family thing—Mom, Dad, me, and Ryan. Then I started playing too and he was proud as." I laughed, remembering the fun times we had when I was playing. "He used to take us all for ice cream every time we won." My smile fell as I thought about Mom and how much I missed her. "My mom was amazing. A complete hard ass, but she was the best too. All my friends said she was their favorite. She would make these chocolate chip cookies whenever she got off work early enough. We used to sit down and eat them with big cups of milk after school. We didn't have a lot of money. Sometimes Ryan would have me over for dinner. It wasn't until I was a teenager and I heard her telling Dad how she'd maxed out the credit card on pizzas for me and my friends that I realized they probably sent me there because money was tight. But we had fun, no matter what we were doing. They were the best."

"It sounds like you had a pretty wonderful childhood." Angelo smiled, and I nodded.

"I ran away when I was sixteen. After Ryan and I… after we…." I stumbled over the words. How did I say that I didn't want him to, but he did it anyway?

"Trent." Angelo interrupted my thoughts. "He hurt you. He was punishing you. He wasn't your first—"

"Yeah—"

"No, Trent. He wasn't. He raped you."

His quiet words hit me with the force of a freight train. I sat there, stunned. I'd seen survivors of rape up close before. I'd treated them. I'd watched it happen to my friend while five men pinned us down and hurt her over and over, rendering me powerless to help. I'd never really put myself in the same category. I'd always put it down to him teaching me a lesson. That he was trying to right my wrongs. That I'd forced him to take action. But I hadn't, had I? All I'd done was be honest with him. I'd shared a piece of myself, and he'd used it against me. He'd taken a piece of me. He'd attacked me.

Angelo cupped my face with his free hand and nudged my chin up. "Oh, Trent," he whispered as he brushed away the tears I hadn't even realized were falling. "You've blamed yourself all these years, haven't you? You ran from him because you thought you'd done something wrong." When I nodded, he took me into his arms and held me close as I cried. Mourned the rest of the childhood I should have had. Cried for the family I'd lost, for the years I'd struggled. For the fear and loneliness I'd suffered through and the heartache I'd put my parents through.

When my tears finally dried out, resolve strengthened me.

"Will you read the letter, Angelo? I want you to know everything."

He nodded and picked up the papers from the bed. "Can I read it out loud? Maybe you can decide if you want to send it to them." God, I wanted to reach out like nothing else. I wished I was strong enough to do it, but so much time had passed. I'd hurt them so much. They probably wouldn't want to see me even if I did get in contact with them. Hell, they thought I was dead. I closed my eyes and nodded, and Angelo began.

"Dear Mom and Dad, I don't even know how to start this letter. I've been gone for years. So much time has passed and I'm different today than the boy I was when I ran away. I'm okay. I've made a life for myself. A good one. I have friends who are the best I could ask for, and I have a good job too. I wasn't sure if it would happen, if I could ever get past that night and the fallout from it, but maybe I have. I don't really know.

"When I left, I stayed in this cheap motel near the train station. I remember thinking how shabby it looked because the stucco was falling off the walls. But it was luxurious compared to what came after. The cops came looking for me. They must have seen the charges on Jake's card, and I ran again. I finally fell asleep in a doorway. I was so scared that first night. It didn't really get any less scary, I just learned the areas that were a little safer. It wasn't really though. My friend... she got hurt pretty bad in a place we both thought was okay. The ambo who helped her inspired me. That's what I do now. I'm a paramedic and during the winter, ski rescue.

"Those nights on the street were all about hiding—from the police, from gangs. It wasn't safe out there and I was always scared. I wish I'd been brave enough to come home. I didn't because I didn't want you to have to choose between us." Memories flooded my mind's eye and I shuddered at the memory of the cold fear that took up residence in me. It didn't leave me for years, even after I'd moved into the group home and finished my high school studies. Angelo paused and took in a shuddering breath. He wiped the tears from his eyes and leaned into me, and I gladly accepted the contact. It was my turn to comfort him and that little thing I could do for him was like a salve to my wounds too. It meant the world. *He* meant the world.

"Is that why you ran? You were trying to protect them too?"

I nodded and clenched my jaw, trying not to start crying again while he continued reading, "I was scared of him. He hurt me. It only happened once, and I know he was trying to teach me something, but I couldn't face him again. He was your best friend and I didn't want to make you end that. So, I chose for you. I know I hurt you and words will never make up for what we all went through, but I'm sorry for my part. I'm sorry I wasn't smarter. That I hadn't kept my mouth shut. I could have avoided you going through hell. I'm so sorry. I don't have a right to ask for your forgiveness, but I wish things could have turned out differently. I think about what it would be like every day to still speak to you. Stopping in to see you, eating cookies and watching the game together. I miss you. So much. I'd do anything to turn back time, but if I did, I wouldn't have my best friend. He's worth going through hell for."

Angelo kissed my throat, my cheek, and finally my lips, and I wanted to fall into him, to block out the world and never leave his arms. "You are, you know? Worth everything I've been through. You're my light at the end of a long, dark tunnel. I've been wandering, lost for years, but you've lit up the path. You've given me purpose. A reason to live my truth."

"I love you too, Trent." We sat there together, holding each other for a moment longer until Angelo went to put down the letter. I reached for him and held in there. I needed him to keep going. To read the next part. So he did. "I saw your Facebook post. I know you think I'm dead, and that's okay. I deserve it after not coming home again. After probably making you think you'd done something wrong to make me run away, then never letting you know I was all right. I don't have a good excuse, a good enough reason that'll make sense to you. But I haven't reached out because I've always been scared to do it. Scared that you'd turn me away or wouldn't want to see me again. I know I've left it for too long."

Angelo rested his head on my shoulder and kissed me again. He breathed deep against my skin and murmured, "I'm so sorry, *mi amore*. I'm so sorry that you went through this. I would do anything to have stopped it happening to you." I tugged him closer. I needed him. Needed to touch him, to feel him against me. To lie in his embrace. I was safe in his arms. Nothing could hurt me. I shuffled back on the bed and pulled him down with me so we were lying together. It was as if Angelo knew exactly what I needed. He wrapped himself around me and rested his head on my shoulder.

After a time he spoke again, "I don't think it's too late, you know. I think your mom and dad would do anything for another chance to see you again."

"How do you know that, Angelo?" I asked. I sounded insecure and afraid even to my own ears.

"Because if I lost you, I'd give anything, everything, to have one more moment with you."

I looked at him. Gazed into his eyes, at the tears shining there. The love and pain. The heartbreak. I took the letter from him and let it fall to the floor before I cupped his nape and brought his mouth closer to mine. I kissed him then, the soft press of his lips against mine, the silken feel of his tongue giving me a high like I'd never had before. His flavor on my tongue, his skin against mine was everything, but not enough all at the same time. I needed to touch him. To feel him against me with every inch of us connected.

I found the hem of his tee and slid my hands under it, his soft skin sliding against my palms. The lithe muscles in his back bunched and stretched, tensed and relaxed under my touch, making Angelo shudder and moan as I ran my hands up and down. But I still needed more. I tugged it up and Angelo rose onto his knees, shifting until he was straddling my hips before pulling it off and tossing his tee aside. I sat up, not wanting us to be parted by even that small distance.

The heat in his eyes, the raw desire stirring there

sucked all the breath out of my lungs. He was beautiful. Damn sexy. His flushed skin and his lips parted and wet from our kiss made me want him more. His chest heaved and the pulse point on his throat thrummed, his heart beating fast. And best of all, he was in my arms.

Angelo threaded his fingers through my hair and tugged me to him. I went willingly. Sighing into his kiss, I mapped his warm skin with my fingertips, running them over his chest and lower toward the waistline of his lounge pants. There were fine hairs on his pecs, and a line that ran down from his navel. Dark hair on tanned skin. The visual had me spinning.

Soaring. Flying as desire ricocheted through me.

I was hard. Achingly so. But it wasn't only that. It was triumph too. For the first time ever, I didn't have to imagine. I didn't have to close my eyes and wish I was with a man, even though I'd despised myself for doing it. It wasn't just Angelo's gender that had me shedding the bonds, the legacy that my godfather had saddled me with. I'd loathed everything about myself for so long, but now I had hope.

I had Angelo.

He'd made me realize I might just be worth loving and that the state of denial I'd been living in was nowhere for me to be in the future. In the now. Kissing him and touching him shone light in all the dark corners, lighting up my world, and I'd be damned if I would close myself in that closet again.

His masculinity turned me inside out in the best way possible. I needed him closer. I needed to touch and taste every inch of his body. As if they had a mind of their own, my hands ran down his back and I gripped his ass. It was the perfect handful, thicker than that of any ladies I'd been with before. Angles and spice rather than curves and softness: it was an unfair contrast to make, a no-brainer for a man like me. A gay man. I wasn't sure if I'd ever get used to calling myself that out loud. But I couldn't deny the obvious. I gasped as Angelo nibbled along my jaw from his position straddling my hips. God, I was so damn hard. Without my blue pills.

I moaned as he rocked against me and I felt his steely length press alongside mine. I shamelessly did it louder when he rocked again, grinding against me. "Fuck," I groaned when he bit down on my lobe and my dick pulsed. "So sexy," I gasped as I slid my hands under the elastic waistline of his lounge pants, pushing them down so they framed his ass. He wasn't wearing underwear. *Fuck me, he's not wearing underwear.*

I pulled him tighter against me and kissed down his chest, licking the flat disk of his nipple as I kneaded his ass, moving closer to his hole with every squeeze. I bit down gently on his pec, and the move made him shudder. Feeling that vibration against my lips, against my body had me primed to implode. I licked him, sucked on his skin, touched every inch of him I could reach. I was insatiable. I was finally loving on him.

The saltiness from the sheen of sweat that'd broken out over Angelo's skin didn't mask his taste. Having his hard cock pressed against my chest as I lazily dragged my tongue over his chest had me wanting more. Had me wanting to taste him in every place.

I tugged down the front of his pants, letting his cock bounce back against his flat stomach. I looked down at him and took my fill, watching as a drop of clear liquid welled at his tip. I hummed low in my throat and leaned forward to lick it away, his taste bursting onto my tongue. I slid my fingers along his crease and reached his hole as I licked again, and Angelo choked out a cry. Pride welled in me, knowing I could affect him like this, and I never wanted to stop.

"Trent," he moaned, and it spurred me on.

I buried my face into the coarse hairs at the base of his cock and breathed him in, savoring the moment. I licked his sac and watched as his heavy balls tightened against his body. Palming them, I moved to his shaft and licked my way up it.

He was long and uncut, his foreskin already pulled back to reveal his corona. I closed my mouth over his glans and tongued the slit, closing my eyes and letting the rapture wash over me. I ran my finger over his tight pucker and pushed gently against it. I wasn't seeking entry, but I was softening him. When he bore down on my digit and his ring swallowed just the tip of my finger, I moaned. It set off a chain reaction, Angelo crying out again and punching his hips forward until I had half his cock in my mouth.

He was hot and tight. Hard. And I was in nirvana. Being with Angelo meant everything. I couldn't deny I was raring to go. My own orgasm was creeping up on me just from touching and tasting him, but I wanted it to last all night. I wanted to wring orgasm after orgasm from the man in my arms, the one threading his fingers through my hair and tugging on the short strands in desperation. Writhing and lost to his own pleasure. I needed to make it better for him. I pulled back, letting my lips and tongue trace the veins along his shaft until his tip popped free of my mouth.

"Oh fuck," he breathed. "I've never... fuck."

"Good fuck, or bad fuck?" I asked with a smile, looking up at him. The moment our eyes connected, the flame burning between us ignited into a wildfire. Angelo kicked off his pants and lowered himself back onto my lap, slamming his mouth against mine. His tongue dueled with mine as he rocked on me. I massaged his hole every time he tried to push onto my finger, but I wouldn't enter him without lube. I couldn't hurt him like that.

Angelo was fumbling between us, tugging at the towel I'd wrapped around me. I wanted to help, but I couldn't let go of him. Couldn't pry my hands away from him. I knew it was free when cool air wafted over my erection, but it was immediately replaced by Angelo's hot, hard cock against mine. He ground down and I gasped, sensation shooting through every one of my nerve endings.

"Trent," Angelo whispered. "I need... Oh, God." His needy moan when he wrapped his hand around our shafts had the words getting caught in my throat. I couldn't get anything coherent out. My brain had short-circuited and white noise filled my mind as pleasure zinged over me.

I fumbled in my nightstand, trying to find the bottle of lube and condoms. I'd bought the rubbers so long ago I wasn't even sure if they were usable, but I'd soon find out. I wrapped my hand around the cool cylinder, and without breaking eye contact with Angelo, flipped open the lid and squeezed it onto my fingertips. Circling Angelo's pucker again, I shuddered as he pressed back against my digits, trying to ride me. "Go slow, Angelo," I begged, not wanting him to hurt himself.

"I can't," he cried, then stilled. "Oh fuck." His eyes wide, he tried to lift off me but I held his hips tight, shaking my head when he tried to move again.

"What're you doing?" I asked. "What's wrong?"

"I'm sorry," he breathed out. "I totally lost it. You touched me and I lost my mind. You asked me to go slow and here I am… not going slow."

"Do I look like I don't want this, Angelo?" I asked, softly, relaxing my grip on him. Relief coursed through me —he wasn't pulling away because of him. He was doing it to protect me. A warmth bloomed in my chest in the wake of the relief. "I want this. I'm ready." I brushed my lips against his, a barely there touch just like our first kiss.

"You are?" Angelo rested his forehead against mine and the tension left his body, his eyes closing on a relieved sigh. Blinking them open again, he looked at me tenderly, touching the backs of his fingers to my cheek. The tingles from that simple touch were transcendental. "I need to hear you say it, Trent. Tell me what you're ready for. Please."

"Everything, Angelo." I brushed my thumbs over his sides, and he shivered. My heart flip-flopped in my chest, and butterflies flew up a storm. Nervous energy assailed me at saying the words. At finally admitting what I wanted. I knew with every fiber of my being if I said I wanted to stop, Angelo would, but that made me want him more. His honesty, his integrity, his gentleness. So, I took a deep breath in and looked him in the eye, ready to make the next move. To take the next step in coming out. My voice was steady when I said, "I want to make love to you. I want to be inside you. I want to watch you as you fall apart in my arms. I want to do the same."

Angelo closed his eyes, a small smile tilting the corner of his lips up. "Then make love to me, Trent."

I didn't need any further invitation. I drizzled more lube on my finger and brought it back to his pucker, slowly pushing past his resistance. We moaned at the same time. His heat enveloped me, and the tight drag of his channel had me sucking in a breath. Angelo arched his back, simultaneously pushing back onto my digit and rubbing his cock against mine. With his head thrown back in ecstasy, I sucked on the soft skin of his throat and hummed when he breathed, "More."

I slid a second finger inside him and scissored them, stretching him ready for me. I'd never forgive myself if I hurt him. He had to be ready, so I took my time preparing him, adding a third finger and enough lube that I glided easily in and out of him. His moans sounded pained, but his leaking cock and the steady rocking of his hips told me that it was the good kind—the kind bordering on desperation. My own dick was throbbing, and I was so close to blowing my wad I was sure I'd embarrass myself as soon as I finally slid home. But I didn't think Angelo was far off either.

I reached out for the condoms again, but Angelo snagged my wrist. His eyes, pupils blown with lust, slowly focused on mine. "I've never done this. I'm negative for everything. Can we skip the protection?"

His words reached deep into my chest and mended so many of the wounds there. Angelo loved me enough that he wanted to do this with me and he didn't even want the latex barrier between us. It wasn't as if it wouldn't already be intimate, but taking that step—the one usually reserved for people who were in a committed, exclusive relationship—meant everything. "He didn't use protection, but I got tested and I don't have anything. I haven't been with anyone since my last test either." I paused, letting the feeling of being so utterly wanted wash over me. "You'll be my first, Angelo. In all the ways that matter, you'll be my first."

"Make love to me, Trent." He kissed me then, long, slow kisses, our tongues caressing and our breaths combining until I couldn't tell where he ended and I began. I gripped my shaft, slathering it with more lube, and shifted so my cockhead was at his hole.

"Tell me if you need me to stop." I kissed Angelo again, guiding him down onto my shaft, a tiny amount. I hadn't breached him and when Angelo tensed, I froze.

"Don't stop. Oh, fuck," he breathed. "So good."

I let him work himself onto me, my corona popping past his resistance on a sigh from Angelo. Silky smooth heat squeezed me tight, making my head swim and my orgasm rush toward me. It was indescribable. Never had I experienced anything like it. Even only partly buried in him, I'd never felt anything so good. Maybe it was the emotion talking, maybe it was watching Angelo toe the line to rapture, but the chemistry between us was incendiary. Powerful yet beautiful, like the majesty of rolling waves on a rocky coastline, or lightning strikes during a summer storm.

I held my hands on his hips, his warm skin tight with tension as Angelo's muscles quivered and he strained with effort. I buried my face into the crook of his neck and breathed him in, his scent calming my racing heart but bringing the inevitable one step closer.

With every small rock of his hips, Angelo sank further

down on me, inching down to the base of my cock. His breathing was choppy and his eyes glassy with desire. His lips, wet from our kisses, tempted me once more, and I kissed him long and slow. My entire being was centered on this man. The one in my arms. The one making love to me with every slow move. Every inch of us was connected. His hands were in my hair again while I wrapped mine tightly around him.

Finally, he was fully seated and I paused, holding him there until he got used to the stretch of my shaft buried in him. But he was having none of it, grinding down harder on me. I gritted my teeth and tried desperately to stave off my orgasm. I needed to make this first time with Angelo as good for him as it was for me. I never wanted him to forget, or regret, waiting for me for years. I squeezed my eyes shut and nuzzled his throat as I planted my heels into the mattress and pushed up, moving Angelo as I tilted my hips as much as I could without using my hands for leverage. I knew I'd hit the spot, the magic P-button, when Angelo gasped and his shaft hardened against my belly. "I'm close already," I confessed, murmuring against his throat.

"So am I," he moaned, and relief surged through me knowing I could do that to him.

"Touch yourself," I begged him, but he shook his head.

"Don't need to." That knowledge had me riding the edge, ready to fall into a blissful oblivion. I wanted to dive in headfirst and never leave if it would be like this between us every time. And I knew it would only get better with experience, with knowledge of what each of us enjoyed. I knew this was only the beginning of our journey. But the only destination I had in mind was making my man, my love, come.

Sucking on the soft skin under his ear and grazing his throat with my teeth had Angelo shuddering. Lifting him and driving him down onto me again, I plunged into Angelo's tight heat and aimed for his prostate every time. Angelo's cries, the whimpers and curses told me I was spot on. That I was sending him into orbit.

I felt the rhythmic clenching of his ass muscles before he cried out, his cum coating my belly as he shot pulse after pulse between us. I had no hope of resisting the pull any longer, not that I wanted to. I surrendered, letting myself get washed away in bliss as I came too. My moans were garbled, completely incoherent as the tingle at the base of my cock expanded outward, sending a buzz through millions of my nerve endings in chorus. With each throb of my shaft, I pumped my orgasm into Angelo and those final binds from my past fell away. I was free. And if freedom wasn't loving Angelo, I didn't know what was.

My body thrummed and my mind soared like an eagle riding the wind currents high in the sky. I could imagine dipping and turning, the rush of wind against my face as I floated, untethered to any of the negativity my past had shackled me with. Having his body against mine and finally being able to express everything to him I'd ever dreamed of was nirvana. Shangri-la. He relaxed into me, and I lay back, pulling him with me. I never wanted to let go. Forever in his arms, sweaty and sticky sounded like heaven to me. My softening cock slipped free of him and we both groaned. "I should get up," Angelo mumbled. "But I don't think I can move yet."

"Stay," I breathed, my voice barely above a whisper.

Angelo nuzzled my throat, dropping a lingering kiss on my Adam's apple. I closed my eyes and breathed him in, holding him tight. He shifted, stretching his legs out and tangling them together. We rolled to the side, lying face-to-face and still pressed together. I watched his eyelids flutter closed as I gently traced the line of his spine down to his ass and followed it to his knee with my fingertips. I kissed him, a press of lips against his and he opened, searching me out. Utterly sated, I tried to show him how he'd affected me. What he'd done by giving me his unconditional love.

For the first time in my life, I wanted to be open. I wanted to walk down the sidewalk holding his hand. I wanted to kiss him in public. To hug him. I wanted to live my truth. I never wanted to leave his arms.

"What are you thinking?" Angelo asked, tracing the line of my jaw. "You look like you're concentrating."

"I want to come out. I don't want to hide anymore. I want this in public." Angelo laughed and I grinned, realizing what I'd said. "Well, not *this* this. But this us." Becoming more serious, I added, "In your arms I'm safe. You give me the courage to do it. I've never had that before." I kissed him slowly and pulled back, resting my forehead against his. "I never want to give you up."

"You never will. I love you, Trent."

"I love you too."

He kissed me then and snuggled down on the arm I had resting under his head. "Let me close my eyes for five and then I'll clean us up," he mumbled.

"Lift up." I kissed his forehead and pulled away, smiling at his grumbling. In my attached bathroom, I warmed the water and wet a couple of facecloths, wiping myself down before taking one to Angelo and doing the same to him. He was sleepy and I didn't blame him. I tossed the soiled cloth aside and pulled the covers over us, pulling Angelo back into my arms. He came willingly, half lying on me as I started to doze.

# CHAPTER 14

## ANGELO

I PULLED IN THE DRIVE, EXHAUSTED AFTER MY THIRD WEDDING in three days. My body demanded that I crash. Curl up and sleep for a week. But I hadn't spent any time with Trent, and despite what I needed, that's what I really wanted. Especially because we'd experienced such a fundamental shift in our relationship only days earlier. Making love to him was something I still didn't have the words to describe. It was an experience I wanted to repeat daily for the rest of my life, but so far, we'd barely seen each other.

The townhouse was dark when I opened the door from the garage, and while I understood Trent going to bed, I wished I could have spoken to him before joining him. When I spied the flickering light of a candle burning in the kitchen, I frowned. It was unlike him to even light one, never mind leave it burning while he was in bed. He was a paramedic—he knew the risks of an unattended open flame. Then I rounded the corner into the kitchen and grinned. Standing there, in a pair of loose fitting, low-hanging pajama pants was Trent, jiggling a teabag in a mug.

"Hey," I sighed as he turned, handed me the cup, and reached for my camera equipment. Placing it gently on the floor out of the way, he took my hand and pressed a kiss to my knuckles.

"Evening." He smiled at me softly with so much warmth and affection in his eyes that it took my breath away. "Come have a soak and get changed. I'm taking you on a date."

I mentally groaned, hoping that I'd managed to keep the sentiment inside my own head. There was nothing in the world I wanted to do more than spend time with Trent, but I was wrecked. My body was crying out for sleep. "A soak would be great," I mumbled on a yawn as Trent blew out the candle and I followed him down the corridor to the main bathroom. The tub was already half full, the remnants of a bath bomb fizzing away and steam curling above the water. Soft classical music played in the background, and more candles were spread around the edge of the tub and on the vanity countertop.

"It's beautiful in here, Trent. Incredibly sweet." I looked around and placed my mug on the counter before moving to unbutton my vest.

"Let me do that." Trent replaced my hands with his and undid the waistcoat I wore. Once he'd slipped it free of my shoulders, he folded it, taking care to lay it gently over the chair in the corner. He tugged at my violet-colored bow tie, and once it was free, he grasped both ends gently and tugged me to him.

His smile was warm and his movements slow and measured, cherishing me with the graze of his fingertips against my cheek. I sighed into his mouth as he brushed his lips against mine in a soft kiss. A gentle whisper of his plump flesh against mine sent shivers through me and made my eyes drift closed. I opened to him and he slipped his tongue inside, only the slightest of caresses against my own. I hummed, a contented rumble sounding in my throat as I chased his tongue back into his mouth.

His lips curved against mine in a smile, and I wasn't sure whether it was his embrace, the steamy room, or that simple action of making him smile that sent a rush of warmth through my chest. But whatever it was, it lit me up from inside.

He pulled me closer, kissing me deeper, and I fell headlong into the magic of his touch. His taste—fresh mint and something uniquely Trent—made me crave him more. I couldn't get enough of him, but I wanted to savor every moment of this connection with him. Trent's touch on my skin, his gentle hands loving me had me leaning closer, wrapping my arms around him. He lifted his hands to my face and I gasped as he kissed me slow and sensuously. I sighed dreamily, loving his undivided attention focused on me. He was a nurturer at heart and there was no doubt in my mind that he'd take care of me that night.

I felt the loss of his hands to my bones when he went back to unbuttoning my shirt. But it wasn't until he needed to tug it out of my pants that he pulled back a fraction and set to work taking it off. I blinked my eyes open slowly, and the look on Trent's face had my breath lodging in my throat. Desire, lust, love written into his features. Pupils blown, lips wet and swollen from our kiss. I wanted to dive right back into him, and when his teeth bit down into his bottom lip, pressing the plump flesh down, I moaned.

My nostrils flared as I sucked in a breath, praying for enough self-restraint not to jump him. Trent smiled, the barest tilt of his lips, and flipped my hands so my wrists were up.

I got the hint and slipped my cufflinks off before tossed them haphazardly toward the sink. They landed with a clatter as the buckle of my belt hit the floor, the leather snaking down and hitting too only a split second later. I admired Trent as he fell to his knees and undid the laces on my dress shoes. I reached out for him, needing the constant connection with him. My fingers connected with his silky hair and I ran them through it, watching the strands slip through my fingers. He waited for me to toe off my shoes before reaching for the button and zipper on my pants. The dark material pooled at my feet, and Trent helped me out of them. The move wasn't sexual; it was infinitely gentle. He took such care when he folded them and placed them on the chair, and it made me smile. I threw my shirt straight into the hamper and tugged off the white singlet I wore underneath, tossing it in the same direction.

Even though I wasn't yet naked, peeling my dark socks off one foot at a time was oddly intimate. More intimate than I imagined it would be. I bit down on my bottom lip, wishing Trent would look up at me. After my second sock followed the first into the hamper he did, and my breath caught.

"I'd really love to kiss you right now," he rasped, his voice low and rough.

"You should definitely kiss me," I responded breathily,

and his lips turned up in a wickedly sensual smile. Pleased, as if he'd set a challenge and I'd passed.

He pressed his lips to my thigh, sending a shiver through me and trailed kisses up to my hip bone. I slid my eyes closed on a moan and let my head fall back, but I couldn't keep my eyes off him long. When our gazes met once again, his dark eyes sparkled with a light I hadn't seen until we'd made love. His almost black hair shone in the candlelight, its light flickering across his perfectly shaped face, framed with a dark stubble that was soft to my touch. I wanted to feel it brush against my cheeks when we kissed. I wanted to feel it between my thighs too, but most of all, I wanted to memorize every detail. I never wanted to forget this moment.

Another shudder passed through me as his hot breath wafted over my thickening shaft and his fingertips curled into the waistband of my black briefs. If I wasn't so preoccupied with the beautiful man on his knees for me, I'd be embarrassed by the tenting in my underwear. But he was a dream come true. Beyond a fantasy. This man, who I'd loved from afar for so long, who held my heart almost from the moment I'd met him, loved me. And he left me in no doubt that he cared with his unhurried movements, reminiscent of unwrapping a gift. He was worshiping me, loving on every inch of my skin he touched.

I ran my fingers through his hair again, needing the connection and greedy for any part of him I could get. Trent tugged the back of my briefs down, exposing my cheeks. Running his nose up my cloth-covered erection, he placed a soft kiss at my crown. I sucked in a breath, sensation rocketing through me. He hummed and did it again before peeling my underwear the rest of the way off.

I wanted his mouth, his hand. Anything. Everything. And Trent didn't disappoint. He took me deep, slowly and so thoroughly licking and sucking me until my toes were curling. He worked me over, bringing me to a climax so strong that my legs were like jelly after I'd come.

When I could open my eyes again and focus on my surroundings, steam no longer curled over the water. I didn't have it in me to be disappointed, but the furrow on Trent's forehead told me he minded. He dipped his hand into the water and pursed his lips. I stopped him when he reached for the faucet again.

"It's okay. It won't be cold." Trent opened his mouth as if to argue but I placed my fingers over his lips. "It probably would have been too hot before. This is perfect."

Reluctantly agreeing, Trent held my hand, helping me step into the water. The heat touching my toes was heavenly, and I sighed when I eased my languid and exhausted body gingerly into the tub. Trent held a waterproof pillow behind my head and I gratefully leaned back into it, reclining as much as I could in the water.

I watched as he soaped up a sponge and started at my shoulders, washing me with gentle strokes of the loofah. He worked his way down my body so meticulously, so carefully showing me how much he treasured me with every movement. I could have stayed in the tub all night but I couldn't hold back my yawn any longer. As soon as I did, Trent began rinsing me and was soon reaching for my hand to help me up. I was shattered, but also kind of excited to see what he'd planned. Midnight had been and gone, but that didn't matter. We had our pick of places to go; Queenstown was always buzzing.

"You ready to come out?" Trent asked, as if he was

reading my thoughts. I nodded, another yawn escaping as he passed me a fluffy towel. "I'll leave you to get dry. Gimme a second and I'll bring in some clothes for you, but once you're dressed wait until I come back, okay?" I smiled at him, a little confused and a lot curious, but I agreed to what he asked and he was gone.

The bath and the orgasm had completely relaxed me, and I scrubbed my hands over my face trying to wake up, but it didn't work. Another yawn ripped free as I finished drying and wrapped the towel around my waist. It was only a moment later that Trent cracked open the door and held out a pair of light gray pajama pants. I frowned, trying to understand why I would be wearing sleep pants if we were going on a date. When I took them though, those thoughts fled. The material was soft to the touch and warm like he'd put it in the dryer. "Thank you," I murmured, trying to stifle another yawn.

"I'll just be another minute."

I nodded my response, already taking off my towel and slipping into the pants. I'd barely had a chance to brush my teeth when Trent came back and opened the door. Placing my toothbrush back in its cradle, I hooked my arm into his and he walked me back down the corridor into the living room. It was lit now, and what I saw took my breath away. Footage of a campfire played on the TV, and Trent's mattress sat on the floor in front of it. Draped over it like a tent was a white sheet with fairy lights hanging off the ends. It was something so simple, but so thoughtful and romantic.

He'd organized a camp out—well, camp in—for our first official date.

"Oh, Trent," I breathed. "It's perfect."

"You've worked so hard these last few days. I wanted to do something special."

"It is special, *amore*. So much better than what I thought we were doing." I laughed, cuddling into his side. Trent wound his arms around my waist and kissed my shoulder.

"What did you think we were doing?"

"Going out. But this… this is heaven."

He smiled, a dazzling, sparkling smile, and warm fuzzy feelings spun around my insides, lighting me up. This beautiful, thoughtful man was mine. After loving him for so long, he was finally mine. I reached up and cupped his face, and even in the candlelight I could see the happy sparkle in his eyes. He looked as radiant as I felt. "I'm so in love with you," I murmured to him, leaning down to kiss my man.

"And I love you," he replied between brushes of our lips together. It was Trent who finally pulled away, taking my hand in his and leading me to the makeshift tent on the floor. He lifted the roof a little so I could slip in and followed me inside.

I went willingly when he patted his pillow and motioned for me to slide into his embrace. "So a nap date was a good idea?"

"I love it." I yawned and rubbed my eyes, trying to stay awake but failing. Trent's warmth and the strength of his embrace, the soft lights and the crackling of the fire on the TV had sleep trying to claim me quickly. I didn't want it to though, and I fought like hell to stop myself, but Trent's soft kisses and his fingertips brushing over my skin relaxed me until sleep won and I drifted away on a dream.

Life had been good these last few weeks. But I was missing Trent. Our paths hadn't crossed that morning. The wedding I'd worked the day before had run late, and I hadn't managed to crawl into bed until one in the morning. Trent's shift started four hours later, so neither of us woke the other. When I'd blinked my eyes open that morning though, I'd been hugging his pillow and lying on his side of the bed. But the smell of him on his sheets wasn't much of a consolation when I'd experienced the real deal.

I only had a few more hours to go and then I'd be able to see him. We were going to Ford's for dinner, all of us trying to mend the rift caused when Trent had seen Ford and Reef together for the first time. Slowly it was being bridged, and I was grateful to be able to help that happen. Ford and Reef deserved friends who supported them, and Trent needed to know that even when he'd done something to hurt someone close to him, he could be forgiven. The relationship could be repaired. At least I hoped he'd eventually get that message, because it seemed like that was a major reason why he'd never contacted his parents.

I wanted nothing more than for him to reconnect with them, but Trent had to do it when he was ready. *If* he was ever ready. I didn't blame him for staying away when his monster of a godfather was their best friend, but I wished he'd confided in them. At least given them the chance to help him, rather than running.

But I understood his fear too.

As a teenager, friendships meant the world. They were everything, and parents were always on the other side. They were always the ones saying no, always the ones controlling things you wanted the freedom to decide yourself. His immaturity in underestimating the love his parents had for him—would still have for him—was tragic, but forgivable. I hoped it was simply immaturity; that they'd never hinted they would choose their friend over him, because that truth was too terrible to fathom.

When the chat icon popped up on my screen, I tapped it open.

**Ford: We still on 4 dinner and movie tonight? 7ish? Just downloaded the new Marvel movie.**

I grinned and keyed in a response. I was dying to meet the new addition, and by all accounts from Ricky, Rufus the puppy was beautiful.

**Angelo: As long as your pup is there**

Three dots popped up on my screen immediately.

**Ford: Rufus is home with us. Mace didn't want to give him back after having him for those couple of days**
   **Reef: He's super cute, Ang. You guys'll love him.**
   **Trent: I don't finish until 7, but I'll get there asap**

The day dragged, and my meeting with the couple choosing images for their wedding album was interminable. But finally I stood on the stoop to Ford and Reef's house, and I was only half an hour late. The heavy timber door gave a beautiful warmth to the muted gray tones of the walls, but I always felt at home in the cottage Ford had built for his winters in Queenstown. Always welcome.

Especially now that he and Reef had made it a home rather than a bachelor pad.

I knocked, and my grin turned into a wide smile when Trent opened the door. He slipped out, pulling it closed behind him, and reached for me. I stepped straight into his arms, but apparently it wasn't enough.

He pushed me gently against the support column and kissed me like his life depended on it. It was as if he couldn't get close enough, needed to feel every inch of me against him.

I sank into the kiss and let his fervor carry me away, pressed against the hard lines of his body, his gentle hands caressing me and his tongue tasting mine. It was like finding a desert oasis after being parched for days. Finally, he pulled back and cupped my face with both hands. The warmth of his palms against my skin, cool from the evening air, was a contrast to the flames of desire that had licked to life with his touch.

Trent, still breathing heavily, whispered in a husky voice, "Hi."

"Hi," I replied, suddenly shy. I smiled at him and he kissed me again.

Movement behind Trent caught my eye and I froze, my lips still connected to Trent's. There in the doorway stood Reef, tea towel in hand with his mouth open. I moved my hands to Trent's chest and tried to push him gently away, but he tightened his grip on me.

"No," he murmured, shaking his head. "I don't care who's there."

"Trent, I'm sorry," I whispered, closing my eyes and looking away. "It should have been your decision to come out, not get busted by Reef."

He gripped my chin gently between his thumb and forefinger and turned my face back to his. "There's nothing to be sorry for, Angelo. I can never be sorry for having you."

He kissed me again, taking his time and showing me with more than his words that he cared. With his head held high, he took my hand and tugged me inside, and the wonderful aroma of whatever Ford and Reef were cooking hit me. My stomach rumbled on cue, and placing a hand against it, I looked around.

Reef was standing in front of us, still looking confused, and Ford had caught on to his partner being out of sorts. With his hand on Reef's lower back, I watched as his gaze bounced to us and then back to Reef, a look of shock crossing his features. Even the laughter and light conversation in the living room quietened down, and it was then that I noticed my brother and one of his boyfriends were there too.

"Uh..." I hesitated. "Hi?"

It wasn't a reply but a bundle of fur zooming toward me that broke the ice. Brown, white, and black Rufus was, at best guess, a Bernese mountain dog cross. His owners had given the mom away to the pound, and when the vets saw she was pregnant, they waited for the puppies to be weaned before adopting out the whole litter and the mom, hopefully, to their forever homes. I reached down to pet him but couldn't resist picking him up for a cuddle. He was a licking and squirming ball of fur with a thumping tail, and I laughed happily as I scratched behind his ear. Trent leaned in, wrapping his arm around me and running his free hand over Rufus's back.

"He's so damn cute," I said to Trent and smiled at him,

reluctantly placing Rufus on the floor when he wiggled around too much. As soon as I was upright again, Trent clasped my hand, linking our fingers together, and I momentarily forgot where we were. I leaned into him, but Ford's response had me instinctively pulling back.

"Rufus is cute," Ford said coolly. "Is this a joke, Trent? Are you tryin' to be funny? Hugging Ang like that? 'Cause it isn't."

Reef put a hand on Ford's chest and shook his head, saying "It's real, Ford," at the same time as Trent got defensive and growled, "I may be an asshole, but Angelo's not. You think he'd do something as shitty as pretending to be together to what? Fit in? Gimme a break."

"So what then?" Ford's tone was a mixture of confused and annoyed. "When Reef and I started seeing each other, you were like the world's biggest homophobe. Now you're with Angelo? I'm trying to understand here, but Trent, I'm having trouble reconciling the picture in front of me."

"Maybe we should go," I murmured to Trent before motioning to the door. "I don't want to ruin anyone's night." Trent wrapped an arm around my waist while I stood there awkwardly, not really knowing what to do with my hands.

"No," Reef interjected. "You're always welcome here."

"Maybe everyone just needs to take a deep breath and put the past aside for a moment," Mace added as he made his way toward us. "You guys have history. We all know that. But Trent and Angelo have just come out. We should be supporting them. Ford, we should be acting exactly how you hoped Trent would act when he saw you with Reef."

Ricky was beside him and he was frowning at me. "It's

always been Trent, hasn't it? That's why you never dated anyone else." When I nodded, he smiled at me and nodded, but sobered as he turned his attention to Trent. "You hurt my brother and I'll hurt you. Look after him and you'll always be my brother." I didn't know whether to be mortified or angry that my brother would say that shit to him, but when he continued, exchanging a smirk with Mace, I couldn't help the laugh that broke free. "Angelo doesn't get two men to double team him. Unlucky bastard."

"Nah, I'm just that good a lover that he doesn't need them." Trent tried to keep a straight face, but the twitching of his lips gave him away. Sobering, he added, "And Ricky? Message received loud and clear."

Caden's words from the doorway of the bedroom he'd just exited had us all turning to him. "What'd I miss?" When Ricky and Mace shifted so Caden could slip between them, he looked our way and added, "Oh," before he smiled and stepped forward to shake our hands. "Welcome to the family, Uncle Trent."

"Who's up for a drink?" Reef asked, motioning to the kitchen. The others cleared off, leaving Trent, Ford, and me in the entryway.

"I'm sorry, Ford. I was an asshole to have treated you so badly. I hated myself, hated that part of me so much that I couldn't stand seeing it. I was so fucking jealous of you and yet I was disgusted at myself for wanting the same thing. It was never you and Reef, and I'm sorry that you guys were hurt because of my actions."

"Why, Trent? Why hate yourself like that?" Ford asked gently. "Why torture yourself?"

I wrapped my arm around Trent and started to speak,

to tell Ford that he had his reasons, but Trent interrupted me. "I came out as a teenager to someone I knew. Someone I thought I could trust, and he punished me for it."

The color drained from Ford's face. "Your parents? They hit you?" Ford's experiences with his own mother and father had been awful, but never violent. Bribery, threats, and manipulation, all to get Ford to walk away from Reef.

"No, another person. He…." Trent closed his eyes, took a deep breath, and squared his shoulders as if he was bracing himself. I supposed he was. He'd struggled with it for so long; I think he was only now coming to terms with the fallout from that fateful night. Trent's arm tightened around my waist and I squeezed him back, trying to show him without words that he was loved. When he opened his eyes again, he focused on Ford and with his chin up defiantly, spoke the words I didn't think he'd ever said before. "He raped me. Tried to show me that I'd hate it, and I did. He made me despise every part of myself, and I mirrored that hatred onto you."

My gaze bounced between Trent and Ford. Trent looked relieved, as if a weight had been lifted from his shoulders. Ford closed his eyes and breathed out, flexing his fists and grinding his jaw. When he opened his eyes, they were filled with pain.

He stepped forward and hugged both of us before pulling back and walking outside. I heard something crash and a shouted "Fuck," and from the corner of my eye, saw Reef go running. I ignored them and turned Trent in my arms and cupped his face.

Trent flinched, his nostrils flaring as he took in a sharp breath. I soothed him, brushing my thumbs over his stubble. Looking into tormented eyes, I spoke the words in my heart. "I love you," I whispered. "I'm so damn proud of what you've overcome, of the person you are. Of your strength. You're so brave."

"I couldn't have done it without you." He wrapped his arms around me tighter and rested his head on my shoulder. I brushed my fingers through his hair, letting the soft strands fall between them and held him close. "I love you, too," he added.

"You guys okay?" Mace asked from the doorway.

I nodded and motioned outside. "Is Ford?"

"Ricky's checking on him."

"He's pissed," Trent whispered. "I fucked up again by telling him. Maybe I should have just stayed quiet."

"Shh," I soothed. "You didn't fuck anything up."

We stayed there for another few minutes, arms wrapped around each other, Trent curled into me. He swiped at his face with the heel of his hand and took in a deep breath. Letting it out slowly, he looked up and gave me a small smile. "Talking about it is getting easier. I told my therapist too, and now Ford. I feel like I'm getting stronger."

I kissed his forehead and smiled against his skin. "You're incredible."

"Did he get put away?" Reef ground out. He had tears in his eyes and clasped Ford's hand, rubbing his knuckles. Heartbreak crossed Ford's gaze when Trent shook his head, and he stepped forward again, wrapping his arms around both of us. Reef did the same, enveloping us in a hug.

When Rufus came charging at us, yapping away and jumping up on our legs, Trent laughed and bent down for him, adding "I think Mace is gonna have some competition to babysit this little guy. I kinda want to keep him."

I smiled at him and at our friends, then looked over my man's shoulder to my brother and his two men standing beside him. My heart full, I took Rufus from Trent and winked at him before hooking my finger into the open collar of his shirt. "Quick, stuff him in here and we can make a run for it."

"You drive the getaway car." He scratched Rufus behind the ears and looked up at me, smiling sweetly. I wanted to kiss him so badly in that moment, so I did. A chaste kiss that ended with us getting licked to death by an overeager pup and two friends who immediately backed away to let us have a moment to ourselves.

"C'mon, let's go find out what's for dinner." I took Trent's hand and placed the still-licking puppy down. He took off in the direction of his masters and we followed. The night had started off on a roller coaster. We'd made it through the loop the loops smoothly enough. Fingers crossed for the rest of the ride that night.

When we walked in, the table was piled high with an assortment of vegetables and a huge pot roast. The others were all digging in, piling their plates up high while Trent and I watched from the sidelines. Ford looked over to us and nodded as if to call us over. We moved into the fold and he handed us two plates. "Dig in. Only guests don't help themselves. Family's at home here."

Trent nodded and smiled, relief painting his features. "Thanks, mate."

Dinner was fun. Good food, great people, and a lightness to the conversation that we hadn't had since Ford and Trent's falling out. Ford made it clear that it was water under the bridge, and Reef was just happy that there wasn't any tension between them anymore.

For the movie, we'd retired to their living room. Ford and Reef were sharing an armchair, curled in each other's arms. Ricky, Mace, and Caden were sprawled out on the three-seater, Gracie in Ricky's arms while he fed her a bottle. That left the daybed for Trent and me, and I couldn't have been happier with the choice. It was big enough that we could sit side by side, but Trent had wanted me close all night, so when I leaned back, he crawled between my legs and laid his head on my chest. I was living a fantasy, real life better than anything I'd ever imagined.

Running my fingers through his hair—one of my favorite things to do—I only knew he was awake from the soft kisses he pressed against my chest. He looked up, and the love shining back at me had my breath catching. I tilted his face up more and kissed him, a slow melding of our lips together. I licked his bottom lip, and he opened to me. Cupping his nape, I kissed him deeper. The movie and the others in the room faded away. I loved his taste, his smell. His rough stubble against my clean-shaven face. His strength and his vulnerability. Everything about him called to me. I'd found my soulmate. The other half of my heart. I held tight and showed him without words that I was totally gone for him.

The movie ended and the lights went up, startling us out of our make-out session. Sheepishly, I looked around and blushed when I saw the others standing there watching us with smirks on their faces. "Welcome back!" Reef laughed.

"As much as I loved watching you two pash, you need to get out. I wanna take my man to bed and it's considered impolite while we have visitors," Ford grumbled, trying for seriousness, but the smile he was failing to hide showed me it was in good humor.

"I thought we were family here?" Trent asked teasingly as he peeled himself away from me and stood, holding out his hand to help me up.

"Dude, do I need to spell it out?" With a shake of his head and a smile, Ford added, "I wanna have sex with my boyfriend. You know, like you two were practically doing on our sofa. Fuck off!"

Mace came out of the spare room pushing a sleeping Gracie in her stroller. "I had to shield her eyes from you two love birds. Mind you, I had to shield Caden's eyes too, so—"

"What? They're hot," Caden interjected. When Mace nodded, Trent huffed out a laugh and tugged on my hand. He was embarrassed, and I couldn't help laughing.

"Guys. My brother," Ricky protested. "Not hot, Caden. And Mace, don't enable him. Please."

We picked up our things and headed out, Ford and Reef waving to us from the doorway as my brother and his family and Trent and I left. I followed Trent home, ready to get him to finally undress me like I'd wanted him to on that sofa. Ready for me to peel him out of his hot as hell uniform and kiss every inch of that bronze skin.

# CHAPTER 15

## TRENT

I'd been living on cloud nine. How did my life get so damn near perfect?

Angelo, that's how.

For years I'd fought my pull to him. I'd despised myself and battled against a part of me that, although only one aspect, was as fundamental as the air I breathed. But things had changed in the few weeks since I finally gathered up the courage to admit the truth to Angelo. We'd moved at lightning speed since then, but at the same time it was at a snail's pace too.

We'd been friends for so long that the slide into a relationship seemed almost effortless. It wasn't, but I was working on it. I was getting more comfortable with myself, constantly repeating the positive mantras my therapist had armed me with and just going with the flow. Touching him —holding him, kissing him—was addictive. We weren't just focusing on that though. Talking, opening up about the things we'd never shared, was coming easier too.

Angelo understood that I struggled sometimes and he was there. He helped.

Therapy was helping too, giving me a safe space to process what had happened and how far I'd come. I'd told Dr. Hansard during our last session that I was coming out, and while she was encouraging, she cautioned me to only do it when I was ready. She didn't want me to come out just to please Angelo.

I hadn't. I'd done it for me.

I'd come out to break that last shackle tying me to my godfather's crime. He had no power over me anymore, and that was more freeing than I could ever have imagined. It also made me feel like I was only tethered to the ground by the slightest thread, ready to float away if it snapped. Or perhaps career spectacularly out of control and crash land if I hit a patch of turbulence. That scared me—the knowledge that coming out could just as easily make me crash and burn as it could make me soar. I had no idea how people would react to me. No idea whether their response would be great, good, or downright violent. And it scared me, but not enough to go back in that closet.

The night I came out I'd needed Angelo. I'd needed his kiss to give me the courage to walk back inside with my head held high and holding his hand. I didn't want to make a big announcement, but when Reef saw us, coming out was no longer something I was hypothetically contemplating and working up the courage to do. It was on top of me and I couldn't get away without everybody making a big deal out of it.

I hadn't expected they'd be so great though. I also hadn't expected to tell Ford any part of my story, but he deserved it and so did I.

Saying the words "I was raped" was as empowering as it was hard. I knew it would be difficult, but the war of conflicting emotions afterward was like a whirlwind. It'd taken me hours to let go of the man who'd become my rock. His touch was comforting and it gave me strength. We lay there on the sofa, cocooned in each other's arms, and I found myself never wanting to let go. So I didn't. I never will.

Three weeks had passed since that night, and I was in another therapy session. Sitting in Dr. Hansard's beige and black office on the sofa near the window, I exhaled slowly. I'd just finished recounting my story to her, and her reassuring words and genuine smile told me she was pleased. I could literally check off the ways I'd followed her advice, and it felt damn good too.

I'd used the tools she'd given me. I'd reached out for support when I needed it, and Angelo had been there for me without question. I'd only told my friends as much as I was comfortable sharing. I'd confronted my fears and was slowly working through each one. I was strong. Stronger than I'd ever felt before.

And I was loved.

It wasn't just Angelo either, even though the man owned me body and soul. No, it was my friends who stood by me and supported me. It was me too. I could finally live my life as me. I could finally be free. I recognized myself in the mirror when I looked now. I didn't look any different, but at the same time I did. I saw the happiness that radiated off me. The confidence, and not the cocky bro'd up front I'd used as a shield for over a decade, but an inner strength.

An inner calm. An acknowledgement of my true self.

It'd taken the years of self-loathing to fall away, but in the rubble that was left, I could see that I was worthy of love, especially my own. I was finally beginning to do exactly that.

"So your letter to your parents was the catalyst for you and Angelo admitting your feelings toward each other?" Dr. Hansard's words were framed as a question, but it wasn't one. "And you've come out to your friends and his family here in NZ too."

"Yep," I replied, nodding. "And his parents and sister in Italy. I know them too." I knew what her next question would be and she didn't disappoint.

"How do you feel about that?"

I wanted to blurt out that I was fine, but she wouldn't let me get away with it. The more I thought about it, though, the more I realized I was okay. I smiled and remembered saying the words. It was as if a weight had been lifted off me when I saw Angelo's mom clasp her hands together and burst into tears with the biggest smile on her face. With all their support, I was better than okay. I was becoming me again.

"I'm good." I nodded and smiled. "Yeah, I'm good. Angelo made it easier, but as much as I did it for him, I did it for me too, and that feels pretty amazing."

She smiled. "I'm glad. We've spoken about your coming out as a process, not a destination. It's not some-thing you'll do once. You'll do it with each new group of people you meet, with your other friends and work colleagues. And one day, if you're ever ready, with your parents. But in the meantime, your life is there to enjoy. Your relationship, becoming this new you. You've come a long way, Trent, and you still have a long journey in front of you, but a key to that is you being happy. Not just in your relationship with Angelo, but in yourself."

"I get it now. I do. And I'm getting there. I like myself now. I'm proud of me, you know?" I hesitated, then asked the question that had been niggling at the back of my mind ever since Angelo read the letter to my parents. "Do you think I'll ever be ready to get back in contact with them? My parents," I clarified.

"That's something only you can answer, Trent. Have you been thinking about trying to rebuild your relationship?"

"Yeah, I have. Angelo said something that's made me rethink every reason I've used not to contact them again." I paused, expecting Dr. Hansard to ask another question, but when she didn't I continued, "I made the split-second decision to run away when I was a kid. I've always thought that Mom and Dad wouldn't want to see me again because so much time had passed. That they'd probably gotten over me." I ran my fingers through my hair, giving myself a moment for the constriction in my chest to wane so I could breathe once more. "They posted a message about me on Facebook. They think I'm dead." My voice wobbled and I swallowed past the lump now in my throat. My eyes stung, tears threatening to escape. "They said they still think about me every day and wished they could see me again. Angelo said something similar. I suppose it got me thinking about reaching out to them. What if I did and they said yes? I might be able to get them back."

"I don't want you to rush into anything, Trent. There's no set time limit that you have to tackle these things in. You've come a long way in a short time. It's important that you're ready before you take that step. Regardless of whether they say yes or no to seeing you, or speaking to you again, it will be highly emotional. You need to be properly equipped to handle that—" She held her hand up, cutting me off as I started to speak. "I'm not discouraging you, but I'm not encouraging you until I feel like you're emotionally stable enough and have the coping mechanisms to be able to deal with that kind of upheaval."

"Okay." I nodded, taking in what she said. It made sense, and I knew I wasn't ready to reach out to them yet, but I also knew that now I'd begun to think about it, I wouldn't be able to let it go. "What can I do until I am ready?"

"Why don't you try updating the letter you wrote? Go over what we spoke about including in it and I'll give you a list of extra things for you to think about adding in."

"Would I have to see my godfather again?"

"No." She shook her head. "We'll make sure he's not with them. If he is, I'd recommend rescheduling so he isn't there. I think with your current state of progress, it would be counterproductive to involve him." She put the pen down she'd been twirling between her fingers and added, "I'd like you to think about who you'd like there as your support person too. Someone who you feel comfortable with."

I didn't even need to think about who I'd want with me. There was only one person: Angelo. But it was more than just asking him to come out for coffee with me as a friend, and even though I couldn't imagine anyone else being there, I didn't want to push the limits of our fledgling relationship too far. "Yeah, okay." I nodded slowly. "It's a lot to think about. So much more than just picking up the phone."

"I'd discourage you from doing that. Let's do this properly, Trent. We'll make sure you're ready, and I'll give you whatever support you need to get you there."

We said our goodbyes, and I mulled the idea over while I was walking to my car. I messaged Angelo, asking if he wanted takeout for dinner rather than cooking. We'd both had a busy week and I couldn't be bothered cleaning up the mess that went with Angelo's masterpieces or my basic survival meals. His message came back quickly.

**Angelo: Can I take you out tonight? There's a new bar I want to check out**

I smiled. It'd been forever since we'd gone out, and never before as partners. I knew I was dropping the ball in the dating department, but with everything else that'd been happening, I'd wanted Angelo to myself. But no more.

I wanted us to be open. Proud of who we were.

I replied and headed to the address he sent me to. It was a traditional storefront from the outside. A basic red brick building with nearly full-length timber windows on either side of the entryway. It was a bank when originally built, and the neon sign over the entry, declaring it to be The Vault, paid homage to that history. Under it, the heavy timber doors opened into a deep room. Along one side, running the full length of the open space, was a bar lit from below with colored lights. Timber floors, black walls, and mood lighting gave the place a modern look, and the gilded mirrors and disco ball sent shards of light sparkling over the empty dance floor and narrow staircase. At the top of those stairs was a round bank vault door that was easily seven feet high. The bar's namesake, I guessed.

There was a small after-work crowd and a few spring-time tourists dressed in much more casual gear than the business people spread out among the tables. The stools at the end of the bar I was standing closest to caught my eye, so I made my way over to them and sat down, ordering a soda when the bartender with bright purple streaks in her hair made her way over to me. I looked around, watching the crowd, but found my gaze drifting to the doors nearby.

I saw him the moment he stepped through, and it only took a moment for our eyes to connect. He looked sexy as fuck as he walked toward me, never breaking eye contact. He could have been stalking me, but the tilt of his smile left me in no doubt that when he caught me, I'd love every second of it. Dressed in navy blue, pinstripe pants and a matching vest, he was dashing. The crisp white shirt he wore gave him a refined, straitlaced business appearance, but the fuchsia bowtie and matching socks I knew he was wearing gave away his playful side, the same one that made his art so unique.

He sidled up to me and stood close. Probably too close for a friend, but I wanted more. My heart raced, my palms sweating as the temptation to touch him rose like a tide within me. I sucked in a sharp breath when he lowered his head to mine and murmured in my ear, "Hi."

I let that one word wash over me and shivered, desire pulsing low in me. Fear mingled in there too though. I wanted to reach out and touch him, but could I do it? How would the biker-looking dude with the younger kid sitting next to him on the table nearby react? I could defend us. I did it more than I would acknowledge for Angelo's sake when we were on call outs, but I'd never exposed that part of myself except to a limited few.

Did I have the courage to reach out to Angelo? To touch him? To kiss him like I so desperately needed in that moment?

I swallowed around the lump in my throat and rasped out a "Hi," too. He leaned in more, no doubt invading my personal space, and I stiffened, cursing myself when Angelo paused.

"Do you like it here?" he asked lowly, his melodic voice and that sexy accent chipping away at my discomfort. All he had to do was keep talking and I'd be putty in his hands. I nodded, unable to say anything, and he smiled. "But you haven't figured it out yet have you?"

The question had me confused, and I looked at him, my eyebrows knitted. "Figured what out?"

"What color was the sign over the door?"

"I didn't take much notice. It was a few different colors. Red, yellow, green, blue. That's it, I think."

"Close. Look at the colors under the bar." I watched them for a moment. Green morphed into blue, then into purple before taking on a red tinge. From orange to yellow then back to green.

"Red, orange, yellow, green, blue, purple on a loop."

"Mmm," he agreed. "The sign too."

Then it hit me. They were the colors of the rainbow.

I looked around again, taking in the people sitting scattered throughout the bar. The biker-looking dude had a skinny blond next to him. Short spiky hair, and wearing a pale blue tee that fitted him like a glove. It showed off every part of his delicate frame. They were sitting closer now, the kid's arm hooked into the bigger man's one. There were two women further away. I had assumed they were friends, but I realized they were more than that when I saw their hands interlinked. "This is a gay bar."

"It is. You okay with us being here?"

I didn't even have to think about my answer. The hesitation, the angst I'd been stuck in slipped away, leaving behind a confidence I'd rarely experienced together with an overwhelming feeling of love.

Angelo had picked somewhere he knew we'd be accepted. Where we'd fit in and no one would criticize us or belittle our sexuality. Where we could be free to exist.

To love.

"I am." I smiled and looked him up and down slowly, wanting to take advantage of being somewhere I instinctively felt safe. I ate up every inch of his lithe frame, and the moan I let out sounded like a purr. "You look… edible."

"You do too."

I looked down at my jeans and collared shirt and shrugged. My leather jacket was slung over the back of the barstool, but that didn't exactly add flair to my outfit like Angelo managed to pull off whenever he was dressed up.

I turned on the stool and willed myself to have the courage to touch him like I wanted to. Nearly two decades of hiding—if you counted the couple of years before I worked up the courage to come out that first time—was hard to kick. But I wanted this for us. I wanted it for me.

I reached out for Angelo and tugged him between my legs, resting my hands on his hips. He startled, his eyes going wide for a moment before a look of pure adoration washed over his face.

I loved that look. Loved when he directed it my way. I'd never get enough of seeing it.

Angelo brought his hand up and cupped my face, running his fingertips over my jaw. It was an innocent touch, but so intimate that I felt exposed. Raw. Strong.

I kissed his palm and he gifted me with that smile I adored before leaning down and asking in a murmur, "Can I kiss you?"

My body reacted like a livewire when he ran his nose down my ear, and I shivered. I felt rather than saw his smile against my cheek as I moaned, "Yes."

Angelo hummed in the back of his throat and brushed his lips over mine in a whisper-soft kiss. I sighed, wishing we were somewhere private enough that I could deepen the kiss, and at the same time loving that we were in the company of strangers.

"Can I get you boys a drink?" the bartender asked us, interrupting our moment.

"Two whiskeys with dry and a wedge of lime please," Angelo answered and motioned to a row of low tables. "You wanna sit over there and eat?"

"Sounds great."

We ordered wings, fries, and sliders for dinner, paid for our drinks, and sat around a table in a quiet corner. Sitting next to each other, we held hands under the table, and Angelo caught me up on the meetings he'd had that afternoon. He knew better than to ask me how my therapy session went. I usually told him, but not for hours after. Not until I wasn't so overwhelmed with the memories we'd dredged up. But the session that day was different. It was a great one, and I couldn't wait to tell him about it.

Our dinner arrived and we ate, sharing the food as I

recapped my appointment. Finally, I added, "I've been thinking about reaching out to Mom and Dad. I don't think I'm ready yet, but will you come with me if you can?"

Angelo put down the wing he was eating and wiped his hands, giving me his full attention. "Of course. Anytime you want, I'll be there."

"I was going to write them another letter. I need to change a few things in it." I reached out for his hand and held on to him like the lifeline he was. "I might send it to them when I feel like I've got it right."

"You'll do it." Angelo squeezed my hand and leaned into me. Pressing his lips gently against mine, he gave me a chaste kiss. Butterflies fluttered around in my belly.

Anywhere else and I would have expected someone to jump out at us and start screaming a homophobic rant. But nothing happened. There were no dirty looks. No under-handed comments. It was liberating.

I leaned forward and kissed him again, this time licking his lip until he opened for me. I wanted to take him home and make love to him, but at the same time I wanted to stay in The Vault, because in that room I was the freest I'd been in a long time. Strangers had become allies, and we shared a bond that made me comfortable enough to reveal the part of me I'd hidden for so long. And it was Angelo who did that for me.

"Come on." I motioned, standing up.

Angelo's eyes flashed with disappointment before he hid it, blinking away the sadness that dulled his eyes and forcing his lips to turn up. I held my hand out and he followed, but instead of leading him outside like I guessed he thought I was doing, I walked backward, deeper into the club and onto the empty dance floor. Music piped through the sound system, but it wasn't loud enough to kill off our conversation.

I smiled. This place was uplifting. Empowering. I didn't care that we'd be the only ones there. "Dance with me?"

I took him into my arms and we swayed totally out of sync to a rock song playing over the loudspeakers. Resting my head on his shoulder, I breathed him in and kissed his throat. It was quick, or maybe not, but it was so right and I was ready to take our relationship to the next step.

I gazed into his whiskey-eyes, filled with the warmth I loved, and asked him the other question that'd been on my mind. "Move in with me?" Before Angelo interrupted me, I explained more. "I know we already live together, but we still officially have separate bedrooms. All our clothes are in separate rooms, and you still have your toothbrush in your bathroom, so we're still not actually *living* together."

A slow smile spread across Angelo's lips, and he tightened his arm around my shoulders before leaning down and pressing his lips to mine. I opened instantly and teased his tongue with my own. His taste, his smell, his strength and love seeped into every part of me and I held tighter, kissed harder, loved louder.

When he pulled back, he whispered, "I'd love to." He kissed me again and moved his mouth to my ear, kissing down my throat and back up. "I want you."

He pulled back again to look in my eyes, and it hit me like a freight train. I was kidding myself. I wasn't loving louder. I wasn't coming out and living freely. I couldn't bottom for him. I couldn't give myself to him in the same way he'd let me into his body countless times. He'd get sick of me and my broken parts. Of my past ruling me. He'd walk away and I'd lose the best part of me: him.

Panic rose in me, sucking the oxygen from my lungs. The blood in my veins turned to ice, and I was light-headed in an instant.

I couldn't lose him, but I couldn't go through an experience like I'd gone through before again either. I didn't realize the bruising grip I had on Angelo until I felt him peel my fingers off his hip and pull his other hand free of mine. He led me to a table and sat me down, and I slumped forward in the chair. My elbows resting on my spread knees, I hung my head low, trying to draw air into my lungs. Angelo pulled up a chair and sat in front of me, holding my hands in his own. They were warm to the touch against my suddenly icy skin, and I concentrated on that connection with him.

"Breathe, Trent. In nice and slow." I did what he said, then exhaled when he told me so too. I trusted him. He grounded me. It seemed like a long time later that I'd managed to stop shaking, and when I did, he asked, "Where did you go?"

"I can't," I whispered. "He hurt me. Bottoming—"

"Oh, Trent," Angelo murmured, cupping my face gently. "Never doubt for one moment how much I love you and how much I want you. But I'll never ask that of you. I'll never push you or make you feel bad for not being able to give me that. I understand why you can't and I'm okay with it. I'm more than okay with what we do." He paused and ran his thumb over my cheek. "I want to kill that bastard for what he did, but he'll never get between us. I'll never let anything get between us."

I leaned into his touch and he moved closer, wrapping

his arms around me. I nuzzled his throat and breathed him in, his spicy scent settling my racing heart. "I love you too," I whispered, my voice cracking. "I'm scared of losing you because of my past."

"I'll always choose you, Trent. Always."

"Can you take me home?" I asked, hating the weakness I felt in that moment. Hating the uncertainty clouding my voice and the cold dread that had invaded my senses when I even thought about any experience possibly being as bad as my first time. No, not my first time. My rape.

Then it dawned on me, this time hitting me like a Mack truck.

My time with Angelo, if I was ever ready, wouldn't be anything like it was with Ryan. He raped me. I didn't give myself freely to him. I was just a kid and he overpowered me, pinned me down and punished me. Angelo... I couldn't even think of him in the same sentence without risking him being tainted by the evil that was my godfather. He and Angelo were nothing alike. My true first time would be the same as them—nothing alike.

"Let's go," Angelo agreed and took my hand in his. I held it tight, needing the reassurance from him as we made our way home.

---

I STOOD AT THE RED AND GRAY POST BOX WITH THE handwritten letter to my parents between my fingers. The warmth from Angelo's hand on my lower back and his body close to mine were a comfort I needed in that moment. My pulse thudded in my veins, and I wiped away the bead of sweat as it ran down my face.

The reality hit me hard.

I had to send this letter, didn't I? I had to get closure. I wanted so badly to have my parents back in my life. But of course sending it terrified me. What if it made no difference? What if they chose to ignore it?

And me.

Or thought it was some cruel hoax.

It'd taken me four months to work up the courage to finish the letter to my parents and send it. Now that I was standing there about to let it go, I was rethinking every word I'd painstakingly written and revised. With every new version, Angelo would tell me the original letter was better, scribbled out sentences and all. When I asked why, he always said the same thing: it came from my heart.

The pages were well worn now, folded and unfolded countless times. I'd tried to copy it out onto new paper, but I hadn't been able to without changing the words, so I wrote another shorter note, explaining why it looked that way. A photo accompanied the letter, one Angelo had taken of me on one of our summer hiking trips. I was happy, smiling at him as I sat down on an outcropping of rocks overlooking the lake, drinking a bottle of water.

"Whatever decision you make here is going to be the right one, Trent," Angelo encouraged me, rubbing his hand slowly up and down my back. "It's natural to be nervous. Scared shitless even. But you're strong. You can do this. Just remember that you're never alone. I'm here every step of the way."

I sucked in a breath, held it, and closed my eyes, gathering my courage. Angelo was right. I could do this. I'd already taken enough time to get to this point. There was no way I was going to back down now. I wasn't that scared boy who ran away anymore. It was time. I lifted the envelope to the slot, slid it in, and let it go. Now all I had to do was wait.

Right at that moment though, I had a shift to begin and Angelo was on his way to meet with clients. We were parked in the lot a block away and would be going in opposite directions when we got there, me up the mountain and him to the outskirts of town. It was good during the ski season; my shifts weren't as long and I didn't swap between night and day shifts, but I rarely saw much of him over the weekends. Weddings weren't just held in spring or summer apparently. So many people were opting to take their vows on or near the snow, or with the snow-capped peaks in the distance, that he was just as busy at this time of year, and even further into winter, as in the warmer months.

Even if I didn't see Angelo much over the weekends, it didn't matter. The months we'd been together were the best I'd ever experienced. I was getting more comfortable in my own skin, and PDAs were getting easier. Something as simple as letting Angelo touch me in public had taken months. I was okay in places like The Vault. It'd become our go-to since our first night there, as much as it'd ended on a downer because of my freak-out. But even though I was better than I had been, showing even the slightest bit of affection on the street was something I'd had to work hard to be able to do. My only explanation was fear, and I hated my godfather for instilling that in me. My therapist insisted that I needed to move at a pace I was comfortable with, that forcing anything too soon would make me anxious and have me constantly looking over my shoulder. She was right, and Angelo understood. He'd been a pillar of strength for me. He never pulled me up on my flinching when he touched me, as long as I didn't shy away from him in places I felt safe. But now, he knew I was mostly okay with his hand on me in the open.

The sidewalk on the main street through Queenstown was cluttered. People poured into town for the beginning of ski season, so I walked close to Angelo. We weren't strictly touching, but I was standing far too close for us to be anything but lovers. That just made this time of year even more special. The hustle and bustle of town, the smiling faces and excited kids. There was something else I was looking forward to later in the year too—Winter Pride. It was getting bigger and better every year, and this was the first year I truly wanted to join in.

My involvement would be more sedate than my other friends', but that's what I was comfortable with. While I'd love to be as loud and proud as Ford and Reef, who were on the organizing committee, or Ricky, whose helicopter tour business was a major sponsor, I wasn't ready for it. My unofficial brother-in-law and his two partners were the poster boys for rainbow families. They'd gained an international following after their interview for an Australian LGBT blog went viral, and #3MenAndAGracie had been trending since. I was proud of them all for over-coming their obstacles, just like I was proud of myself for coming so far. I still had a long way to go, but I was a work in progress.

My next step, depending on whether I heard anything back from the letter I'd just posted, was trying to rebuild the relationship with my parents.

We reached Angelo's Mini and he leaned against the door, pulling me close to him. I ran my hands down his red suspenders, following their length. Like me, he wasn't wearing a coat, but my black ski pants and red Alpine Rescue polo were nowhere near as classy as his black dress pants, red bow tie, and crisp white button-down shirt. His sleeves were rolled up, exposing his forearms and that, paired with his hot nerd getup, had desire pulsing through me. We were a study in contradictions, but our mismatched looks were only surface issues.

He was my best friend and the love of my life. I leaned in and kissed him chastely, but Angelo's quiet moan had me going back for more, holding his nape to keep his lips pressed against my own. I steeled myself, waiting for the anxiety of kissing him in public to hit me, but it never came. I kissed him longer, gently touching my tongue against his, tasting and teasing each other. I sank into his embrace, pressing my body to his, every dip and valley of Angelo's lithe frame fitting perfectly against my own. The stiff length of his shaft alongside my belly had me in a tailspin, my own cock hardening impossibly. Desire swept over me and our kiss turned desperate. My hands were in his hair, tugging at the short strands, and his fingers pressed into my shoulder, kneading the muscle there.

He pulled back, sucking in a lungful of air, and I did the same. Pupils blown with lust and his kiss-swollen lips nearly had me diving into him again, but his words stopped me. "You never stop amazing me with your strength. That took guts. I'm proud of you."

"Kissing you?" I asked, confused. My brain had turned to mush from his kiss and his strong hands on mine.

Angelo huffed out a laugh and ran his hand down my side, making me shiver. "You kissing me, yes. But sending the letter too."

"Oh." I smirked. "I… yeah. But it feels good too. Reaching out, I mean. And kissing you," I stuttered.

Angelo laughed and leaned down to kiss me again, and I didn't hesitate to respond. A flood of relief, of awareness washed over me. Standing in that parking lot, among the cars out in the open, I'd pushed past a major hurdle. I'd broken through years of fear. Years of self-loathing to acknowledge in public who I was and who I wanted. I smiled against Angelo's lips and kept kissing him, never wanting to let go. Joy filled me, innocent and pure. I was like a teenager with a crush, like a kid feeling that first rush of achievement when he tried something new. I felt like a man who'd had nothing finally getting what meant the most to him.

Love. Affection. Self-respect.

I held Angelo tight and we kissed until we were breathless once more.

"I love you," I whispered against his throat before kissing a line up to his ear. Sucking on his lobe, I scraped my teeth over it and hummed. Angelo's grip tightened and his shaft pulsed against my stomach.

"You're a damn tease," he grouched before kissing my cheek. "And I love you too."

"We better both get to work, or I'm going to test how comfortable I am in public," I mumbled against his skin.

"Mmm." He gently pushed me away from him and tried to discreetly adjust himself while I did the same.

I waited until he was in the Mini and the engine started before I made my way over to my beat-up truck and headed up the mountain for a shift.

An hour later, I found myself doing paperwork, signing off on an incident report, and sorting through the other documents I needed Ford to countersign. It was peaceful in the rescue center. We had one patient keeping Ford busy, and the radio was silent. I'd slipped into my own world, remembering Angelo's lips on mine and his needy whimpers as he pulled me close. It had me smiling like a loon. I loved being able to kiss him, and doing it in public made the butterflies flutter around my belly.

"Aw, Trent's all loved up," Ford exclaimed from the doorway.

I jumped, my heart thudding in my chest. Ford's remarks wrenched me out of my daydream. Hand on my heart, I laughed at myself. "Busted." I grinned, no doubt with hearts in my eyes.

"I'm happy for you, Trent. You've been smiling a lot lately. It's a nice change."

I couldn't deny that I was smiling more. I was undoubtedly happy and ridiculously in love. "I am happy." I looked up at Ford and found myself blushing. I scrubbed my hand over my face and huffed out a laugh.

He came and sat down opposite me, crossing his ankle over his knee, and smiled a knowing smile. "Feels good, doesn't it?" It wasn't a question. He became more serious and tilted his head to the side, studying me. "You doing okay with everything? You know I'm here to talk if you ever need to."

I smiled. "I kissed him today. In public."

"First time?"

I nodded and bit my lip trying to hold back a grin. "It was good, Ford. I felt free. He's given me that. I never thought...." I shook my head and huffed out a breath. "I never thought I'd have that, ya know?"

"Yeah. I get it. With your past, it can't have been easy opening up."

"It hasn't been, no." I scrubbed my hand over my face, all the happy feels gone the moment I thought about my godfather. "I still struggle with a lot of things, but therapy is helping and Angelo's a far better man than I deserve."

"No." Ford shook his head. "He's exactly the kind of man you deserve. He's a good man. The best."

"He is. I love him." I smiled. Thinking of him did that.

"It's obvious." He paused, but I knew he had more to say. I didn't have to wait long. "How long have you been in love with him?"

I huffed out a breath. "Years, but I wouldn't admit it even to myself. Especially to myself. I hate that I hurt him while it took me so long to come to terms with it."

"You did the best you could, Trent. Jesus, you survived. That's… that's enough. It's okay to need help."

"I know that. Well, now I do anyway." I paused, needing to gather the nerve to tell him why I was in town kissing Angelo to begin with. "I, ah… I reached out to Mom and Dad. Sent them a letter today. I have to wait now to see if they respond. It's gonna suck—the waiting I mean—but maybe they'll call me."

Ford stood up and walked around the desk to me. I watched as he ruffled my hair and pulled me to his side. "I'm proud of you. You did good."

Our conversation was interrupted by the crackle of the radio and the bell on the entry door. We jumped into action, each of us heading to where we were needed. I appreciated Ford's words more than he could know. His support meant more than he could ever imagine. He'd hated me, and he had every right to. I'd nearly ruined his chance with the love of his life. If anyone did that to Angelo and me, they wouldn't still be standing. I'd hunt the bastard down.

To think that Ford forgave me, that he put aside the hurt I'd caused him and Reef the moment he understood why I reacted that way, just proved to me he was the kind of friend I wanted to be.

# CHAPTER 16
## TRENT

The wait was killing me.

Three days. Two hundred and fifty-nine thousand, two hundred seconds. And I felt every single one of them.

I couldn't sleep, but I was exhausted. Every time I closed my eyes, my mind ran in circles faster and faster and faster and faster until I was damn near dizzy. It was like the opening credits of *The Big Bang Theory*.

Even when I was awake, I couldn't think straight. It started as me being preoccupied about Angelo and the kiss we'd shared in the parking lot and turned into obsessing about when the mail would be collected. I should have paid for tracking on the letter so I could see exactly where it was at, but I thought I'd be better. I thought I'd handle it. Within a few hours, Ford sent me home. I didn't blame him. I nearly ran over a couple of kids building a snowman just off the beginner run when I took the snow-mobile out to check on a skier. He was having as good a day as me—falling over trying to get on the ski lift wasn't something I'd done before, but in my dysfunctional state, it wouldn't surprise me if I did.

I didn't eat either. Even the smell of food had me wanting to barf. My stomach churned at the same speed as my mind. I lost count of how many cups of coffee I'd had until Angelo cut me off somewhere around the forty-hour mark. I was still jittery, but I didn't know whether that was the nerves or the caffeine in the espressos I'd downed like water.

Angelo's hovering was making me insane, but I couldn't bear to have him far away either. He'd come close and I'd walk away, then I'd go straight back to him and crowd him until I was practically sitting on his lap. I could see him getting frustrated. He didn't know what to do with me, but he was doing everything I needed. I didn't know what else to do. What to feel. I'd placed my entire relationship with my parents in New Zealand Post's hands. There was literally nothing I could do until they delivered the letter and I got the call. *If* I got a call.

I paced the living room floor, trying to rationalize a plan in my head if I didn't hear from my parents for days or weeks. Or maybe never. If I truly had burned the bridge between us by running away all those years ago, I had to face up to them not wanting anything more to do with me.

The thought stung. I'd wanted it for so long. I'd missed them so damn much, but my therapist was right. I had to work up to it. I hadn't been brave enough or strong enough to have sent the letter before. Now I was, but I was also impatient to know. I had to remember that I'd had a while to come to terms with this. I was springing it on them. They might need time to get used to the idea I wasn't dead, too. I had to remember that they might not even believe me, or want me, and ignore the letter altogether. I scrubbed my hands over my face and ran my fingers through my hair, groaning in frustration.

At any other time, seeing me like this, Angelo would have dragged me to the gym for a sparring session. But this time he knew it wasn't what I needed. I wasn't angry, I wasn't letting out frustration. I was scared. Nervous. Excited. Hopeful, but fearful too.

"Trent," Angelo called quietly. I heard him, but when I didn't answer straight away, he stood in front of me, blocking my pacing. "Hey." He reached out, clasping my arms gently.

"What?" I snapped, regretting it immediately. I blew out a breath and grasped his hand. "Sorry, I don't mean to take it out on you. I'm not good at this."

"I wouldn't be either." He cupped my face with his free hand and pressed our foreheads together. "You need to get out somewhere peaceful. Why don't you put your gear on and we can hike along one of the trails?"

I closed my eyes and relief washed over me. He always knew exactly what I needed even when I had no idea myself. "That sounds perfect." So that's what we did. A few hours later, we were on one of our favorite trails overlooking the town. High up in the mountain air, the cold fall breeze buffeted the slope, and I pulled my beanie down lower over my ears. The pack on my back wasn't heavy, but it was a little awkward, being filled with a rolled-up blanket and a couple of foil wraps, torches, and a first aid kit. Angelo insisted on carrying the food and drinks, a much heavier bag.

The rocky terrain made it slippery underfoot and I had to concentrate hard not to lose my footing as we maintained our punishing pace hiking up to the snow line. I was exhausted, breathing hard in the thin air and completely out of energy. It wasn't surprising, given my lack of food or sleep in days. The lactic acid buildup was making my exhaustion worse; I needed to sit down. Angelo beat me to it, pointing to a huge boulder over-looking the valley. "Up there. I need a rest."

"Sure you do." I smirked as best I could while trying to get enough air in my lungs to power the last way up the slope. "But I appreciate you not calling me out on needing a break."

I sat on the pitted surface of the rock. It was ice-cold, the chill instantly seeping through to my bones. While Angelo fussed over the food, taking containers and flasks out of his pack, I pulled the blanket out of mine and laid it over the rock. Sitting back down, I shifted to make enough room for Angelo to join me and we sat there together. We didn't speak, but I appreciated it. It was the first time my mind had quieted in days. Angelo handed me a flask of sweetened tea he'd brewed before leaving, and we broke open the fruit, nut mix, and candy bars.

"Thank you," I murmured. "For being there through this. I've been a mess. I didn't realize how hard it would be. The waiting is killing me." I'd barely finished my sentence when my cell rang. I stilled, then looked at Angelo.

"Answer it," he encouraged, digging it from the side pocket of my bag.

It was an Auckland number. My heart thudded in my chest and my palms were sweaty. This could be it. It could be them. Nervous excitement pulsed through me, warring equally with fear. I had no idea what to say or do, but I knew one thing. I had to speak to whoever it was on the other end of the line. I swiped to answer it, saying, "Hello?" My voice came out at a higher register than I intended, betraying my nerves. I cleared my throat and repeated myself, "Ah, hello."

"Hello, my name is Amanda Weathered from Bakersfield, McKenzie & Weathered in Auckland. May I ask to whom I'm speaking?"

The name sounded like it was a firm of lawyers. *Oh God, no. Please no. Please don't let anything have happened to them.* I reached out for Angelo's hand and he clasped it, threading his fingers through mine and holding tight. "I'm known as Trent Campbell now, but my full name is Keir Trenton Campbell." My voice wobbled, emotions making it crack. Angelo shifted, wrapping his arm around me and holding me close.

"Did you send a letter to Mr. and Mrs. Campbell recently?"

"I did. They're my parents. I… I was trying to reach out to them." I sucked in a breath, willing my heart to steady. When I spoke again, it was barely a whisper. I had no idea whether the woman on the other end of the line even heard me above the whistle of the wind. "Am I too late?"

"Sir, I'm following up on behalf of my clients." She sounded businesslike. Not cold, but a no-nonsense professional. She didn't beat around the bush either. "They received a letter this morning and telephoned me. My instructions are to ask you some questions that only Keir would know the answers to and to pass on those answers to my clients. If they're satisfied with them, they'll make contact directly with you."

"Okay." Relief filled me. I assumed if they were

instructing her, that they were okay. I hoped. I nodded, knowing she couldn't see me, still freaking out about the possibility that I was too late.

"Tell me, what was your favorite thing to do with your sister?"

"I'm an only child. I don't have any siblings. Mom and Dad tried for years before they had me. Then they tried again, but it never happened." I paused, my brow furrowing as I put the pieces together. "But you know that, don't you?"

"I do, Mr. Campbell. Can you describe a memory from one of your childhood holidays with your family?"

I thought for a moment, reaching back into memories I'd buried long ago. Ones that were of happier times. Ones that were too painful to think about now.

"We never went on holidays just the three of us. My godfather was always with us. I remember one time going camping at this creek. The campsite was at a bend in the stream. I was so excited about going there that I went down to the water and fell in. I twisted my ankle on the rocks and had to sit down for most of the weekend. Dad and my godfather took me fishing instead of swimming and hiking like we'd planned. It was the first time we'd gone. Between the three of us we caught one fish—it was Dad who hooked it. But it didn't swallow the hook. It was too small to have done that. The hook got caught on its fin. When we got back, Mom made a big deal about not having any dinner to cook, but the whole time she was smiling. We had dinner, then ate enough marshmallows toasted on the fire to make me want to puke."

Angelo was rubbing my back, smiling at me. "That sounds like a wonderful memory."

"It was a fun trip. I had a good childhood."

"Thanks for telling me that, Mr. Campbell." The lady asked me a few more questions, some to trip me up and others to get more details from me to verify my identity. When she hung up, the only thing she promised was that she'd pass on my answers and someone might be in touch.

I was restless again, hopeful but nervous, and unsurprisingly Angelo picked up on it. "Let's head back down the mountain and have a hot shower together." I smiled at him and nodded.

"Yeah, I'd like that."

My cell rang again when Angelo was pulling my truck into the drive of our townhouse. The number flashed up on the screen, and I swallowed hard. It was another from Auckland, but this one was familiar. It was one I'd memorized as a kid, ironically in case something happened and I needed to call home. It obviously worked; I could never forget it. I closed my eyes and reached for Angelo. He clasped my hand, squeezing tight when I swiped the answer button. "Hello?"

A gasp came through the line and a lady started sobbing. "My God, it's you," she said, and I recognized my mom's voice instantly. My eyes burned and I didn't even try to stop the tears from flowing. Angelo was there, reaching out for me when I needed him most and for that I was grateful.

"Mom?" I cried. "Is… is Dad there too?"

"I am, son," he answered, and I cried harder. Hearing their voices was like a dream come true. Something I never thought I'd hear again. They sounded the same, but different too. Time would do that, I supposed. I'd given up hope of speaking to them again, but there I was, all four of us crying.

Mom added, "We knew it was you as soon as we saw the photo, but we couldn't get our hopes up. We thought you were gone."

"I miss you," I blurted . "I'm sorry. I'm so, so sorry."

"Hush, son. There's nothing to be sorry for. You came back to us." My father's words were to mollify me. I knew that we'd have to work through the issues I'd caused. No, the issues my godfather had caused with his evil act. But it was still nice hearing they were happy I'd called them.

"Can you send me a photo of you?" I asked. "I haven't seen you in so long. You only ever share photos of me on Facebook." I huffed out a laugh at the irony of my parents sharing my photos and me not even being on social media.

"I'll text you one now," Mom said, still sniffling. "Can we see you, Keir? Come and visit you? Or maybe you'd like to come to us?"

"Ah…." I hesitated, but that was enough for Angelo to step in.

"Trent, go at your own pace. Remember what you've been working through. Maybe get them to come here." He spoke the words against my temple, mumbling more than speaking, but it was what I needed to hear.

I nodded. I wasn't ready to go to Auckland yet, mainly because my godfather might be there.

"Is there someone else there with you, Keir? Should we call back another time?" Mom asked, uncertain.

Before I could answer, Angelo spoke up. "Hello, Mrs. Campbell, Mr. Campbell. I'm Angelo. Please don't go. It's not an inconvenient time. I just told Trent that perhaps you might like to come to Queenstown. It's lovely at this time of year. It's not the cheapest time to come here though, with ski season about to start."

"Oh, hello, Angelo," she replied, more of a smile in her voice. "We'd love to visit Queenstown. Can you recommend somewhere to stay?"

Angelo looked at me and smiled, wiping the tear tracks from my cheek. "I'll text you through a few names of the hotels closest to our house after you hang up."

"You two live together?" my dad asked, and my gut sank. I didn't want to lie to him. I was out to everyone who mattered, but fear clasped a cold hand around my heart and squeezed it. I'd only just got them back. How would I handle it if they didn't want anything to do with me when I shared that part of me with them?

I opened my mouth, then closed it again, torn between telling them how important Angelo was to me and lying to them. I was saved from answering when Angelo did it for me.

"We're roommates, yes. We've been friends for years." My eyes popped open and I looked at him, worry sweeping any trepidation away. Why had he done that? Why did he just jump back into the closet with me? He smiled and ran his thumb over my cheek again before kissing me softly on my forehead.

"We're happy you're friends then. It's important to have that," Mom said with a hint of sadness in her voice.

"Angelo's… he's amazing," I explained, needing to tell them in my own way how important he was to me.

We spoke for a while longer, the conversation staying on safe topics. Things like work and Dad's recent retirement, whether I still fished, and how our team was doing in the football. I didn't have the heart to tell them that I didn't really follow the games anymore because of the memories they dredged up. But I did ask them whether they'd kept in touch with my childhood best friend, Jake. They had. He visited them whenever he was back in the country. He'd apparently moved to Australia for college and had stayed there. I wanted to ask them about Ryan too. To check whether they were still as close as they used to be, but I dared not mention his name. I wasn't sure what it meant when they didn't speak about him either.

Throughout the whole conversation, Angelo held me close, running his fingers through my hair and letting me know with soft caresses that he was there for me. When we said goodbye with promises to speak again in a couple of days, I closed my eyes and laid my head on his shoulder.

"You need some sleep, *amore*," Angelo murmured against my hair.

"Why did you tell them we're roomies rather than partners?" I asked quietly. I wasn't sure whether I wanted to know, especially considering how we'd fought so hard to feel comfortable enough to have our relationship out in the open.

"It's a lot to take in at once—finding out you're alive, hearing your voice again, arranging for them to visit. I was trying not to overwhelm them and to protect you from having so much emotional stuff happening all at once. I'm sorry if I hurt you by saying that."

"No, it's okay. I just... I was scared to tell them, but I didn't want to lie either." I looked up at him and took a steadying breath. "I can't lose you. I'm scared they'll hate me, but I can't lose you."

"Shh," he soothed, running his fingertips down my face. "I'm not going anywhere. I'll always choose you."

I closed my eyes to his touch and felt his warm breath before his lips ghosted over mine. The move was intimate and lovely. Sweet and soothing, his love wrapped around me like a warm blanket. I found myself smiling that dreamy smile I had whenever I thought of Angelo, but I needed him in my arms. I blinked open my eyes and motioned to the townhouse. I didn't need to say anything further. Angelo got out and I followed, meeting him at the front of my truck. We left the bags in the car and went inside, stripping off our coats and scarves as we passed through the living room. Angelo paused outside the main bathroom and grasped my hand, pulling me inside.

"I've got a better idea than a shower." He pulled out a couple of Lush bath bombs, started filling the tub, and lit one of the scented candles we had in the room. "Let's get you undressed." He was on his knees undoing my hiking boots and pulling each off, my socks following soon after. I helped him up after he'd taken off his own, and he reached for my sweater, leaning in to kiss me first.

Our tongues tangled as he inched it up my body and I moaned into his mouth. His hands were on me; fingertips dancing over my stomach had it fluttering. He pulled back, only to lift my thin sweater over my head, my T-shirt following immediately behind. I tugged off his thermal Henley, leaving us both bare chested in our waterproof hiking pants. His olive skin and the dusting of hair over his chest and down his belly had my mouth watering.

I kissed him again, moving my mouth along his jawline and down his throat. Kissing and licking my way across his chest, my tongue lashing his nipples and down his taut stomach to his navel, I relished his taste. His soft skin and those strong hands threading through my hair. He wasn't pushing, just pulling me close to him. Anchoring himself to me. I loved that. I loved knowing he was as desperate for my touch as I was for his.

Falling to my knees, I popped the button on his pants and lowered the zipper, tugging both his pants and underwear down his legs. I helped him out of them and tossed the clothes to the side out of our way. He was hard, but I turned away from his shaft, kissing his thigh and hip, across his belly over to the other hip. Angelo's groan had me looking up at him. My tongue still against his inner thigh, I grinned wickedly when I saw his drunk-with-desire but pained expression. Precum leaked from the tip of his cock, and I couldn't resist a taste. I swiped my tongue over his slit and hummed when his flavor burst onto my taste buds.

"Get up here," he rasped, tugging on my wrist.

I let go of his hips and stood up, kissing him hard when we were again chest to chest. He pushed me against the vanity basin and fell to his knees. I leaned back and looked down as he ripped open my pants and stuffed his hand down my boxer briefs, jacking me as he worked my remaining clothes off my hips. His tongue lashed my balls, and I hissed at the contact. He was bringing me to the edge far too quickly.

I pushed gently against his forehead and he immediately pulled back. Hurt flashed across his features, but he quickly covered it up before breathing out a "Sorry."

"I don't wanna come in your hand like a randy teenager. I wanna love on you." I smiled at him, cupping his face in my hands. "I wanna mess up our bathroom." I smirked at him and flicked off the faucet before stepping into the warm water.

Angelo followed me in, and I tugged him down on top of me. Spreading my legs, he slipped between them, lining up our cocks as he brought his mouth back to mine. He ground down and I thrust up, sliding our shafts against each other. I gasped at the friction created by our hardness pressing together, then moaned in ecstasy as I wrapped my hand around them and encouraged his movements with my other hand on his ass.

Water sloshed around us as we moved together, lost in each other's kisses and the synchronized dance of our bodies. I squeezed his perky ass cheek before moving my fingers to his crease, rubbing over his hole. Circling his pucker, I pressed gently, but not enough to enter him. That was all it took. Angelo stiffened over me and his shaft hardened impossibly, grinding against my own. It pushed me over the edge too, my orgasm flowing over me like the waters of the Niagara River crashing over the edge of the falls. Our cum pulsed out of our cocks together, both of us struggling for breath as we soared high above the clouds, or maybe tumbled in a barrel with the rushing waters.

Our softening cocks still in my hand, Angelo let his weight rest fully on me. Pinned below him in the warm water, my legs spread and his mouth close to mine, I was the most comfortable I'd been in days. My eyes closed, and I tilted my head up to his for another kiss. This one was slow and sweet. Lazy swipes of our tongues and brushes of lips. It was heaven.

Angelo looked up and around, surveying the damage, and grinned. "We didn't lose too much water." He lifted off me and reached for the soap, drizzling the liquid over my belly.

Using steady hands, he rubbed the bubbles over my skin, washing away the evidence of our orgasms and the sweat from our hike. He tended to every inch of me, from the tips of my fingers to my hair and down to my toes, unhurriedly caressing my skin. I lay with my eyes closed, enjoying his gentle touch. His hands left me, and I opened my eyes to watch him vigorously scrub himself with soap, not taking anywhere near the care with himself as he did with me. I reached for him and tried to help, but he playfully swatted my hands away. Taking the hand-held showerhead, he pulled the plug and rinsed us both down before passing me a towel from the cupboard.

"I feel like I could sleep for a week," I mumbled, my words already slurring with exhaustion. I did a half-assed job of drying myself, and Angelo led me to our bedroom, pulling down the covers and taking me into his arms. Head resting on his shoulder, I hooked my leg over his and held him close, sleep taking me just after I felt rather than heard his happy sigh and the press of his lips to my forehead.

It was only a few weeks later that I found myself standing next to Angelo in the lobby of one of the nearby hotels. The nerves jangling around in me were a stark contrast to the surrounding calm. Soft music played from hidden speakers, and the staff processed the line of people checking in and out quickly and quietly. The high ceilings and square columns accented with steel beams, black light fittings, and gray walls gave the lobby a modern warehouse feel, but the rich red-gold of the polished timber floors added a welcome warmth.

I looked around for the sign to the café my therapist suggested we book at. Apparently, it was the perfect setup for private conversations, and at this time of morning, the café was usually quiet. Angelo pointed to the sign, and we headed up the curved stairs to the café. Dr. Hansard was waiting for us just outside the entrance with her colleague who would be acting as intermediary. "Trent, hello," she greeted me warmly as I stepped off the stairs and we made our way over to them. "And you must be Angelo. I've heard so many wonderful things about you. It's lovely to finally meet you." They shook hands, and Angelo smiled politely.

"Hello," he mumbled, his cheeks flushed. He shot a glance my way, and I reached out for him, brushing the back of my hand against his. I swallowed hard and closed my eyes, my nerves in overdrive. I'd been semi-okay up to that point. I could tell Angelo was worried, watching me while I got dressed and on the way over to the hotel. He'd driven us here, and on the elevator ride up from the basement parking lot, he didn't take his eyes off me. I'd assured him then I was okay.

Now? Not so much.

My gut was busy doing a gymnastic tumbling routine that would rival that of an Olympic gold medalist, and my heart was thudding hard in my chest. *It's really happening. I'm really seeing them again.* I smoothed my hands along my black, button-down shirt and made sure it was still tucked into my dark gray dress pants. Angelo insisted I looked good. I'd liked what I'd seen in the mirror before we left, and he was right—I was comfortable and more confident in the tailored clothes. But while the clothes made me look put together on the outside, inside I was a quivering, swirling, freaked out, nauseous, nervous mess.

Angelo stepped a fraction closer to me. Anyone who didn't know us wouldn't even look twice at the picture we painted—two friends standing shoulder to shoulder. But his being slightly in front of mine was his subtle way of protecting me, like he could push me behind him and shield me from whatever I needed an out from. I appreciated his presence more than he could ever know. I wasn't strong enough to do it alone. But that was okay. I knew my limitations now, and this was one of them. I needed him as my support person, and Angelo was exactly that. He was my person.

I admired him from my peripheral vision. His navy blue slacks were paired with a pale-blue check shirt and a navy bow tie. Matching check socks, brown leather shoes, and blue suspenders finished off the outfit. He was carrying his suit jacket in his left hand and he had his camera with one of the smaller lenses slung over his right. He turned and smiled warmly at me, and my heart flip-flopped in my chest.

Dr. Hansard studied me closely, her expression filled with genuine concern. "How are you doing, Trent?"

"I'm nervous. Scared about their reactions and them not understanding why I ran away. I'm more scared of my godfather being here."

"He's not." Dr. Hansard's colleague spoke with an Indian accent. "I introduced myself to them when they arrived. They're sitting down waiting for us, but you take your time going in. We'll wait for you to be comfortable before starting, okay?"

I nodded, and my mind wandered as they continued talking with Angelo. When I looked up, they'd left Angelo and me alone at the entrance. There were other people around, but not many, so Angelo pulled me to the side and spoke quietly, with no judgement in his tone. "You zoned out. He's Dr. Ankur Bhat." This time I did reach for him, threading our fingers together and squeezing his hand.

"I'm scared, Angelo."

His smile was soft, his eyes full of love when he encouraged, "You can do this, Trent. You've come so far. You're strong enough for this, and I'm right here. Always." Instantly my nerves settled. He grounded me. I wanted this. I wanted to meet them again. I was scared, terrified even, but I couldn't let it stop me from walking through that door. Angelo pulled me close for a moment, hugging me hard.

Before he moved away, I whispered, "Thank you." Hands shaking, palms sweating, I drew a deep breath in and entered the café with Angelo close behind. The maître d' met us and guided us to a table in the back corner. Like Dr. Hansard had promised, each area was designed into a private nook. Some were larger than others and over-looked the main street and towering mountains beyond, the view framed by picture windows. Others were just an armchair and small side table enclosed between tall book-shelves packed with books of every description. Paintings and sculptures were dotted around too, giving the place an eclectic, artistic vibe, and the smell of roasted coffee beans and fresh-cooked pastries permeated the air. My stomach growled, uncaring that I'd been too jittery to eat much of anything that morning.

The maître d' showed us the table that my parents and Dr. Bhat were seated at. Dr. Hansard hovered nearby, but I didn't take much notice. All I could focus on were my parents. Dad had a full head of steely gray hair now, and his face was no longer smooth. Wrinkles had aged him, and he'd lost some of his bulk. He was still broad shouldered, but the muscle had started to turn soft. Underneath though, I saw the same strong man I'd idolized as a kid.

We gazed at each other and he slowly stood up, stepping out from behind the table. Mom followed, pushing her glasses up her nose as she stood. She hadn't worn them when I was younger. It wasn't the only change either. She looked frail. Much thinner and more hunched than she was all those years ago. Her hair was streaked with gray like Dad's, and her hands bonier too. She moved a lot slower now, and Dad held out his hand to help her walk. Tears ran tracks down her wrinkled cheeks as she placed a hand over her mouth and choked out a cry.

"Keir," she whispered like a prayer, my name sounding strange on her lips after all this time.

Angelo's hand on my lower back rubbing small circles had my legs reengaging, and I acted on instinct, pulling both of them into my arms. I was taller than them now, broader than Dad too, but I felt sheltered like I did as a child when he hugged me. Mom's frailty didn't show in her hug, her arms winding around me in a vise grip.

I cried hot tears. Years of pain and longing, of missing my parents, of fear and betrayal by my godfather washed over me. Powerless to stop, I trembled in their arms, wishing I hadn't waited so long. Wishing I'd been stronger. Braver. Mom and Dad cried too, all three of us clinging desperately to each other.

"We never thought we'd see you again." Dad spoke through his tears, and my already broken heart shattered into a million pieces. "I was waiting for them to find your body. We've waited so long, but you're here. You're really here."

"I'm sorry, I'm so sorry." It was the only thing I could say, but it was nowhere near enough. Shame mixed with that self-loathing for fucking everything up threatened to drown me. I hated that I'd hurt them. With everything in me I wished I could turn back time and change how things happened that night and the shit storm that ensued.

But I couldn't.

I'd known in my gut that I'd hurt them, but hearing the words crushed me. Weighed down by them, I reached blindly for the one person who could pull me up. Angelo. His hand on my shoulder steadied me, and I breathed again. That simple touch was enough to haul me from the depths of despair so I could take a gasping breath.

I don't know how long we stood there, crying and holding each other tight, but when we eventually pulled away, I looked for him again. He was still there, right next to me. He squeezed my shoulder, but it wasn't enough. My emotions were running close to the surface and as much as I needed his touch, I needed to comfort Angelo too. Pain laced his features and I needed to soothe it away. His eyes, glassy and red, cried tears for me, and seeing his hurt broke my heart.

Angelo's free arm was wrapped around his midsection, shielding—or maybe comforting—himself. I reached for him, pulling him into my arms. The moment I did, his love enveloped me. All I hoped was that I could give him the same comfort he gave me with a simple touch. Angelo's grip around my shoulders tightened, and he buried his face in the crook of my neck. I breathed him in and Angelo did the same as I held him close, never wanting him to pull away.

"You okay?" I whispered.

"I should be asking you that," he huffed. "Seeing you with your parents was beautiful. Heart wrenching, but beautiful." He patted me on the back, a move so unlike Angelo that when he pulled back

I looked at him, making sure he was all right. I knew he was doing it to protect me, but I suddenly hated not being open about what he meant to me. I hated that he thought he needed to.

"Mom, Dad." I motioned to the man standing next to me and smiled at him. "This is Angelo."

"Your roommate, I remember. Hi," Dad replied, holding out his hand.

"Pleased to meet you, Mr. Campbell. Mrs. Campbell, hello." They shook hands and Angelo pulled out our chairs, the four of us sitting down with Dr. Bhat at the head of the table.

I looked to the doctor, who motioned for me to speak. I remembered that he would only participate if he thought he needed to. He was, for all intents and purposes, an observer.

"So…," I began, not knowing how to start the conversation between us. I had so much to say, but no idea of where to start. The initial awkwardness didn't last long though. We all started talking at once, then stopped and laughed. It broke the tension, and I let Mom and Dad go first.

"We were so happy you reached out." Mom held out her hand from across the table, and I slipped mine into it. Her warm fingers closed around mine, the difference in her Maori tones and my half-white coloring more pronounced in the winter when I had no tan. She squeezed tight. "We thought the worst when it'd been so long. We tried everything we knew to find you, but you'd disappeared. When we got your letter…. I didn't believe what I was reading until I saw your photo. It left me in no doubt."

Dad spoke then. "Our psychologist told us to call anytime we ever needed anything. When I told her about the letter, she wanted to reach out and make initial contact. I'm sorry if that upset you."

I shook my head and added, "No, I understand. It was out of the blue on your end. I'd been working up to it for months. Years, really."

We were interrupted by a waiter taking our order for coffees, and when we were alone again, Mom asked, "Why did you leave, Trent?" Dr. Bhat went to interrupt, but before he could get a word out, Mom put her hand up and shook her head. "Never mind. That doesn't matter. What's important is that you're here now and we can keep up contact again."

"We're probably supposed to stick to safe topics today, but I do want to explain. I need to, so you know it wasn't your fault." Angelo squeezed my shoulder and I leaned into his touch, taking the strength I knew he was offering. "It was Ryan. He hurt me." I sucked in a breath, trying not to drown in the memories. My voice cracked as I tried to push through and keep the story going. "It was… awful. Every moment's burned into my memory. I wish I didn't remember, but I do."

I closed my eyes and tried to center myself. Focusing on Angelo's comforting touch, I kept going, my voice barely above a whisper. "I couldn't go back there. I couldn't see him again. I knew you wanted me to go and apologize, but I didn't understand why. I was ashamed. Scared it'd happen again. Scared of him. I just reacted. I ran. I hid. I was trying to get away from him. I didn't mean to hurt you. I never wanted that." I huffed, disgusted at myself. "I didn't want to make you choose between us. So I made the choice for you."

Dad shook his head, his jaw clenched tight. He closed his eyes and visibly relaxed his fists before running his hands through his steely gray hair. I knew I'd said the wrong thing the instant he did it, and my gut sank. Mom squeezed my hand tight, almost crushing my fingers, and she sobbed.

"We found out. I saw your clothes in the bathroom. I saw the blood in your underwear and on your sweatpants." Dad wrapped his arm around Mom and pulled her to him, and she cried softly against his chest. He continued, "We came looking for you, but you'd already run. We called everywhere. We drove around the streets yelling out for you. Begging you to come home. Every one of your school friends was out looking for you too. No one had seen you—"

"No one?" I asked incredulously.

"No." Mom answered, sadly. "The police told us that you'd seen Jake, but he never broke your trust."

The same waiter reappeared with a tray of coffees, and

tea for Dr. Bhat. The doctor stood and looked after the check while we sat there quietly for a moment. I stirred my latte, remembering my childhood friend. I'd wanted to reach out to him so many times, but I was scared of my godfather knowing I was alive. Of him discovering where to find me. Jake had kept my secret, and I was so very grateful to him for protecting me like that.

Dad broke the silence after a beat, adding, "You'd only been missing for an hour when we called the police. They came straight away and interviewed us." Dad looked away and closed his eyes. Clenched his jaw and blew out a breath. I couldn't see his free hand, but I was sure he'd made a fist again. It was hard seeing him like that. So obviously in pain from something I'd done. From memories I'd left them with.

Mom took up where Dad left off, seamlessly continuing like I remembered they always did. "They interviewed Ryan too. He promised them that you'd drunk all the beer in his refrigerator without him knowing it. You were drunk and hurt yourself falling down the steps. It might have been a reason for your black eye, but it didn't explain your other injuries."

"He let me have one beer, but he was drinking all night. The refrigerator was almost empty by the time the game was nearly finished." I blew out a breath, nauseous from the memory of the smell of it on his breath as he'd spewed his hate-filled words at me. "I haven't been able to drink it since," I said quietly, ashamed that he still had that control over me.

"We'd handed over your clothes to the police that first day. But Ryan kept insisting that the last he saw of you, you were stumbling home. I was so angry with him."

Mom shook her head, rage flashing in her eyes. "I confronted him. Told him we'd handed everything over to the police for testing. That if he'd hurt you, I'd kill him. He sneered at me and I lost it. I remember kicking and punching him. Scratching him and yanking out his hair. Your father walked into the house and pulled me off him. I'll never forget what he did then."

"What?" I asked, my voice barely a whisper. Strangled by the soul-deep anger my godfather evoked in me.

"He got two plastic bags from the kitchen and taped them over my hands, hair and all, and we went straight to the police station. They collected the DNA evidence under my fingernails and the hair and sent it for testing against the samples they'd collected. It came back positive." Tears pooled in her eyes and fell down her cheeks. On a whisper, she added, "We just wanted you back. We wanted to help you heal from what he'd done to you."

I hung my head in shame, and the tears fell again.

They knew.

Angelo wrapped his arm around me and I turned into him, crying into his shoulder. He held me close, his touch a comfort. His warmth, his smell, and the hand on my back rubbing circles was home. He was love. It was a bitter contrast between the topic of our conversation and the gentle way Angelo handled me. It made one thing stand out in stark relief: I wanted to tell them who I was so badly. I wanted the nightmare of my past gone and to look forward again.

"He's dead, Keir," my dad announced. His words were cold. Clinical.

Shock surged through me, and relief wound its way through my bones. I lifted my head from Angelo's shoulder, tears still staining my cheeks. I looked between my parents, stunned. Dad was still hugging Mom, his arm tight around her shoulder. Tears ran down their cheeks, ageing them even more. My body went numb, shock paralyzing me. I had no idea how to feel. What to think.

He continued, "He killed himself. We figured he knew he'd be arrested. Bastard was too scared to face up to what he'd done."

"When?" I whispered, unsure if I wanted to know the answer.

"A few weeks after you ran away."

I sucked in a sharp breath, and my head spun. Angelo cupped my nape and massaged me there firmly. It kept me grounded. My elbows on my spread knees, I rested my head on the table, trying to suck in much-needed air. My lungs burned, my stomach churned, and my head felt like it would explode, the dull throb quickly turning into a wrecking ball. Blood pounded in my ears as the news sunk in.

He'd never hurt anyone again.

I'd never have to see him again.

But everything I'd gone through for those seemingly endless months sleeping on the streets and the years afterward were for nothing. The fear and the horrible things I'd seen. The struggle to feel safe again. To learn to trust again. The hunger and thirst. The complete and utter loss of my dignity. The disappearance from everyone's radar.

I'd become invisible, slinking into alleys and hiding in plain sight. People walked past me and ignored me. They looked at their cells, they turned away. The brave ones who looked at me rather than through me always gave me pitying glances. I felt like a hollowed-out shell. As if I was a ghost. Invisible to most people and written off by the others. All of it could have been avoided. I could have been safe at home in my bed. I could have finished school and gone to university like a normal kid.

But I wasn't normal anymore. Not after he raped me. I'd changed. How could I have gone back to my old life when something so fundamental about me had changed? Everyone would have known. They would have talked about me as the weakling who bent over for his relatives. I would have been branded as the queer kid who was up for it with anyone without them even knowing how true at least some of their words were. But looking back, it seemed like a small price to pay.

Angelo moved closer and hugged me tighter. If I hadn't gone through all that, if I hadn't lived through hell and clawed my way out of it, would I have been standing on the bridge at the exact moment I needed to be? When the man sitting next to me came to photograph the bungee jumpers? Would I have lived in Auckland and been with Mom and Dad, but missed the most important part of me?

I slipped my hand onto Angelo's leg and took the strength I needed from his never-ending support. Lifting my head from the table, I sat up straight and looked at Mom, then Dad. "I came out to him. To Ryan. I told him I was gay." I paused, waiting for them to react. Mom closed her eyes and more tears fell. "He hit me." My voice wobbled, but it didn't break.

I let anger fuel me. Rage push me. The fear he'd instilled in me give me strength.

"He told me that no boy of his was a good-for-nothing faggot. Then he raped me. Said he was teaching me a lesson. Proving how much I'd hate it, and I did. He fucked me up for nearly two decades. I've only been able to talk about what happened in the last year. Only confessed it to Angelo when I understood how badly he was still fucking me up. How he was ruining the best thing to have ever happened to me."

"Oh, son," Dad whispered, his eyes shimmering. "Were you scared to tell us? Did you tell him because you were afraid of us?"

My eyes stung when I nodded, more tears threatening to fall. Angelo was right there, his arm around me again. I sucked in a breath and waited, not really knowing what I was waiting for.

"All we ever wanted for you was to be happy," Mom said. "To love and be loved." Mom smiled at Angelo before continuing, "If this young man is who you love, then we're happy you found him. Especially after what you've been through. All we ask is that you care for each other, you don't willfully hurt each other." Mom reached for my hand again and grasped it tight when I slipped mine into hers. "And you tell each other how you feel at every chance."

I nodded, this time my tears spilling over. I hadn't cried this much before in my life. Emotions overwhelmed me. While it'd been hard taking a walk down memory lane, and especially hearing what Mom and Dad went through, this part—my coming out—the very reason the whole clusterfuck had happened in the first place, was uplifting. The weight of nearly two decades of suppression had dislodged when I'd come out to Angelo, and the last heavy chain had just shattered. Fallen to the ground. It was as if I could straighten to full height for the first time. I was free to be me.

I looked at Angelo and gave him a watery smile, which he returned. I tugged him down to me and rested my forehead against his. He cupped my face and brushed his lips, ever so softly, against my own.

I murmured "I love you" to him and closed my eyes, basking in the warmth of his hands. Letting his gentleness and his whispered words of love back to me seep into my soul. Slowly I opened my eyes and turned to my parents. It was one thing knowing your long-lost son was gay and quite another seeing it. But there was no hesitation in their acceptance, and no distaste in their loving smiles.

"You're okay with this?" I asked, still questioning what I was seeing.

"Yes," Dad replied simply. "We just wish we could have told you this as a teenager. But now that we can say it, we will. It doesn't matter to us who you love, as long as they treat you right and you do the same. We'll never judge anyone for following their heart. Look what it did for us—we got you."

My coffee sat untouched on the table, and so did everyone else's. Only Dr. Bhat had drunk his tea by the time the waiter came back to ask if we needed anything. I motioned for him to take my mug and sat back in my chair, rubbing my eyes.

"You look exhausted, Trent," Angelo said from beside me.

"I am," I mumbled. "I haven't been sleeping properly." Looking up at Mom and Dad, I added with a tilt upward of my lips, "Excited about seeing you again."

"We have all the time in the world, Keir," Mom responded, then added, "Or do you prefer Trent now?"

"I don't mind what you call me. Everyone here knows

me as Trent, but you chose my name, so I'm happy for you to call me Keir."

"Okay." She nodded, and Dad smiled. "As I said, we have all the time in the world. We can catch up again tomorrow or the next day if you'd like to rest. Seeing you again, I finally feel like I can sleep right again too."

I closed my eyes and blew out a breath, once more ashamed of the hell I'd put my parents through.

"Hey, none of that," Dad chastised. "You survived as best as you knew how. We wish things were different, that we hadn't lost all this time together, but we're grateful you're in front of us now, happy and healthy. We would have given anything to see you again, and here you are. We came together again, and that's what's important."

I stood then and went around the table to Dad. He met me behind Mom's chair and we hugged hard. I remembered his smell: Old Spice aftershave. I couldn't believe he still wore it. But it was comforting that he did. He was the dad I remembered. The more we'd talked, the more the differences in age fell away. We wouldn't be able to pick up our relationship and run with it without working through the baggage we still held. There'd be anger and guilt we'd have to work through, grief, and we'd need a way of looking forward. To rebuild our relationship without constantly dwelling on what happened and what could have been, but today was a huge step in the right direction. I'd waited so many years for it to happen.

"They look alike don't they?" I heard Angelo say to my mom. Dad and I pulled back and watched Mom and Angelo speak. They'd both stood from the table and were holding hands.

"They do," Mom replied fondly. "We'd love to hear

how you two met and how long you've been together. Maybe next time we catch up you can bring some photos and tell us your story." Mom pointed to the camera Angelo had hung over the chair, and Angelo smiled.

"I'd like that." Angelo nodded. "Can I take a photo of the three of you together now?"

Mom's smile was bright when she agreed, and she stood on the other side of me. I hugged both of them and we smiled as Angelo took a few shots.

"You too now, Angelo," Dad said, waving him over. "Doc, can you help us out?" Dr. Bhat smiled and took the camera off Angelo, who went to stand next to Mom. Frail or not, she manhandled him, pushing Angelo gently toward me so I could stand next to my man. I grinned happily having him in my arms again and smiled when she hugged Angelo to her side.

"Smile," Dr. Bhat said and took a few photos before checking the screen on Angelo's camera. "Looks good to me."

# CHAPTER 17
## TRENT

I untucked my shirt and sat down on the bed, resting my elbows on my knees. Angelo was behind me, on his knees on our mattress, rubbing my shoulders. "Tell me what you need, Trent."

"I have no idea." I sighed and scrubbed my hands over my face. "I'm tired."

"Why don't we lie down then?"

"You're probably busy. Don't let me stop you from working."

"I've got the day off." He dropped a kiss on the back of my head and muttered, "My boss is a tight ass, but he gave me the day off."

I huffed out a laugh and smiled, shaking my head. "You do have a nice ass, and if you're all mine for the day, then yeah, I wouldn't mind having a lazy one."

"Let's get you out of these clothes then." Angelo reached around my shoulders and began unbuttoning my shirt. I undid my cuffs at the same time, and he slid my shirt off my shoulders when he was finished. A whisper-soft kiss at my nape followed, and I leaned into him, letting my weight rest against his lithe body. Angelo held me close for a moment before shifting. "Come on, strip so you can be comfortable enough to sleep."

I stood up and took off my pants, hanging them over the chair in the corner while Angelo shed his clothes too. Dressed only in our underwear, we slid under the covers and I cuddled into him, needing his arms around me. Warm and comfortable with my head on his shoulder, our legs wound together, and Angelo's fingers tracing patterns on my back, I soon drifted off.

The sun was lower in the sky when I woke, my back pressed against Angelo. His arm still securely around me, I was the little spoon. Not something I was used to, but I loved it. I blinked open my eyes and stretched out my legs, humming when Angelo pressed a kiss to my shoulder. "You didn't have to stay here with me while I slept," I croaked, my voice still rough from sleep.

"And miss out on cuddling you?" Angelo huffed out a laugh. "I wasn't going anywhere."

Curiosity sparked at his words and I turned my head to see him. "Do I give you enough affection? I want to give you what you need."

"You do, *amore*. I love how generous you are. You make me feel loved every time we're together."

"That's because you are," I whispered before wrapping an arm around his neck and kissing him. Angelo splayed his hand on my hip and deepened the kiss, a wildfire sparking between us instantly. Desire pooled low in my belly and I reached for my cock, but Angelo batted my hand away, instead rubbing his over my hardening length.

Angelo was hard too, his shaft resting along my crack. I

thrust into his grip, Angelo's dick rubbing against my ass giving us both a hint of the friction we needed.

I sucked gently on Angelo's bottom lip and let it pop free from my mouth. Angelo didn't hesitate, licking and nibbling a path up my jaw to my ear and trailing his tongue around it before sucking and biting my lobe.

He didn't stop there, kissing and dragging his teeth along the sensitive skin of my throat to my pulse point. My hand went to his head then, holding him in place as he sucked a mark into my skin. I moaned and angled my head away, giving him more room. Angelo rocked against me, rubbing and kissing me, and I gasped and ground back against him. He shifted, pushing me onto my back and hovering above me on straightened arms. He was readying to straddle me, but I held him tight, making him pause.

Pupils blown, he looked down at me. His lips were parted and wet; his hair flopped over his forehead. He looked kiss drunk, and love swelled in my chest.

"I... I want...," I stuttered, not knowing how to put words to what I really wanted. The day had been filled with emotional upheavals, but I was lighter than I had ever been. I wanted to make new memories. To start fresh. To experience love rather than pain and hatred. "I'm ready, Angelo. For you." It was the best I could do, and Angelo stilled, searching my face. He was looking for something, but I had no idea what.

"You want to make love to me?" Angelo asked tentatively.

I nodded and squeezed his forearm tight, seeking his strength to help me get the words out that I needed to say. "I want you inside me this time."

Without words, he kept searching my face before leaning down to brush a soft kiss on my lips. "I won't hurt you, Trent. If we do this, you need to tell me what's going on in your head. You need to tell me how you're feeling."

"I will," I promised.

"We'll take it slow. I won't push you. We only do what you're ready for. Okay?" Angelo was serious. He wasn't teasing me or trying to talk sexy to me. He was setting the ground rules so they were crystal clear. He expected me to communicate with him. I could expect him to stop the moment I wasn't comfortable with anything that was happening. He waited patiently, giving me time to decide. It was time I didn't need. I wanted this. I just hoped I could give it to him. And give it to myself too. "If you're uncertain," he started, but I held my fingertips to his lips.

"Yes. I want this." I nodded and sucked in a breath when he rested more of his weight on me. I widened my legs, waiting for him to slip between them, waiting for him to reach for the lube.

Instead, he pressed a kiss to my lips. Then another to my cheek. And another until he'd licked and kissed every inch of skin on my throat. He moved down like we'd done to each other before, mapping my body with his fingertips and tongue. But this was different too.

He was worshipping me, taking care to show me just how much I meant to him.

The soft scrapes of teeth and the swirl of his tongue over the same spot, or soft kiss pressed there, and gentle fingers exploring the valleys and ridges of my body had me reaching for him. He was addictive, as potent as a drug, and I was high on his touch. Threading my fingers into his hair, I held him to me, never wanting to let go. It wasn't until he reached my abs that he shifted between my legs, and I spread them wide to accommodate his shoulders.

"Is it okay if I take these off?" he rasped, tugging on my underwear.

"Yes," I replied, my voice rough.

"Can I kiss you here?" he murmured against my inner thigh after tossing my boxers over his shoulder. I nodded and he stretched up over me again, hovering above me on locked arms. "Can you tell me rather than nod? I don't want to misread anything."

"Yes. To both. I want you there, Angelo." There was a hint of desperation in my tone, like I'd die if he didn't touch me, and truth be told it wasn't too big an exaggeration.

Angelo sunk back down to his haunches and laved my cock with his tongue. Sucking me, deep throating me, gently nipping the soft skin of my sac with his lips, he worked me up again, leaving me wanting and close to coming undone. Angelo spread my legs a little wider and laved his tongue along my crack. He didn't touch my hole, just worked his way around it, giving me time to adjust and get comfortable with exposing myself.

"More," I moaned and felt rather than heard Angelo's hum of approval. A gentle swipe followed. Soft and slow. Not probing, just tasting. Loving on me. Then more of the same until my hips were moving without conscious thought and my moans were incoherent. I was reacting on instinct. Free to feel. To experience.

He pulled away, and I missed his heat immediately, especially when he crawled over to the nightstand for the lube. He handed it to me and shivered when I trailed my free hand up his side. Leaning down and kissing me gently, he ordered softly, "Squeeze some of the lube on my fingers, *amore*."

I did, expecting him to push straight into me, but Angelo took his time, letting me get used to him there. Letting me adjust to this new position. I closed my eyes and arched my back, impatient for him. But he stopped moving.

"Open your eyes, Trent. See me. Really see me."

I did and watched him as he gently pressed against me. I had been relaxed, but the pressure there had me tensing. Logically I knew it wouldn't hurt as much as it had that day. You work a muscle, warm it up, and exercising it wouldn't hurt. I knew that. But persuading my body was another matter. The second I tensed, Angelo pulled back, moving his hand up to my balls. Giving my shaft a pump, he distracted me with his kiss until I moaned into his mouth, desperate once more for his touch.

I was ready with the lube this time, squeezing more onto his fingers. Bringing my hand to his face, I trailed my fingertips along his cheek when he reached my hole again.

"Breathe out, *amore*. Tell me if you want me to stop."

"For fuck's sake, don't stop," I begged, shifting my leg and opening myself to him more. This time when he gently pressed into me, he pushed past my resistance and sank in. His finger wasn't uncomfortable, but I wasn't exactly seeing stars. I supposed that was what it would be like for me.

Maybe I was broken. Maybe he'd ruined that part of me.

"Trent," Angelo warned. "Get out of your head. Talk to me."

"You're not hurting me, but it's not…."

"What? Not amazing?"

I nodded, and he smiled softly.

"That's because I'm not moving. I was letting you adjust." He pumped his finger, slowly moving in and out in a torturous slide, and I gasped. Every nerve ending lit up, and a full body shudder passed through me, my eyes closing as he pressed deeper.

Angelo paused and my eyes snapped open to his again. Looking at him, seeing him there above me kept me grounded. It kept me in the moment. He smiled warmly, liking whatever he saw in my expression, and pressed against what must have been my p-spot. Fireworks exploded though me, hardening my untouched cock and pulling my balls up to my body.

I choked out a cry and pressed down onto his fingers, trying to get him to brush the spot again. Angelo chuckled and rasped, "Now you know how I can come without you even touching my cock."

He brushed my prostate again, but didn't linger, only giving me tastes of what I could expect with him inside me.

"More, Angelo," I pleaded, and he withdrew, holding his fingers out for more lube. I squeezed a generous amount of the slick onto them and held my breath waiting for him to press into me.

Angelo's gentle touches shouldn't have surprised me, but they did. I kept waiting for him to slam into me. To be rough. For it to hurt. But that wasn't Angelo. He was more of a man than Ryan had ever been. His protectiveness, unwavering support, his mission to make this experience one to override the bad memories of my one and only other time told me how much he cared.

It wasn't long before he started stretching me for his third digit, and I was ready for him in less time. When he slid into me again, I moaned and pulled him harder against me. I needed his touch. I needed to feel all of him. Angelo draped himself over me, his hard length pressing into my hip and his warmth surrounding me. I was pinned under him, but instead of feeling trapped, I was cocooned. Safe.

"Angelo," I gasped as he hit my p-spot again. My shaft leaked in my hands, precum slicking the path for my hand to follow. "Please," I begged.

Angelo paused and murmured against my ear, "Lube me up if you're ready for me. Or use it on you to make yourself come."

"I want you."

He pulled back and looked me in the eyes, and I slid my slicked-up hand between our bodies. His eyes rolled back and he thrust into my fist as I closed my hand around him.

"Oh, God," he rasped. "Fuck."

I let go of him and shifted his weight so he was lying between my legs. He pulled back and looked around us before grasping his pillow, lifting my hips and sliding it under me. "The change in angle will help," he murmured.

"Come inside me, Angelo."

He grasped his cock and gazed down at me, eyes full of love. I was riveted to his face. Captivated. He shifted and I held my breath, anticipating the burn as he pushed into me, but it didn't come. Angelo went slowly, letting me get used to our new position and watching me closely. I loved that about him. Asking for my consent every step of the way made me realize how much he treasured what we were doing. I acted on instinct, wrapping my legs around him and savoring the heat of his body pressed against mine.

"Please," I whispered. Angelo inched forward, taking his time to breach me. He was thick, and it took everything in me not to tense, but he'd prepared me so thoroughly that there was barely a sting.

He paused, breathing hard, his nostrils flaring, and I watched in wonder as Angelo fought for control. Long moments later, he began moving.

There was no frantic pumping of his hips, no slapping of bodies, no porn-style cries. It was soft gasps and long kisses, slow rolling hips and tangled legs.

Anchoring himself with a hand on my shoulder, the other holding my face steady as he kissed me, Angelo moved in me. The stretch, the fullness, the shot of bliss every time he pressed against my prostate soon had me moaning for more.

"Stroke yourself," he instructed me as he kept up the slow dance of our bodies.

Our breaths mingled and sweat beaded and Angelo never loosened his grip. Gentle arms around me held me tight, reminding me of how loved I was. How cherished. I closed my hand around my shaft and pumped it, shuddering as my sensitive flesh pulsed and my orgasm swept over me. I moaned, and Angelo reacted in kind, burying his face in my neck and crying out.

Breaths sawed in and out of my lungs and my heart hammered in my chest as I floated in the clouds. Wrapped securely in Angelo's arms, his weight resting on me, I never wanted to move. This right here—in his arms after making love—was where I wanted to be for all eternity.

Angelo looked up at me, and I smiled serenely at him. "I love you," I whispered.

"Love you too." He kissed me softly, just a ghosting of his lips against mine. I groaned when Angelo pulled out slowly before rolling us to the side. With his arms around me, I sighed contentedly and snuggled into him again.

"How are you feeling, *amore*? Sore?"

"Sore, no." I hesitated, and it was enough for Angelo to prompt me, pulling back with a look of concern marring his features. I smiled at him and voiced what was in my heart. "I feel safe. Cherished. He took that from me, but you've given it back. I'm free. For the first time in years, I'm really free of him."

"Oh, Trent," Angelo whispered, tightening his arms around me once more as I burrowed against his chest. "You are cherished. So much." I drifted then, falling asleep once more in the warmth and security of his arms.

## ANGELO

*Three months later*

I WALKED DOWN THE STREET HAND IN HAND WITH TRENT. Rainbow flags adorned every window and lamp post. Excitement hummed in the air like electricity. Music pumped from each venue we passed, and no one blinked an eye at the drag queens walking along the street or the twinks, cubs, and daddy bears checking each other out.

We'd all travelled our own journey to get to this point, but we understood each other. We'd faced obstacles to get there. Some we'd overcome, others we were working on. Everywhere I looked I saw acceptance. Not just tolerance, but true acceptance.

Knowledge that I had a tribe, and I truly belonged. *We* truly belonged. Holding Trent's hand so openly was something I had never dared to hope for, but in the months since he'd regained contact with his parents, he'd changed. He'd grown more confident. More open. As if he received strength from acceptance. From our love. And boy, did I love him. Even more now than I had before.

Seeing his true self, seeing him live like he was no longer afraid, was such a beautiful thing. I squeezed his hand and smiled his way. Trent responded by tugging on mine and pulling me close, wrapping an arm around my waist. It was awkward in our coats, but I wouldn't have it any other way. It was Winter Pride and for the first time in my life, I was walking down a street toward a rainbow-colored pedestrian crossing hugging the man I loved.

We were meeting everyone at The Vault to celebrate Pride with a family dinner. It was still early—little Gracie's bedtime dictated that—but that didn't matter. I looked across the road to the other side of the rainbow crossing and noticed our friends and family waiting there for us. I grinned and waved at them, and Trent tugged me onto the street.

Traffic stopped in both directions to let us pass, but Trent paused right there in the middle. "What are you doing?" I asked, grasping his hand and trying to tug him to safety. He smiled and dropped to one knee right there, unhurriedly reaching into his coat pocket. He pulled out a gold band, and I put a hand to my mouth, laughing in a panic. "What are you doing?" I asked again, my voice higher than my normal register.

"I'm asking the man I love to marry me. Right here, in front of all our family." Trent held his arms out wide and announced loud enough to capture the attention of everyone within a half-block radius. "I'm proposing in front of the whole damn town." Quieter then, speaking just to me, he continued. The sincerity in his voice had me reaching for him once more. "You saved me that day on the bridge. You opened my eyes to a world filled with color and love. You gave me all the things in my life I thought I'd lost."

I squeezed his hand hard, proud of the bravery he'd shown every step of the way as he fought to overcome his past.

"You gave me courage and strength. You've stood by me through everything, good and bad. You gave me my parents back"—he motioned with a tilt of his head to his proud parents standing there waiting for us—"and together, you freed me from the chains I was still bound by. You made me be proud to be me. To stand up and actually live. To admit I'm gay and be able to tell you how much I love you. There's nowhere else that I want to be than by your side loving you. I want to grow old with you, holding your hand like I am right now. I want to be your best friend and your person forever, because I'll always choose you too. So, whaddya say? Will you marry me?"

I stood in stunned silence for a moment until my brain caught up with what I'd heard, and my heart flip-flopped in my chest. "Yes." I nodded, laughing as unrepentant joy filled my soul. "Yes," I shouted happily.

Trent stood up and slipped the ring onto my finger as the crowd around us cheered and clapped. Someone whistled, and another person honked their horn. The noise, close by, made us jump, and we jogged the rest of the way across the road to safety. Trent pulled me into his arms and spun me around, laughing. His radiant smile matched my own, making my heart brim with happiness.

My man. My soon-to-be husband.

Everything but him faded away. He was beautiful in every way—his mind, his body, and most of all, his heart. I'd given mine to him and I knew without a doubt that I had his. I leaned down, resting my forehead against his, and he cupped my face as I ran my fingers through his hair.

"My Angelo. I love you," he murmured against my lips.

I traced my thumb down his cheek. "And I love you."

He kissed me then, a soft brush of lips against mine. A barely there touch that was filled with the purest of love. With the promise of a future together, filled with sweet touches and soft caresses. Of home and family. Laughter and slow dances and nap dates. I closed my eyes and deepened the kiss, holding the love of my life close to me, the way I always would.

# EPILOGUE
## ANGELO

## THREE YEARS LATER

I smiled when Trent pressed Play and the strains of Lukas Graham's "Love Someone" came through the speakers. It was our song, played at our wedding picnic as we danced under the canopy of the tree while the sun set behind the mountain range. Lanterns had been strung through the wide branches that night, but we didn't need them now. The sun was still high in the cloudless blue sky on the warm summer day.

Trent pulled me into his arms and we swayed together, enjoying the sounds of the birds chirping in the branches above us and wind swishing the long grass at our feet.

Quiet surrounded us, and a sense of peacefulness settled in me. It was one of our favorite places to walk through at any time of year and exactly the reason why we were married here. The two of us, our closest family and friends, a minister and a photographer—no more than twenty people shared our day, but we wouldn't have wished it any other way.

It was perfect, just like our lives had been in the three years since. I closed my eyes, remembering the moment I'd laid eyes on him as he walked down the aisle.

*I shook my hands out, trying to stop them shaking. My heart thudded in my chest, but I wasn't nervous. Excitement pulsed through me instead. The shade from the tree's canopy and the breeze off the lake gave us some reprieve from the heat of the day, but I could only think of one thing. Trent. The long grass swished, the air silent except for the call of a bird and the engine of a lone four-by-four as it wound closer. Trent had nearly arrived.*

*It was late afternoon, the sun on its way to setting. The lanterns hanging in the branches of the tree above me flickered on, and I turned to the sound of the car pulling up. Our guests let out a collective "aww" as Trent stepped out from behind the vehicle. My breath caught. My heart did a somersault in my chest, and a broad smile split my lips. Our eyes met and it took everything in me not to run through the collection of picnic blankets to him. He grinned at me, a bright spark in his eyes that I'd only seen in those last few months. I loved being one of the reasons he smiled so joyfully.*

*Dressed casually like me, Trent wore tan-colored chinos and a white linen shirt. He may have gone for cool casual, but he was smoking. He walked to me, his eyes never leaving mine and his smile never dimming. He was flanked on either side by his mom and dad; they were ecstatic. It didn't surprise me. Their beloved son had come back to them, and they were celebrating something they'd admitted to giving up on the possibility of ever having.*

*I waited impatiently at the base of the tree for my man to join me, and, finally, he did. "Hi," I whispered to him as I reached for his hand. He slipped his into mine and threaded our fingers together, squeezing momentarily.*

*"Hi," he murmured back. "Waiting long?" He smirked, and I brought my free hand to his face, cupping his cheek.*

*"All my life."*

*"No regrets?" He brought our clasped hands to his lips and gently kissed my knuckles.*

*"Never." I shook my head and ran my thumb along his stubble, staring into those fathomless brown eyes that were filled with warmth and love.*

*"Good. Me neither." He smiled again and added, "But we need to work on your definition of casual."*

*I laughed and looked down at myself. I'd paired light brown slim-fit pants, rolled up just above my ankles, with a pale blue short-sleeved shirt and a navy bow tie. "What's wrong with what I'm wearing? It's casual. You can even see my legs."*

*"You're perfect just the way you are. But, baby, a bow tie isn't casual."*

*I quirked my lips up at his words, his tease making me smile. His husky, "Here, let me," had me swallowing hard. Trent tugged on my bow tie, undoing it and opened the top button on my shirt, then another. "This little patch of skin right here," he murmured as he fingered the dip of my throat, "is sexy as fuck."*

*"There are innocent eyes here," my brother interrupted, "so if you're going to start stripping give me plenty of notice."*

*"Gracie won't even remember it," I quipped without taking my eyes off Trent.*

*"It's not Gracie I'm worried about. It's me!" he retorted, making Trent roll his eyes. I smirked and motioned to our celebrant with a tilt of my head.*

*"You ready?" I asked, and with Trent's smile and nod, we turned to the lady we'd chosen to help us say our vows.*

"Happy anniversary, baby," Trent crooned as we slow danced together.

"I can't believe it's here again. The years have flown by," I mused. "But I wouldn't change a thing."

Trent looked to the buggy sitting in the shade of the giant tree we were under, its branches reaching out as wide as it was high. "I wouldn't either. I never dreamed that this would be my life."

Our baby boy, Luca, would be four months old in two days. He was getting bigger with every day that passed, and his personality was starting to shine through. He was a happy bub, and Trent doted over him, something I adored watching. The wonder in Trent's eyes the moment he saw him made me fall in love with my husband all over again. Seeing the three generations of Campbell men sitting on the sofa together watching the rugby set my heart to bursting. It was a tradition they'd resumed when Trent's parents had moved to Queenstown in the springtime before we were married and something I was so grateful they'd been able to do.

Trent spent almost as much time with them as he did with me. He would stop in after work a couple of times a week, and his parents came over weekly to watch the game. I still didn't understand rugby, but I sat in on every match just to see Trent and his father interact. Now to witness that same bond being mirrored in Trent's love for our baby boy was something I couldn't miss.

"You never deserved anything less, *amore.*" I leaned down and kissed him, our lips pressing together gently before I opened and he met my tongue with his own. I'd never get enough of this man. He was a gentle soul, so caring and tender, yet so strong. He had an iron will but a soft touch. Every time we came together, even now after years of making love, he looked at me with such wonder in his eyes that I never doubted his adoration. We'd shared so much, come so far, and I loved him more today than ever before.

Our life together was simple and happy. My business was still doing well, and I'd hired an assistant to do most of my editing for me. It meant that I had more flexibility to spend time with Trent and Luca. We'd finally managed to buy our very own house and we lived in a cozy cottage on the same street as Ford and Reef and around the corner from my brother and his family. Trent's parents lived a five-minute walk away, and Caden's father, Gabe, lived next door. Trent still loved working with Ford in the winter but had stopped working as a paramedic during the warmer months. Now he was mountain rescue year-round, looking after hikers and mountain bike riders who traveled to Queenstown for the summer season. It was a better fit for him—it kept him in the mountains, which he loved, and avoided the crazy night shifts he used to do.

Luca let out a cry, and Trent pulled back, bringing our joined hands to his lips and kissing my knuckles before making his way over to the buggy and lifting our dark-haired baby boy from it.

"Hey, bubba. Daddy's gotcha," Trent cooed. "Papá's right here too."

I sat next to them on the picnic rug we had spread out and mixed a bottle of Luca's formula while Trent changed his diaper. Freshly dry and redressed, Luca gurgled happily when I tipped the bottle to his mouth and held it for him. His hands balled into fists, he clutched the bottle as Trent cuddled him close.

Brushing his fingertips over our baby boy's face, I watched as Trent smiled gently at him. I leaned in closer and kissed Trent's temple, breathing him in. He leaned into me, and I cradled the two great loves of my life in my arms. A warm breeze rustled through the grass around us, and I pressed my lips to my husband's temple again, showing him just how much I loved him. I cupped my baby's little head and closed my eyes, thankful every day for the gift our surrogate had given to us.

Thankful for both of them, because our life was like this quiet moment together—perfect.

It'd been a long time coming, a difficult road to navigate. But now that we were here, now that we were coasting with our windows down and the top off, with the wind in our hair, I knew dreams did come true.

Mine were in my arms. And that's where they'd stay.

# ACKNOWLEDGMENTS

If you read the dedication, you'll see that my former student inspired Trent's story. I knew when I was writing *Whiteout* that there was more to this complex man. His reaction to seeing Reef and Ford together for the first time was a window into something so much more profound. BB, thank you for sharing your story. I can never express how much I admire your strength and resilience. Keep sparkling.

To all the men who have shared their stories and all the resources that organizations like RAINN, the NSW Health Education Centre Against Violence and 1in6 provide to male survivors of sexual assault, thank you. Your support in putting this story together made it possible.

Another thank-you also needs to go to my critique partner who looks at all my work and always sets me on the right path. Kariss, thank you, beautiful. I always appreciate your eyes. Thank you also to Liv and all the ladies at Hot Tree for your eyes and feedback on the various drafts of this story.

For my A-Team, who were there to commiserate and encourage me when Trent was so damn stubborn that I was begging him to listen to me, and yet he insisted on doing things his own way. Thank you always for your friendship and encouragement. You're always there and I appreciate you to no end for it.

I'm so grateful to Hubby and my boys. I desperately needed those hugs when I was crying over Trent and Angelo, and you were always there to give them to me. You never questioned it. You were just there for me, and I love you to the moon and back for it. I swear, the next book I write won't be so heartbreaking. Probably. Maybe?

Finally, an especially huge thank you goes to all the readers who pick up my books and bloggers who show so much love for the book community. I can never thank you enough for your support over my years of writing. The time you take to buy, read, review, reach out and share your thoughts about my books is so very appreciated. Thank you for pushing me to be a better writer with every word I type.

Ann xx

# ABOUT THE AUTHOR

By day Ann Grech used to live in the corporate world and could be found sitting behind a desk typing away at reports and papers or lecturing to a room full of students. She graduated with a PhD in 2016 and is now an over-qualified nerd. But the grind got old, and the voices got louder. She still has the librarian look nailed, but she's a little freer to be herself now.

She's never entirely fit in and loves escaping into a book—whether it's reading or writing one. But she's found her tribe and loves her book world family. She dislikes cooking, but loves eating, can't figure out technology, but is addicted to it, and her guilty pleasure is Byron Bay Cookies. Oh and shoes. And lingerie. And maybe hand-bags too. Well, if we're being honest, we'd probably have to add her library too given the state of her credit card every month (what can she say, she's a bookworm at heart)!

In 2019 she was an Award-Winning Finalist in the Fiction: LGBTQ category of the 2019 Best Book Awards sponsored by American Book Fest for her story *In Safe Arms*.

She also publishes her raunchier short stories under her pen name, Olive Hiscock.

Ann loves chatting to people online, so if you'd like to keep up with what she's got going on.

Join Ann's newsletter:
http://anngrech.us8.list-manage2.com/subscribe?u=
0af7475c0791ed8f1466e7fd9&id=1cee9cdcb6

Join Ann's reader group: https://www.facebook.com/
groups/1871698189780535/

Visit Ann's website for her current booklist:
www.anngrech.com

twitter.com/anngrechauthor
bookbub.com/authors/ann-grech

# ABOUT THE PUBLISHER

**Hot Tree Publishing loves love.** Publishing adult romantic fiction, HTPubs are all about diverse reads featuring heroes and heroines to swoon over. Since opening in 2015, HTPubs have published more than 300 titles across the wide and diverse range of romantic genres. If you're chasing a happily ever after in your favourite subgenre, HTPubs have you covered.

Interested in discovering more amazing reads brought to you by Hot Tree Publishing? Head over to the website for information:

WWW.HOTTREEPUBLISHING.COM

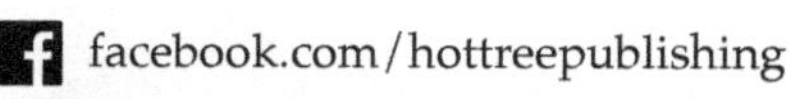

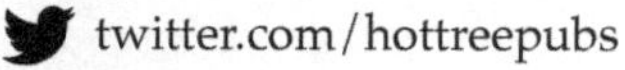

www.ingramcontent.com/pod-product-compliance
Lightning Source LLC
Chambersburg PA
CBHW061046190726
48286CB00006B/1634